The Conversion of Rudy

By
Paul L. Weingartner

Just One Publishing
— If Just One life is changed, it will be worth it all.

Published by Just One Publishing, Inc.

LIBRARY OF CONGRESS CATALOGING-IN-PUBLICATION DATA
Weingartner, Paul L
The Conversion of Rudy/Paul L. Weingartner.
p. cm.
ISBN 0-9676457-0-0
1. Conversion–Fiction   2. Religion–Fiction   I. Title
1999

Just One Publishing, Inc.
2031 West Rose Garden Lane
Phoenix, AZ 85027
Phone: 623-780-2480
Fax: 623-780-2571
www.just-one.net
John@just-one.net

Printed in the United States of America

PUBLISHERS NOTE:
This novel is entirely a work of fiction. Any resemblance of people, places, or events in this novel to actual persons living or dead, places, programs, or events, is entirely coincidental.

All biblical quotes from King James Version.

This book
is dedicated
to:

The grace of the Lord Jesus Christ,
The love of God and The communion
of the Holy Ghost.

I Corinthians 13:14

IV The Conversion of Rudy

CHAPTER 1

Neal sat on the hot metal folding chair at the front, right-hand corner of the football field. On this scorching, graduation day the band played the ceremonial songs with a vacant, faint sound leaving the audience with a disquieting need to turn up the volume.

Each delay in the program irritated Neal because it pushed back his valedictory address, which distracted him from the other parts of this, his ceremony. He was beginning to doubt the content of his speech. (He planned a boldly honest speech—always a hazardous approach.) Finally, as if time had cruelly waited until Neal's anxiety was at its peak, he was introduced. As if jolted out of a dream, Neal became aware of himself walking across the lawn and up the wooden steps like he had practiced.

"Thank you, Dr. Turner, members of the board of education, parents, and graduates of the class of 1993," Neal began. "I am here because tradition requires that the student with the highest grade point average make a speech to the class. This speech is usually eclipsed by the keynote speaker. I intend to make sure that that does not happen this year. I intend to tell you all about the meaning of life."

Neal spoke about his faith in Jesus Christ and how His teachings were robust and continued to provide the most reliable moorings for modern problems. He spoke frankly and unashamedly about the coincidence that as the world pulled more and more away from biblical teachings, the social problems it had to cope with increased. His speech resembled a powerful sermon—to the discomfort of some. In short, he used this opportunity to witness to this audience about the teachings and purpose of Jesus Christ.

Neal made his speech quickly and, he thought, with little repetition. He stopped abruptly. The audience came to a stunned realization that the speech was over and that they should clap. After a tense moment of silence there was applause. Neal was grateful that the applause lasted until he got to his seat.

After the tension of the ceremony Neal had to use the restroom. As he walked into the bathroom he overheard someone inside say, "I didn't understand a word the little jerk said. Who's he think he is preaching like that, Billy Graham or something?"

Neal turned on his heel and shot out before the speaker could come around the wall and notice him. He walked to his car and drove to the party for him and his friends. He would use the bathroom there.

The graduation party was anticlimactic, subdued, and quiet. Parents wanted the graduates to make a big fuss, but the graduates wanted as little fuss as possible. Still, they got gifts, which did not happen that often. Neal took in a little over two hundred dollars, some assorted books, clothes, and photo equipment (photography being his latest interest).

Neal had no way of knowing that he was about to meet someone who would change his life forever.

On the way home from this party Neal had to drive past a bar well known for the sexual activities that went on there. Just beyond the parking lot he saw a guy about his age lying unconscious in the taller grass. Neal felt an unfamiliar urge to help. He pulled off the road to see if the fellow needed any help. He sensed in himself an absorbing interest in this stranger tugging against fears that warned of trouble.

He waited a few seconds that seemed more like minutes. He was in something like a panic but finally decided to help, whether it proved to be right or not. He got out of the van and walked toward him. He nervously glanced toward the bar to see if anyone might be coming out to get him. Seeing no one, Neal moved closer to see what he could do to help.

Neal was raised in a conservative Christian home and, therefore, naive about sex and drugs. It looked like he was going to get a crash course in both. This person had no visible markings on his body and wore no jewelry. He was athletically built and good looking. He was in worse condition than Neal thought.

"Are you all right?" asked Neal in a quivering voice. There was no answer. "What's your name?" Still no answer. "Hey," shouted Neal in a voice which was becoming a little annoyed, "Can you hear me?" The youth opened up a little from a fetal position at this louder sound. His head turned in the direction of the sound. Neal considered him no threat so he bent over and shook his shoulder. "Hey, buddy, can I help you?" he asked.

There was no discernible reaction. Neal wondered if he should call the police. He ruled that out because he did not want to get this guy in trouble. Neal thought of calling the rescue squad. He rejected this too, because of the attention it might draw. Neal decided to take him home, give him a good meal, and a good night's sleep. Neal would remember this decision later and would never be able to explain why he was not more afraid of what the person might do, or what his parents might say.

Neal tried to shake him on the shoulder, but he didn't stir. Neal had a blanket under one of the seats in his van, which he wrapped around the guy. Neal carried him over his shoulder and put him in the back of his van. The youth laid down in the van without appearing the least suspicious about where he was going, or what Neal was going to do with him.

After Neal got him on the van floor and shut the door another problem occurred to him. How was he going to get this guy into his room at home in the condition he was in? He thought he could carry him up the metal fire escape stairs but there would have to be no one watching. How could he possibly explain this to anyone? Again he considered just calling the rescue squad and getting out of this situation. He could not understand why he felt it was so important to help this person. It was like he was being forced to do it. He decided to take some time driving home. Perhaps this person would regain some consciousness.

Neal checked the area one more time for anything this person might have dropped, or for any friends who might be looking for him.

Seeing nothing, he pulled into the light traffic on the road at this late hour. The noise and jostling of the van caused the youth to move about, and as Neal spent twenty minutes driving around, he woke more completely. He began looking around slowly. He seemed totally relaxed. There was no evidence of panic or fear. Being naturally cautious, Neal could not understand how anyone could be so unconcerned about where he was, or what was happening to him. When the youth realized he was moving in a van he sat up slowly and looked out the windows.

"Where we going, man?" asked the guy. "Where is this?"

"I'm taking you to my house where you can sleep and be safe," Neal offered. "That is, if you want to. I could take you to your place, or back to that bar if you want."

"Where are we?"

"We're on Route 104 near Stamford. I found you lying by the road. I thought you might not be safe lying there so I picked you up.

"Too far."

"What do you mean, too far?" asked Neal.

"It's too far to take me home tonight. I don't want to make you drive that far."

"Where do you live?"

"In the city," was all he volunteered.

The first piece of the puzzle was put in place. On the East Coast "the city" meant New York City. Neal was seeking other pieces to answer his many questions. He was near his home and noticed that his guest was responding more quickly to his questions. It seemed that he was much more alert. "You mind staying at my house tonight? If not, I can take you somewhere else. I'd even be willing to take you into the city."

"No. That's fine. Your house. You got anything to eat?"

"Not in the van," Neal said. "I can get you something at home. You wait in my room and I'll bring it up."

The youth seemed alert now. He did not seem worried about who Neal was or where they were going. He acted like this happened all the time. They pulled into the long driveway of Neal's house. Fortunately there were no lights on. Neal's parents had gone to bed. Neal guided him through the house and up to his room.

"Dude, you got anything to eat? I'm starving."

"Oh, yeah," said Neal, "I'll get you something. You wait here." The guy nodded and Neal went cautiously down to the kitchen. He found some cookies, cheese, crackers, fruit, and two bottles of soda. When he got back to his room he found the guy sitting patiently in an armchair by a bookcase. He was looking at some of the titles when Neal walked in.

"Here we go," said Neal. "Dig into some of this." To Neal's amazement, the guy ate everything he brought.

"Why'd you bring me here?" the guy asked.

"I thought you were in no condition to be left alone, and I didn't want to call the cops."

"That's cool, thanks," he said, with a sincerity that surprised Neal, whose curiosity grew with each exchange. He hoped he would not be in a hurry to leave in the morning. Neal wanted time to ask him some questions. He looked like he was drifting back to sleep so Neal helped him into the extra bed. (He had twin beds because it was common for him to have friends overnight.) The stranger fell into a deep sleep as soon as his head hit the pillow. Neal stayed up for a while and watched him sleep. He was silent and motionless except for some shallow breathing. Neal could not help but think the guy looked so innocent and childlike.

As was Neal's custom, he knelt down by his bed after he was sure the guest was asleep, and began to pray. "Oh, Lord, Lord, what kind of a situation am I in now? Help me to do the right thing by this stranger. Lord, please show me what I can do to help him out of his troubles. Let me be a help to him in some way. Let me show him Your light."

CHAPTER 2

The morning was bright, clear, and breezy, a perfect June day in Connecticut. Neal awoke before his guest. He got little sleep that night imagining many possible stories about his guest. He finally decided that his guest was poor and from a broken home who found that being a gigolo was a way to make big bucks fast. In his naiveté he even thought that this guest might take the money home to his mother.

Neal's naiveté stemmed from the fact that he was a born-again Christian from a conservative denomination with an Amish/Mennonite background. His parents sheltered him from some of the harsher facts of life. This denomination emphasized a genuine conversion experience as a condition for membership. Neal made such a conversion and was genuinely involved in this Faith. He thought it was the perfect choice for life and wanted to share it with others. The frustration Neal often felt was in not being able to express the uniqueness of his faith before people wrote him off as a religious fanatic. Frankly, Neal did not know how to explain his faith successfully to avoid such a characterization. Most people knew enough about religion to prejudge what he was trying to say and pigeonhole him before he could explain the differences.

Neal feared that his guest would do the same, so he planned a big breakfast to give him more time. Neal had the house to himself; but grew anxious about what his guest might do after he woke up. Would he be violent? Would he leave as fast as he could? Would he steal things from the house? A sense of fear shook Neal for the first time, as he began to realize the dangers of bringing this stranger to the home. Neal had to admit that he knew nothing of him, not even his name.

Finally the stranger did roll over in bed and fell with a loud thud on the floor. He gave a muffled moan through the sheets that were pulled over his head, and groped around with his hands to learn which way was up. He pulled himself up and sat on the edge of the bed rubbing his eyes, and pushing his hair back.

"Good morning," chimed Neal as he entered the bedroom, nervously checking on the condition of his guest.

"Morning," he said in a patient, easy voice. "Where am I?" He looked around the room and up at the ceiling.

"You're in my house, or my parents' house. I'm Neal Ebler. I found you lying unconscious along the road last night looking like you could use some help, so I picked you up and brought you here."

"Thanks," he said in a sincere and oddly calm way showing no fear.

Neal used a direct approach. "I wish you'd stay here a while, have breakfast, and talk."

"Sure," the guest said without hesitation.

"What's your name?" Neal asked.

"Rudy," he said, not yet lying because his real first name was Rudyard, a name given by his father for his father's favorite English writer, Rudyard Kipling. "Rudy Horace." Again, not quite lying because "Horace," his father's first name, was Rudy's middle name.

"Well, Rudy, welcome to my home. Why don't you take a shower, and then we'll have breakfast."

"Oh, OK, thanks."

"I'll get started on breakfast."

Neal made fried eggs, toast, bacon, juice, and coffee. Even working slowly he got done long before the water stopped running in the shower. This Rudy sure is slow in the bathroom he thought to himself. He tried to keep things warm in the oven until, finally, Rudy appeared. They sat down to eat and Neal spoke up.

"It's my custom to say a prayer before eating."

"Great!" Rudy said with real enthusiasm, not getting the hint that he should pray too.

"Would you like to pray with me?" Neal asked.

"You go ahead. I'm not much of a praying person."

"Would you like me to pray for both of us?" Neal asked.

"Whatever you want," Rudy answered.

So Neal began, "Dear Heavenly Father, before we eat this meal we want to turn to You and thank You for it. We know that all good things come from You. Thank You for protection in our sleep. I am thankful to You for the gift of this guest in our home. Help us to learn more about each other, and become friends. This we pray in Jesus's name, Amen."

"That was great," Rudy said enthusiastically. It was said the same way you would say "nice shot" after a successful tennis stroke. "Are you a preacher? Are you one of those who goes around saving people out of bars?"

"Oh, no," Neal answered in an embarrassed, laughing tone. "You've never prayed? Don't you go to church?"

"You picked me up off the street outside a bar and you ask me if I go to church? Church people don't act that way," Rudy argued with no anger or tension.

"I think some do. There's a lot of hypocritical church people in the world," Neal said.

This seemed true to Rudy but also slightly traitorous that a person who talked so much about church would say that.

"The church that I go to emphasizes a literal view of the Bible. In that respect it's unusual. It's one of the things I like most about my church," Neal offered.

"It's good to hear someone talk like that about their church," Rudy said with genuine sincerity. Neal noticed that Rudy ate with flawless table manners. This, along with Rudy's poised conversational style, caused Neal to revise his theory about who Rudy was.

"Tell me about yourself. For instance, where do you live in the city? What do your parents do? What do you do?"

Rudy did not begin immediately. Many questions were going through his mind. Here was someone who seemed to be unselfishly concerned about him. On the other hand, Rudy did not believe that people like Neal existed. He decided not to drop his guard and so lied about his family. "I live in an apartment on the middle West Side. My father is in business and my mother works in accounting for a small company. I just graduated from high school and am scheduled to go to college in the fall. How about you?"

"I just graduated too. I'm scheduled to go to Ohio State University in the fall. I plan on studying Psychology. My father works for a Swiss pharmaceutical company and my mother does lots of volunteer work. What do you plan on studying?"

At this comment Rudy bristled slightly. "Psychology? Why are you interested in Psychology?"

Neal sensed this change in emotion. "You seem to really freak at the mention of Psychology. Did you have a bad experience with a psychologist or something?"

"You might say that," Rudy cut him off. "How many people are there in your church?" he suddenly asked.

Neal was delighted that Rudy brought the conversation back to his church. While Rudy was quickly grabbing at anything that would get the conversation off himself, Neal took it as genuine interest and said a short prayer of thanks to God.

"Well, our church is different from most churches," Neal answered. "We have around a hundred members but on a typical Sunday morning there are more like a hundred-and-fifty or two hundred who attend."

"Why is that different?" Rudy asked.

"Well, most churches have a large membership, but only a fraction of the members attend regularly," Neal explained. "Our church requires more of a Saint Paul-type conversion experience before a person can become a member. Many people attend for years before going through this conversion experience. Some never become members even though they attend all their lives."

"Oh, you're one of those 'born-again' Christians?" Rudy guessed.

"Yes—in a way." Neal went on. "Our church has been empha-sizing a born-again experience since the early 1800's when we were founded. We're a little disturbed at how the meaning of the term 'born-again' has been misused recently."

"Well, what does it mean?" Rudy asked. "You can't go back into your mother's womb and be born again?"

"You know, you just asked the exact same question that a man during Christ's time asked," Neal said. He just could not believe how easy this was. "Being born again refers to a spiritual renewal of your mind. It's as if you wash out all the thoughts that mess you up and receive a mind that is clear, fresh, and new. Old problems, bad desires, hatreds, and everything else that does not please God, are forgotten and lost. Your mind desires new things that are spiritual, unselfish, and good."

"And who decides what's good?" Rudy asked, not believing anybody really thought this way. He was becoming concerned that Neal was some kind of religious zealot. He liked Neal. Neal was nice to him. Neal did not act fanatical. He seemed more thoughtful, but Rudy was keeping his guard up. He was glad he did not reveal his true identity.

"Two sources decide what is good," Neal went on in a voice of assurance and authority that surprised Rudy. "The Holy Scriptures and the Spirit of God."

"What are the Holy Scriptures?" Rudy asked. "There are many ancient books filled with wisdom. How do you know which ones are the Holy Scriptures?"

"We use the Holy Bible," Neal said. "And as to which ancient book to use we only know that following the direction and advice in the Bible gives a life of excitement, fulfillment, and inner peace, along with the hope of eternal life in Heaven. There may be other books that do that too, but we're not interested in how many there might be. We just emphasize what we know about."

"There's a refreshing honesty in your answers," Rudy volunteered. "I've never met anyone like you before."

"Why don't you spend the weekend here? You could meet some of my friends and maybe even visit the church on Sunday," Neal asked.

"OK, that'd be cool," Rudy agreed.

Neal had the stunned experience you get when you realize you've won some great prize. You don't really believe it. You want to ask for clarification to be sure that you heard correctly, but you're afraid that asking will change the results.

"Great! I can take you to town to get your things and bring you back. I've got nothing else to do."

"No. I'll take a train. It's too much hassle with a van."

"That'd be silly when I can drive you in. I don't mind doing it."

"OK, just drop me off near my apartment, you can kill some time while I get my stuff, and I'll meet you later."

"No problem," Neal said, a little curious about Rudy's secretiveness.

Neal loaded the dishes in the dishwasher while Rudy wandered around the house.

"You've got a nice place here," Rudy yelled from the living room.

"Thanks. I'm glad you like it."

Rudy noticed a piano in the family room. He played a few notes, noticed music books all around, and concluded that music was important in this home.

Neal heard the piano, came into the living room and asked, "Do you play the piano?"

"Oh, some," Rudy answered.

"Well, try this," Neal said showing him the song book his church used. "In the middle there are some beautiful anthems."

Rudy opened to one and began playing it. It was far from the most technical sight reading he had ever done, and he got through it with no errors.

"Wow!" Neal said with genuine amazement. "You really know how to play a piano, don't you?"

"I've been playing for a long time. I've had lots of lessons. I guess it's something I'm good at."

"You certainly are. You played it perfectly. That must've been the first time you've ever seen it, right?"

"Yeah. But I can sight read pretty well. This seems like a nice book."

"Keep it. If you can play like that you'd like the other songs too. You might also study the words. They're full of meaning." Neal inscribed the book with his address and phone number.

"Thanks. This is a special book."

They went out to the driveway and climbed into Neal's van.

"Why do you drive a van?" Rudy asked. "Guys in the suburbs are supposed to drive sports cars. Stores drive vans for deliveries."

"Oh, I'm sort of the unofficial bus driver for our church's youth group. Most of the kids don't drive so I sort of take them around."

They settled into the van while Neal drove into the city. They talked sparingly, both perfectly comfortable with long silences. How, he wondered, could Rudy seem so normal today when yesterday he was passed out on the side of the road?

They got to Manhattan with no difficulty. Rudy wanted to pay for the gas but Neal told him to forget it. Rudy told him to stop on a block in the low 70's and Central Park. He got out and told Neal to meet him at this same spot in three hours.

As Neal pulled away he saw Rudy shrink in the rearview mirror. Neal worried that Rudy might not be there when he returned. Maybe this was his way of ditching Neal. He decided to go to the

Museum of Modern Art. It took nearly thirty minutes to find a parking place. He tapped bumpers as he jockeyed back and forth with only six inches to spare.

Rudy grabbed a cab to his parents' apartment building. He asked the doorman for the cab fare. This was routine for the doorman who knew Rudy's lifestyle too well by now.

Rudy took an express elevator to his apartment complex. He had to ring the bell to get in. The staff were busy cleaning the apartment. No one talked to him. It was well-known that he hated all the chit chat and false enthusiasm. He was certain that they really resented him and thought him a rich, mixed-up kid who would never amount to anything.

Little could they have guessed that he had earned three points less than a perfect score on his college entrance exams, and had been accepted at Harvard in pre-law.

CHAPTER 3

Rudy's mysterious behavior, lying about his name and family, and not inviting Neal up to his apartment, was to keep Neal from learning his true identity. Rudy Horace was really Rudyard Horace Peterfield, the only surviving son of Dr. Horace Alan Peterfield, Jr., one of the most prominent and influential psychiatrists in New York City. The name "Peterfield" was a household word for two reasons. He inherited one of the world's larger industrial fortunes, and—perhaps because of this—he became something of a public figure who was frequently quoted by the media on the mental health impact of current affairs. This gave him the prestige to attract a glamorous and influential clientele. In short, he was a mental health institution.

It was Rudy's experience that when people heard of his famous father they were no longer able to see him as an individual. He was unable to establish his own identity. He was only "Dr. Peterfield's son."

Dr. Peterfield was the only child of a world-class European industrialist, Horace Alan Peterfield, Sr., who became one of the richest men in the world. Peterfield went to medical school and, with the benefit of his father's wealth, received an international education.

In spite of Rudy's father's remarkable education, he was an unsuccessful father. Rudy's mother, Carol Ann Peterfield, was a borderline-alcoholic fashion plate who was in the highest demand at "A" list parties all over the world. She was a great patroness of the arts.

Horace, Jr. and Carol had three children: Horace Alan Peterfield, III who died some years ago; Julia Lynn Peterfield, who was twenty; and Rudyard Horace Peterfield, who was eighteen.

The money this family controlled tainted every relationship they had and tended to make any problem nothing to worry about. Rudy watched as it ruined his older brother and sister, and by the time he met Neal, it had nearly ruined him. He learned that he had to hide his true identity if he wanted to be treated normally.

Dr. Peterfield was distinguished, gray-haired, tall, and athletically built. He was always dressed in custom-tailored suits and rode in a chauffeur-driven Rolls Royce limousine that was conspicuous even for New York. Because he feared kidnapping, he never permitted photographs of his children to get out of family hands. Because of this, Rudy was able to move about Manhattan and beyond freely, as long as he did not use his real name. This was a luxury he reveled in. For complicated reasons, Rudy did a lot of reveling, which is what took him to Stamford the night Neal met him.

Rudy's sister, Julia, also rebelled against Peterfield. She joined a bizarre religious cult in Central Africa at the age of seventeen and had not contacted the family in more than three years.

Rudy still lived at home. Like his story to Neal, home was an apartment in New York. But unlike his story, it was the most ostentatious apartment in a city of conspicuous apartments and took up the top three floors of one of the finest apartment buildings on Central Park South. Rudy found it impossible to take friends there: the effect was overwhelming. The place had an inside and an outside pool, huge natural gardens, and all the electronic gadgetry imaginable.

Peterfield was an eccentric figure who liked to dine formally in New York's most baronial private dining room: his own. He had the thick, hand-carved teak paneling for this dining room brought in from a Welsh castle.

Both of Peterfield's parents and his father-in-law were deceased. His mother-in-law spent most of her time between a London suburb and Jamaica, where she wintered. She frequently visited and was the only person who spoke her mind to Peterfield. She could be merciless about his failings, and he listened respectfully to everything she said.

Dr. Peterfield was a victim of his education as much as a beneficiary of it. He held a view on parenting, popular during his college years, that believed in letting children learn for themselves in a nondirected atmosphere of discovery.

He was so nondirective, that his children could rebel outrageously without even a squirm of embarrassment on his part. One example was when the Peterfields were having a large buffet in their home. There were fifty guests from the mental health and medical professions. Peterfield was lionized at such affairs because he was clearly the most famous and the richest. He embodied the secret fantasy of each of the other guests though—or perhaps because—their professions, well-paying as they were, could never take them to his heights of wealth.

During this buffet Rudy stepped onto the table, walking down the length of it occasionally knocking plates of food to the floor, and stepped into the punch bowl like it was a footbath. The tension in the air was paralyzing as all thoughts turned to Peterfield. The guests were too polite to stare at him, but their curiosity about how he would handle this situation added exponentially to the tension.

"Oh, good, Rudy. How entertaining. I'm sure you've behaved just like a trained monkey. Everyone is amused at the antics of the more primitive species, won't you stay and do something else shocking?" Dr. Peterfield said in a voice that could only be described as sweet and charming. Because Rudy didn't like to follow directions, the suggestion of staying caused him to leave, after a few other rude antics and gestures on his way out. The guests were relieved and the fun and conversation returned as quickly as the tension had come.

Peterfield's approach may have been appropriate if he had followed it up with a private conversation with Rudy. The awful thing was that Peterfield did not believe it necessary to follow it up. His next conversation with Rudy might be a week later, and he would not mention the event. This was the treachery of Peterfield's parenting. There was no emotional connection with his children. Everything he did was done in the antiseptic, rubber-gloved, artificiality of theory.

Rudy's way of dealing with this was to get away and have experiences on his own. His father encouraged this freedom. Rudy had lots of it. Rudy would be gone for days, sometimes even weeks, and come back with no mention of his whereabouts. Rudy soaked up experiences with a Faustian thirst for knowledge. Like his father, he was extremely bright and had an interest in people. So sticking around with Neal for a few days was not unusual for Rudy. He liked to immerse himself in other people's lives to learn what made them tick. He may have been searching for a life of his own. The changes that Neal's influence would make on him, however, he would never have believed possible.

CHAPTER 4

Neal returned early to pick up Rudy. He was waiting in his van when Rudy's cab returned to the block where he got out. Rudy instructed the driver to go uptown a few more blocks where he got out and walked back to Neal's van but, improbably, Neal noticed.

"I can't believe you're back," Neal blurted out unable to disguise his fear of being stood up.

"I told you I was coming."

"Well, where to?" Neal asked Rudy.

"I don't know. It's your trip," Rudy said. "Let's get something to eat."

"Here or in Connecticut?"

"Let's get out of here," Rudy said, wishing to put some distance between himself and where he lived.

Neal swung the van around the block and headed north. The blocks were blurs of sidewalks, shops, and people milling around. Above the shops were apartment windows of nameless people. Each block seemed both unique and the same and nearly endless. When they got in the faster lanes the blocks just blurred by. It was a sunny day, warm, and clear. There was little humidity in the air, rare for this time in New York.

Neal pulled into a diner not far out of the city. He loved to eat in diners. They reminded him of the previous generation, which he romantically believed to be more authentic than his own. He visualized people eating in a diner just before thumbing their way out to Oklahoma to begin a new life. He made up a fantasy that this was a more honest life than just staying in Connecticut and slipping into the high-tech career world he was probably destined for.

Neal and Rudy sat in a booth near the window. They watched as traffic passed by, heading somewhere in a hurry.

"We're lucky to have this time off, aren't we?" Neal asked Rudy.

"Yeah, I guess," Rudy agreed not really getting the point.

"So much of life is so planned out for people. Barf! I never want to get like that."

"Barf!?!" Rudy repeated laughing.

"Oh, that's just something my friends and I started. It seems to express the emotion just right," Neal offered as a feeble explanation. Rudy did not look convinced. They waited ten minutes before a waitress came over. She handed them worn, plastic-coated menus with several layers of tabs stuck over previous prices. "Can I get you boys something to drink?" she asked.

"What'ya have on draft?" Rudy asked.

"Very funny. I'll be back," she said and went to wait on other customers.

"What're you gonna have?" Neal asked.

"I don't know. This was your idea," Rudy answered.

"I love the taste of a cheeseburger, French fries, and a chocolate milkshake all together. It seems so basic and good," Neal said. "I used to eat it a lot when I was a kid, and every now and then I go back to it. It's great."

So they both ordered that.

"So what should we do?" Neal asked.

"I don't know, it's gonna get pretty hot, maybe we can go to the beach or a pool?" Rudy offered. "Do you know anyone who has a pool?"

"Yeah, Jim's got a pool. I can call him and see what he's doing," Neal said.

"Who's Jim?" Rudy wanted to know.

"Jim's a friend of mine, Jim Stander. He goes to my church. His father is a doctor in New York, a surgeon. They have a big house and a pool. Let's see if he's home."

Rudy wondered if Jim's father would know his father. There are lots of surgeons in New York City, Rudy reasoned. It's unlikely that this one would know his father well enough to have seen a picture of Rudy, or to have been invited to the Peterfield's apartment. Rudy didn't want to get caught in this deception; but he calculated that this was safe.

Neal returned from the pay phone. "It's all set. Jim's going to play some tennis with Jack Powers, another friend. I told him we'd meet them at the tennis court, maybe play a little tennis, and then go back to their house for a swim. How's that sound?" Neal asked.

"I don't have a tennis racket, and I'm not too good at tennis," Rudy said.

"We've got extra rackets, and we aren't too good either. The main thing is to have fun. We don't take the game too seriously," Neal reassured him. "You'll have a great time."

"OK," Rudy agreed. The waitress brought their orders. Neal bowed his head in silent prayer. Rudy watched. When Neal finished, Rudy asked, "What did you say to God?"

"I asked God to bless this food and drink, I thanked Him for meeting you, and prayed that He would direct me so that I could be a real help to you," Neal admitted in absolute candor.

"Thanks," Rudy said. "I need all the help I can get."

"Why do you say that?" Neal asked.

"No special reason, just a joke."

"I find that in most jokes, there's a trace of truth. Perhaps you wanted to say that you needed help."

"Perhaps," Rudy said and by this admission failed to strike at the bait Neal put out.

After finishing the meal Rudy had to agree that the combination of a chocolate milkshake, French fries, and a cheeseburger did leave a nice taste in his mouth.

There was a little argument about the bill, but Rudy insisted on paying since Neal had provided breakfast and transportation.

Neal noticed that Rudy paid with a fifty dollar bill, and appeared to have quite a few others in his wallet. Rudy tipped the waitress about the same amount as the meal cost itself, and they went out to the van.

Neal wondered how Rudy got this kind of money. He checked out Rudy's clothing. It had an expensively casual look to it. He was not wearing a watch—often a barometer of wealth—and no other jewelry. He wore a fashionable summerweight shirt widely open and baggy. He wore tight jeans, obviously well worn, faded, and deck shoes with no socks.

He threw a backpack that was rumpled but new in the van. It had never seen any real camping trips. He had no other luggage, and the backpack was not overloaded. Neal worried that Rudy wasn't planning on staying long.

"Have you lived in the city all your life?" Neal asked.

"Yeah," Rudy answered. "I'm about to go to college, but except for some vacations I've lived there all my life. Have you lived in Connecticut all your life?"

"No. I was born in Elgin, Illinois," Neal said. "My parents came to Elgin from Austria where my older brother was born. We have a church in Elgin. My parents moved here for a better job and because they had some friends from Europe who moved here too. People in our denomination make a lot of decisions based upon where our other churches are located. Did anyone in your family ever go to a church?"

"Oh yeah," Rudy admitted. "My grandparents on both sides of the family were religious. My sister's religious, I think. I don't really know a lot about what she's doing. She's living in another country now."

"What country's that?" Neal asked.

"I'm not sure. One of those poor ones in Central Africa. She's trying to find the meaning of life. I think she's also trying to get back at our parents," Rudy offered.

"Why would she want to get back at your parents?" Neal asked.

"I don't know. She doesn't make any sense."

Neal backed off, glad for a few more bits of information, but trying not to pry too hard. In forty minutes the van pulled into the parking lot of a tennis court. Jim and Jack were already playing tennis.

"Do you have tennis stuff?" Neal asked.

"Yeah. In my pack."

Rudy changed in the back of the van and they joined the others on the court. Neal introduced Rudy to Jim and Jack. Jack was the president of their church youth group. Jack offered, "We'll take on you two, OK?"

"No chance," Neal protested. "How good are you, Rudy?"

"I haven't played for a long time. I stink, really," Rudy made clear.

"You're really too good for us," Neal bargained. "Why don't you split up and the sides will be more even. Rudy, why don't you play with Jim? He's the best out here today."

"OK," Rudy agreed. "I hope Jim doesn't mind being handicapped in this way."

"No problem," Jim assured. "These are just friendly games anyway."

Rudy played hard, but was right about his tennis skill. Jim was too diplomatic to show any disappointment. Like Neal, he realized the importance of making Rudy feel accepted in the hope that Rudy would visit and take an interest in their church. Neal and Jack understood this without speaking.

Rudy was aware that he was not playing well, and was getting angry with himself. After the games, Jim and Jack were complimentary. They slapped Rudy on the back and told him it was a good game.

"You play much tennis?" Jim asked Rudy.

"Nah! I mean, you saw me play. Would you say that was a person who played much?" Rudy asked revealing a slight impatience with the false compliments.

"I guess not. You really put a lot of effort into it, though," Jim added sincerely.

"Let's hit the pool," Jack shouted. "We can talk about the game while we cool down in your pool."

With that they picked up their things and headed for the cars.

"Why don't you ride with me, Rudy? We're not that far away," Jim offered. Rudy climbed into Jim's car. Jack hopped into Neal's van. Jim's car was a standard transmission and Jim should have been an automatic transmission driver. He shifted too early, burdened the engine at slow speeds in too high a gear. He betrayed no skills at driving. The car, though only two years old, was making all kinds of groaning and humming noises.

"You're not gonna point out all my faults as a driver?" Jim asked.

"Nah. You're doing fine," Rudy said sincerely.

"You probably don't know anything about driving," Jim offered.

"I don't. I don't know how to drive."

"You don't know how to drive?" Jim asked disbelieving.

"No."

"How do you get around?" Jim asked.

"Someone's always taking me. I never want to go somewhere where no one else is going," Rudy explained, wondering if he was sounding ridiculous.

"Well, don't you like to get away when you want to? What if you want to leave before the others do?" Jim asked.

"I never seem to want to. Besides, it doesn't really matter how long I stay somewhere. I don't work on a tight schedule," Rudy answered.

"Are you in school?" Jim asked.

"I just graduated."

"High school?"

"Yeah."

"Me too. Got any college plans?" Jim continued

"Yeah."

"Where ya going?"

Rudy thought for a minute. Was he telling too much? He didn't want to lie and get caught up in some awkward story. He decided that there was no big problem with telling him this. "I got in Harvard. I'm in pre-law."

"Oh, Harvard! Wow! That's great," Jim said. "You must be a brain."

"I did all right," Rudy acknowledged.

Neal watched Rudy and Jim talk through the back window of Jim's car as he followed them in the van. He was glad that they had such an animated conversation. He prayed that Rudy would like his friends and would want to spend more time with them.

"Where'd you meet this Rudy?" Jack asked. "He seems like a nice guy."

"I picked him up on the side of the road. He looked like he needed a ride. We just started up a conversation. I think he might be interested in our church," Neal said.

"Where's he from?" Jack asked.

"He's from the city. I'm not sure exactly where. Somewhere in midtown, I think," Neal said. "I don't really know too much about him yet. I just met him last night. He stayed overnight, and we've been bombing around this morning."

"I'll bet his parents are loaded," Jack suggested.

"Why would you think that?"

"I don't know. He acts like a rich kid. I mean, the real rich," Jack guessed.

"No, I doubt that," Neal protested. "Why would a real rich kid waste time with us?"

"Maybe he wants to see how the other half live," Jack said.

"You remember *The Prince and the Pauper* don't you?"

"I guess that's possible, but I doubt it. He did seem to have a lot of money in his wallet, though," Neal admitted.

"Oh, that's a bad sign," Jack added. "Rich kids never have any money. They're always leeching off others. That's the funniest thing. Still, I'll bet he's a rich kid."

Neal thought this suggestion improbable, but he filed it away as a possibility.

They pulled into Jim's parents' driveway. Jim's parents were well off. His father was a surgeon, and they lived in a nice, new house on two acres of land. Their back yard had a big inviting pool. Jim pointed out the dressing rooms and ran into the house to get his bathing suit. Neal and Jack carried their trunks into a dressing room. Rudy, just stood beside the pool, pulled off his shirt, kicked off his shoes, and dropped his pants. He was wearing bikini underwear, which doubled as a swimsuit.

Jack and Neal came out of the dressing room and were stopped in their tracks by this outfit. They quickly tried to act casual, but looked around to see if Jim's sister was around. Jim came out and dove into the pool first. Jack and Neal eased into the pool from the shallow end. Rudy headed for the diving board. He threw some water on himself to check the temperature. He then hopped up on the board, checked the bounce with a few jumps, and executed the most effortless one-and-a-half dive the other guys had seen outside of diving meets.

"Get a load of that suit," Jack exclaimed while Rudy was still safely under water. "Can you believe this guy?"

When Rudy climbed out and headed for the board again Jim said, "Now we know what you do. You're an Olympic diving champion."

"Right, Jim," Rudy agreed in a mocking voice. "You're so full of bull you'd compliment your executioner on the hone of his ax," he joked.

Neal noticed how quickly Rudy felt at ease talking with people in a most familiar way. He assumed a quick friendship.

Rudy climbed out of the pool, climbed back onto the board, and walked out to the end. He turned around and stood there a few seconds working out toward the end of his feet. He executed a perfect back flip keeping his body perfectly straight, arching around in a huge path. He slipped into the pool with only the slightest ripple.

The others joined him in diving.

"Where'd you learn to dive like that?" Jim asked.

"What! More of your flattery?" Rudy joked.

"No really," Jack supported, "you're really good. Were you on a swim team or something?"

"Yes, I was," Rudy said. "I've always been around the water a lot. My parents have a place where we get out of the city in the summers. It's by a lot of water and I guess I've always enjoyed diving."

"Well it shows," Jack said.

Rudy tired of diving after about a half hour and climbed out of the pool. He walked over to a lawn chair, adjusted it to a lying position and flopped down on it.

"There are towels on the bench by the dressing room," Jim told Rudy.

"I'm OK," Rudy said waving Jim off sort of lazily while lying there.

Jim, Jack, and Neal kept swimming for a while and talking. They decided to dive for objects on the bottom, play some water tag, and other water sports. They only later noticed that Rudy fell asleep. They walked over and noticed that he was still sleeping when they finished their swimming.

"Should we throw him in the water?" Jim asked.

"No you shouldn't throw him in the water," Rudy answered without moving a muscle. "I'm all dried off, and don't want to get wet again."

They all had a good laugh, then decided to go in the house for some refreshments. The guys got dressed in the dressing rooms again. Rudy just pulled on his clothes over his suit.

Neal thought, "How efficient. He doesn't need a suit, he doesn't need a towel, and he doesn't need a dressing room. He's ready to jump in the water wherever he is."

CHAPTER 5

That evening, as Rudy and Neal drove back to Neal's house, Neal was struck by the fact that Rudy showed no hesitation in meeting his parents.

"Won't your parents miss you for dinner?" Neal asked.

"I left them a note. They're used to me being gone a lot. It won't bother them."

When they pulled in they parked near where Neal's father was sitting in a lounge chair on the back patio drinking iced tea and reading the paper.

"Come over here, I want you to meet my dad," Neal directed. "Dad, this is Rudy Horace. Rudy, this is my dad."

"Nice to meet you, Mr. Ebler," Rudy said. "You really have a great house here."

"Nice meeting you, Rudy," Neal's father said. "We like it. Make yourself at home." John Ebler shook Rudy's hand while leaning far forward in the lounge chair.

"Come inside, I want you to meet my mother," Neal urged his friend.

The kitchen had a painting of an old man sitting at a simple table holding his hands together in prayer. On the table were a cup and a small loaf of bread. It was a popular picture found in many Christian homes. On an opposite wall was a plaque that asked the question, "Why worry when you can pray?"

"Mom, this is Rudy Horace. Rudy, this is my mother." Mary Ebler was working at the kitchen sink on dinner. She was a warm, friendly looking, older woman.

She said, "I won't shake your hand; my hands are such a mess. We're glad you're here. You are staying for dinner?"

"Thanks. I'd be glad to stay. It smells inviting."

Neal walked up to the sink and grabbed a few carrot sticks. He offered several to Rudy, who refused. They walked into the living room where Neal flopped down on the sofa and picked up a magazine. Rudy walked more slowly into the living room trying to take in all the details of the place. It was tastefully decorated in a popular, Early American style.

Rudy saw a few books on a coffee table in the living room. The most prominent among them was a Bible. Rudy was about to pick up the Bible when Neal's mother called everyone to the table.

Before eating Neal's father announced, "Let's pray. Dear Heavenly Father, we thank Thee for the bounty of this table. We thank Thee for our health, our home, our family, and friends, and the faith that Thou didst make possible through the death of Thy Son, Jesus Christ. Help us to cherish and understand that miracle more and more each day. Lord, we don't ask that our life be made easy; just that Thou wouldst give us the strength to bear it. Amen."

Neal's father made sure that Rudy received each serving dish first, which he took without the protests of false modesty that Neal expected. He seemed to know that to accept this honor and pass the plate on would be quicker and more polite than to argue. In this, as in so many other ways, his manners seemed to be flawless, tasteful, and invisible. Neal made a point of improving his own manners.

"Where do you live, Rudy?" Neal's father asked.

"In New York," Rudy answered. "We live in an apartment on the middle west side. We could certainly use a beautiful lot like you have around your house," he added.

"Thank you, Rudy," Ebler said. "The yard is Mary's special project. She loves to put in lots of beautiful flowers."

"All that, and an excellent cook, too," Rudy said. "This is cooked just right, and nicely seasoned."

"Why thank you." Mary Ebler said noting that he had not mentioned the food until he had eaten at least one bite of everything. One could not gainsay his sincerity.

The meal went comfortably; Rudy fit in perfectly. Neal wondered how easily his parents would have accepted Rudy if they had seen him the night before, or knew where Neal had picked him up.

It was only around the question of what Rudy's father did for a living that there was the slightest hint of tension. Rudy made a clumsy answer of his being "a professional."

The Eblers, Rudy knew, were the kind of people who would be far too impressed with his father to remain objective about Rudy. Once again, he found it wiser to remain silent.

The conversation was comfortable, light, and revolved around what the boys did that day, and what they were going to do. Rudy noticed no tension in the room. How different this was, he thought, from his parents' dining room table.

The last time he ate a meal at home with his parents you could cut the tension in the air with a knife. His father had just come home from a professional trip where he had been recognized for his contributions to his field. On these occasions his family knew never to bring up anything controversial because it irritated him considerably. Rudy's maternal grandmother happened to be visiting.

Peterfield had an unaccountable respect for this woman. She was the only one who could talk to him and be sure that he would listen. Her name was Dorle Kupferschmidt, the daughter of a wealthy German industrialist, Hans Bern. She married a wise businessman, Werner Kupferschmidt, who took his wife's fortune, and continued to build on it in his lifetime. It was Dr. Peterfield's fantasy, however, that her husband was an unremarkable intellect and that it was his wife who was responsible for preserving the family wealth. This misreading of the facts was the basis of Peterfield's great respect for her. In her he could see no faults, a situation she took unfair advantage of at times for her daughter's and her grandchildren's sakes.

The Peterfield's dinner, by contrast, began with no prayer but was conducted with an almost religious formality. There was a soup course and salads, various wines were served in and around the courses, all on expensive pieces of china, crystal, and silver. No plate ever held more than two items of food, and waiters were constantly tending to them. Dr. Peterfield seemed to relish a constant fuss being made around him.

One memorable dinner conversation began, "I think you should give more direct advice to Rudy about his college education," volunteered Dorle Kupferschmidt without warning.

"Why do you think that, mother?" Peterfield asked.

"Well, Rudy has done so well on his exams, that I think he could do whatever he wanted to do," she said.

"That's true, mother," Peterfield agreed.

"Well, we all know that you want Rudy to go into psychiatry and follow you in your practice," Dorle bluntly said.

"Mom!" said Carol Peterfield.

"That's all right dear," assured Peterfield. "How do we all know that, mother?" he asked with a cold steel edge in his voice that his mother-in-law did not bother to notice.

"Because we live together and know each other," she answered with conviction. "I've watched you over the years and you've failed as a parent. You've not given your children the kind of guidance they needed. You were blessed with wonderful children: normal, healthy, and bright. Still, all that intelligence in children needs to be challenged and directed by loving, caring parents. You have adhered too closely to that advice you find in your books and all three of your children have suffered from the lack of direction."

"Mother, please." Carol protested in a convictionless way, just barely a whisper. She regretted saying even that as soon as she had said it. She found in times like this it was best to withdraw into the table and dishes, to say nothing, and hope that she could go unnoticed. She reached for her empty wine glass sparking an immediate move on a waiter's part to fill it for her.

"You're going to blame my children's adjustment problems on me?" Peterfield asked in a sterile, clinical voice.

"Your oldest son is dead. Your only daughter is running around barefoot and pregnant in an African tribe somewhere, and now, Rudy, your only remaining child is at the point where he needs guidance from you as a father. He is dying to have from you the one thing, and the only thing, you'll never give him, some direct advice. Tell him to go into medicine."

No one else in the room would have dreamed of making a comment at this point. It was like all the amateurs in a room had cleared a wide space in the center for the two best to fight it out. No one else becomes involved because the two in the center are perceived as being evenly matched, and a true contest is about to take place. Neither Rudy nor his mother would ever contribute to this conversation between Horace and Dorle. It was their special world of extremely personal, yet strangely unemotional, verbal debate.

"I cannot give him the advice you suggest because I believe that he has to make decisions about his future himself," Peterfield argued, making a point that at least a dozen parenting books would back him up on.

"How does any child decide what he wants to do with his life?" asked Dorle. "He bases it on a lot of the advice he gets from others. Not that he takes advice directly, of course, but he uses that in the greater formula he uses in making up his own mind. You don't flatter yourself to think that he will obey your advice upon just giving it once, do you?"

"I'm not sure why you think it is so important for Rudy to go into medicine?" asked Peterfield in a plaintiff tone of voice. "Maybe Rudy doesn't even want to go into medicine."

"Have you ever asked him?" Dorle returned not missing a chance, or giving an inch.

"No, I've never discussed it with Rudy. What do you think, Rudy, do you want to go into medicine?" Peterfield asked his son.

Rudy worked up the most sarcastic tone of voice he could and said, "I thought I'd go into trial law and have you doctors working for me," Rudy tried to discourage any further interest in having him participate in this conversation. "I guess there's plenty of time to decide. I can always change horses after I start."

"Now that's reasonable," added Carol. "Can we talk about your recent trip, darling? Tell us about the honor they gave you." She tried to take Rudy's lead and change the subject.

As Rudy's thoughts were so keenly focused, he was unaware of the conversation around the Ebler's table. There was a long silence which jolted Rudy back to the present and caused him to realize that something was expected of him.

"I'm sorry. Was something said to me? My thoughts were a million miles away. Excuse me," Rudy explained.

"Yes, Rudy, Neal was just talking about you and said that you're interested in visiting our church. He said there was a trip coming up and that you may be able to go along," Neal's mother, Mary, said.

"Oh, sure. I'd be glad to go on that trip," Rudy said with genuine enthusiasm.

"But you don't even know where it's going to be," Mary remarked with amazement.

"Well, where could it be?" Rudy asked.

"We're planning to go to Ohio for a youth rally," Neal said. "It would be just great if you could make it. I wanted to ask you about that all day but thought I'd wait for the right opportunity. I can't believe that you'd be willing to go without needing to know more about it."

"Why not?" Rudy asked. "I'm up for some new experience."

"Don't you have a summer job?" Neal's father asked. "How can you just take off like that?"

"I don't have a summer job. I didn't try that hard to get one. My dad's paying whatever college expenses are not covered by scholarships. I don't really need much money. What do people do at youth rallies?" Rudy asked. He imagined it was some sort of athletic competition or something.

"Well, we get together on Saturday afternoon and talk. You know, renew old friendships and make some new ones. Then we have supper together, and have an evening program made up of singing, including some quartets and things. Then a guest minister usually gives a sermon followed by more special numbers. We all go back to people's houses and stay overnight. On Sunday there's a big Bible study for everyone, and then there's another sermon. There's afternoon services, and evening campfire, again, and we all go back to our host's homes. On Monday morning, there's a breakfast at some park, some activities, and everyone leaves for home whenever they have to. It's a long weekend, but it's great," Neal explained.

"Why do you go all the way to Ohio for that?" Rudy wanted to know. "Can't you just meet with a bunch of people here in Connecticut for that?"

"We don't have many churches in Connecticut, Rudy," explained Neal's father. "We're a small denomination and we keep in close touch with all our churches. Ohio happens to be the state where we have the most churches."

"Why don't you just get together with some other churches here in Connecticut?" Rudy asked.

"Well, we don't view the Bible the same way as most churches. We think it would be confusing to get together with churches of other denominations." Neal's dad explained.

"Well, how do you view the Bible that's so different?" Rudy asked. This sounded kind of odd to Rudy.

"Well, for one example, the Bible teaches that there is only one acceptable reason for divorce and that is adultery. It further teachers that if someone puts away his wife and marries another he commits adultery, except if the divorce is for the reason of fornication. This strict teaching about marriage is not being observed in most churches today. The Bible also teaches that people should not kill, but love their enemies and pray for them that spitefully use you. John the Baptist told soldiers to do violence to no man. Those who would follow the Bible, therefore, must be pacifists. Most churches today ignore this. There are many examples like this where modern Christianity has preferred to not observe basic, black and white teachings of the Bible. They don't see the Bible as the absolute, infallible word of God anymore. They explain much of it away as cultural."

Later that evening, Rudy, Neal, and Neal's father went into the living room. Ebler showed Rudy where many of these teachings were located in the Bible. One by one, they covered a long list and after each one Rudy was amazed at how clear and simply it was stated in the Bible. He had always believed that the Bible was a mystical book that was hard to understand. He had read portions of it, but assumed that it was all written in some oblique symbolism. He did not expect to understand it.

"But why the Bible?" Rudy asked. "There are lots of ancient books. My father likes to quote from the Rubayat by Omar Khayam. How did you pick the Bible to follow so closely?"

"That answer is hard to understand," Neal's father went on. "Since the original teachings of Christ, there has been a small number of people who have tried to follow His teachings closely. Those teachings enable you to escape being separated from God and allow you to return to God. This provides a great blessing of peace and a renewed, divine nature. Christ's teachings are found in the Bible. The rewards of literally following them far outweigh the self-sacrifice that is also required."

"What do you mean returning to God?" Rudy wondered. This sounded like an out-of-body experience to him. "And what do you mean about a divine nature?"

"According to the Bible, Rudy, God is holy and cannot come into the presence of sin. God walked and talked with mankind in the Garden of Eden until sin came into man's life. At that point, sin separated man from God. God withdrew Himself from man and cast him out of the Garden of Eden. Man became progressively more and more evil until God destroyed him with a flood. After the flood, God gave mankind a set of laws to live by until He would provide a Savior to restore mankind to a fellowship with Him. Those laws, however, were also incomplete. Finally, in God's plan, there was a need for a sacrifice of His Son, Jesus Christ, to become the righteousness for mankind, since they were unable to have any righteousness of their own. For that reason Christ came into this world to die and shed His blood that mankind could, one day, be reunited with God in Heaven."

Rudy thought he was hearing a joke but Ebler wasn't laughing. He had learned a little respect for Ebler; however, this sounded like an adult version of a Saturday morning cartoon. Could Ebler actually believe this? he asked himself. He had to be careful. At several points he almost laughed because Ebler said things that would have been said for jokes among his friends. Ebler's mood was absolutely serious, which caused Rudy some confusion in trying to understand what was going on.

"This is all clearly written in this book, Rudy," Ebler ended. "I know this sounds fantastic to you. This book also says something about that. It says, the preaching of the cross is, to them that perish, foolishness. If you have thought at any point in this short explanation that this was foolishness, that would be perfectly understandable."

Rudy marveled at how Ebler knew the Bible so well—and seemed to know his own thoughts, too.

"People say this book reads you more than you read it," said Ebler. "There are certain books within the Bible that seem to do that better than others. The book of Romans, for example, is particularly good at that. You might start reading that book. It has a lot to say about repentance, and the process of becoming reinstated with God through the grace of His Son, Jesus Christ, and through the Power of His Holy Spirit."

"That would be the Father, Son, and Holy Spirit that people talk about, wouldn't it?" Rudy asked.

"Exactly, Rudy. They are one, and yet they have three separate functions—but, that's getting into material a little more complicated than we need to think about now."

"Are you a preacher in this church, Mr. Ebler?" Rudy wanted to know.

"No, Rudy, I am one of the Bible class teachers, but I am not a minister."

"You seem to know the Bible so well. I just thought that you must be a minister," Rudy added.

"I think you'll find that most of the people in our church know the Bible that well. It's important that people know it that well. It puts you in touch with the Power that will get a person to Heaven."

The time flew by and shortly Ebler excused himself saying he had to get up early to go to work. Rudy and Neal stayed up a little longer. They sat in the living room but said little. Neal did not know what to say. He was afraid that anything he might say would be too much. He seemed to realize that Rudy had a lot to think about and knew it was wise to let him absorb it before distracting his thoughts with more conversation.

Rudy was satisfied to sit in silence, too. It strangely did not seem uncomfortable to sit in this unfamiliar living room with Neal, someone he had only met the day before and think about religious thoughts.

"Well, I have a lot to think about," Rudy finally said breaking the silence. "Do you believe all that, just the way your father said it?"

"Yes. I think dad put it pretty well," Neal answered.

CHAPTER 6

The next morning Rudy and Neal slept late. Again, Neal got up before Rudy. Neal noticed that Rudy left his clothes anywhere they happened to fall. Neal thought, for someone with such good table manners, Rudy's a real slob with his clothes.

"Tell me what it's like being Rudy Horace," Neal said deciding upon a direct approach.

"What do you mean?" Rudy asked.

"You know. Tell me about your life and I'll tell you about mine. I have an idea," Neal said, "Let's talk for fifteen minutes about you, and then fifteen minutes about me. That way I can learn about you, and you can learn about me. After all, you must be a little curious about me or you wouldn't stay here this long. You want to start, or shall I?" Neal asked.

"I don't know about this. I haven't got that much to tell, really," Rudy hedged.

"Let me start by asking you a bunch of questions, then," Neal suggested. "Why do you want to be a lawyer?"

"Oh, that's easy," said Rudy. "I've always been pretty good at it. I liked debate in school. I like persuasion and thinking quickly on my feet. I think that's what lawyers have to do."

"Yeah, I see what you mean," Neal acknowledged. "Do you mind if I ask some personal questions."

"Probably," said Rudy. The quickness of this response took Neal by surprise. "It depends what it is."

"I've been dying to ask how you got outside that bar the other night?"

"Oh, that's what you want to know," Rudy sighed. The relief in his voice puzzled Neal, who wondered what other area Rudy would consider more difficult to talk about. "I was tagging along with someone I met in the city. She seemed real nice at first. She lived in Stamford and offered to take me home. I tagged along for something to do. Then she dropped me for someone else in the bar. So I got hammered and I guess I wandered outside to sleep it off."

"Do you have an active sex life?" Neal asked.

"No, I guess I'm just normal. I run around with some pretty fast friends, though. Most of them are older than me."

"What did you think I was going to ask you about?" Neal asked.

"I thought you were going to ask about my family. I don't like talking about them. I hope you understand," Rudy said.

Neal didn't understand. This secrecy made Rudy more mysterious. What could it be about his family that Rudy would not want to tell? Was his family involved in crime? Neal wondered.

"What were you like as a little kid?" Neal asked.

"Oh, I rebelled a lot. Mostly against my parents," Rudy admitted. "I used to get in lots of fights, lots of vandalism. Then I learned it's better to be a lover than a fighter."

"What caused you to learn that?" Neal asked. "Did you have some big scare with the police, or something?"

"Yeah, something," Rudy tossed back. "I guess it would have to be the death of my brother. That was a pretty big jolt."

"I'm sorry," Neal said. "How did that happen?"

"He killed himself in a car crash," Rudy said. "He used to drink a lot, and he had this real suped-up 'vette. He was driving way too fast and crashed into a garbage truck in Greenwich. I guess that's why I still haven't learned how to drive yet."

"What kind of a 'vette was it?" Neal asked.

"It was a '65 Stingray, metallic blue. The engine was modified to deliver twice the horsepower. It was fast. My brother used to scare the shi-uh-daylights out of me on rides through the country. I guess I always had the feeling he would kill himself in a car. Our folks used to say that, too.

"One day he was at a party and had been drinking too much all evening. When the party broke up, around three in the morning, he decided to go for a fast ride. One of his friends went with him. My brother was known to be the life of the party, kind of wild, unpredictable.

"He got out on some of those back roads and pegged the speedometer. He flew over a small hill and slammed into one of those big green garbage trucks broadside. Moved the garbage truck about twenty feet. The highway patrol estimated that he was going about 160. Can you imagine that? 160 miles an hour. He must have abandoned all hope of seeing the end of that trip through the country. Some said he wanted to commit suicide. They said that that was the only way to understand it. Some were really angry with him for taking a friend with him."

Neal saw Rudy's eyes starting to water up. He didn't actually cry, but the intense feeling was almost electrical.

"What do you think?" Neal asked.

"I think he was too drunk to know whether someone was in the car or not. I don't think he wanted to commit suicide. I can't believe he wanted to commit suicide," Rudy argued.

"Would he have had any reason to commit suicide?" Neal asked, hoping that Rudy would stay in this open mood.

"Well, he was unhappy. He'd flunked out of his second college in two years. He had no idea what he wanted to do with his life. But I never got the impression he felt he had no hope, or no options," Rudy added.

"Just think of that, moving a garbage truck twenty feet in a corvette," Rudy said. "He never had a chance. Everything burst into flames, and there were parts of the car all over the neighborhood. I never did see him after that. There wasn't enough to find to show in a casket."

"That's terrible," Neal said with sincere conviction. "I've never heard of an accident like that. Did he have a lot of accidents before?"

"Oh yeah. He was always bouncing his cars off things. He was the world's worst driver. Hey, your time's up. Now I get to ask some questions about you," Rudy said, seeming to wake up from deep thought.

"I guess that's what I said," Neal agreed, wondering if he could get Rudy back into that serious mood when his turn came again.

"Do you get along well with your father?" was Rudy's first question.

"Oh, yeah. He's great," answered Neal.

"Haven't you ever gotten mad at him, or wanted to run away from home?" Rudy asked.

"I've been mad at him lots of times. He always thinks he has to tell me exactly how to do things. It's like I haven't got any brains at all. He goes into endless detail at what he calls 'plans' for Saturday projects, or other work detail. I've done the things before, but he still thinks he has to spell out every step."

"Have you ever wanted to run away from home?" repeated Rudy.

"No. Not really," admitted Neal. "I guess I realize that most people don't have it as good as I've got it. I really have no reason to run away."

"Why do you think you get along so well with your father?" Rudy asked.

"For a person who doesn't want to talk about his family you ask a lot of questions about mine."

"Well, skip it if you don't want—"

"No, that's all right. I guess it's because my father's a Christian. That means he's got to be honest. He's never lied to me, and he's always been a good example of everything he's wanted me to do. You know, it's not like he's ever asked me to do something he doesn't do himself."

"I haven't found Christians to be all that honest," Rudy challenged. "Are you sure that Christians have to be honest?"

"Well, true Christians do," said Neal. "I don't think that everyone who calls himself a Christian necessarily *is* one. Here, again, I guess it's 'cause of the church we go to. Our church emphasizes a pretty literal interpretation of the Bible. When the Bible says, liars won't inherit the kingdom of heaven, we take that literally."

"You mean no one in your church lies?" Rudy asked in a skeptical way.

"None of the members of the church do intentionally, at least," Neal said. "We also do not bear arms in military service. The Bible instructs that we are to love our enemies and pray for them who spitefully use you. We think it's a little hard to pray for someone while you're sighting them down the barrel of a rifle. We've got members in our church that I could introduce you to who were sentenced to death in Europe for their refusal to bear arms in Hitler's army.

"I have a friend whose father was sentenced to death for refusing to bear arms. They had him in jail for several months waiting execution. For all he knew he was going to be shot by firing squad. Then, at the last minute, they needed ambulance drivers so they made him one of those. While he was in the army jail he used to sing hymns. The guards trusted him so much that they would leave the jail doors open tempting him to escape. Somebody must have gotten the bright idea that people this honest could be used for some kind of work so they made him an ambulance driver instead of executing him. Others were executed.

"See, our church doesn't believe you're a Christian until you've made a thorough conversion. A thorough conversion means being convinced that you are a sinner, being genuinely sorry for your sins, repenting for them, confessing them, and making restitutions for them. After you've made restitutions for as many of your sins as you can recall, and are living peaceably with all men as much as you can, then God will give you His Divine Nature, and His Divine Peace. That peace is the most precious thing on earth. It's something everyone is looking for, but only true Christians find it. The Bible says it's a peace that passes all understanding. It's a feeling of direction, a feeling of confidence, and a feeling of hope in the future. Not only an earthly future, but a Heavenly future with God," Neal explained.

"Have you made that kind of conversion?" Rudy asked.

"Yes, I have."

"When did you have that conversion?"

"Two years ago." Neal said. "I guess about the same time you were changing from a fighter to a lover, so was I in a way. That brings up another important point. We believe that these conversions cannot occur before a person reaches the age of accountability."

"When's that?" Rudy asked.

"About thirteen or so. Before that, a person is really too immature to understand the complexities of conversion," Neal added.

"That makes sense to me," Rudy added to Neal's surprise. "I've read about those child ministers at six or so, and I wondered how this kid could know about all the pressures and influences on people."

"That's exactly right. And you see, our church realized that one hundred and forty years ago when it started. It wasn't because we were so smart. It's because it's in the Bible," Neal said. "OK your time's up. My turn again."

"No wait, I think I've got a few more minutes," Rudy said in mock protest.

"You'll have to wait till next time," Neal joked. "Tell me, how do you get along with your father?" Neal could see Rudy bristle with this question.

"Not as well as you and your father," Rudy said. He seemed to calculate that if he made some brief, superficial remarks, Neal would get off the subject.

"Well, do you do things together?" Neal continued.

"No. Sometimes we don't see each other for days," Rudy answered. "We don't have much in common."

"What does he do for a living?" Neal asked thinking that this would be a more comfortable question than the others; not knowing that this was the most sensitive area.

There was a long silence where Rudy seemed more perplexed than at any other time Neal had seen him. "I don't want to tell you what he does. It's nothing illegal, or anything like that. I wish you wouldn't try to figure it out. Maybe I'll tell you some day, I don't know." Rudy knew he sounded like a dope to Neal.

"Well, are your parents rich?" Neal asked, surprising even himself with this question.

"Let's just say they're comfortable," Rudy said, realizing that Neal was not going to be satisfied without some vague answer. "This is the subject I really hate to talk about because I guess I really hate my father. I know you're supposed to honor your father and mother, but if I had to be honest with you, I hate my father more than anyone on earth. My father never does anything with his children. He's as cold as ice. He's about as distant as the Matterhorn and just as cold. I think that's the reason my brother killed himself in a corvette. I think my brother needed some love and guidance from our dad and he never took the time to help him. He's so busy helping everyone else that he has no time for his family. I wish I could think of a way to make him pay for that."

"How about your mother? Is she more involved?"

"Not really. Although with her you get the impression it's because she doesn't know how to be. On the few times she's tried to stick up for us, my dad has put her down so badly that she just withdraws like a child herself. My dad really intimidates everyone in the house. He's a killer. He's killed my brother, and he's nearly killed me.

"I'm sorry about this appalling scene," Rudy confessed. "I told you I didn't want to talk about this. Please, don't let this spoil things. Let's change the subject. Let me ask you some questions."

"It's not your turn yet. I'll change the subject," Neal insisted.

That's the way the conversation went on for the whole morning. They never got back to Rudy's family, but they got to know each other quickly.

CHAPTER 7

Neal and Rudy talked at the breakfast table until nearly two o'clock and would have gone on longer if the phone had not interrupted them. The call was from Jim Stander. He and Jack Powers were going to New York and wondered if Neal wanted to go along.

"What're you going to do?" Neal asked.

"We're going to go to a couple of camera stores, and maybe check out a museum," Jim said.

"Rudy's here, too," Neal said.

"See if he can come," Jim offered.

"You want to go to New York? Jim and Jack—you met them yesterday—are going to go to a couple of camera stores, and maybe a museum," Neal said to Rudy. "You want to go with them?"

"Sure, why not?"

"OK Jim. Who's going to drive?" Neal asked.

"I'll drive. Your van's too big to park," Jim said. "I'll pick you up in a few minutes. We're on our way now."

Neal hung up and began picking up the breakfast plates. "They're on their way. Do you like photography?"

"Sure. I haven't done much of it, though," Rudy admitted.

Jim's car pulled into Neal's driveway and he gave an unnecessary honk on the horn. Rudy and Neal climbed into the back. The conditions were crowded and uncomfortable, particularly as Jim missed few chuck holes. Jack missed no opportunity to howl and mock his driving.

Once in a while Neal would explain to Rudy that they should not be taken too seriously. He explained that they always poke fun and mock each other.

"What religion are you, Rudy?" Jim asked. Neal was surprised that Jim would be so direct, and surprised that he had not asked the same question.

"I suppose I'm agnostic. My parents have never taken me to a church except for weddings or funerals."

"Haven't you ever been curious about the different churches?" Jack asked.

"No. I guess I've always thought that no one under seventy-five ever went to them. I thought of them as places for those who were afraid of death to go and get comfort," Rudy answered. "I find yours interesting, of course. That's why I'm hanging around Neal's so long. I guess I'm getting to be a pain."

"Not at all," Neal said with great sincerity.

"I'm sure Neal's right, Rudy," Jim agreed. "Our church believes in evangelism and we're thrilled that someone would show an interest. We're a little uncomfortable with standing on street corners and doing that kind of evangelism, but when someone wants to know more about our church, we're delighted to explain it to them."

They were now sitting in a huge pack of cars stuck in traffic, stopped somewhere in the middle of the pack with cars in both directions. "What a crowd for this time of day," Jim mentioned. Jim didn't have air conditioning so their windows were rolled completely down. Jim glanced out his side window and about six feet away he saw the tail pipe of another car bent so that it was aiming right at him.

"I wonder what the air quality index is on this spot right now. The air has to be ninety percent carbon monoxide. I wonder how people can live in this," Jim said with disgust.

"It seems real bad," Rudy agreed, "but people seem to live just about as long in New York as they do out in Ohio."

"Why did you pick Ohio?" Jack asked.

"Neal was talking about it yesterday," Rudy admitted.

"Have you ever been to Ohio?" Jack asked.

"Listen, if you're from Ohio, I didn't mean to insult your state. Make it Iowa."

"No, I'm not from Ohio, but that's the state where we have the most churches. We travel there once or twice a year for youth rallies and other activities. It's a great state," Jack said.

"I guess it must be," Rudy agreed. "Neal's dad said the same thing about so many churches being there. I've never been there. Didn't you say that's where you're going to school, Neal?"

"Yeah. And there's going to be a youth rally there in a couple months. Maybe you can go with us to visit then."

"Yeah, and how about Eastern Camp?" Jack asked. "Rudy should go to that if he really wants to know what our church is all about."

"What's Eastern Camp?" Rudy asked.

"Oh, about a thousand people from our churches around the country get together in Virginia for a week of fellowship around God's Word. There are lessons, forums on interesting topics, sermons, campfires, and lots of time to just visit," Jack explained. "It's a great way to get to know lots of people in our churches in a big hurry."

They rolled toward midtown and their conversation continued around the rich cultural background of their church, and how many things they enjoyed about it. Rudy was impressed to see that all three of these guys were equally sincere and devoted to their church. They seemed like intelligent guys to him. He didn't believe that anybody thought that way about their church.

After driving around for about twenty minutes in the area of the camera store, they finally followed a pedestrian who was walking to his car. When he pulled out they parked in his spot. (The average lifespan of an empty parking space in New York being approximately thirty seconds.)

Jim locked his car and they walked several blocks back to the camera store. After getting in, they found it hard to talk and move around with the crowd. Rudy stayed with Neal as Neal looked over some of the merchandise hanging on stands or lying on tables.

"Wow, I'd sure like to have one of these," Neal said pointing to a close-up billows for a Nikon camera outfit. "I'll have to save up for that."

Rudy just barely caught himself from buying it for him. He certainly bought much more expensive things for people who were far less nice to him in the past. He could have popped it on his dad's credit card and no one would have given it a thought. He knew he should repay Neal's kindness, but he didn't want to tamper with their friendship by throwing money around too easily. He would try to set his budget where Neal set his.

"Do you need a camera, Rudy?" Jim asked him. "It's a pretty big hobby for us."

"Well, I don't know. I don't have one. I've never really thought I needed one," Rudy answered.

"It's a great way to record memories," Jim added. "You sort of keep a record of important things in your life."

"I can see that," Rudy acknowledged. "I guess I just never

developed the hobby."

"If you want one, I can help you get a good beginner's outfit without wasting much money before you really know what you want," Jim offered.

"Thanks, but I'll wait. I don't usually care where I've been, or want to remember it all that much." Rudy regretted that as soon as he said it, hoping that he didn't sound too jaded.

Rudy watched as his new friends looked over the store's merchandise. How different they were than any of his other friends. They lacked a bitter sarcasm that most of his other friends had. They seemed to get a genuine excitement and interest in this activity. Their purchases were minor, not amounting to more than fifteen or twenty dollars each. In fact, Neal didn't buy anything. Rudy began debating again whether he should buy Neal those billows. He felt selfish just taking advantage of these guys and not paying them something, yet, somehow, he sensed that giving them gifts would spoil the sense of equality that they had so unselfishly given him.

When they finally left the camera store they decided to leave the car where it was and walk to a gallery. Along the way they looked in the windows of many stores, restaurants, and businesses. They also passed several street-corner lecturers passionately preaching their beliefs.

At one corner someone stopped Neal and engaged him in conversation. Neal was too timid to know how to stop him. The rest only noticed that Neal was missing after walking about halfway down the block. Rudy was the first to walk back to the corner.

"Did you tell this person you weren't interested?" Rudy asked Neal in a harsh tone of voice.

"Yes, but he just kept on talking," Neal admitted.

Rudy put his face about six inches away from the preacher and said, "He said `No!' don't you understand English?" Rudy said this in such a threatening and vicious tone of voice that he scared his friends. The preacher backed off immediately and apologized to Rudy.

The group walked back down the street with Rudy trembling in rage. "You've got to be tough with those people, Neal," he said. "They just push themselves all over you if you let them."

"I guess you would know, living in the city," Neal said.

Jim, Jack, and Neal noted how upset Rudy had become. It was

unlike anything they had seen in him up to that time. He still hadn't quite calmed down by the time they got to the gallery. They rode up the elevator in silence and got out in the small lobby where the gallery was.

"You're going to love this gallery, Rudy," Jim said. "You can actually look through mounted photographs of some of the greatest photographers in the world. They have actual prints right there and you can buy them if you have the money."

They went in the gallery and found it practically empty, a common experience most of the time. There were shelves of photography books and stands holding stacks of photos.

The guys spent about an hour quietly viewing while Rudy, finally, became bored. Rudy was not interested in photographs of the old masters, and most of these were black and white, on top of it all.

Finally, Jack noticed that Rudy was getting bored and said, "Have you had about enough?"

"Yeah," Rudy agreed. "Haven't these guys heard that they invented color photography? I can't see what the fascination is all about, can you?"

"Not really," Jack admitted.

"Why do you come here, then?" Rudy asked.

"Well, it's something to do. We usually have a lot of fun. What would you like to do now?" Jack asked.

"Let's take the Staten Island Ferry," Rudy suggested.

"Why do that?" Jim asked.

"It's fun to watch the captain try to dock the thing on each side," Rudy said.

So they hopped on a shuttle subway to the IRT line, took the IRT down to the southernmost point, West Battery, got off and walked to the dock. They paid the quarter each for a round trip boat ride. They walked around on the boat and watched as it went close to the Statue of Liberty. Rudy showed them how to walk to the front on the car level just as they were getting close to the dock on the other side. The underwater currents were stiff and it took an experienced pilot to drive the ferry precisely between the two walls of poles used for guiding it.

Often the pilot would misjudge and the boat would run into the wall of poles, which would bend greatly against the weight of the boat. After giving some, they would straighten out and push the boat toward the dock. After banking off the side a few times the boat would pull up to the dock where heavy walkways would be lowered onto the deck. Attendants then removed chains and let the people walk off.

It wasn't speed boating, but it was something to do, and it was a relaxing boat ride. The other guys claimed to enjoy it. It was a success. They hopped the subway back to Times Square, got out, and looked for their car.

CHAPTER 8

On the way back to Neal's house they were quiet from the rigors of hiking around New York. Rudy was thinking about what they had been doing for fun. It was the kind of life he was inclined to mock with his friends.

Rudy thought that if he had been with some of his friends and bumped into these guys he wouldn't even notice them. Alone, he found himself entertained by their ideas of fun. Such was the nature of the subtle prejudice in Rudy who thought himself above peer influence and prejudice.

After returning to Neal's home they went up to his room. Neal suddenly remembered, "Oh, tonight's youth group. You're going to like that, I think."

"Well, why not?" asked Rudy. "What do you do at youth group?"

"We sing a few songs, have a brief business meeting, and then we have a guest speaker come and talk, usually."

That evening Neal's mother served another delicious meal. Rudy was thoughtfully complimentary.

Later they climbed into Neal's van to begin Neal's self-imposed bus duties. Neal drove nearly fifty miles picking up kids to go to youth group. The kids were younger than Neal and Rudy. They all seemed innocent and childish to Rudy. It was hard for him to see them as people or personalities. Neal had no trouble relating to them as individuals. He knew details about them that revealed a special interest in them, not just the grudging duty of being the youth group bus driver.

The time went fast and Neal's van pulled up along a curb in an older residential neighborhood where the houses stood close together. A heavyset, older woman with a heavy German accent cheerfully met the young people with Rudy and Neal at the door. She exuded warmth and love as she let them all in. Inside the house there were many crafts and decorations. It seemed to Rudy that the woman was the creator of all these crafts and that she had gone well beyond an appropriate proportion of crafts for the space they were placed in. There were family pictures hanging on the walls of the living room, along with plaques of religious sayings. The living room formed an L shape with the dining room and was arranged with folding chairs in preparation for the meeting.

Rudy was introduced to the owners of the house. Rudy told them how nicely decorated their house was. They told Rudy what a nice looking boy he was.

The house quickly filled. Neal made Rudy sit toward the front by sitting there himself. Neal's friends, Jack and Jim, showed up shortly after. Someone tossed out song books to all those sitting in chairs. After singing several songs, the meeting began. Rudy noticed that Jack was the president. He began the meeting with the usual reports from the secretary and the treasurer.

Rudy noticed that all the girls wore dresses, and small doily-looking woven things on their heads. The guys wore conservative clothes and short hair. They sang heartily and seemed eager to be there. There was a lot of kidding and teasing. They all had a glow of health and innocence that reminded Rudy of a Norman Rockwell painting come to life.

Rudy thought to himself, "There's no doubt about it, Rudy, you've found yourself a real cult here, boy. What set of steps in brainwashing could get everyone to behave this way?" He didn't feel threatened though—he believed himself to be immune to "unhealthy" influences.

Jack was an efficient president. He handled some old business, talked about transportation to the upcoming youth rally in Ohio, made arrangements for a car wash to raise funds for sending their younger members, and discussed sending bandages and other supplies to Brazilian and Argentine missionaries with no resolution at this time. Someone complained that they never do these things, just talk about them. Someone else suggested forming a committee that could make recommendations to the group. Then Jack, sensing that the business meeting had gone on long enough, abruptly stopped it. He asked a young person Rudy did not know to pray.

"Let's rise for prayer." he said. "Dear Heavenly Father, we're so thankful to You that we could gather together tonight. We ask your blessing on the speaker tonight. We ask your blessing on the family that invited us into their home. We pray that each one who came out would receive a blessing from You. Amen."

They all sat down and Jack introduced the evening's speaker. Jack introduced him as, "Elder Brother Theo Venzel."

Theo Venzel stood in front of the group. He was short and thin and seemed old to Rudy. His small features were covered with wrinkled skin. He was bald with a narrow horseshoe of closely cut hair around the back of his head giving the impression of a bow of laurel twigs like the ancient Olympic athletes used to wear.

Theo spoke with a thick German accent in a quiet, meditative voice. He had a wise, patient, and constant smile on his face. His small face was dominated by thick glasses that magnified his eyes. His pupils appeared to float and slide around loosely as he shifted his focus from side to side. He struck Rudy as possessing great kindness and gentleness.

He spoke in a voice that suggested great respect for the youth and that he knew he was talking to intelligent, well educated people. He advised them that the Lord was looking upon them carefully to see who was wise among them.

He expressed concern that many of the young were not making progress in conversion. He was concerned that many young people were content to just attend church and not make a permanent commitment to Christ. He was anxious that they understand that this was not satisfactory to Christ. In fact, by their failure to accept the invitation call of Christ, they were putting themselves in the most condemned group mentioned in the whole Bible. To prove this point he asked them to turn to Matthew 10 and read some verses from that chapter.

It turned out as they read around the room that it fell to Rudy to read verse 15 which was, "Verily I say unto you, It shall be more tolerable for the land of Sodom and Gomorrah in the day of judgment, than for that city." After the reading was ended Theo Venzel elaborated on the verse that Rudy read. He mentioned that the twin cities of Sodom and Gomorrah were among the most wicked in the world. But without elaborating on that, he went on to say that even though God made it rain fire and brimstone on Sodom and Gomorrah, he will take a more tolerant view of those people than the young people sitting in that room if they fail to respond to the loving call of Jesus Christ to be their Savior and Guide.

"Make no mistake about it," Theo said using an expression that Rudy would learn he frequently used, "This is a serious business.

No one comes into the presence of the preaching of the Gospel and walks away innocent in God's eyes. You will be required to give an account for yourself as to what you did with Jesus Christ. Did you cry 'crucify him,' or did you bow down to Him and call upon Him to give you the power you need to become a son or daughter of the Living God and a joint heir with Jesus Christ of the Heavenly Kingdom?"

The man never raised his voice once in the entire thirty-minute talk, Rudy observed. He used none of the splashy techniques for holding people's attention; yet, he had everyone wrapped in attention. No one stirred while he spoke. And after he stopped, as if suddenly realizing that, everyone shifted in his seat, coughed, and in other ways seemed to come back to life.

Rudy was thunderstruck. He had never seen anything like this in his life. This was the closest to how he imagined Christ Himself would have taught. This was how he had heard the Tibetan gurus were described. Yet here was this guy talking in an older middle class home in Stamford to a small group of nerd-like kids for free.

While these thoughts were turning through Rudy's head, the group had chosen another song to sing out of the songbook and had actually begun singing before Rudy realized it. Neal noticed that Rudy was deep in thought, too, and believed it to be a good sign. Neal thought, "How fortunate that on this first night we have Brother Theo. This has been a good introduction for Rudy."

Rudy was impressed that Venzel declined to elaborate on the practices of Sodom and Gomorrah. Some people condemned them so loudly and long that it suggested a morbid fascination with the practices they were condemning. In fact, Venzel was saying that these nice, clean cut, Norman Rockwell-type kids were worse than those who practiced sodomy. Rudy was not sure he agreed with this; but he found the teaching consistent with the scripture used, and he found it unique.

After a closing song, there was another prayer by a young man in the group and the hostess served refreshments. These consisted of excellent pastries of a German and Austrian origin and punch. Rudy noticed that these kids enjoyed hanging around together and stayed forty-five minutes after the program ended. It was obvious that these people enjoyed each other's company and shared many interests in common.

After dropping off their passengers, Rudy and Neal were finally alone in the van.

"Well, what did you think?" Neal asked. He thought that Rudy would be impressed.

"That dude's cool," Rudy said.

"Yeah, I thought you'd be impressed with him," Neal agreed. "He's probably one of the leading elders in our entire national church."

"Does he represent the opinions of the whole church?" Rudy asked.

"Pretty much," added Neal. "He's been around a long time. He's lived through a lot."

"He just seemed to really know what he was talking about. It would be hard to jump on him for anything he said tonight," Rudy said.

That night, after getting ready for bed, Neal knelt beside his bed to pray as he always did. Rudy felt the urge to kneel down and pray too. Several times during Neal's silent prayer Rudy nearly slid out of bed and knelt to pray. Two things kept him from doing it: he felt Neal would read too much into it if he did, and he was not sure what he would say anyway.

As Rudy was falling asleep he kept wondering what Theo meant when he said that no one comes into the presence of the preaching of the Gospel and walks away innocent in God's eyes. Rudy could understand that he was not innocent; but he could not understand how hearing the preaching of the Gospel was the key to taking away one's innocence.

Rudy's thinking about God in the past was limited to a belief that God said He was love and Rudy assumed that He'd forgive everyone for anything they did. He began to admit to himself that there may be some fine print in that huge book called the Bible that he should read—but he was afraid to.

CHAPTER 9

The next morning Rudy decided he had worn out his welcome and planned to go back to New York. He knew telling Neal would be difficult. He'd have to choose his words carefully. He was surprised and amused at his concern to not hurt Neal's feelings. This was a new emotion to him.

He tried to plan his words as he walked down the stairs. He was greeted by the smell of bacon and eggs.

"Neal," Rudy began while watching closely for Neal's reaction, "I don't know how to thank you for all you've done for me. I don't just mean putting me up and making me breakfast, I mean taking me to your youth group and letting me meet some of your friends."

"Sure, Rudy, glad to do it," Neal answered and began to suspect that Rudy was softening him up for something else.

Rudy noticed the worried look and quickly added, "I'm sure you'll deny it, but I feel I've stretched my welcome. I think I'll head back home today, but I'll definitely keep in touch."

"Oh no," Neal protested, "you haven't worn out your welcome. My parents probably don't even know you're staying here. They're gone before we get up and we're gone when they're around."

"We've had some meals with them," Rudy said. "They've got to be wondering how long I'm staying. Besides, I really want to get home for a while."

"Why don't you wait till after this weekend? This weekend you can visit our church. After that, I'll be satisfied that you've had a proper introduction to our church," Neal argued.

"I want to come to your church this Sunday. I just don't want to stay at your house all that time. I wouldn't feel right. I've got to get home and do some thinking," Rudy said.

"But what if you get home and decide that it's too much of a hassle to get up to our church on Sunday. It'd be easier to stay here. How are you going to get there?" Neal asked.

"I'll come. I promise you I'll come, OK?" Rudy assured him. "I can take a train and a bus. Just tell me where the church is. I'll check the schedules and get there."

"I can pick you up in my van," Neal said. "Maybe I can even

visit you later this week to work out the details."

"Maybe we can do that later," Rudy held his ground. "For now, let's just leave it this way. I'll head back home today and meet you at your church on Sunday. Don't worry. I'll be there."

But Neal was worried. Neal couldn't be sure that this wasn't a farewell. He began having doubts. He thought, "How could Rudy be interested in such an odd church?" At the same time he was hearing Rudy promise to be there. He decided to believe him. One thing was clear, Rudy wanted to go home after breakfast.

"So, how are you going to get home?" Neal asked. "I can take you in the van."

"No, that's too much driving." Rudy protested.

"Maybe Jim or Jack are going in anyway?" Neal continued.

"I'll just take a train. Let's check the schedules."

They enjoyed a leisurely breakfast before Neal dropped Rudy off at the train station. As Neal pulled away and saw Rudy in the rear-view mirror, he wondered if Rudy would keep his promise to be at his church that next Sunday. He had given Rudy the address and the schedule of the services. That was about all he could do.

Rudy sat by a window on the train. He looked out the window half seeing the houses, the trees, and the buildings slide by his view. He was deep in thought about his life and the lives of Neal, Jim, and Jack. Occasionally some observation would impose itself on Rudy's thinking. There were the two little boys playing "Dodge cars" with their bicycles in the parking lot of the grocery store. There was the loud steady rumbling and hum of the train's machinery. Finally there was the tacky home-made sign on the little ma-and-pa hardware store on one of the blocks they rolled by.

They made good time getting into the city. When the train screeched to its final stop, Rudy grabbed his backpack and ran up the stairs two at a time to the street level. He decided to walk to his parent's apartment after sitting in the train so long.

He felt a strange blend of contentment and hostility. He was surprised to feel an urge to keep his promise to Neal and visit his church. But he also recognized a small sense of encroachment because he never kept these kinds of promises with other people he met.

As Rudy got closer to his apartment building the sidewalk became more crowded. Afternoon luncheons were breaking up from the expensive restaurants along the way. Shoppers were milling around, sidewalk venders were setting up their stands, and limousines lined up two-deep much of the length of the street.

He passed a man who had set up an easel with a white board upon which he had written an elaborate chart explaining some religious view. The man stepped right in front of Rudy and asked him to look at this chart and listen to what he had to say. Rudy drew himself up to his full height and with all the indignation he could produce, flipped his middle finger about six inches from the man's face and yelled "Get out of my way!" The man moved quickly, fearing that Rudy might become more violent. Rudy surprised himself with this reaction. He seemed to be a volcano of hate. Rudy was confused by such a flash of temper in himself so recently after all the love and kindness he experienced with Neal.

Rudy was more worried about his growing tendency to judge his own actions. Would he return to Neal's church? Was he rude to that street preacher? Since when did he ask himself so many questions about his behavior?

Rudy walked into the lobby of his building and overheard the security guard and a woman talking. The woman was in her forties and was talking about a church building her small congregation had purchased and was refurbishing. Rudy stopped to listen, too, for no particular reason. He was on friendly terms with the security guard, a compassionate older woman in her sixties who was a good listener.

"...so when we looked at the stained woodwork after it dried," the lady said, "we noticed that it was not the same color as the other woodwork in the sanctuary. We were so disappointed until someone noticed that it matched perfectly the stain on the doors of the bathrooms. So the molding and trim could be used around the bathrooms and it matched perfectly. Isn't that something? It's like a miracle; like it was just meant to work out that way; like it was supposed to be that way." The lady enthused like she was telling someone of the parting of the Red Sea.

"You mean that God arranged for the color of the wood to come out that way," Rudy interrupted.

"Well, yes. That's exactly what I meant. I really believe that," the lady said.

"Well you said that 'it' just worked out that way. What you

should have said was that God worked it out that way. 'It' didn't work it out that way. God did it," Rudy added. "Either you believe in God or you believe in 'it,' but something worked it out that way, either God or 'it.'"

"Oh, you're that shrink's brat son, aren't you?" she attacked.

"No," Rudy said with all the arrogance he could arrange in his voice. "I'm the son of god," he said as he walked to the elevator and threw his pack in the corner while still five feet in front of the doors. He entered, turned around, and waited while the operator took him to his family's floor.

"Isn't that a shame?" asked the woman of the security guard. "All that money and it just spoils the children."

Rudy walked across the foyer of their apartment and noticed that his mother had her discussion group in the living room. He stopped in the entrance to the living room, held his fist high over his head in the style of the "black power" salute, and yelled, "Praise Jesus!" as loudly as he could. He walked over and kissed his mother, took several finger sandwiches that were on a huge, glass-topped coffee table, and walked back out toward his rooms.

"What do you do with teenagers?" his mother asked rhetorically. "His father has too many ideas on how to raise him and I have none."

"Well, I told my kids that I was going to survive child rearing whether they did or not," volunteered one woman.

Rudy threw his pack in the corner of his room and headed for the outdoor pool. He kicked off his shoes, stripped off his shirt and pants, and dove into the pool. He swam several laps before crawling out of the pool and walking back to his rooms. He passed several cleaning ladies who showed no signs of shock at his dripping water on the carpet. They were used to his habits, which were eccentric at best and almost animal-like at worst. One of them simply picked up a rag and wiped up the water where she could.

Another cleaning lady went out to the pool and picked up his clothes and carried them to his sitting room. Rudy would be looking for those things before leaving later, and he knew that they would be brought to just that spot.

Rudy punched a few buttons on his stereo counsel with the same speed and familiarity that an airline pilot punches the buttons on his control panel, and his bedroom was filled with music. He flopped down on the bedspread of his bed, getting it wet, and pulled several pillows out from under this cover. There he dozed for several hours.

He might have slept longer but his phone rang. His answering machine droned out its faithful message, "Hi, this is Rudy. Drop dead if you think I'm going to do anything for you, but if you want to do something for me, leave your name, number, and a brief message. Wait for the beep, dummy." Rudy winced at the tough sound of his message. He wondered, had this visit with Neal changed him this much? Was he that tough before?

"Hi, Rudy, this is Renee. Where've ya been? Let's go dancing tonight. I'll pick you up at ten. Call me either way," and she hung up. Rudy just reached for the phone as she hung up.

"Shoot," Rudy said. Now I'll have to call her, he thought as one of his favorite songs started on the radio. He reached for the remote control and cranked the volume up to ear-splitting levels. He flopped back and forth on the bed to the rhythm of the music.

When the music stopped, he hit the remote control and the room got quieter again. He dialed Renee's number. While he was waiting for the three rings to start Renee's answering machine he noticed that there were several messages on his answering machine. He reached down and rewound the tape without listening to the messages. The next few calls would record over those and he wouldn't listen to them either.

"Hi. This is Renee. Like, I can't answer the phone right now but, uh, like, your call is very, important to me, OK? So leave a message and I'll call you back."

Renee picked up the phone when Rudy started talking and they agreed to meet at a popular nightclub in midtown between ten and eleven. They picked one that catered to a highly varied crowd. It was huge, popular, and had lots of rooms for different kinds of groups.

Renee's father was a television news anchor for a major network, and her mother was the daughter of a senior partner in an aggressive law firm. They were divorced and Renee lived with her mother. Renee's grandfather and Rudy's father were well acquainted. Peterfield had used the law firm on numerous occasions because of their ruthless reputation. (It was said of that firm that just answering a threatened suit on their stationery often discouraged the other party from pursuing the suit any further.) Peterfield didn't know Renee's father, however, and did not know that Rudy was Renee's friend and occasional lover.

Rudy showered, shaved, and splashed on lots of talc and cologne. He pulled on tight jeans, and an oversized shirt which he fastened with only one button near the middle. He dug around in the corner of his closet and found an old, worn down pair of cheap, rubber thong-type sandals for his feet—the kind that people wear in public showers to keep from getting athletes foot. He got his wallet from his pants and added a few more hundred dollar bills. He also removed his credit card, and any other form of identification so that if he lost everything he wouldn't have to run around and replace things.

Rudy grabbed his backpack and dumped the contents out on the floor. The maids would clean anything he had laying loosely on the floor. Along with his clothes the small black hymnal that Neal had given him fell out.

That reminded him of the train schedule. He looked up the number and called but the line was busy. He decided he had time to call later.

Rudy went down to the kitchen to see what was cooking, and who was home to eat it.

"Hi Paulette," Rudy said as he walked in the kitchen. "What's the grub?"

Paulette was an older French cook who had been with the Peterfields since before Rudy was born. She loved her work and was considered one of the best gourmet cooks in Manhattan. Her specialty was sauces and she knew exactly what Dr. Peterfield liked. She understood that he was the one member of this family with strong feelings about food. If she made him unhappy, her work was finished.

"What do you mean grub?" Paulette responded faking horror in her voice. She explained the meal to Rudy. Rudy looked at a small television monitor on the counter. This was a closed circuit television system so that the kitchen would know how quickly the guests were going through the courses of food. During the longer courses even the waiters were supposed to go to the kitchen and leave the guests alone. There were signals Peterfield worked out that would inform them when guests might want more wine, or anything else. This television system had no sound, which kept conversations confidential, and this required someone to be watching the television nearly all the time.

"The old man's eating alone tonight?" Rudy asked.

"Your father is eating alone. You might go in and keep him company," Paulette corrected knowing full well how Rudy would receive this advice.

"Yeah and I might cut off my right arm, too," Rudy said. "Let me have a plate here at the counter."

Paulette adroitly set a complete place setting on the counter with the same china Rudy's father was eating on. She made it look effortless.

Rudy shared his father's love for fine food and was generous with praise to Paulette. For this reason, she tolerated and overlooked his boyish antics and shocking expressions. She made nearly as big a fuss for him as she did for Peterfield—which included access to wine.

This evening Rudy drank more wine than was usual.

"You pour the wine down like you don't want to go wherever you're going tonight," she observed.

"No, I'm looking forward to getting out tonight," Rudy insisted, but wondered to himself if she was right. Did he have doubts? He was aware of some self-examination on the question that would not have been there before. Where, he wondered, did that come from?

"No, Paulette, it's just that debauchery is such hard work that I need to get somewhat numbed before beginning it," Rudy joked.

"I think you better check the meaning of debauchery," Paulette said. "A person your age should not be involved in debauchery."

"Only people my age have the energy for debauchery," Rudy joked.

Paulette shook her head in mock disapproval.

Rudy finished his last glass of wine and decided it was time for him to go. He checked the television screen to make sure that he wouldn't run into his father on the way out and headed for the front door and the elevator down to the rush of the city. A cab rushed him to the door of the club he mentioned by name. Rudy climbed out and stood in the line that was already forming. This club was famous for rejecting people at the door, thereby creating a specially blended mix of people to play together in this adult sandbox of drugs, drink, and debauchery.

Rudy never had any trouble getting in, since the owner was a patient of Rudy's father.

The line was composed of every character type in the city that night. There were prep school types with boat shoes, khaki pants, and sweaters with the long sleeves pushed up to the elbows. There were bums with filthy clothing reeking of sweat and dirt. There were those in off-the-shelf suits from department stores who were nervously trying to look rich. There were those in tuxedos rented or owned who were trying to look above it all. Rudy's tight jeans, open shirt, and rubber sandals were surprisingly middle of the road for this crowd.

Rudy descended the long stairs into the inferno of people that were waiting below. The first sensation was the loud rock music, which made any sustained, intimate conversation impossible. It was the kind of rock music that emphasized wild, frenetic guitar solos against an almost industrial background of rhythm. The beat was about twice that of the human heart beat and suggested excitement and abandon to the all too willing crowd.

The next sensation was the smell of smoke and booze. Finally there was the crowd. The club seemed to have an uncountable number of levels and rooms. There were bars stretching along several walls, sunken sections, elevated sections, and sections separated by thin walls, shutters, strings of beads, and more substantial walls.

The place was already crowded by ten-thirty. Rudy walked through the center of the room heading for one of the bars. He ordered a screwdriver and had no difficulty getting it even though he was three years under age. After paying for it and getting a huge wad of bills in change, he turned around and waited for Renee. Several people said hi to him as they walked around, suggesting that they get together soon. Rudy nodded and said anytime.

Rudy knew that he'd be here first because Renee was always late, but after two screwdrivers he became impatient. He walked over to someone both he and Renee knew. "Have you seen Renee?" he asked.

"Yea. She's over at the bar," the friend said pointing to a bar on the opposite side of the room.

"Thanks," Rudy said and walked over to see Renee sitting on the end of the bar drinking a beer.

"Where've you been?" Rudy asked. "I've been waiting over

there for a half hour."

"What?" Renee said, not hearing Rudy for the noise.

Rudy leaned over to speak right into Renee's ear. Renee mistook this for a desire to embrace and hugged Rudy affectionately. Rudy returned the hug and noticed that Renee was more passionate than usual. By talking into each other's ears Rudy learned that Renee was upset because her father wanted to get married again and have the whole family come to the wedding in Europe. It would knock three or four weeks out of her summer, and would require her to do a lot of family things that she hated.

"So don't go," Rudy suggested.

"My dad's not like yours," Renee argued. "He doesn't ignore everything I do. He overinterprets everything I do. If I don't go, he'll freak. He can make life real rough for me."

Rudy ordered another round and they turned around to watch the crowd. It was the usual mix of exhibitionists, thrill seekers, parasites, fun lovers, and people with attitudes.

"I've got to take a leak," Rudy told Renee.

"Me too," Renee said.

They found the washroom and walked in to relieve themselves. There were dozens of stalls around the room with lots of traffic wanting either drugs or sex—both of which were in great supply.

Renee grabbed Rudy and gave him a hug and a big wet kiss. "Not so fast," Rudy protested.

"Oh, we're in a mood are we?" Renee asked.

"I don't know, I guess I am."

They returned to the main room only to find that they had lost their seats at the bar. They walked to another section of the club where people were into dancing energetically. The music played on and the place kept getting more crowded.

"Let's get out of here," Rudy suggested.

"Now?" Renee asked.

"Yeah, now," Rudy said. They got to the street and quickly found a cab to take them to the next club. Traffic was not bad so they got there quickly.

Renee was not getting anywhere with Rudy. He seemed distracted and only wanted to drink. She wanted to go to bed with him and the thought of that reminded him of Neal and his friends. How differently he looked at this now. As a result of this distraction, he seemed miles away to Renee.

"Hey, what's the matter?" Renee asked.

"Nothing," He was surprised to notice tears forming in his eyes. Were these tears of exhaustion, tears of stress?

"Hey, you all right?" Renee asked as she looked up at him. "What can Renee do?"

"Let's just drink for a while," Rudy said.

"Sure, Rudy. Let's do."

"I'm sure glad you understand me," Rudy said. "I'm glad we can just sit here side by side and not even feel we have to talk all the time. It's comfortable just sitting beside someone you love."

Rudy thought of Neal and how much kindness he had shown him, and he thought of Renee and couldn't remember one act of kindness Renee had shown him except for physical love. The act of saying this to Renee showed him how untrue it really was.

After a few more drinks they decided to go to another place with a little more energy. So they walked back out to the street and hailed another cab.

Rudy picked a place that was even more high energy than the first place, hoping to pump some life back into the evening.

It was after the second day of this that Rudy realized he was looking at seven in the morning on Sunday, the day he had promised Neal he would visit his church.

CHAPTER 10

Rudy was startled to recognize that it was Sunday morning. He was still in a club. He had forgotten to check the train schedule. He faced the prospect of letting Neal down. He had that same knotted-stomach feeling that a schoolboy gets when he realizes he forgot to do some important homework. At the same time he was confused. He didn't know why he worried so much about disappointing Neal.

He shook his head to think clearly. How could he get there? A cab would be too expensive and the driver wouldn't know Connecticut anyway. His folks' cars would be busy. He finally struck upon the idea of an airport limousine. They could take him there with no trouble. Rudy arranged for one to pick him up in front of his parents' apartment in an hour. He took a cab to his apartment, quickly cleaned up, and changed.

He wisely decided upon conservative clothing: a dark, Wall Street broker type suit, white shirt, and red tie. It had been some time since he wore a suit, and he was pleased with how serious and intimidating he looked.

He walked through the kitchen to grab something to eat.

Paulette, who was beginning breakfast, looked up and commented, "Well, look at the junior arbitrageur. Are you off to a funeral?"

"No, church," Rudy answered. He grabbed a croissant and a cup of coffee and headed for the elevator, leaving Paulette speechless.

Rudy finished the croissant and coffee during the long delay for the limousine. He was about to call when it pulled up. The term "limousine" was a joke for this rust bucket. Rudy cautiously climbed into the rattling van and told the driver where he wanted to go. The driver assured him that it was no problem, so Rudy went back looking for a bench seat that he could stretch out on. He tried to find one where the plastic upholstery was not torn too badly so that the stuffing would not get all over his suit.

Lying on the seat he was floating half way between being awake and asleep. He slept better than he thought, however, because the driver woke him when he pulled furiously into a gas station cursing the crazy roads in Stamford. The driver had no idea where he was. Meanwhile, these delays made Rudy late for church.

Neal was disappointed, but he could not honestly say he was surprised. The church had a forty-five minute Bible study before the main worship service. There was a ten-minute break between the two. Neal still hoped that Rudy would make it for the worship service.

Though Neal realized that Rudy was probably not coming he still looked up when anyone came late. Each time it was someone else. And as some law would have it, when Rudy did arrive it was the one time Neal did not look up. Rudy walked into the church through the main doors and saw no one in the hall. He noticed the Bible study in a room off the hall. He found where the back of the group was sitting and went in that door.

Rudy noticed a seat next to Neal that he had, obviously, kept open for him. The Bible Study teacher continued his lesson without interruption while Rudy confidently walked up the aisle and sat down beside Neal. Neal couldn't believe his eyes.

"I thought you weren't going to make it," Neal whispered.

"I told you I'd be here, didn't I?" Rudy asked.

"Sure did," Neal said.

They sat there quietly listening to the remaining few minutes of the Bible Study. Rudy discreetly looked around the room. He noticed about a hundred people. They were all conservatively dressed. Rudy spotted Jim and Jack, nodded slightly, and smiled, acknowledging their presence.

The Bible study ended and they slowly walked to the sanctuary. Several people walked purposefully up to Rudy and introduced themselves. One older man was friendly, half hugging him and patting him on the shoulder. He spoke with a heavy German accent but the message was of welcome. He kept saying how happy he was that Rudy was a guest.

Someone announced that it was time to get started and they filed into the sanctuary. Rudy noticed that there was a genuine hush of reverence and that nearly everyone bowed their heads as they sat in the pews and said a brief silent prayer. Quiet organ music played for a few minutes when, without waiting for it to stop, a song number was announced.

Neal pulled out two hymnals, just like the one he gave Rudy, handing one to Rudy. Neal sang heartily, as did nearly everyone. The effect was awesome. This group was quite sophisticated musically. They sang four-part harmony and sounded like a prepared choir, even though someone just announced an unrehearsed song.

When the song was completed, several men in the first row began conferring together in hushed whispers. Two of them walked up to chairs that had been placed behind an elevated pulpit. Once they sat down they, again, bowed their heads and had a short, silent prayer. They then conferred again to decide who would deliver the sermon.

Rudy recognized Theo Venzel sitting in the first row and figured that he was not going to preach today. Rudy would have a chance to hear another preacher from this church.

The preacher stood behind the pulpit for a few seconds in quiet contemplation. "Let us pray." he said. "Lord, we stand before thy Holy Word as an empty vessel waiting to be filled from Thee. We draw together seeking instruction from Thee and not the wisdom of men. We are thankful for the opportunity to gather in peace, unmolested from without, or from within. We are thankful for a good government that allows us to gather in worship freely. And we want to pray for our government as Thy Word instructs us to do. Divide, now, Thy Word to a place that seemeth good to Thee. For Thou dost know the needs of Thy children and friends. We promise to listen to the teaching of Thy Good and Holy Spirit; and to let none of Thy words fall to the ground. We promise to be not only hearers, but doers of Thy Word. This we pray in Jesus's name, Amen."

After the prayer the preacher opened the covers of the Bible and the pages fell open. He looked at the page for about five seconds and announced, "The Bible has opened to II Corinthians, chapter three. Let us read and meditate from this passage for our text this morning."

He gave everybody a moment to find that passage in their own Bibles. Rudy pulled a Bible out of the rack mounted to the back of the pew in front of him and looked in the index for II Corinthians.

"Page 189," Neal whispered to him.

"Thanks," Rudy said.

After reading the chapter the preacher suggested another hymn to sing. This was followed by a prayer given by the other minister. For this second prayer the congregation knelt on the floor with their arms resting on the pew in front of them.

Rudy thought this was all interesting. He sensed in these actions and words a paradox of great formality yet devoid of ornament or ritual. Rudy noticed no traditional Christian trappings in the sanctuary. The inside was tastefully decorated but plain. It reminded him of a black tuxedo, plain but formal.

After the prayer the congregation settled back into the pews for the meditation. The first minister returned to the pulpit and talked without notes about the chapter they just read together. He spoke frankly with boldness, clarity, and honesty. It seemed to Rudy that he was speaking only to him. Rudy was impressed by how this man could make this ancient text come alive and be relevant to today.

Rudy became lost in the message. It seemed like he was the only one in the building. He looked into the eyes of the minister and it seemed like the minister was looking only at him. During the course of the sermon Rudy did not move a muscle.

After twenty minutes the preacher stopped. He invited the other minister to add to the sermon, which he declined to do. When the preaching stopped Rudy shifted his posture. Others did the same. It became obvious that few, if any, had moved during the sermon. Such was the concentration people were paying to these wonderful words.

After they sang another hymn, the preacher invited a "brother" to conclude the meeting with prayer. Just behind Rudy sat an older man who announced, "Let's pray." He then proceeded to thank God for the sermon, and the opportunity to get together. He prayed for those who were too sick or shut-in to come to church. He concluded his prayer by expressing his thanks for those who visited the church including some for the first time. Rudy was a little embarrassed that he had been singled out in this way, but was also impressed that these people appreciated guests.

After the prayer the minister made a few brief announcements and then asked, "Are there any greetings for the congregation?"

"Greetings from Upper Marlboro, Maryland," came one voice.

"Greetings from Windsor," came another.

After each of these announcements the preacher said, "Thank you."

After a short delay, Rudy suddenly caught on and said, "Greetings from New York."

Neal nearly laughed and leaned over and whispered, "No,

that's only for members of the church visiting from other places where there are churches. But that's OK" The preacher thanked Rudy as well, wishing to treat the misunderstanding as casually as possible. Church was then dismissed and all were invited to eat a light lunch in the multipurpose room.

"Let's go out for lunch," Rudy suggested to Neal.

"Well, there usually isn't much time," Neal explained. "They have a brief lunch and an afternoon sermon that starts at one."

"You go to both sermons?" Rudy asked. He thought the afternoon sermon was for those who didn't attend the morning sermon.

"Oh yes," Neal answered. "And there's a midweek service on Thursday evenings. Once a month there's a family night when we have Sunday evening singing with special numbers. You might say we're an active church."

"I'd say that," Rudy agreed. "Are all the sermons this good?"

Neal was delighted to hear Rudy's reaction to the sermon. "Yes, mostly. Of course some are better than others."

The group sprung into action, getting the tables and chairs out and the food ready. Everyone had a small job to do, and the work flowed so naturally, with such an economy of effort, and so efficiently, that it was obvious that they did this often.

While they ate, church members tossed friendly jokes back and forth. Someone commented on Rudy's suit which, when attention was called to it, was discovered to be of the highest quality. This tended to confirm the theory that Rudy was from a wealthy family.

Following the afternoon service, people went their own ways. The young people got together to visit older folks. Once a month the church had a family night supper with a program of songs, musical numbers, and a brief talk. Rudy happened to come on one of these Sundays.

During the supper that evening Rudy sat across from an older woman. Neal and Jim sat on either side of him. The woman had a pleasant, unwrinkled face. She was short, overweight, and wore an old derby-style hat which made her look like Winston Churchill. She had an untroubled look of contentment.

"What a nice sermon we had this morning." she said to Rudy while smiling warmly. Rudy agreed.

"Where're you from?" she asked.

"New York," Rudy answered, feeling slightly admonished for

not introducing himself. "I'm Rudy Pete-uh Horace. I'm just visiting here."

"I know. We're always glad to have visitors. It cheers us up," she said. "I'm Anna Bauer." She offered her hand. Rudy rose to his feet to shake her hand.

"I'm glad to meet you. Where're you from?"

"I'm from Mitrovitsa. It's in Yugoslavia. I was born there. I've lived here for the last thirty-five years."

Rudy asked her many questions about how she got to this country, why she left, and what she has done here for thirty-five years. Neal noticed this and was, again, quietly impressed with Rudy's manners. He also noticed that these questions went beyond mere politeness. It seemed like Rudy had a genuine interest in this woman. Neal observed how easily Rudy just started asking her questions, and how much she was enjoying the interest.

After the meal the church, again, sprang into activity like a beehive, clearing the tables, doing dishes, putting away tables and arranging the chairs.

The evening program consisted of general singing and mixed groups of vocals and instruments. One violin quartet of children played several hymns. They were obviously just learning the violin and the screeching was bad. This struck Rudy as funny. He wanted to laugh but realized how rude that would be. In trying to stifle his laugh, he found he had to laugh more. He bent forward to hide his face behind the back of the person sitting in front of him and his face turned red. He pulled out a handkerchief to act like he was blowing his nose. He was desperately trying to get control of himself. Fortunately the songs they played were short. Neal and Jim saw the whole thing and laughed at Rudy's predicament.

Toward the end of the program, an older man gave a five-minute talk. One comment caught Rudy's imagination. The man said, "Many times people wonder why they were put on this earth." Rudy could agree with that. He had wondered that many times. "Well," he went on, "God is love, and we are put on this earth to reflect God's love to others. We are to carry out God's love through our hands and feet, through our voices and minds. We are to be an agent of that love to the world around us."

That statement seemed to sum up what Rudy was seeing in these people, in this church.

CHAPTER 11

Rudy woke up late Monday morning in his own room. His last three days made sleep a necessity, not a luxury. He stared at the ceiling and was in no hurry to move. It was time to reflect on the last few days. He felt like he had visited a foreign country. He wanted to review his memories before allowing them to slip into unconsciousness.

His thoughts kept returning to the kind of fun Neal and his friends had. They didn't do drugs, sex, or rock and roll. And, yet, he liked being with them. He found them interesting. He felt that they had something that he wanted. What could it be—the religion?

Rudy remembered a conversation his father and grandmother had about religion. His grandmother attended church regularly and suggested that Peterfield do the same with his children, since she believed that it was important for children.

"That's just it, it's exclusively for children," Peterfield said. "Just like Bugs Bunny and the Road Runner, religion is a myth, a cartoon to give people the illusion of things working out right in the end."

"You're equating religion with a cartoon?" she asked.

"Yes. Life's a huge cosmic joke. And if there is a God, which I can't believe, He'd be laughing till his sides ached from the sight of those who practice religion in His name."

"Everyone believes in God when the going gets rough," she said. "People cry out to Him just before crashes, disasters. That must mean something."

"It simply means that they've been taught what everyone in our culture's been taught. It hardly proves there's a God. Did God save them from the accident?"

"There's no doubt in my mind that there is a God," she continued. "And a Jesus Christ."

"Yeah, well, Jesus told you to have only one coat, and if you have two to give one away. Shall we walk over to your six closets and check out your supply?"

"Don't reduce the argument to absurdities," she argued. "Of course we live in different times. I merely think it would be helpful for you to take your family to church for some exposure to religious training. Normal people find it most wholesome for families."

"Evelyn Waugh found it to be the province of inhibitions and complexes," Peterfield argued.

"Evelyn Waugh was converted to Catholicism in his life. He obviously thought it appropriate."

"Freud said religion was an opiate for the mind."

"And I say that you have an unhappy family, and you don't take them to church. Maybe there's a connection. That's all," she huffed in one last effort.

"Purely coincidence. I suppose if there was a big solar flare the day you got the flu you would think that solar flares caused influenza," Peterfield countered.

The conversation went downhill from there. Peterfield was unmoved. His mother-in-law was unprepared to argue with him on the subject. Just how unprepared, however, was what Rudy was going to learn.

Even though Rudy's father felt strongly about religion, he knew enough about business not to make those feelings public. The last thing he wanted to do was become a spokesman for atheists and alienate his public audience. Peterfield was a cautious man. He prided himself on planning to avoid regrets.

Rudy knew he couldn't talk to his father about religion. He didn't feel he could talk to his mother either. She never expressed a firm opinion about anything. Rudy knew if she ever did have any opinions, twenty-five years of marriage to his father were enough to kill those. His mother just did parties. She worked on volunteer projects for what were, to Rudy, totally meaningless causes like the New York City skyline, saving old buildings, and graffiti art shows.

Mrs. Peterfield had been beautiful in her youth and was still strikingly good looking. She was thin, fragile-looking, frequently bored, and easily exhausted. She seemed more like a vision, an apparition, incapable of touching things, only floating around them gently, softly influencing people with the influence of her poise, wealth, and social position which she knew how to use powerfully. Everything was such an effort to her. She had help for everything. She reduced herself to just a will giving directions for others to carry out. Rudy exhausted her. She loved him greatly but was afraid that his energy would somehow impose itself upon her and draw her into some burden she would rather avoid. Rudy suddenly realized how alone he was. There was no one for him to talk to about his recent experiences. He didn't even know if his father was in the country. For all he knew, he could have taken the Concorde to Paris for the day.

Rudy was not physically neglected. He was a precocious child and his parents encouraged him in many interests. His father even took him to cub scouts. One night the director decided to play a group game. Everyone was supposed to take off their shoes and throw them into a pile in the middle of the room. The lights were turned off and people had to find their shoes in the dark.

Rudy's father was purple with rage at this familiarity. They left as soon as they possibly could, and that was the last program he ever came to in scouting, or any of Rudy's other interests. All of his father's involvement had a flavor of being a grudging conformity to role type without emotional conviction.

When Rudy reacted to this distant, sterile parenting with rebellion, his father sent him to psychotherapists. The first was when Rudy was eight. Rudy was prepared for this visit by being told that this person did the same thing his father did. Rudy went cooperatively without fear but with some confusion as to why it was necessary.

During the first round of treatment he took the matter seriously and tried to comply with what he thought the therapist wanted. The problem was that there was no real reason to go. Rudy's comments were remarkably naive, open, and innocent, while the therapist was looking in vain for signs of pathology. When the therapist could find no signs of pathology he became increasingly alarmed, fearing that they must be extremely well protected by a brilliant ego. The therapist never doubted the original assumption that Rudy needed therapy since it came from Rudy's world-famous father. To contradict him was to begin a career change.

This first encounter with therapy was conveniently discontinued when Rudy went on an extended European vacation with his mother and siblings. There was a mutually polite verbal dance around the belief that Rudy was much better, and that he might be able to discontinue therapy.

The second course of therapy began when Rudy was eleven. Rudy was now painfully aware of how uninvolved his father was, and he was angry. He vented his anger on his father by getting into all kinds of trouble. He broke valuable things in the house, damaged property, and began stealing. His most flamboyant rebellion was stealing a car and smashing it into the showroom window of a Rolls Royce dealership, hitting several of the new cars on display.

Though these misbehaviors were getting bigger, Rudy's father was taking his usual hands-off approach. He had secretaries keep things out of the papers, and made cash settlements to keep people from pressing charges. Finally, he sent Rudy to another therapist for more counseling. When the misbehaviors continued even during counseling, he was sent to a residential program. This move got to Rudy and an unspoken truce was reached with his father. Rudy would not destroy things outside the house, and he could make the therapist's life a living hell on earth during treatment.

Rudy had several strategies for doing this. He moved around the office, often behind the therapist's chair, making rapid movements with his arms while yelling abusively. He asked the therapist what he would do if Rudy jumped out his sixteenth-story window. He threatened to beat up the therapist if be brought up certain subjects. He tried to turn nearly every subject the therapist wanted to talk about into forbidden territory.

Because of these behaviors, Rudy went through a series of therapists, male and female. None could work effectively with him. None really had any idea what was wrong with him. Clearly he had many problems, but the source of the problems was rarely suspected, even when Rudy broke from his usual oppositional behavior and told them directly that he thought his father was a monster. So great was the influence of Peterfield that no therapist could imagine that *he* could really be the source of the problem. Most therapists envied his children and assumed that Peterfield raised them perfectly and in the lap of luxury. Rarely have the facts been farther from the fiction.

Again, vacation plans rescued Rudy from treatment in his early teens. They did not resume after the summer vacation.

The final effort at psychotherapy for Rudy was at sixteen when he became sexually promiscuous. Rudy's mother was the most upset by this development. She was not a prude, but she believed that Rudy's experiments had a dangerous self-destructive purpose to them. In one of her rare moments of assertiveness, she insisted that

Rudy receive psychological treatment for this and she selected the psychologist herself. Her husband was delighted by this suggestion, as he wanted out of the matter altogether.

Rudy's mother made a fortunate selection. She was given the name of an elderly psychologist in Manhattan who took on a grandfatherly role in Rudy's life. His name was Keller. He was licensed years ago when doctoral degrees were not necessary and was operating under a grandfather clause in the licensure laws.

It had helped that Rudy had had as much psychotherapy before as he had. He exhausted all his games at meeting therapists and approached this old, bewhiskered, heavy-set psychologist with a blank slate.

The first session with Rudy was unusual. No sooner had Mrs. Peterfield sat down in the waiting room to look over the wrinkled, smudged magazine selection, than Keller and Rudy came out, walked right past her, and left the office building. Keller took Rudy to a nearby ice cream shop where they ordered two fancy sundaes.

To Rudy this seemed to waste the first hour completely. Keller asked him few questions, and Rudy volunteered little information. Keller's reactions to things Rudy said seemed to be real, genuine, and spontaneous, not the cold, predictable remarks of the other therapists. Rudy found him remarkably attentive. Rudy believed that the old man cared deeply, although he could not say how he got that opinion.

Time seemed to stand still for this old man, Rudy thought. He effortlessly spoke of things Rudy thought unimportant. Rudy was extremely on guard for something the old man might be doing in a sneaky way, but he could detect nothing dishonest in the old man's behavior. Keller patiently paid the check, left a generous tip, and they walked back to the office building. By the time they got back to the waiting room the fifty-minute hour had ended.

Keller indicated how nice their first session was and directed Mrs. Peterfield to the receptionist for payment and to arrange the next appointment. The old man captivated Rudy. Perhaps he was the grandfather Rudy never knew, perhaps he was some miracle worker. Perhaps it was because his mother had made the arrangements instead of his father, perhaps it was because he was a psychologist and not a medical doctor. One thing was clear, Rudy liked him.

Mrs. Peterfield believed that Rudy made a great deal of progress with Keller. Rudy opened up to other people, seemed to be less strident, more relaxed. In spite of all these successes, however, Rudy still was openly and actively promiscuous. After several months of treatment, Keller insisted upon meeting with Rudy and both parents. During this meeting he suggested that Rudy was promiscuous to get even with his father. Keller informed Peterfield that he had to come to treatment with Rudy for the next several months, and that even then he was not sure if the treatment would be successful. He made it graphically clear that Peterfield had neglected many important fatherly duties, had been too cold in his treatment of Rudy over the years, and that he had a lot of work to do in a hurry.

Mrs. Peterfield could never remember what happened after that interpretation. Peterfield went into a wild rage, something no one had ever seen before. He began a fifteen-minute diatribe against Keller that would have curdled blood. He stood over Keller, purple with rage, blood vessels swelling in his neck, and pointing a finger within inches of Keller's untroubled, gentle, face. After accusing Keller of nearly every legal and ethical violation in the book he left without paying for the session, or rescheduling.

In spite of Rudy's interest, and his mother's faint pleadings, Rudy never went back. Behind the scenes there were big shoot outs between Peterfield and the New York Board of Psychology about Keller. Peterfield used all the power, influence, and money he could to run Keller out of town, but Keller had been around a long time and had powerful friends in the highest possible places in state and city politics. In fact, Keller ended up threatening to file a law suit to get Peterfield to pay for the last session.

Between these courses of therapy, Rudy was sent on retreats, to private schools, to camps, and on private expeditions for his stimulation, and education. These private expeditions included mountain climbing, sailing, scuba diving, camping, hiking, white water rafting, mountain biking, dirt biking, snowmobiling, fishing, hunting, fossil hunting, and dozens of other activities that could be done in and around the private school calendar.

As a result of all these activities, Rudy could be a comfortable conversationalist with anyone. He possessed a broad fund of knowledge, and did well on college entrance exams and games of trivia.

Yet for all of this, Rudy realized that he did not have a normal upbringing. He realized how different he was from his new friend, Neal. Rudy knew he could talk freely with Neal. He just had to decide if that was what he wanted. He had been down so many other paths. There had been so many other false hopes. He was not sure he wanted to try this one.

CHAPTER 12

Rudy woke with a powerful appetite. Paulette prescribed and dispensed a huge omelet, toast, and coffee.

"What has Master Rudyard been up to these last days?" Paulette asked in a mock formal way.

"I've been going back and forth between nightclubs and fundamental churches," Rudy answered honestly. "My life has gotten a little crazy lately."

"Those sound like pretty wide extremes," Paulette agreed. "Aren't you afraid they're too extreme?"

"Yes, to be truthful, I am," Rudy admitted. "I don't know what I want. Where're the folks?"

Paulette was the one person who had the best track on where his parents were. Everyone in the family could talk freely to her. She easily inspired confidence and respect.

"Your mother's at Columbia for an all-day meeting, and your father's in his office today."

"Will dad be home for dinner?" Rudy asked.

"I think so; but it'll be late."

"Does he have plans for lunch?"

"Not here," Paulette said.

"Are they planning to go to the cottage soon?"

"No, I don't think so," Paulette answered with a growing curiosity.

"I'm thinking about going up to the cottage. I need to get away and think for a while," Rudy volunteered sensing her curiosity.

Rudy phoned his dad's office and asked to have his dad call home when he got a moment. He called their travel agent and made arrangements to go to the cottage.

Going to the cottage meant going to the Peterfields' forty-room mansion on Martha's Vineyard. The place was more than two hundred years old and had seen several major additions and renovations. It was perched high on a hill overlooking Edgartown Harbor. Their neighbors were famous writers, newspeople, and rock musicians. The neighborhood was a colorful blend of old world conservatism and nouveau riche youthful excess.

The travel agent arranged the plane fare and contacted the

cottage to have someone pick up Rudy at the Vineyard's airport. The cottage kept a small staff year round to keep up the grounds, clean, and cook. It was a coveted assignment because the Peterfields rarely went there, and when they did they never stayed long. Peterfield was always too busy in New York, and Mrs. Peterfield, if she left New York at all, was interested in going further away than Massachusetts.

The phone rang and Rudy answered it quickly.

"Rudy, this is your father, what's up?"

"Thanks for calling right away. Do you mind if I go to the cottage for a while?" Rudy asked. "I need to get out of the city and clear out my head."

"No. Have a good time. Thanks for telling me where you'll be," Peterfield said. "I've got to run, is there anything else I can do for you?"

"No. Thanks," Rudy said, and they hung up.

Paulette took this all in from Rudy's side of the conversation. She thought he was acting more deferential than usual, and wondered what was up. She loved him like a mother and conveyed that to him many times. He felt it and loved her back.

The travel agent called back and said Rudy could catch a plane at noon but he would have to move fast. He told her to book it, and went upstairs to pack. He found a Bible his grandparents had given him in his bookshelf and packed it with a handful of shirts, shorts, underwear, and some warmer things for the evenings. His mother's car was available so he took that. It was a robin's egg blue Mercedes limousine with white leather seats. He sunk into the back seat while the driver whisked him off to Kennedy. He looked over his mother's personal things in the car. She had several ladies magazines, a current popular novel with a page turned back approximately one-third of the way through, and a well-stocked bar.

He was dropped off in good time at the departing flights area of the commuter airline that served Martha's Vineyard from New York. He picked up his tickets, grabbed another cup of coffee, and went to the gate to wait.

There was an odd collection of people walking around the airport. The other passengers waiting for the flight to Martha's Vineyard were mostly mothers and children. There were two passengers about his age on board: a boy and a girl, but no one seemed to know each other.

Rudy sat on the vinyl bench seat at the airport gate drifting in and out of deep thought. He was comparing what he knew of Neal's life with his. As he was thinking, he looked up to see an older man in a dark suit and white clerical collar walking past in the hallway. Rudy ignored him but shortly he saw the man pass by again. He bore a striking resemblance to Keller, Rudy's last therapist.

Rudy approached him, "Excuse me, sir, can you help me?"

"Well, I don't know. I'm from Illinois," the man said, thinking that Rudy was going to ask him for directions.

"I noticed that you're a preacher, and I was wondering if you could answer a question about the Bible," Rudy said.

"Again, I don't know. That would depend upon what you want to know," he said, bracing himself for an insult. Since he was so clearly identified as a man of God by his costume, he frequently had to endure wise cracks, insults, and dirty jokes told in his presence loudly enough for him to hear. Looking at Rudy's clothes, and his age, he expected he was in for another such experience.

Rudy asked, "If a person is just starting to read the Bible, how should he go about it? It's such a big book. Is it best to start at the beginning and read all the way through?"

"What an intelligent question, young man," the older preacher said with a noticeable sigh of relief. "No, I wouldn't advise you to start at the beginning. You should start with the Sermon on the Mount found in Matthew 5, 6, and 7. Then you should move on to Luke and read the entire book, and then you should read the entire Book of Romans. After that you may want to read the rest of the New Testament before getting into the Old Testament. Do you have a Bible?"

"Yes, right here in my pack," Rudy answered, pleased that he asked the man.

"Are you familiar with the books of the Bible?" he asked.

"No I'm not," Rudy admitted.

"Well then I'll write this advice on the back of my card. If you have any questions you can call me and I can try to explain it to you." The preacher not only wrote down the books and chapters, but he took Rudy's Bible and found Matthew 5 and stuck the card in there so that Rudy could find it easily to get started.

"All the books of the Bible are in the index in the front," he went on. "You can look up where Romans is when you finish the first two readings."

"Thanks," Rudy said. He pulled out his wallet and pulled out a fifty dollar bill and handed it to the preacher. "I hope this covers your fee for this advice."

The old man paused for what seemed to Rudy like a long time and looked him knowingly and squarely in the eye. "Son," he said with a shaking, emotional voice, "are you from a rich family?" There was something in his tone of voice that suggested that a yes answer may not be good news.

"Yes. I guess you could say that," Rudy admitted.

"Well I will pray for you that you really do read these passages that I have recommended and that you read them seriously and honestly. Our Lord said that it is easier for a camel to pass through the eye of a needle than for a rich man to enter the kingdom of heaven. But He also said that with God all things are possible. Not many rich people feel the need for religion. I think I see that you are different. I pray that I am right."

With that the man pushed away Rudy's fifty dollars and walked away. There was something slightly eerie about this experience. Rudy wasn't used to being unqualified for something. He sensed a slight resentment welling up at the suggestion that he might not be "right" for religion. Yet he recognized the man's words as kind.

Rudy's plane arrived. It was a square-bodied propeller plane that could only handle about twenty-five passengers. It was mostly empty. After the stewardess passed out the honey-roasted peanuts and the soda, Rudy pulled out his Bible. He opened it to where the preacher had stuck his card. He read the note on the back of the card again, then flipped the card over. He was startled to see that there was nothing on the other side. He turned the card back over half expecting to see that the note had also disappeared. It was there, however, clearly guiding him to read sections in the Bible. He was beginning to doubt his senses. Didn't this preacher say he could call him if he had any questions?

The plane rattled and rumbled along the coast most of the way and then pointed toward Martha's Vineyard. They landed easily and rolled up to the tiny terminal. The terminal had the usual blend of high-tech desks, logos, and power colors but they did not create the usual respect or formality that they do in bigger airports. Here they were out of place in a building that people insisted upon using more casually.

There was a big square of park benches with their backs to a chain link fence on one side of the building. Here people waited in the breeze frustrating the institutional preference for a more formal, air-conditioned atmosphere. There was something friendly and accepting about it, as if to say, now that you have gotten onto the island, you are given permission to relax with us.

Rudy waited there until he saw the huge brown Ford wagon with simulated wood panels. It was nine years old but it had low mileage and no rust. It spent most of its life in a garage. Rudy threw his pack on the passenger side of the bench seat and climbed in. The car rolled massively but slowly toward Edgartown on the two-lane highway.

"How was your flight, Rudy?" asked John the gardener-turned-chauffeur.

"Oh, fine. I don't remember much of it. I was reading a book the whole way," Rudy answered. "What's going on around here?"

John listed several cultural events that were scheduled for the week, which included performances by folk singers, art, and photography exhibits, and other educational programs.

They pulled in the driveway and behind the house. The landscaping was quite mature and well maintained. One could not tell from looking at the house that the owner had not set foot in it for at least a year. "You've done a great job with the shrubs," Rudy volunteered. "You must stay with it every day."

"Well, it does take some time to do the job right," John added with genuine modesty in his voice. John, like most of Peterfield's employees, seemed to almost worship the doctor. They worked with a zeal betraying a belief that they were helping the doctor be better able to help others. They held the belief that if they make things perfect for Peterfield, he would be left unhindered to do his work—which is so extremely important. The feeling went beyond merely being dedicated to a high standard of excellence. It took on an almost missionary fervor in serving this special man, Dr. Peterfield.

Rudy benefited too, because they believed that if they made Rudy comfortable, they were helping Peterfield as well.

Lucy, the maid/cook, met Rudy at the door. She took his pack and followed him to his room. She put his few clothes in his dresser and laid his Bible on top. She noted that it had a card marking a place, and was surprised. She did not remember that he was particularly religious. She inquired if he would be there for dinner, and what his plans might be. Rudy indicated that he was there for some quiet time to think.

For most of this stay, Rudy slept in late in the morning, took a shuttle bus to one of the beaches, or did a little light sailing in the afternoon. He ate alone in the family dining room reminding himself, with a little shock, of his father.

During the evenings he would read the Bible. In a matter of days he got through the sections prescribed by the mysterious preacher he met in the airport. He then was faced with the task of working on the Old Testament.

This introduction to the Bible impressed Rudy that it was basically an introduction to a new way of living to the world by One reported to be the Son of God. The way seemed clear and uncomplicated. This was not what he had heard about religion. He thought religion to be one of the most complicated things.

This way, called the Gospel of Jesus Christ, seemed to be elegant in its simplicity. Rudy got a powerful feeling that there was a tremendous wisdom hidden in this book. To follow this book literally, however, would require him to make many changes in his life. According to this book he was a vile sinner and not eligible for entry into Heaven. He was not at all sure, yet, that there was a Heaven.

Rudy enjoyed the slower pace of the island, mainly because he had a clearly prescribed reading assignment. Now that he was facing the Old Testament he was not sure where to start. He decided to call Neal and ask for his advice. The first time he called Neal was not home. He didn't leave a message but called back later and got him.

"Hey, Rudy, where are you? I haven't heard from you for a while," Neal said with enthusiasm when Rudy finally did get through.

"I'm at my folks' cottage."

"What are you doing there?" Neal asked.

"Well, you won't believe this but I'm reading the Bible. I've covered the New Testament but I don't know where to start in the Old Testament."

"Wow. That's a lot of reading in a short time," Neal said. "It's impossible to absorb all the meaning that quickly; but I guess it's good to read it through once to get a sense of the whole."

"Yeah. I never realized the Bible was a complete system," Rudy admitted. "It's really a fascinating historical story."

"It's really great that you read it like that, Rudy. People spend lifetimes reading the Bible over and over again," Neal encouraged. "When're you going to be back? We need to get together again. It'd be neat to talk about what you're learning from the Bible."

"I don't know. I'm about done here. I'll call you when I get back in town. Oh, where should I start reading in the Old Testament?" Rudy asked.

"Oh, there's lots of places. Some people say the Psalms. Some people say start with Genesis. Actually the first two books are pretty exciting. Then you could jump to Joshua and read a few books. Then jump to the Psalms. Chronicles and Kings are full of history, too. Just jump around like that."

"Start with the first two books." Rudy repeated. "Then jump to Joshua and read a few books, and then jump to Psalms. OK, that's what I'll do. I'll call you in a day or two. We'll get together then."

Rudy went on to ask Neal about Jim, Jack, and the church. He talked without thought of the long distance charges. Neal was distracted by the cost mounting for Rudy's call. He was grateful that Rudy valued talking that much but couldn't ignore a certain faint anxiety that the cost was growing.

Shortly, in spite of his interest in talking to Rudy, the anxiety of knowing that the meter was running caused Neal to casually suggest that this was costing Rudy quite a bit. It was one of those situations where there was no way to avoid it. He was a victim of his conservative upbringing. He didn't want to end the conversation. He didn't want to offend Rudy. Yet, he heard himself speak those regrettable words.

The conversation ended shortly after, with Rudy assuring Neal that the bill didn't matter. After they hung up, Neal regretted not talking as long as Rudy would have wanted to. Neal marveled at how easily one's upbringing and biases can work against one's purposes.

Rudy was awakened that same night by a bad dream. He dreamt that he was on a ladder suspended over a bubbling lake of hot, molten lava. He dreamt that the ladder was slowly moving downward toward the lava and as the end of it was hitting the lava it was burning off from the heat. He had to climb the ladder to stay above the heat. The task was made more difficult as the rungs of the ladder were getting further and further apart, and the rate with which the ladder was moving downward was increasing.

Rudy was impressed by his lack of emotional reaction to this dream. He did not panic. He was just amazed at this predicament. He wondered what it might mean.

The next day he made arrangements to go back home. Lucy told him how nice it was to have him there and John drove him to the airport. Again, there was little traffic. He was coming and going at just the opposite times of the traffic. He was looking forward to asking Neal about a few of the things he read.

CHAPTER 13

Rudy returned on a Friday afternoon. He took a bus to midtown, and a cab to his parent's apartment. He planned on walking but the sidewalk was a zoo. The traffic was also bad but at least he was sitting down.

The cab was a new model but already seriously banged up. The driver was friendly but looked like a dangerous criminal. He kept a pencil poked into the cushioned dashboard. It was striking how function outweighed form in this way: families that purchased this model car would have been horrified with a hole in their dash so quickly.

Rudy hadn't eaten in a while so when the cab stopped outside a small French lunch spot he paid the driver and got out. He walked down the five steps into the restaurant to begin, as it turned out, an agonizing wait for service. He sensed that the management didn't take him seriously. Finally he had had enough and let fly a series of French profanity and insults that would make a French dockworker blush. He demanded a table and some fast service all in perfect French with a natural accent.

When the management heard his French, they bent over backwards to take care of him. No effort was too much. He loved great service. In this respect he was much like his father; but he hated it when others pointed this out to him.

After lunch he walked the few blocks home. As he walked into the apartment he noticed that the place was buzzing with activity. People were cleaning every conceivable surface and the kitchen was alive with activity. Huge trays were being prepared, pots and pans were on every burner. There were fresh-cut flowers everywhere.

Rudy walked to his mom's sitting room where she was working at a fancy glass-topped desk. "Party time, huh mom?"

"Oh Rudy," she said, "how nice to see you." He walked over and kissed her on the cheek. She ran her fingers through his hair on the back of his head and kissed him on his cheek too. "My beautiful son. What are you up to? I heard you were at the cottage."

"Yeah I needed to get away for a while."

"Oh, your life is so difficult," she teased. "Are you going to be home tonight?"

"That depends on who's coming. What dog-and-pony show is dad parading through here tonight?" he asked.

"Well, actually, I'm having a thirty-year reunion party for some of my Smith friends tonight. I'm expecting about sixty people. It'll be a genuine delight. Can you stay?" The message sounded more like, you may want this advanced notice to see where you can go instead.

"I was planning on skinny dipping in the pool tonight. Will that be all right?" Rudy asked.

"Oh, that'll be great. My friends'll love it," she said, playing along with the joke.

"I'll make a few calls," he decided.

He got to his room and called Neal. He was told that Neal wasn't home from work yet. He had gotten a summer job doing maintenance work in a factory. Rudy found out when he was expected to be home and planned to call again. He went back to his mother's desk and asked to use her car.

He called Neal again. He made arrangements for Neal to pick him up at a diner near Neal's house. He arranged the time for a half hour later than Rudy would arrive so that he could send his mother's car back before Neal saw it. He dumped the dirty clothes out of his pack and stuffed some clean ones in. He also folded up a jacket in case he decided to go to Neal's church.

At the diner Rudy ordered a hamburger, French fries, and a chocolate shake, something he ordered with Neal before. Neal was right, the flavors went well together, and you got a certain satisfied and full feeling finishing the shake.

Neal came to the diner a little early. He sat down opposite Rudy and said that he and a few friends had decided to spend the night at Jim Stander's parent's cabin, which was on a small lake in western Connecticut. Neal said they could go swimming, fishing, and even a little boating. So they agreed to go.

The cabin was old but comfortable. It was paneled inside with well-finished, native wood. It had a lot of old furniture that was overstuffed. There were three bedrooms, a large living room, a small kitchen, and an eating area. The cabin was on posts on the side of a hill, which created a large crawl space under the floor where boats, fishing gear, and lawn chairs were stored. Everything was old but well maintained.

It was this feature of well-maintained age that was most unique to Rudy. He had to think that if his father had this place, he would push over the cabin and build something new. Rudy really liked the rustic quality of it. The plumbing fixtures were old and inconvenient. There was a separate hot and cold faucet in the bathroom lavatory. This required you to either wash your face in cold water, or wait until the hot water started coming and burn your hands. Rudy learned to mix cold and hot in cupped hands.

The stove had gas burners and a lethal-looking oven. The knobs on the oven were so old that the numbers could not be read. What had at one time been shiny plastic with sharp neat edges was now a porous, dull looking material with rounded edges. The floors were not quite flat, and no two floors were on the same level. The cabin had seen several remodeling additions that created some outside-looking walls on the insides of some rooms. Light switches, when there were some, were on inconvenient walls. Other lights were turned on and off by a string, giving the place the charming quality of a huge puzzle, immediately comfortable in its simplicity, casualness, and coziness.

On an inside wall of the living room was a huge fieldstone fireplace with a deep fire box, a wide hearth, and a huge wooden mantelpiece. It had an iron hook hinged from the side for holding a pot of water over the fire. It had a wide grate with big squatty andirons resolutely standing at attention on either side of the front of it. The fireplace was not old enough to really be used for cooking; but it was clear that it was intended to be realistic down to the smallest detail.

There was nothing cheap about this cabin, just old, worn, and comfortable, like a well-worn pair of shoes. Jack, Jim, Neal, and Rudy would spend the night there, but some others came for the evening. They decided to go swimming and play a game they invented called "ball tag."

The water was cold, but the exercise kept them warm. They played for nearly two hours, well after dark. No one really wanted to quit, but the mosquitoes were getting bad, and it was cooling off.

Rudy fit into the group easily. He was made "it" about as often as anyone else. People dunked him under the water, pushed him off the deck, and splashed him just as much as anyone else. It would have been imperceptible to anyone watching that he was new to this group.

Later that evening they sat around the living room talking about coming events for their church. One guy asked if they were all going to the youth rally in Ohio. It turned out that everyone in the room was going if they could find a ride, except Rudy. He admitted that he didn't know what a youth rally was.

"It's a blast, man," one guy volunteered. "You drive there Friday night. On Saturday you go canoeing, or hiking, or something like that. The rally actually starts on Saturday night. There's a dinner in some rented school building, then they have a sermon. After that there's a campfire with lots of special numbers and personal testimonies. On Sunday they have a sermon in the morning and afternoon just like our usual Sunday schedule, and a campfire that night. There's usually a picnic breakfast on Monday morning, and then everyone heads home. It's great. There are about a thousand people there and you really have a great time."

"You should go, Rudy, you'd like it," piped in another guy.

"I wouldn't miss it," added another.

"Well, we'll see," said Rudy. "It sounds good. You mentioned it to me before, didn't you Neal?"

"Yeah. I'll be glad to take you."

Jim and Jack made a fire in the fireplace. They had a nice fire burning before long, and everyone was sitting in a semicircle around the fire.

"I wish we had some marshmallows," Jim said. "But we'll just have to watch the fire."

"You know, someone once said that people going to church are like the coals in a fire," one of them said. "As long as they are grouped together they are glowing, red hot, and on fire. But you take one of the coals out of the pile and place it on the hearth alone for a while and, even though it was red hot, it'll cool off and eventually go out. It's the same with church. People need to go to church regularly to stay on fire for the Lord."

Neal looked over at Rudy to see if he was listening, and if he appeared to agree with what was said. He was pleased to see that Rudy was listening and looked impressed with this comment.

"Do you go to a church?" someone asked Rudy out of the blue.

"Oh, yeah, we're Episcopalians," he said. "But I can't remember when I've been to church last."

"Well, you were in our church just a week ago," Jack pointed out. "And we're real glad to have you."

"Yeah. Please keep coming," another said.

"Don't you guys think it's pretty unusual to go to church? I mean, do you think more people go to church or don't?" Rudy asked.

"Oh, most don't go to church," they agreed. "But that doesn't make it right. People are commanded by God to go to church. `Do not forsake the assembling of yourselves together as the manner of some' is what the Bible says."

"Well, a lot of people violate that advice," Rudy allowed.

"I can't blame a lot of people for not going to their churches," said one. "If I had to go to some of the churches of this world, I would be the first one out the door."

"Do people have to agree with everything their church teaches to stay in the church?" Rudy asked

"Yes. Absolutely," one of them said.

"No, wait a minute," said another. "I don't think everyone agrees on everything in any church, even ours."

"Ideally the members of a church should agree on most everything. There's a certain commandment for unity in the Bible, after all," argued another. "But it's probably impossible to agree on everything."

This conversation went on for quite a while when someone noticed that it was getting late. Everyone except Jim, Jack, Neal, and Rudy gathered up their stuff and left to get home on time. Rudy learned that they had a curfew imposed upon them by their parents of around eleven. It could be a little later if the parents knew that they were with other church youth group kids.

How different, Rudy thought, from his own friends and their parents. It seemed like things didn't get started until after eleven. Most of his friend's parents gave up on keeping track of where their children were a long time ago.

After the dust settled in the driveway, a calm settled over the cabin. There was a much lower energy level in the cabin, less need to speak and keep the conversational ball going. They were aware of a wonderful quiet with only the crackling of the fire, the chirping of crickets, and their occasional shifting in their chairs.

"Does anyone wanna go for a walk?" Jack asked.

"No, I'm too tired," admitted Jim.

"I don't want to go either," added Neal.

"I'll go with you," Rudy said.

So Rudy and Jack walked down the driveway. There was little traffic so they walked along the road quietly. There were no street-lights but their eyes adjusted quickly to the moonlight.

"What we do for fun must be pretty different for you," Jack said.

"Yeah, it's different," Rudy agreed. "But it's fun. I never thought of ball tag before."

"Don't your folks have a cottage near some water. I thought I heard . . . ."

"Yeah, they do. But no one ever thought of ball tag. I guess we do some boating, some diving, stuff like that. Who thought up the idea, anyway?" Rudy asked.

"I don't know. It just developed. I suppose someone had a ball and threw it at someone. They got mad and threw it back and missed. It probably just grew from there," Jack answered.

"You guys seem to have more fun than the guys I hang around with. It's like old-fashioned fun, home-made games." Rudy said.

"I'm glad you said that," Jack answered. "I was wondering what you thought of us. I guess our church could be viewed as old-fashioned.

"Most churches have a preacher who studies the Bible and preaches sermons in the form of a lecture. In our church all the members know as much about the Bible as the preachers do. It's neat the way people have such well-thought-out beliefs on the Bible.

"One reason for that is that our church requires a Saint Paul-type conversion for all their members. Becoming a member is not a simple matter of making a public statement, signing up, and paying dues. Each person is required to go through a thorough conversion experience."

"Yeah, Neal was telling me that same thing. Did you go through that kind of experience?" Rudy asked.

"Yeah. Mine isn't dramatic," Jack said. "But I did have a conversion experience."

"What happened to you?" Rudy asked.

"Well, I first felt the call of God at one of our camps when I was thirteen," Jack began. "I'd gone to camp most of my life, and I was raised in our church. I'd gone through Sunday school. I'd known about the plan of salvation since I was a child. Some of my friends were converting, and one night, during a campfire, I felt a big load of guilt. I realized that I was a selfish person, trying to act tough, lying to my friends, and being a hypocrite. At school I was cussing and telling dirty jokes to act tough, and at church I was considered this good little boy. I felt ashamed of that, and knew that I had to decide one or the other. I wasn't doing a good job at either.

"So that night, after a campfire, I stayed behind and talked to a minister. He was nice and patient. He told me that only God could put that conviction in my heart, and only God could give me the power to convert. He said that God would lead me to confess my sins, and make restitutions for all the things I could remember doing wrong. I had to ask forgiveness from God for all the sins in my life, too.

"I confessed my sins that night to that minister. It wasn't as hard as I thought it'd be. He made it seem like everybody had told him pretty much the same thing and he was used to hearing it all. He told me to pray to God for help from the Holy Spirit and pointed out the sinner's prayer: `Lord have mercy on me, a sinner.'"

Rudy listened with genuine interest. Jack saw that in the expression on his face.

Jack went on, "The minister said that nobody could go through with a conversion without the power of the Holy Spirit because we're wrestling with the power of Satan. And Satan wants to keep you a servant of his. There's a verse, somewhere, that says, `We do not wrestle against flesh and blood but against powers and principalities and spiritual wickedness in high places.'

"I can't tell you how true that is. I didn't fully understand that when I started out; but no one can become converted on his own power. He has to surrender his life to the power of God through the Holy Spirit. In a way you go from one spiritual possession to another. You can't escape the possession of Satan without the power of the Holy Spirit. Everyone tries it, though. It takes a while, and some frustrating experiences of your own to really learn that for yourself.

"I went back home after camp and started reading my Bible more at first. But I didn't tell my parents, and I didn't start doing any restitutions. I started back in school that year and fell back into old habits. I got away from reading the Bible, and just slid back into old patterns. The following year at camp, during one campfire, I heard a testimony from a friend of mine about my age. He said he'd started to repent and gave up several times. He said that it was only when he told some other friends and his parents that he was able to stick with it. He said that it was important to tell a few people close to you so that it sort of forces you to keep at it. But the most important thing is to read the Bible and pray for the strength and the will to see it through to the end.

"That year I went home and told my parents that I wanted to convert. It was unbelievably hard to tell them even though I knew it was something they were waiting to hear. I know now that it was the power of Satan trying to keep me from telling them because he somehow knew that that would be a major help in my seeing it through. It's kinda scary when you think about it. You're that close to these spiritual powers. You're a pawn in the middle of all these forces.

"I also asked my parents to forgive me. They were both happy, of course. They said that they'd been praying for this from the moment they knew that they were going to have a baby, before I was even born, and that they had prayed for this every night of my life. So I started making my restitutions."

"What do you mean by restitutions?" Rudy asked. "I heard Neal talk about that too."

"Restitutions are going back and making things right," Jack explained. "If you stole something, you went back and offered to pay for it. If you hurt someone's feelings you went back and apologized for it. If you lied, or cheated, you went back and confessed it and offered to do something to correct it. I didn't have too many by the age of thirteen. I have always been raised in a protective home, I guess, but I had some things to do. Here, too, the Devil makes it hard to do. It seems like each time you do it, though, you gain more strength to do the next one. They are little victories over the Devil which raise you higher and higher out of his grip or influence. It's like you are climbing up a cliff out of the pit of hell and with each restitution you are a little further out of his reach. His call is slightly fainter.

"I stole a toy car from a toy store once. It was years before and I was sure that the clerk working there at the time was not even the clerk at the time I stole it. But I went back and explained that I was becoming a Christian and that I needed to pay for something I had stolen years before. The clerk said that she didn't even know how much the thing cost, so she told me to talk with the manager. So I had to explain the whole thing, again, to the manager. The manager estimated the cost to be about fifty cents and told me that that would probably cover it.

"I remember thinking at the time that the manager should've just told me to forget it. Lots of times that's what people do. I remember even thinking at the time that he was a little picky by expecting me to pay. It seems odd and embarrassing now, but I still had a little too much pride at that time, even while doing that restitution. I mean, here I was asking to pay for something I had stolen and being a little offended when the clerk allowed me to pay. It just shows you that the process of conversion is a gradual one, and you learn a lot as you go along.

"Now I think the clerk was right in requiring me to pay something. It seems like you have a stronger feeling of completing the task when there's some cost. But there are situations where it's impossible to pay. We hear lots of stories in our church about difficult restitutions. But back to my story. I made all the restitutions I could think of and still didn't have peace."

"What do you mean by peace?" Rudy asked.

"Well, the Bible calls it a peace that passes all understanding. People describe it as a powerful feeling that comes over you when you realize you're accepted by God as a child of His, and that your sins are forgiven and cast into the sea of forgetfulness."

"Wait a minute," Rudy interrupted. "There's a sea of forgetfulness?"

"Yeah. It's in the Bible. God'll remember your sins no more.

"There's a general teaching in the church that you shouldn't consider your conversion complete until you experience this great feeling of peace. It's true that you get a measure of this peace a little bit at a time as you do your restitutions. Each small victory brings you closer to your goal, and brings a small measure of peace. You're removing, bit by bit, the things that condemned you. But it's important to remember that this is not possible to do alone. You need the power of the Holy Spirit to accomplish these things.

"One section in the Bible that was shown to me at this time

of my conversion was the first six verses of Romans eight. This is where Paul explains that there is no more condemnation to those who have forsaken the flesh and walk after the Spirit. This period between finishing all your restitutions and before receiving peace varies widely from person to person. It took nearly a year before I thought I could say I received that peace. Others take longer, and for others it's only a short time.

"It seems like even during your restitutions you're confused about how they're done. You sometimes take your focus off Jesus Christ and think that you did them under your own power. After they're accomplished, there's usually still one obstacle that you're trying to do yourself. After fighting against this for some time, you finally collapse and give up. That's when The Spirit finishes the work and gives you that wonderful peace. Once you've received that there's no mistaking it. You start out on a life of obedience to God, working with God in a father-son relationship."

"Does that mean that you're perfect and that you never have a problem again?" Rudy asked. He couldn't believe that such a thing was possible.

"No. You still have ups and downs, but you know where to turn, and you live in a continuous communion with God. You become a soldier for God. That doesn't mean that you don't have losing battles at times, and that you don't get discouraged in the trenches. It means that you can return to the camp of Jesus and get pumped up by His grace when those discouragements come. And you know that your team will, ultimately, win."

"What do you mean your team'll ultimately win?" Rudy asked.

"That's a long story, too," Jack answered, realizing that he'd been talking for a long time. "Let's talk about that with the other guys. It has to do with the end time prophecies. Christians believe in a great resurrection of all Christians living and dead. After the great resurrection, there'll be a great tribulation, followed by a millennium of peace where the Gospel will be preached without persecution for a thousand years. Then, Heaven and Earth will be destroyed, and new things happen which I don't really understand all that well. In fact, there isn't universal agreement on these things. They're written about in the scriptures here and there and even though people try to study them carefully, there are vastly different opinions about just exactly what will happen."

"It sounds a little fantastic," admitted Rudy. "Why do you believe it?"

"I believe it because the Bible says it. I think the Bible is the inspired Word of God. As you read the Bible more and more you get more and more amazed at it. It's prophecies are all coming true, and it has been confirmed in so many mysterious ways over the years. The Bible's the book to live your life by. I know there are many other good books, and I know that there are many other ancient books that large groups of people live their lives by, but for me, the Bible is the final authority."

"That's really great," Rudy said. "It's rare to find someone with things so clearly thought out." Rudy was only beginning to appreciate how true this statement was. He marveled at how solid these guys' faith was. They didn't seem to have the same drifting feeling of hopelessness that his own friends had. But they weren't the holy roller types either. They weren't forcing their beliefs on others, or even on Rudy. They were explaining, when asked, what they believe, and they knew exactly why they believed it.

CHAPTER 14

While Rudy and Jack were on their walk, Jim and Neal sat by the fire enjoying the peaceful atmosphere created by the calm after physical exertion. They were entranced by the fire and its reddish glow on the wood paneling.

"So, tell me about Rudy," Jim asked.

"What do you want to know?" Neal asked.

"Where's he from? What do his parents do? What does he think about religion? You know, stuff like that," Jim clarified.

"Well, I don't know that much about him. He lives in the city. I don't know what his parents do. They have a cottage near some water, and he's done a lot of swimming. That's about all I know."

"That's it?" Jim asked.

"Oh, one thing, he really hates his father. It's the only time I've seen him real emotional. His father sent him to some kind of psychologist or psychiatrist for a while and he hated that, I guess. I think his family has some money or they wouldn't have sent him there."

"There's something about him that you really like, isn't there?" Jim asked.

"Yeah. I don't know quite what it is. He's friendly and open. Yeah, maybe that's it, he's so open and honest."

"Do you think he's interested in coming to our church?" Jim asked.

"Oh, yes. Very much so. He called me a few days ago from his father's cottage and told me that he was reading his Bible. He wanted to know where he should read in the Old Testament because he had read the entire New Testament."

"He read the entire New Testament since we saw him last?" Jim asked, not quite believing.

"That's what he said. He found some minister in an airport and asked him how he should read the Bible. The man told him to start with the Sermon on the Mount and then read Luke, or something like that. Well, Rudy did that, and then he read the entire New Testament. Then he called me and asked me how he should read the Old Testament. I told him to read the first two books first, and then jump to Joshua and Judges and then jump to Psalms."

"Do you think he can grasp all that reading that fast?" Jim asked.

"I told him it was good that he read it so fast, but that now he should re-read sections more slowly. I think he's interested," Neal explained.

"He's friendly. He seems to fit in well."

The conversation swung to other subjects in a lazy winding way as they waited for Rudy and Jack to return. They thought of playing Monopoly but decided not to. They thought of cleaning up the cabin but decided not to. They just sprawled over the furniture watching the fire die down.

The walk back for Rudy and Jack was much quieter. It seemed like Rudy was deep in thought. He would occasionally interrupt the silence to ask Jack a specific question about his conversion. Jack seemed talked out and was happy to answer the questions briefly and then walk along silently until the next question came up. They had been quiet for some time when they came upon the cabin. They decided to sneak up on the cabin and see what the other guys were doing.

The conversation inside had turned back to Rudy. They were talking about the chances of his becoming interested in the church. Jack was relieved to hear that the comments about Rudy were complimentary so he decided to remain silent and let Rudy hear them.

"I think it would be a miracle if Rudy could find the Lord in our church," Jim said.

"I know," agreed Neal. "I really hope and pray that he can. It'd be so encouraging. We could really use him. You know he plays the piano beautifully."

"Is that right?" asked Jim. "I wouldn't have guessed that. How do you know that?"

"He sat down at our piano one day when my parents weren't home and played from sight right out of our song book. It was as if he'd played them for years. He's got a real gift."

"There's something about him that seems so real. He seems so open to religious ideas," added Jim.

"I just wish it could happen. I wonder what the chances are?" Neal speculated.

Jack signaled for Rudy to walk away from the cabin. "We better go back a ways and walk up to the cabin making some noise so they hear us coming."

They walked back the lane and stopped by a short section of split rail fence. They sat on it when Jack brought up the question directly to Rudy.

"So what are the chances that you'll come to our church regularly?"

"Pretty good. I think Venzel's cool," Rudy admitted as Jack struggled to choke down a burst of laughter. Cool was one of the last words Jack would use to describe Theo Venzel. "You guys seem to have things so clearly thought out. You seem to really know where you're going. And I've never met people who were so friendly."

"Is that so unusual?" Jack asked.

"Yeah. I don't know anybody that's got such a clear idea of what life's all about. Most of my friends are agnostics, I guess. They have no idea Who God is or what He wants."

"Weren't they brought up in a church?" Jack asked.

"No. Nobody I know goes to church. Some of us were baptized. Our grandparents insisted on that, but our parents never go. They put it in the same category as astrology, or some other superstition. Only the poor believe that stuff. It's not cool to do religion," Rudy explained.

"Why your grandparents?"

"Well, most of them went to church. I can remember a big argument my grandmother had with my father about going to church. My grandmother thought it was pretty important, but my father didn't. Like most arguments, my father won."

Jack and Rudy talked longer than they planned. So they went back to the cabin. "You guys've been gone a long time. Did you get lost?"

"No," Jack answered. "We just had a long talk."

"Well, we better get to bed. We've got a long drive to church in the morning, and we've gotta get this cabin closed up before we leave," Jim added.

They gave Rudy the nicest bedroom by himself. Everyone but Rudy fell asleep quickly from the activities of the day. Rudy lay awake for some time thinking about what Jack told him. It wasn't so much what he said but how he said it. He was absolutely convinced. He had firm, definite opinions about what he was talking about. All these guys seemed so sure of their beliefs.

Rudy read about the Apostle Paul's conversion on the way to Damascus. He now knew what Neal and Jack meant when they referred to a "St. Paul's conversion."

The account of Paul's conversion had another message for Rudy. It was that even the most improbable people sometimes convert. In fact, he thought he wanted to. He was still not clear about how to go about it in this church. He reached over to the bed stand and picked up a Bible that was left on the edge by someone in Jim's family. There was a purple ribbon attached to the binding that was used as a bookmark. Rudy opened it to where the ribbon was and saw a small verse highlighted in Colossians 2:3 which read, "In whom are hid all the treasures of wisdom and knowledge." He looked at the previous verse to learn that this was speaking of Jesus Christ.

Rudy realized that he had read that verse when he read the entire New Testament, but he had not paused to reflect upon what that verse might mean. He wondered how all wisdom and knowledge could be hidden in Jesus Christ. He thought about all the philosophers, physicists, chemists, biologists, and others and wondered how all this wisdom and knowledge could be hidden in Christ?

Rudy laid the Bible on the bed stand, open, with the ribbon lying across that page. He wanted to remember to ask about that in the morning. He wondered what all they must know that he didn't know. He wondered how much more he needed to learn.

He had the feeling that he was outside a big stone wall prying open a rusty steel door. Inside this door was a lush tropical garden full of unusual flora. Each plant was interesting by itself; and its placement amongst such a huge garden overwhelmed the viewer. It was the excitement of finding a new interest and realizing that there was so much to learn before you could reasonably converse with those who have been interested in it for years.

In short, it was exciting. He felt a warm feeling of success and fortune. That feeling of expectation and adventure ushered him into a deep, restful sleep.

In the morning, there was a flurry of activity getting equipment hauled into the crawl space under the house and locking it up. They decided to eat breakfast on the road so that they wouldn't have dishes to clean.

They had two cars so Rudy rode with Jim, again, and Jack rode with Neal.

"Hey Jim," Rudy began. "I read a verse last night before falling asleep that I don't understand."

"Yeah, great. What was it?" Jim asked.

"It said that in Christ was hidden all the treasures of wisdom and knowledge," Rudy paraphrased. "What does that mean?"

"It said that?" Jim asked. "Say that again."

Rudy repeated the verse and was surprised to learn that Jim had not heard of it before.

"Have you read the New Testament?" Rudy asked.

"Yeah, most of it, I guess," Jim answered. "I don't read it like a novel. I jump around and read all over the Bible. I probably read that verse while reading other verses and never paid attention to it. I have a guess about what it means, though."

"Go ahead," Rudy urged.

"Well, I think that when you become a Christian you come under the direct influence of the Holy Spirit of Christ. The Holy Spirit actually lives in your heart. This Holy Spirit leads and directs your life. It guides you in ways you can't understand but which prove, later, to be extremely wise. So it isn't like you actually possess the wisdom or knowledge that the verse is talking about. It's that you benefit from the huge pool of wisdom and knowledge when it affects you, and when you listen to it.

"Wow," Rudy reacted. "Can you give me an example?"

"I can give you an example in medical biology," Jim asserted. "God instructed the Children of Israel not to eat anything from a pig. The people were not given the reason why at the time. They were just told what not to eat. Those that followed that advice were protected from trichinosis. Those that didn't obey may have gotten sick. If someone insisted on knowing why before obeying he may have been in trouble. It is not all that important that you understand why."

"I never thought of it that way," Rudy admitted with some fascination in his voice. "That's really amazing. Can you think of a modern-day example?"

"Well, let's see, our church believes that women should cover their heads while praying and prophesying. This is found in I Corinthians. We believe that that covering needs to be something more than just a woman's long hair. Now I don't honestly see a good reason for that. I don't understand why God would require that of women only. Some have suggested that it was just for that time because of the sinful conditions in Corinth. They feel that women were advised to cover their heads for that time only to avoid being mistaken for women of the world in early Corinth.

"Personally, I don't think God would have preserved it in the Bible in such a direct instructional way if He intended it to be only for that period of time. I think the obedience to that requirement may have a healthy psychological affect on women for some reason unknown today. It may do something mentally healthy for the relationship between men and women.

"One thing is certain, people today are just as offended by this requirement as people must have been about being denied pork in ancient times. But that's often a common feature in God's plan. He asks people to do things that test their faith. He asks them to do things that test their humility and their willingness to obey.

"In the Old Testament there's a story about a famous military man named Naaman. He developed leprosy and was doomed to die because it was incurable at that time.

"He had a Jewish maid working in his house at the time and she suggested that a prophet in her country could heal his leprosy. So he went to this prophet who wouldn't even come out and talk to him personally. He sent a messenger out who told him to go wash in the muddy Jordan River seven times. When he heard that he was furious. He knew there were rivers in his homeland that were cleaner than the Jordan. It was insulting and degrading to wash in such a muddy river.

"One of his advisors gently spoke to him and reasoned that if the prophet had asked him to do something real hard he would have done it, so why not give this plan a try. What did he have to lose? So the military man did wash seven times in the Jordan and his leprosy was completely cured."

Rudy exclaimed. "What a fascinating story. Is that in the Bible?"

"Yes it is. The point is that God wants to see humility and obedience in His followers."

They rode in silence while Rudy's thoughts raced. He marveled at how each of them knew the Bible so well. It was clear to Rudy that this was not a church where people just sat in pews and listened passively. These people actually studied the Bible and thought about it.

"Let me tell you," Rudy quipped, "the women's movement wouldn't like your idea about why women should wear head coverings."

"Maybe not," agreed Jim. "But we're not dictating what all women must do. We're simply saying what we think the Bible says. The reasons are not known to us. The practice seems to be clearly spelled out in I Corinthians. If a woman doesn't agree with that, she has the right to believe any way she wants to."

What a full day of lessons to be learned, thought Rudy, and this only on the drive to church.

CHAPTER 15

After a busy Sunday, Rudy rode back to New York on the train. Neal wanted to take him but Rudy declined, again.

While riding the train he worried about how he was ever going to explain his true identity. His disguise embarrassed him, but he knew it was necessary.

It was not a new problem that he, alone, suffered. He had been to private schools with other children of notable families who complained of the same thing. His anonymous identity worked well for him.

He reflected with genuine satisfaction on the comments he overheard Jim and Neal making about him in the cabin. He was grateful that he made a good impression on them. He liked knowing that he earned this on his own. He hated to see this end. Rudy had earned some hard-to-get credentials in his own right. He had done extremely well on ACT testing. He was accepted into Harvard in the fast track where many courses were waived due to his test scores. He won many competitions while sailing alone. No matter how famous his father was he could hardly have influenced the outcome of the race, or the speed of the other boats. Rudy won amateur competitions on the piano, and had earned the respect of Neal just casually playing in Neal's home.

Rudy was naturally gifted and excelled easily at many things. In any other home he would have earned sincere praise and admiration. In his father's home, however, these were eclipsed. This was made more difficult because his father was an intensely political person. He knew he had tremendous influence and he was comfortable with flexing it at will.

When Rudy was young he didn't understand this. He was easily taken in by the ready praise for his work whether he earned it or not. Over the years he learned that whether he put forth great effort or not, he was continually getting the highest praise. This compounded, for him, the already difficult identity struggles of adolescence.

This experience with Neal, Jim, and Jack, was his most successful sojourn entirely on his own. He was excited about how well it was going. He wanted to learn all he could from the experience, and did not want to end it too early.

Rudy believed that this group, more than most, would be least likely to be influenced by his father's fame. This church's emphasis on things spiritual, and not on things material, might help. Still, he was not ready to reveal his true identity.

Rudy rode up the elevator so deep in thought that he didn't even say hello to the security person, something highly unusual for him. As he walked into the apartment he was met by his mother.

"Oh, Rudy, how nice to see you, dear. Are you going to be home for dinner?" she asked.

"I guess I could. What's up?" Rudy asked.

"Well, your father will be home, and I thought we could have a nice family meal."

"Sure. Fine," Rudy said. "That'll be nice."

"Maybe we can all catch up on what we've been doing for the last few weeks. I'll tell Paulette the plan," his mother said with noticeable enthusiasm in her voice. "We dine at eight, and you should dress."

That gave Rudy some time. He debated going to a gym, or just swimming in their pool. He decided on the gym. He didn't really want to do that more, he just thought it would sound more ambitious when his dad asked him what he did.

He took a cab to the private gym, which was mainly used by serious athletes. There were guys there who ran three or four miles every day. These people took a zealot's interest in sports.

Rudy walked past the person at the desk and was buzzed into the gymnasium. He walked around the outside edge of the gym floor watching for flying balls from the two full court games going at the time. The men playing were intense athletes, dripping with sweat, running back and forth with all their effort, their gym shoes making ear-piercing whistling sounds every time they stopped, or changed directions. There was also a thunderous hollow wooden sound as the ball and their feet pounded the hardwood floor.

Rudy walked along a hall overlooking racquetball and squash courts. Here, too, were the sounds of gym shoes squeaking loudly on the highly waxed floors, the rifle-loud sounds of rackets drilling balls into the front walls, and the groans of missed shots. In some courts people were playing handball where the racket sounds were, mercifully, missing, but the sounds of feet pounding the floors to chase down the difficult shot were still there.

Occasionally several players would walk along talking excitedly about their games. They would grunt to Rudy as they passed, but there was, somehow, an awareness that Rudy was not quite a full member there. They seemed to know that he wasn't driven to athletic efforts. Even though Rudy had been a member there all his life he felt like an outsider.

He walked up to a big door with an odd, numeric keyboard of buttons above the knob. He punched in a simple triangular pattern that was easy to remember and the lock started buzzing. He pushed on the door but it did not open. He realized you still had to turn the knob so he reached for that and turned as the buzzing stopped. Again, it didn't open. There was a clumsy bumping of the door telling everyone inside that a novice was working the door. His second try easily opened the door.

Rudy found his locker in the middle of the room and started turning the dial on the combination lock when an odd feeling of self-doubt hit him. When he finished the combination, his worst fears were confirmed. He had forgotten the combination. He looked nervously down either direction of the row of lockers. There were a few people standing at their lockers who were too well mannered to stare at him, but the awareness seemed almost written in the air: here was someone who forgot his combination. Here was an impostor among these dedicated athletes, someone who comes so rarely he forgot his combination.

Rudy discreetly walked to the office of the masseur where the files for the lockers were kept. He asked the man for his combination. The man politely read him his combination never hinting at how unusual it was. He knew Rudy well. One of the only reasons Rudy kept his membership in this gym, in fact, was because he liked to get massages from this man. That was exactly what he did this time. Rudy showered, sat in a steam room for a while, and got a half-hour massage. He then went back to the steam room to sweat out the oil, showered, dressed, and left his clothes, bag and all in the locker in case he ever needed a change of clothes there.

Rudy stopped in a snack bar connected with the gym. He ordered several bottles of sparkling water and a banana. The snack bar had lots of junk food, but most of the patrons ate healthy things while there. Rudy enjoyed the contented feeling after a good massage and a steam. Time seemed to slow down, and life seemed to get simpler. *He* tended to get lazier and signaled for a phone. The waiter brought a phone and plugged it into a jack at the table.

Rudy called home and asked for a car to be sent around. His mother told him that his father was on his way home soon and would swing by and pick him up. Rudy walked out to the curb so as not to keep his father waiting. The locomotive-sized Rolls Royce limousine pulled up. The deep black paint finish was so well polished that it reflected the building behind Rudy as clearly as a mirror. Rudy climbed in the back before the driver could get out.

Rudy's father acted pleased to see him. He was halfway through a tall gin and tonic. Rudy guessed that it was not his first for the afternoon.

"Can I have one of those?" Rudy asked.

"Sure. Help yourself," Peterfield agreed.

Rudy leaned forward and found a glass, a wedge of lime, and all he needed. He poured himself a double and settled back in the seat beside his father. He took a big gulp and sighed, "Ahh, mother's milk." His father finished his drink and asked Rudy to make him another.

Rudy poured his father a double and handed it to him. "How's this?" he asked.

His father took a sip and in mock horror asked, "Did you put any gin in this?"

Rudy offered to step it up, but Peterfield admitted he was joking. It was fine.

His father told the driver to make a loop through the park. That explained to Rudy how he was going to finish that drink before they got home. They were only blocks from the apartment. "I love riding slowly through the park," his father admitted. "So you've been to the gym. How ambitious of you, son."

"Not really. I just got a massage and sat in the steam."

"Oh the waste of youth." Peterfield said. "You can afford to ignore your body now, but the day will come when you, too, will exercise."

"I'm sure it will, father," Rudy agreed not wishing to get into an argument.

They drove through the park in silence. Peterfield finished his drink and then grew restless to get to the apartment. He even told the driver to pick up the pace. The big car leapt noticeably to a faster pace, passing several cars. When the massive car pulled up to the apartment, the doorman had his hand on the handle before it completely came to a stop. Rudy let his father climb out first and followed him into the building. There were lots of hellos from the staff to the great man. He returned them with sincerity as he walked briskly toward the elevator. Rudy leaned over and tipped his index finger at the security woman with a conspiratorial wink. She laughed thinking that he was in some kind of trouble.

His mother met them at the door. She and her husband embraced and gave each other a slow kiss. Then they paused, leaned back slightly, and both said simultaneously, "I love you." This was a routine practice Rudy had seen all his life. But there was something too mechanical about it for Rudy. Like so many of Peterfield's domestic efforts, it had an incontestably wholesome appearance to it—until you learned that it was a daily unaltered routine. It was also likely to be his only intimate effort.

They went to the patio by the pool for still more drinks. Peterfield and Rudy had another gin and tonic. His mother had her usual. It was a drink Rudy memorized since he heard her order it so often: a vodka martini, dry with no olive, and a shot of scotch poured on top. This lethal concoction was her regular drink.

They sat on the patio for nearly an hour while Peterfield read his mail, looked over several papers, thumbed through several magazines, and conversed absentmindedly with his wife.

"So, Rudy, what are you doing with your time these days?" Peterfield asked. "We see little of you."

"I've made some friends in Connecticut," Rudy explained. "I spent all last weekend at their cabin on a lake."

"You were also at the cottage," Peterfield added.

"Yeah. I needed to get away and clear my mind."

"Get away from what, Rudy?"

"This whole scene: the parties, the clubs, my friends."

"Well, did you clear your mind?"

"I guess."

"And what is your clearer mind entertaining now?"

"Well, I've been reading the Bible," Rudy said. "I never realized how much sense it made."

Rudy thought he noticed the slightest grimace of disapproval in his father's otherwise stony face. Then he asked, "Does it? I never thought that."

"I know there are lots of odd balls out there preaching various religions; but I'm talking about those who follow the Bible literally," Rudy said.

"Yes, there are some who follow the Bible literally," Peterfield agreed. "But most people get quite confused by religion. It's full of infighting, prejudice, and hatred. I shudder to think of the death and destruction that's gone on all over the world in the name of religion. In fact, it still goes on. Look at the tension in the Middle East."

"Well, your grandmother will be pleased to learn that you're reading the Bible," said Rudy's mother.

"Yes, indeed," agreed Peterfield. "How was the cottage? Was it well maintained?"

"It was perfect. The place never looked better. John's put in a lot of time on the shrubs and everything. You really should go up and see it," Rudy added.

"We're going up this weekend, aren't we, Carol?" Peterfield asked. "Will you be going too?"

"No, I've got some plans with these guys from Connecticut. What's the occasion?"

"There's a big race this weekend. We thought we'd watch part of it. I guess I need to get out of the city, too. Maybe to clear my mind too."

"I'm sure you do dear," his wife said with empathy. "You need to take more time to relax."

"Dinner is served, sir," reported the butler.

They walked into the cavernous dining room. The table was set with the precision and cleanliness of a hospital operating room. Everything was to Peterfield's peculiar specifications. He liked a lot of room between people. He liked to dine in the highest possible formality. The china was priceless. The dishes were slightly larger than usual and delicate. The silverware was heavy, substantial, and comfortable in the hand. The crystal was ornate, thin, and fragile.

The table and chairs were massive, solid, and extremely comfortable. One had the impression of settling into a cradle for a pleasurable, leisurely meal. Everything was designed to pamper, soothe, and relax. Courses of the meal were served slowly. Because of Peterfield's signaling system with the kitchen, there was never a feeling of being rushed or of having to wait. The effect was a well-choreographed dance between those dining and those serving.

Conversation was also soothing. Peterfield subscribed to a custom of only talking about pleasant things at the table. He ate slowly so that, even though he never took second servings, his guests had plenty of time to do so if they wished. The entrees were almost always French; but the final course was always Austrian.

Peterfield knew what he was doing when it came to dining. One had a wonderful feeling of contentment and peace after such a dining experience. Many felt that such a carefully orchestrated meal put them under a spell. Those who had eaten there counted that meal their most memorable. The secret was in the presentation of the food and wines. The beauty and the grace were hypnotizing.

Rudy was familiar with the effect. He usually considered it a waste of time. He sat in his chair patiently this evening, however, because he was watching his father more closely than usual. He wondered what motivated his father. He saw his father, suddenly, as strangely superficial. Although that was a term no one else would apply to him, Rudy was being overwhelmed with the conviction that this was tragically true. Here is a man, he thought, who has such a well-ordered and routine life that it has become superficial. Where are his challenges? Where is his growth over the last ten years or so?

"Rudy, you seem to be staring at me," his father complained. "You must stay home more so you know what I look like. What's on your mind?"

"Oh, sorry," Rudy said. "I was just wondering, do you have any goals? I mean, do you have any challenges?"

This question seemed to worry his father a little. His eyebrows moved slightly together and downward in a way that was barely perceptible. He glanced at his wife who seemed unaware of the conversation. She had long ago learned not to listen emotionally when anything sounded the least bit controversial. It was as if she had a switch that turned off when something might be tense or unpleasant. She would fix the smallest possible smile on her lips and be sure to move her head back and forth with the speakers—but she was a million miles away.

She had learned two rehearsed answers for when anyone asked for her opinion. First she laughed nervously and told them not to get her involved. If that didn't work, she said something idiotic, like she thought they were both right in a way. These two strategies got her out of almost any conversation.

"Well," Peterfield began trying to anticipate what Rudy's point was. "I'm at a different time of life than you are, Rudy. People my age are not making new goals for themselves as a rule. They're planning for retirement."

"Yes," Rudy continued, "but you aren't planning on retiring, are you? Don't you have any challenges?"

"What do you mean? Like, do I want to sail across the ocean like Bill Buckley? Do I want to change careers? Do I want to climb a mountain? No, I guess I don't have any challenges like those."

"Do you ever worry that your life is a little too routine? Do you ever get bored?" Rudy pressed further.

"Well, yes. My life has its routine, but I don't get bored. I think I have a pretty stimulating life. I work on lots of different projects. I guess I've found a few things I'm interested in and I keep doing them. I'm not bored because I find them interesting, but they are somewhat routine. I've been doing them for years. Has this line of questioning got something to do with your college plans?" Peterfield asked. He was growing irritated with this interrogation at the dinner table.

"I don't know. Maybe. I guess I've been giving my life a lot of thought lately."

"Well that's a healthy sign," his father said hoping to change the subject with something encouraging.

Dinner was finished with a new dessert that Peterfield discovered on his last trip to Vienna. He brought the recipe back for Paulette to experiment with. It was a fabulous success. Peterfield had no obligations that evening so, shortly after supper, both he and Rudy decided to go swimming in the pool. They swam and dove, and they even splashed around a little. Rudy enjoyed it. It reminded both of them of years gone by when Peterfield would throw Rudy into the air above the pool while Rudy giggled and drank in cups of pool water. Rudy's mother went to her sitting room and watched TV.

CHAPTER 16

After swimming Rudy and his father toweled off and sat near the pool. There was a quiet warmth to the mood. Both were aware of the rareness of this time together. They felt some pressure to talk about something but were afraid to disturb the mood. They sat there deep in thought. The only sounds were the gurgling of the water filtration system, the rushing air of the ventilation system, and Rudy's mother's television in the distance.

"This is great," Peterfield began. "I guess we should make more time for this."

"Yeah. It's pretty rare," Rudy agreed.

More silence continued to the point where it was making Rudy uncomfortable. Rudy wanted to ask his father about his thinking about religion, but he was afraid.

The newness of this religious interest was starting to wear off. He had stayed with Neal and his friends longer than he had ever hung around any other groups. He liked to immerse himself in different groups for a short time; but he usually left quickly. Now, he sensed that he was at a plateau. To hang around longer would require some personal sacrifice. It was as if he hoped that his father would discourage him that he jumped into this subject.

"I'd kinda like to know what you think of this religious thing," Rudy asked his father.

"What religious thing?" his father wanted to know.

"Well, I've found this group of people in Connecticut who are really a lot like the Amish, or Mennonites. I've been hanging out with them and I've learned a lot about them. They really seem to be genuine people. They're not religious fanatics; there's something genuine about these people."

"Really?" Peterfield noticed with concern the conviction in Rudy's voice. "What do you mean, genuine?"

"Well, they're real nice to everyone. They don't play all those social games everyone else does. They seem to be above trying to impress each other. You get the feeling that when you talk to them you really know them," Rudy explained.

"You sound like you're impressed with these people," Peterfield observed.

"Yeah, but there's nothing halfway about these people. With them it's either all or nothing. I'm not sure I want to get more involved with them. I mean, they lead such a narrow life."

"So who says you have to?" Peterfield inquired.

"I guess something inside me says I do," Rudy admitted. He was being much more open with his father than he had intended to be. With this last remark he even surprised himself.

"Really?"

There was a moment of silence while Rudy thought about this. The silence was perfectly comfortable for both of them. Rudy wondered if this was how his father did therapy. Shortly Rudy broke the silence by adding, "It seems like these people really have life figured out. They're not as shallow as my friends. I really envy them— and I'm talking about guys my age."

"Have they really figured anything out, or are they blindly following a social order?" Peterfield asked gently. There was no mockery in his voice. It was a logical question belonging at this point in the conversation.

"Well, I don't know. I mean, is anyone ever sure of life? How old do you have to be before you decide that this is the way you're going to understand it? The thing that stands out is how secure they feel. There seems to be no doubt in them about life. They seem so, I don't know, I guess contented might be the word for it."

"I'm a little concerned about guys your age being so contented. Doesn't it seem a little early?" Peterfield ventured, being careful not to betray his great skepticism. The last thing he wanted to do was give this group underdog status.

"It does seem a little early," Rudy admitted. "But there's something so appealing about their lives. I met their leader. They call him an elder. He seemed incredibly wise."

"How did you get that impression?" Dr. Peterfield inquired.

"Well, he was so patient. He didn't get distracted by the popular things to do and say. He was so original, so thoughtful. One side of me really wants that for my own life," Rudy confessed.

"You say one side of you," Peterfield observed. "What does the other side want?"

"Oh that side would mock these guys. Call 'em dorks, or

nerds. That side wants to laugh them off. Walk away from them and go on to something else."

"One side of you wants to laugh them off?"

"Yeah. They're a little scary. Their life is different. I don't know what I should do," Rudy admitted.

"Which choice would give you the most future choices?" Peterfield wanted to know. He thought he found his approach.

"I don't know. I'm tired of my life. I haven't actually been going anywhere," Rudy admitted.

"Not going anywhere?" Peterfield asked betraying a little emotion at last. "Where do you think Harvard is, nowhere? You've done some great things with your life so far, Rudy. You do well at anything you put your mind to. Look at sailing, the piano, your scholarship."

Rudy was pleased to hear his father saying such encouraging things to him.

"Look, Rudy, you've met some interesting people. They'll be just as interesting in six months or a year. Why don't you give it a chance to cool off for a while. If there's anything in their life for you, you can always renew an interest in them later. Give it a year. Go to school. See what you can make of yourself. If you want to take your life more seriously, go ahead, but give them a break and see if your feelings are as strong later as they are now. You could use that as a test."

That was it. Actual advice. Rudy could not believe the monumental importance of this moment. He was receiving direct advice from his father. Because of that he was unable to weigh the advice for himself. Because of its rareness Rudy was inclined to take it hook, line, and sinker.

"I can do that," Rudy admitted. "You know what that is, dad? That's direct advice."

"Yeah, I know," Peterfield admitted. "Well, even I can slip up now and then."

"I guess I've got lots of time. You're right," Rudy admitted. "I'll let it settle and see what floats to the surface. But I'll tell you, this was unlike anything else I've experienced before. There was something that seemed so right about it."

"I suppose it's something like sales resistance," Peterfield added. "You see something you want to buy badly. If you can walk away for a day or two and think about it, maybe you don't really want it as badly as you did when you were first looking at it. I've never had any doubts that you would find your own way, son, and that may include this group, but give it some time."

There was a twinge of fear that rushed through Peterfield. Perhaps he had just oversold the advice. Would he live to regret saying, "…and that may include this group"? He was sorry he said it.

Rudy was under no obligation to return to Neal's church, so it seemed like a natural place to put some distance between them. Rudy decided to do some sailing. He returned to Edgartown and inquired around about some racing teams, and got caught up in the summer activities on the Vineyard.

He met some young people on the beach who were doing summer jobs on the Vineyard and who were going to Harvard. He asked lots of questions about getting along at Harvard such as where the best spots were, what to avoid, how to handle the administration, where to shop, where to eat. He quickly earned a place of esteem with these new friends because he had so many basic courses waived due to his test scores and academic record. At a school that is exclusively made up of brains, they could easily size up that Rudy was a major brain.

While there he also met some other students from Yale, Columbia, and Dartmouth. They formed sailing teams and had some friendly competitions. They also did a lot of partying. At one of these parties the conversation turned to what Rudy had been doing this summer since graduating.

Rudy told them about this unusual religious group. Before he was able to describe the group fully others in the party started condemning formal religion viciously. Rudy was surprised at the intensity of their emotion.

"Wow! Man," Rudy protested, "I only mentioned that I met these people. Don't freak out."

"We're not freaking out," some girl argued.

"I don't know," Rudy continued. "The way you're reacting, you'd think I'd suggested returning to prohibition."

"Well, ugh, Rudy, I mean, have you ever spent any time with those Jesus freaks?" another girl asked him.

"They're weird, man," a guy added. "I've got a cousin in Tennessee who's really into that, you know. He's a pain. He comes to family reunions that are held on Sundays, right? And what does he do? He refuses to eat anything. At a family reunion, right? He says he always fasts on Sundays."

"Fasts, what's that?" asked another.

"That's where you don't eat, you know, like Ghandi and his hunger strikes."

"Well, anyhow, this guy doesn't eat, right? But he stands around and makes a big pain of himself. It's like he's somehow better than the rest of us, or at least he thinks so. Everybody mocks him out, man. He's a number one idiot."

"He probably thinks you're persecuting him by mocking him out," volunteered another.

"Yeah, but I mean, nobody's impressed. It's just that he's kinda this big embarrassment to the family. I asked him once if it was ever written in the Bible that he had to fast every Sunday. You know what he said? He said it wasn't. It was entirely everyone's choice."

"Weird!"

"So you know what I told him? I said, how come you gotta do it at family reunions? And you know what he said? He said it's a silent witness of a Christian life. He said I'm supposed to ask him about it and he's supposed to tell me all about Jesus.

"I told him I'd rather eat a bug than hear about Jesus and I don't like looking up from a reunion buffet and seeing some guy acting holier than thou and strutting around for everyone to see. Then I really cut loose with a string of obscenities just to irritate him. I don't know why I did it. He just made me mad, I guess. I hate those guys."

"Well, these guys weren't like that," Rudy volunteered. He was unafraid of speaking up in their defense. He felt no peer pressure from these people to go along with the thrust of the conversation. "These guys were real cool. They seemed to be having a good time, but in a simple kind of way."

"Simple is the word," piped in another. "They don't drink, they don't smoke, they don't party. They don't have any fun. You've gotta be a little simple to be like that. Don't get involved with 'em, man."

"It's a dead end street," agreed another. "Religion's what

grandparents do."

"I'm not saying I'm getting involved with them. I just never met people like that before. I found them kind of interesting. They seemed so honest," Rudy added.

"Where've you been brought up?" asked another. "I thought everybody knew about these Jesus freaks."

"Right here, for one place," Rudy added. "My family's been coming here all my life. I live in New York City."

"Well, I think you're lucky if you've never been around those people. They're real creepy."

"Come on," Rudy protested. "You make it sound worse than it is."

"Are you kidding, man?" asked another girl. "I'll tell you what. You go to a religious bookstore and look around at the people in there. I'll bet it'll be full of people in polyester clothes, with long, straight, greasy hair, wearing old, bent, metal-frame glasses sliding down greasy noses, and they'll have a plastic liner in their shirt pocket with five or six pens and pencils clipped in a neat row. It's freaky, man. It's like some Martian team came down here in the fifties and pulled out a store full of people and held them in suspended animation for thirty years and returned them back into a religious book store all at once."

"You can't be serious," Rudy protested.

"You wanna bet money on it?"

"Get off it, Rudy," another guy said. "You can't be serious. Nobody's that dumb." His tone of voice suggested that the conversation must move on, that it would be boring to talk about this subject anymore. And the one thing that this group cared about was to not be bored.

The conversation did move on to other things. But Rudy's thoughts stayed there. How strongly these people felt against religion! Rudy had the sense that it was irrationally strong. It had all the flavor of bigotry in that it was arbitrary, strong, abrupt and unthinking—except that it was not directed at a racial or cultural group. Rudy believed that these same people would be intolerant of anyone generalizing about any other minority group in the country. They would likely jump to the defense of any other minority group, yet they lumped all religious people into the same category with no hesitation or embarrassment.

Rudy debated bringing up the subject again to make this observation but wisely decided against it. He was depressed. He didn't like to learn that people who were otherwise sophisticated and tolerant could be so firmly against Christianity. He didn't like thinking that he might become involved in such an unpopular movement. Even though Rudy was perfectly comfortable with taking an unpopular stand now and then, he always did it with the confidence that he, personally, was popular and much admired. He lived in the mainstream, and he enjoyed instant popularity nearly everywhere he went. That was the reason he could risk taking an unpopular stand now and then. He was troubled with this beginning awareness that he could select an interest, or a life choice, that would make him just as instantly unpopular as he had once been instantly popular up till now.

The days passed leisurely for Rudy. He got up between nine and ten, had a big breakfast, then did some sailing. He then grabbed a late lunch and headed out to one of the beaches. He lay in the sun or threw a Frisbee with some friends. Late every afternoon he met friends at a harbor view restaurant for beers. (Rudy, because of his age, had to drink soda.) They sat around for several hours talking about events of the day or about people who were not there. Rudy frequently tried to get the conversation back to Harvard so that he could learn all he could about the ins and outs of the place before going there.

They passed several hours at this bar. The small glass-topped table resembled a surreal chessboard with green and brown beer bottles the chess pieces moved around in battle. There would be eight or ten people sitting around one of these little tables drinking and gossiping until exactly 7:10 p.m. That was when they fired off the cannon at the Edgartown Yacht Club and lowered the flag. This became their signal to move on to dinner and the evening activities.

Everyone in this group seemed to be in the same social circle. No one acted impressed with Rudy's living arrangements. Everyone seemed to understand all the same things. Rudy felt perfectly comfortable with this group. He didn't have to watch how much money he spent like he did with Neal and his friends. On the other hand he didn't feel comfortable talking about religion again.

This was how he spent his summer. Several times at the beginning of the summer he thought of calling Neal, but didn't. He didn't want to complicate things. He was surprised and curious to recognize a certain guilt in himself about not calling Neal. He wondered where the guilt came from. Neal was kind to him, that was true—but why did he feel he owed Neal so much?

After a few weeks Neal and his friends came into his thoughts less and less. Some days would go by where he would only think of them in the quiet of the evening after the day's activities had ended. He wondered if he would ever contact Neal again. As each day passed it seemed less likely; yet, there was a faint belief that this would be regrettable.

As Rudy was thinking these thoughts, Neal was having similar thoughts. He wondered what had become of Rudy. He didn't have Rudy's telephone number so he had to wait until Rudy contacted him. He was irritated by how Rudy controlled this.

Neal's friends and family asked him what had happened to Rudy. This was irritating because Neal felt dumb saying that he didn't know. All they could do was pray for him—which they did every night by name.

CHAPTER 17

As the summer wore on Rudy grew more restive with the routine on the Vineyard. He was eager to get to Harvard. He was a young man in a hurry, so he packed and moved to Cambridge early. His father had leased a third floor apartment on Bow Street.

Rudy slipped easily into the social whirl of Cambridge. His apartment was much nicer than the accommodations of most of his fellow freshmen. As a consequence, he played host to many planned and unplanned functions.

Rudy was eager to get started in his program. He enjoyed many of the elective courses, particularly literature and history, because of the interesting professors teaching in these areas.

In history he discovered an eccentric professor named Rice. This man was tall and lanky. He could have been the prototype for Ichabod Crane in "The Legend of Sleepy Hollow." He had long unruly hair and wore women's huge octagonal glasses which kept sliding down his nose. He walked around with at least five books under one arm—bookmarks haphazardly jutting out of them in several places. His other arm was devoted to carrying a big coffee mug.

This history professor would arrive in class late, place his books on one side of the desk, his coffee mug on the other, and sit awkwardly in the middle. He would lean forward over the edge of the desk, appearing to defy gravity, and lecture in a soft voice. He used no gimmicks to entertain his students, but he did have an exhaustive fund of information about all the personal and private facts about the characters of history.

His classes were large. He spoke softly, however, so that students had to listen carefully. Those that did were richly rewarded. He acquired all his information by spending years of study in the archives of Europe reading through original documents, letters, and diaries. Rudy was amazed at his ability to hold all this information in memory and retrieve it at will. Rudy never met anyone with such a powerful memory.

Professor Rice was liberal with his time and approachable to students. Periodically Rudy would visit his office. He said something to Rudy once that had a lasting affect on Rudy's life. When Rudy was asking him so many opinion questions he turned it around and asked Rudy his opinion. "After all," he said, "in a couple of years you'll be the expert." This comment would stick with Rudy all his life. It may not have been actually true, but it was generous and it provoked much thought in Rudy. This was Rice's true gift. He was able to get students to believe that they were able to think.

Rudy took as many courses from this man as could be scheduled. Coincidentally, the other professor that he had great respect for was also named Rice, but they were not related. He taught English Literature and was also peculiar looking. He was stooped over with a spinal problem. His neck didn't move freely and jutted out forward. To look around he had to move his whole upper body. He smoked heavily, and his drinking was legendary. Students made jokes about not lighting a match around him. He sometimes missed classes but when he came, and when he stayed long enough to get into the material, he was inspirational.

This Professor Rice also directed a student-run theater on campus. He had a brilliant sense of the dramatic. He read a lot of poetry to his classes, timing the endings so that he would finish a class with a powerful line, look up, and say, "I think we've worked hard enough for today." This was the signal that the class was over.

This Professor Rice also worked on public debates held for the students. He would do much of the organizational work and write the resolutions. He frequently used resolutions that were designed to embarrass the administration in some way. This made the debates quite popular with the student body.

Rudy participated enthusiastically in these debates and did well, which called him favorably to the faculty's attention. His first year was a success at getting involved in more than the typical freshman.

Rudy took study seriously. He was good at it and believed it necessary to becoming a useful person. He wanted to be that expert the history professor was talking about. He liked being able to get his arms around an idea by researching it, understanding it, and then being able to write or act upon it in a way that would earn the respect of his colleagues and professors. This process came easily to him and it was a way for him to further distinguish himself.

Freshmen were required to take a physical education class specializing in one sport. Rudy gave this some thought. He was good at swimming, diving, squash, and tennis. He decided to take a sport that he had not played yet. There were obscure sports like lacrosse, or rugby, but he decided to take a sport that he might play later. He took golf.

He was at a disadvantage, because everyone else played it for many years. He could not exactly explain why he had never played it before. There were, obviously, no golf courses in Manhattan. It just never worked into his life.

Rudy was naturally athletic and discovered a natural aptitude for golf. He made rapid progress but never got on the varsity team. He liked golf because it was leisurely, it could be played at his own pace outdoors on acres of carefully manicured grass. He liked the smell of a golf course. He liked the scenery around a golf course. But amidst all this beauty there were tremendous frustrations. It didn't take Rudy long to learn what he should be doing. What did take some time was actually *doing* it.

Rudy got involved in other student activities. His English Professor Rice got him to try out for a small part in a play. His friends had a lot of fun with that. They went to football games, lectures, and other activities of college life. Rudy enjoyed the public lectures, since Harvard drew an impressive list of speakers. Rudy's opinions were far to the right of the average Harvard undergrad. He found himself often arguing the minority view.

There was a philosophy professor, by the name of Scatina, who was always on the opposite side of the aisle from Rudy on debate issues. Some of the topics seemed so ridiculous to Rudy that he wondered how a thinking person could take the opposing view. Rudy, therefore, avoided philosophy where possible, and certainly avoided Scatina's courses. He didn't avoid him socially, however. They knew each other from the after-debate activities. They went to eating establishments and reviewed the debates with a small group of participants after each one. A core group of students and faculty evolved that enjoyed being together and discussing topics of interest on the campus.

Rudy even played golf with Scatina. A foursome decided to play one Saturday morning. It was Rudy, Scatina, another student, and the academic advisor in Education. This last participant was a good golfer. In fact, she had spent a short time on the women's professional tour. She ended up beating them all easily. Scatina was unbelievably bad at golf. It was difficult for Rudy not to laugh out loud at his unconventional swing. He was short, and overweight. Consequently it was difficult for him to swing smoothly. He thought he was accommodating for this—but actually he made things much worse. He sank deeply by bending his knees at the top of this backswing. When he started his swing downward he straightened out his legs, which almost guaranteed that the club head would not pass the ball near where it was addressed. This made for incredible accuracy problems. It was routine for this man to shoot in the double digits on half the holes per round.

There were many vacations or long weekends in the college schedule. Rudy's friends frequently made short trips and he went on some of these. One popular thing was to take a ferry to Provincetown. It had a long history of being an artistic community and that appealed to their budding intellectual curiosity. Rudy invited them all to his parent's cottage for one long weekend but only a small group went because of transportation difficulties.

For the Thanksgiving holiday Rudy decided to go back to New York. He had invitations to go with friends but his mother's youngest brother, Ueli, and his family were going to be at his home for a big family meal. Rudy really liked Uncle Ueli and his family. They had three small children who were a lot of fun to watch at holidays. Rudy took a genuine interest in them. He always played games with them and they really loved Rudy in return. Rudy had unlimited patience with them.

A large group gathered around the dining room table for the Thanksgiving meal. Paulette prepared what had to be the largest turkey in New York. Ueli quipped, "I'll bet if you carried it past Macy's they'd try to tie ropes on it." Peterfield carved it with great ceremony and the meal went well. Rudy's cousins were somewhat active but held themselves together in this intimidating, formal atmosphere through the main part of the meal. They were dismissed before dessert with the promise that they could have all they wanted in the middle of the afternoon. The children felt paroled.

After dessert, over brandy or coffee, the discussion turned to Rudy's Harvard experiences. Both Peterfield and Ueli had been to

Harvard. They asked questions about various faculty and were amazed to learn that some were still there. They were impressed with Rudy's success so far. One of the faculty took the trouble to write a kind note to Peterfield. Ueli expressed complete approval of his choice of law. Ueli was a chemical engineer by training and the president of a German-owned manufacturing firm in the South. He was particularly amused by Rudy's choice of golf for a sport, since he was an avid golfer. Plans were made for Rudy to go south over the Christmas break and play on some good courses. He thought the story of Rudy's Philosophy professor excessively funny and laughed so hard that it annoyed Peterfield.

Ueli gave Rudy some specific advice about Harvard: where to go, where not to go, what to watch out for. Most of it seemed accurate to Rudy. It had not been that long since his uncle was there. Ueli was on the crew team and that developed into his current passion of speedboat racing. Rudy thought this was quite a leap from rowing, but probably a lot more exciting.

The evening was filled with fun and interesting stories. The visit of this special uncle and his family made this a special Thanksgiving for Rudy. The only disappointment was that they had to return home the following day. It was a short visit and the rest of the holiday promised to be dull.

As Rudy was thinking of how to salvage the holiday his thoughts turned to Neal and his friends. Rudy had stopped thinking about them as often and was preoccupied with thoughts of school. Rudy also thought of Renee. He tried to get in touch with her first but was told that she was in Europe for the holidays with her father. Rudy left a message to have her call him when she got back.

CHAPTER 18

With Renee out of the country, Rudy decided to call Neal. He couldn't remember the number and it wasn't in his appointment book. He thought of calling information, but remembered that Neal put it in the song book he gave him. "Trust Neal to think of everything," Rudy chuckled to himself. He dialed the number and wondered what Neal had been up to. It was the Friday after Thanksgiving and no one answered. Rudy called later.

It was late that afternoon when Neal's mother answered the phone.

"Oh, Rudy. How nice to hear from you. Neal's not here right now. He'll be so disappointed that he missed you. Let me have your number. I'm sure he'll want to call you when he gets home," she said.

"Thanks, Mrs. Ebler." Rudy returned. "It's nice to hear your voice too. Is he somewhere where I could call him?"

"Well, he was going over to Jim Stander's. I'm sure you remember him. Perhaps you could call there." Mrs. Ebler gave Rudy the number and forgot to push harder for Rudy's number.

Rudy called the Standers to learn that Jim and Neal had gone over to Jack's. Rudy tried Jack's number and Jack answered the phone.

"Hi, Jack, this is Rudy."

"Rudy!" Jack practically shouted into the phone.

"Sshhh!" Rudy insisted. "Don't let Neal know this is me. How ya doing? I haven't seen you guys for a while."

"Yeah, we missed you."

"Thanks. I got caught up in family stuff and then I was off at school. How about you?"

"The same," admitted Jim.

"Is Neal there, can I talk to him?" Rudy asked.

"Yeah. he's here," Jack answered. "I'll go get him."

"Be sure not to tell him who it is, OK? I want to surprise him."

"OK, that's cool. I'm sure he'll be surprised. We wondered what happened to you. Let's get together."

"OK. We'll try to work something out. I just want to surprise Neal first. Don't let on who it is. He didn't hear you shout out my name did he?"

"I doubt it. They're downstairs playing Monopoly. You know how loud they get playing that. I doubt if he heard anything."

Jack went downstairs and told Neal that there was someone on the phone for him.

"Who is it?" inquired Neal.

"You'll have to ask him yourself," Jack said allowing Neal to believe that he didn't know.

Neal climbed the steps wondering who would chase him down to Jack's house. He decided it was his father.

"Hello," Neal said with a somewhat unfriendly tone of voice. He imagined that his father was calling him home for some work.

"What kind of tone of voice is that?" Rudy asked. He wasn't trying to disguise his voice.

"I'm sorry," Neal said. He still couldn't make out who it was. It wasn't his father's voice, but he had heard the voice before. "I can't quite make out your voice."

"You don't know who this is?" Rudy asked enjoying Neal's predicament.

"It sounds like Rudy Horace. Is that possible?"

"It sure is," Rudy said, relieved that Neal sounded so eager to hear from him. "What've you been doing with yourself?" Rudy asked.

"I've been in Ohio going to school."

"Oh, that's right," Rudy remembered. "How do you like it there?"

"It's big," Neal said. "They treat you like a number there."

"Sounds bad," Rudy said.

"Well, there's lots of good things, too. I'm doing fine. I like it. It's just an adjustment to go to a school that big. How do you like Harvard?"

"It's great. I'm having a blast."

"Glad to hear it," Neal said. "Hey, can we get together and share stories? I'd like to hear all about Harvard. I've got lots to tell you about Ohio State."

"Sure. I'm home for Thanksgiving. Well, I guess you are too. Most of my family went back home today so it's pretty boring around here. How can we get together?" Rudy asked.

They arranged to meet at the train station in Stamford. The train ride gave Rudy time to think. He wondered at his mood. He was really eager to meet these guys again. Still, there was a slight feeling of trepidation. He wondered if he had exaggerated their qualities in his memory. He wondered if he would be disappointed. He wondered if he would still like them as much as he thought he did. He never got to any churches in Cambridge or Boston. He rarely read from the Bible. He let this experience lie dormant in his mind since that last Sunday with these friends.

The closer the train got to the station the more anxiety he felt. He wondered if this was a wise move. In spite of this anxiety he noted that he made the call, had gone to some difficulty to track Neal down, and had agreed to come up for the weekend. Obviously he wanted it to happen, he reassured himself.

Rudy was met at the station by Neal, Jim, and Jack. There was some pushing and shoving as they gave him a friendly welcome. Beneath the kidding was a tremendous relief that Rudy called them. Neal feared that he had seen the last of Rudy.

Neal's old van rocked back and forth with their assault on its peaceful rest. The motor sprang into action and with the crashing sound of the sliding side door, they lurched out of the parking lot. They decided to get pizza. They ordered too many, ate all of them, and drank a small river of soda. With the satisfied feeling of a full stomach, they climbed more slowly into the van again and headed on.

They decided to go to a boat basin, walk along the docks and look at the boats. The weather was bracing but they kept warm by walking.

"So what have you been doing in Boston, Rudy?" Neal wanted to know. "How do you spend your time?"

"I spend a lot of time in the library, if you can believe it," Rudy confessed. "There's so much to learn. I've got some great professors who really turn you on to their subjects. You really want to perform for them to get their attention, I guess, and to get them to notice you."

"Well, do they?" Neal asked.

"Yeah, some of them do," Rudy admitted. "I got involved in the public debates and a few of them stick around after the debates and go to a coffee shop with the students to discuss what went on. How's it going at Ohio State?"

"Much different," Neal admitted. "The place is so big you

feel like a number. There are some classes that are so big they just put up about six television monitors in a crowded auditorium and you watch one of those. They've got a bunch of graduate students assigned to help you if you have any questions, but most people don't bother asking them."

"Sounds bad," Rudy agreed. "Do you go to any games, concerts or stuff?"

"Oh, some," Neal agreed. "I've been to some plays, and I went to one football game. I got tickets, which isn't that easy to do, and I took a friend along. We sat right behind a big "I" beam. We were so far up you couldn't see where the football was. You needed binoculars to see what was happening."

"But the Buckeyes are a great football team, right?" Rudy asked. "At least you got to watch a great football team."

"Yeah, I guess so," Neal agreed. "What about you?"

"I went to a football game once," Rudy remembered. "It was at Columbia so I got back to New York. Columbia's got this huge, new stadium and a terrible football program. And their band is even worse. They only had about twelve legitimate instruments in the whole band. One guy was marching around with a sponge rubber mop that would open and close from the handle. One guy had a bicycle rim hung around his neck with a string. He was beating on it with drum sticks. Some guys were using large soda bottles as drums.

"The whole thing was a big joke, but at least they knew it was a joke. Anyhow we beat 'em."

"Sounds pretty dumb," Neal suggested. He couldn't imagine the great Ohio State marching band using makeshift instruments like that.

"I'll say it's informal. There was one critical point in the game with the team defending a fourth down and inches situation. It was a critical time and the band was too busy clowning around to know what was going on. They didn't even bother cheering. We really clobbered 'em."

"Wow! Look at some of these boats," Jim observed.

"How'd ya like to have one like that?" Neal asked.

"That'd be neat," agreed Jim.

Rudy noticed that the boats weren't as big as his father's. This was a gentle reminder to him to keep his identity secret. He began to wonder if he could ever tell them who he really was.

"It's getting kinda cold," remarked Jim. "Let's get out of here."

So they walked back to Neal's van.

"You guy's hungry for anything?" Neal asked.

"No way," cried Jack. "I couldn't tamp anything down with a wooden spoon."

"Get the heater going," Jim ordered. "Maybe we could get some hot chocolate somewhere."

"That sounds good," Rudy agreed.

They bought some at a drive-through and headed out to Jim's cabin.

"Remember last summer when we came here to play ball tag in the lake?" Jack asked. "That'd sure be cold now, wouldn't it?"

"I don't know—we've swam in some pretty cold water out here."

"We always seem to get in in May. I'll bet the water isn't any colder now than last May," Jim suggested.

"Do you want to go in, Jim?" Rudy asked.

"No way!" Jim hastened to clarify.

No one wanted to go down to the water that night. Instead, they sat around a table and played Monopoly. They all considered themselves good. The game ground to a halt in the middle because they couldn't agree on any trading and bargaining.

They decided to get some sleep. The next day they were going hiking during the day and had a campfire planned with the youth group in the evening. That night Rudy wondered why he thought these guys were so much fun. He tried to remember what they did. He wondered why walking past some boats, eating some pizza, and playing Monopoly at some cabin out in the sticks of Connecticut was fun. He couldn't seem to come up with an explanation. He couldn't keep his mind focused on the question long enough to figure it out. Something in his thoughts just wouldn't permit him to finish the equation in his head. It just was fun, but he didn't know why.

When he forced himself to think it through, he could only decide that these guys were nice. They weren't critical. They didn't run other people down the way his friends at school did. Their thoughts and humor seemed refreshingly simple. It wasn't the kind of simple that meant undeveloped or slow. It was the kind of simple that meant free.

Rudy's thoughts drifted to his Harvard friends. He wondered what they would have thought of these guys. These weren't the type that they described as being in a religious bookstore. These were normal looking guys. He wondered if his Harvard friends had ever meet people like these. He wondered if he could get these guys to come to Cambridge and meet them. It wasn't exactly a drive across town. Then he remembered that he couldn't keep his last name secret if they met his friends at Cambridge.

With these thoughts he drifted off to sleep. A sleep aided by the fresh cabin air, the coolness, and the silence of the countryside. He slept soundly with no worries. He felt perfectly comfortable with these guys. He could trust them. He realized that he could have left his wallet with a thousand dollars out on the kitchen table and it would still be there when he woke up in the morning. No one would steal it for drugs. This was a good enough reason to sleep soundly.

CHAPTER 19

Rudy woke to the smell of Canadian bacon in the kitchen. It took a minute to remember where he was. How improbable he would have considered it, last spring, if someone would have told him that he would be in a cabin in Connecticut with some Christians during the Thanksgiving vacation that same year.

He had a little trouble getting out of bed. The bedrooms were cooler than the rest of the house. He pulled on some clothes and headed toward the bathroom. Since this required going past the kitchen he was buffeted with a bunch of cheerful morning greetings. He had trouble sounding half as cheery. After a shower he did better.

"It sure smells great!" Rudy said.

"Thanks," said Jim the cook. "You're just in time to dig in."

"How can I help?" Rudy asked.

"You'll get a chance when we clean up. How're you at washing dishes?" Jack asked.

"I don't know. I've never done it."

"Right," the guys joked

Rudy sat down to a huge plate of food and started eating like he always did.

"Don't you want to say a prayer first?" asked Jim.

"Oh, yeah, I guess I do," Rudy agreed. He was embarrassed that he had forgotten this practice. He tried to smooth it over with a joke: "But I want you to know that it's not because you cooked the food." He bowed his head and gave thanks for the food.

"Eat a hearty breakfast, Rudy. We're going for a long camera hike with some of the other guys from the youth group," advised Jim.

"What's a camera hike?" Rudy asked.

"It's where everyone has a camera with a short roll of film in it. Everyone has to shoot the entire roll of film during the hike. Then the rolls are developed and everyone has to show every frame that was developed, whether it turned out good or not," Jack explained. "Then they vote to see who did the best with the limited number of shots they had. It's just for fun. There aren't any prizes or anything."

"Well, I'm sort of at a disadvantage already 'cause I don't

have a camera," Rudy admitted.

"You can use one of mine," Neal offered. "I've got an extra one." This was true. Neal was a camera nut. He was always taking pictures. "I'll give you some pointers about how to use it."

While cleaning up, about twelve people from the youth group arrived. They stood around waiting for the organizers to give the directions.

Two vans drove the group out to a huge stone quarry. Jim explained that all the photographers must stay in the stone quarry, that they would have six hours in which to take their pictures, and by five o'clock everyone must be back at the vans and ready to go.

There were the usual adolescent questions trying to further structure what was intended to be an unstructured event. They were the kinds of questions that could all be answered with, "That's entirely up to you. Use your imagination."

Neal took a few moments to teach Rudy about "f" openings, shutter speed, the light meter, and depth of field. Then he took a stab at composition.

Rudy recognized many of the details about composition, which he had learned taking oil painting classes. The more technical information about depth of field was lost on him. He paid special attention to how to use the light meter. He figured that would be enough to get by.

Rudy and Neal then split up. Neal took the assignment seriously. He planned to win. Everyone expected him to win. Only Neal believed that there was a chance of someone else beating him. Rudy walked toward the center of the stone quarry. There was a huge iron and corrugated metal building with railroad tracks running under it. It was like a grain elevator, only for gravel. It had huge conveyor belts, pulleys, chutes and cranes.

It was clear that this building had been unsued for many years. It was merely a skeleton of its former days. Most of the corrugated metal sheeting had been torn away by high winds. There were solid metal beams holding the floors up. The floors were made of thick wooden planking. Here and there were big holes in the flooring that dropped through several floors where a chute might have been. Some of the boards were dangerously loose, some had nails sticking up through them, and some were beginning to rot. The building was a study in contrasts of light and shadows with the bright sunlight coming through the many holes in the siding and across the floors.

Rudy climbed to the top of this building and watched the activity below. He wanted to be unnoticed by the others and just watch them. He watched what others were doing with their cameras. Some took the assignment seriously. Some were casual. Some crawled around and took pictures from unusual angles. Others just snapped pictures quickly.

Finally Rudy got tired of sitting in one place. He climbed down and took a few pictures. He returned to the vans for lunch. They packed a picnic lunch with lots of soda in a cooler full of ice.

There were only a few of the younger kids at the vans when Rudy got there. They were shy when Rudy walked up.

"Having any luck with these pictures?" Rudy wanted to know.

"Yeah. We're all done," admitted one of them. "I don't see why it takes five hours."

"How can you be sure you didn't miss something?" asked Rudy.

"What can you miss?" asked another. "It's just one big field with a stone quarry in the middle.

"Have you ever been here before?" Rudy asked.

"No."

"How do you know there isn't something you missed? You should scout it out first."

"I guess we could except we took all our pictures," admitted the first boy. "How many pictures have you got left."

"About half," Rudy said. "Hey, let me take a picture of you guys sitting here."

Rudy hung around the vans hoping to run into Neal, Jim, or Jack to hang around with after lunch but they never showed up. He found out that Neal had taken his lunch with him in his coat pockets.

The weather was perfect for photography. There was a deep blue sky with tufts of white clouds scattered around, enough to give the sky some character, a Northern Canadian kind of sky. There was a remarkably crisp freshness to the air. It was chilly but healthful being out in this.

Rudy decided to use his remaining pictures on the people in the group. He saved the last two frames to get a picture of the whole group when they got back.

On the way back to the cabin Neal told about an exciting place he found. It was a storm sewer that he climbed into. He had gone about three city blocks when he ran into a junction of smaller connecting pipes. When he turned around and looked back he saw a pitch black tunnel leading back to the bright light at the end. Every hundred feet there was an overhead pipe leading up to a culvert. This produced a circular ring of light evenly spaced along the dark walls of the tunnel. It looked like concentric circles around a spot of bright light in the middle.

After dinner, back at the cabin, they formed a circle around the living room and sang a few songs from a camp song book. A few small groups sang special numbers. Rudy was impressed with the natural, spontaneous way they enjoyed singing. He was emotionally moved by the words of the songs and the feeling they put into them.

Rudy had always believed that religion was filled with unimportant events that preachers or priests tried to attach important meaning to. He believed that only the clergy took the events seriously. He believed that everyone else honored a tacit agreement to let the clergy be so worked up about religion because it gave a nice formality to major events in their lives, like births, weddings, and death. It was as if religion was the service called upon to walk us through these moments in our lives, so that we would not have to be embarrassed at how we handle them alone. Like the frame around a picture, religion provided an unnecessary but agreeable boundary to experiences at these moments that was ornamental but not to be taken too seriously. And when anyone took religion too seriously, the frame around a painting became too fancy, creating an indecent lack of proportion where the frame eclipses the painting.

It was in this last point where Neal's church was different. They put a great emphasis on religion but it didn't have that insipid quality that Rudy's friends joked about. These people were heavily involved in religion but it seemed to make sense for them. If he could grasp the reason for this he might be able to understand these people and explain them to his friends. But even this desire to understand these people, and to explain them to his friends, was something he didn't understand. Why was he so interested in them? Why did he care?

CHAPTER 20

During the campfire Rudy had several experiences that caused him to wonder if others in the group could read his thoughts. It seemed like everyone who spoke said things directed solely at him. He looked for a way to get out but realized that getting up and leaving wouldn't be cool. His thoughts raced to figure out what his next move was. He decided that it was to be cool, sit still.

One speaker hit a nerve when he asked, "Is Christianity cool? Does anyone in the group hope for Christianity to be cool?" He said that if they did, they were fooling themselves. He said that was the trouble with popular Christian movements. "They're being distracted from the Christian fervor in their wish to make Christianity look cool to people.

"What's cool about getting stoned like the Apostle Paul after preaching the truth to a bunch of people?" he asked. Rudy was distracted by the word "stoned." He wondered if the Apostle Paul ever got high. This gave Rudy a kind of jump. Then he realized that the speaker meant having stones thrown at him and being left for dead. Rudy felt a certain disappointment. He couldn't relate to it. He did know what it was like to get high. He felt a slight regret that the speaker was not referring to this more contemporary meaning of the word.

Then, like a miracle, the speaker said, "Well, I don't know anything about getting stoned the way the Apostle Paul did, but I've been stoned on booze and drugs before.

"When I was in high school," the speaker went on, "I decided this church was all wrong. It seemed like the other kids were having a lot more fun than I was. So I decided to stop coming to church and youth group. I grew my hair long, I got into heavy metal music, and I hung out with the bad kids in school.

"My parents were real upset with this but I didn't listen to them. We got in lots of screaming fights but I learned that if I could ignore that, they couldn't do much to me. Well, this went on for a while and then it suddenly stopped being fun. I don't really know when the fun stopped, or if it ever was as much fun as I thought it was. I think it was really fun at first but slowly the fun stopped. It wasn't something I noticed, but eventually I was going to more and more trouble just to get the stuff, and it wasn't as good as it was at first.

"I remember one night I gave up drugs for the hundredth time; and I tore up the phone number of the guy I usually bought stuff from. Then, late that night, I changed my mind and I had to have some. I couldn't remember the guy's name clearly but I tried to look it up in the phone book. There were lots of people with that name so I started calling some of the numbers trying to find the guy. It was three o'clock in the morning and I was calling all these people.

"Well, people were getting real mad and I was getting real frustrated. I remember standing in that phone booth and hitting myself in the head trying to remember that guy's number. I must have looked crazy. I was hitting myself in the head as hard as I could swing inside a phone booth. Then, suddenly, I saw myself in that situation. It was like I was outside the phone booth and was able to see this person in the phone booth hitting himself in the head and looking like a crazy person.

"I suddenly realized that this was not what I thought I was going to live like when I left the church. I thought I left the church for fun. I wanted to have more fun than the church people were having, but this didn't look much like fun. I wondered, who watching me would believe that I was having fun. It was like I couldn't keep lying to myself anymore. I admitted that this was stupid. I told myself that I was a jerk to do this. I had always thought of myself as a smart person and here I was hitting myself in the head so hard that when I reached up and felt my scalp it was full of lumps.

"I remember I hung the phone up and started crying right there in the phone booth. I slowly slid down the glass box until I was squatting on the floor sobbing as loudly as I could.

"I went to my parents' house. It was about four in the morning and I realized that I had to tell my parents about my decision to give this life up. I realized that I had to tell them right then or the next day I'd be tempted to put it off and go back to drugs. So I walked in my parents' bedroom and woke them up. I told them I was coming home, which sounded a little ridiculous to me, but they understood what I meant. They hugged me and cried too.

"That was the beginning of my conversion. I found the grace through the mercy of the Lord to come back to church, give up drugs and all my old friends, and live a life for Jesus. And I just want to tell you that religion is not just for old people about to die. Religion is not about feeling good and having a cool time. Religion is about Jesus Christ and His mission on earth. Religion is taking up His cause and working for Him. It may not always be that glamorous. You may get ridiculed, but it feels good to work for His cause. It feels good to serve Jesus Christ. So don't get involved in some of the things that I did. Save yourself all that. Just go straight to Jesus Christ and get busy for Him."

The boy sat down and Rudy felt totally numb. He felt like he was the only one sitting in this room and that this person was speaking directly to him. Rudy was aware that he had not even stirred in his seat during the entire time this guy was talking. It was not just *what* he said. It was the interaction between what he said and what Rudy had been thinking.

This mood was interrupted by some movement in the room. A quartet got up to sing the final number which was "Why Not Now." This song asked the question, "Why not come to Jesus now?" Rudy thought about this. He thought about talking to this guy immediately after the campfire meeting. He considered asking him if he could speak to him for a while. But he did not. Rudy also realized that he was only going to be here for another day. Tomorrow afternoon he would take the train back to New York and later head back to Cambridge and school.

It took a while for Rudy to come down from this experience. Slowly the bustle of the group and the refreshments brought Rudy back to the present. Shortly the group broke up and all but Jim, Neal, Jack, and Rudy left for home. There was a silence in the cabin that seemed comfortable to all of them. This was not a time for boisterous talk. They were all tired. There was a general agreement to make an early night of it.

Rudy wanted to get to bed, lie there, and think. He looked forward to some quiet so that he could put his thoughts together. He laid on his bed in silence. He had the impression that his thoughts were racing and that he had a lot to think about, but he couldn't seem to bring any of these thoughts into focus. He was aware that there were some powerful impressions floating around in his brain but he couldn't seem to freeze any one of them long enough to take a closer look at it. It was like all this thought was in some foreign language and that one part of his mind was thinking about it in that language, but that the other part of his brain didn't know that language.

He was aware of a disappointing fear that this information was somehow lost, yet a faint belief that it would not be. He felt like part of his brain was cheating him from thinking about these things. The thoughts that he had were fading quickly, like the body of the Cheshire cat, but the feelings, like the smile, remained to tease.

The morning began with great activity. Some quick doughnuts for breakfast and off to church. There was no chance of staying at the cabin. Their whole focus was on the Sunday activities. All their activities, friends, and associates revolved around this church.

During lunch Rudy explained his need to get back to the train for home. Neal took him back in his van alone. He wanted to talk to Rudy some. Neal was not comfortable leaving all future contact up to Rudy. He wanted Rudy's phone number and address. Rudy was reluctant, but Neal pressed him hard.

Rudy decided that since he was renting his own place in Cambridge there would be no trouble with mail addressed to him as "Rudy Horace" instead of "Rudy Peterfield." The phone number would be no problem, either. It was not like he lived on a dorm floor where other students would know his real name. So he decided that there was no risk in giving Neal his address and phone number.

He was relieved that he had this separate address to give Neal. He didn't want to give him the New York info and fortunately Neal didn't press for that.

After a friendly farewell, Rudy settled into a corner of the train for the ride to New York. He wanted to relive some of the experiences he made this weekend but, again, found them oddly difficult to recall. They were giving him no satisfaction at all. So he slipped into making plans to return to Cambridge and his studies. It was like a giant page was turned in his mind and his thinking returned completely to Harvard and the growing tapestry of friends and relationships he was making there.

Still, he couldn't help but be puzzled by his seeming inability to retrieve the thoughts and feelings he had at Jim's cabin. He wondered how he could have such powerful emotions and not be able to relive them? He wondered how something that had obviously been such a strong part of him could now be lost to him. He didn't like this. He didn't like not being able to think about what he *wanted* to think about. This disturbed a vanity he held that he was in control of his thoughts and feelings.

That night, as he lay in his own bed, he was struck by the big change between Jim's cabin and his own apartment. He covered a world of change in that short time. How different, he realized, these two worlds were. How did they get to be different? Did they have to be different? That was to be the last thought he would have of Neal and his friends or his church for weeks.

CHAPTER 21

On returning to Harvard Rudy noticed that his mailbox was filled with invitations to parties from friends who stayed in Cambridge. His answering machine was, too. While listening to the messages he remembered that Neal now had his phone number so he changed his message to something more tame and rewound the tape.

Rudy enjoyed getting back to school. He felt comfortable with the world of ideas and responded to the demands and deadlines placed upon him by professors. To his friends he seemed all work. They complained that he had no social life, that he was asexual. Rudy realized there was some truth to these remarks. He had tried to call Renee many times, but she was never there. He wrote letters and cards but none were answered. This was typical. She was intense when you were with her; but too preoccupied with herself to write or call.

Some of Rudy's friends staged a mock kidnapping one night. They carried him off to Trecaso's, a small Italian Restaurant run by three old Italian brothers who loved wining and dining customers, whom they treated like guests at a big private party. They didn't keep a close eye on the bottom line, but their love for their guests showed and gave them a brisk business.

This restaurant also had an elaborate cellar. As long as the students drank wine they were rarely carded. If they ordered hard liquor, they were. The place was small and plain. It had linoleum floors, formica tables with metal and plastic chairs, cheap blond paneling, and old fluorescent lighting hanging precariously from a high ceiling which was made of beautiful, elaborately pressed tin panels. Most patrons never saw the ceiling but Rudy noticed it immediately. He advised the owners to clean it up and put some light on it which they had no intention of doing.

Each booth had a remote juke box. It had a Plexiglas semi-circle and six pages of music selections that you could swing back and forth. They had an unusual selection. There were birthday songs, anniversary songs, polka selections, one or two religious songs, some old Beatles songs, and others. One that quickly became popular with Rudy and his friends was "Lay Lady Lay" by Bob Dylan. One of

Rudy's friends, named Craig, could imitate Bob Dylan perfectly singing this song.

Craig was a fascinating character. He was bright. His parents were of modest means and lived in Ohio. They placed a high value on education, however, and sent him to expensive Eastern private schools. This placed him in with a lot of rich kids. He was as bright or brighter, but felt far inferior because of his modest background. These feelings of inferiority developed into a tremendous wit, a biting sarcasm, and an acid tongue.

Rudy recognized Craig's inferiority complex and admired his humor. Rudy made Craig feel like an equal and Craig liked Rudy for that. Craig couldn't play a game or sport without turning it into a battleground to prove his superiority. He was above average at sports and games but believed himself to be the best. This produced a comical effect as he tried to use sports to establish his superiority when everyone but Craig knew that it wouldn't work. They also knew that his true superiority was intellectual, but that he failed to recognize this himself. The ironical need to prove his superiority, coupled with his failure to recognize the arena where he was truly superior, made him naturally funny.

So a pattern developed where Rudy and his friends would meet at Trecaso's for some good pasta and lots of wine. They would sit there for hours drinking heavily. When they finally left, their legs would hardly straighten, which they found hysterically funny.

From this beginning it wasn't long before the group got into more drinking and some experimental forays into drugs. They were more respectful of drugs, however, and stuck primarily to alcohol.

Rudy was used to drinking. He had drunk wine all his life with his family. His parents were never stingy and he never wanted much. This drinking with his friends was different. This drinking seemed to make possible an openness and an expression of feeling that none would be willing to do otherwise. In fact, this group's unofficial motto was *in vino veritas*. This they said to themselves as they slid past the point of inhibition.

One Saturday morning Rudy was sleeping in late from an evening of such drinking. At eleven-thirty his phone rang. Uncharacteristically he answered the phone before his answering machine turned on.

He practiced saying hello several times before picking up the phone so that his voice wouldn't crack, "Hello?" he said.

"Hello, Rudy, is that you?" the voice on the other end said.

"I think so," Rudy admitted. "Who's this?" he didn't recognize the voice.

"Guess," challenged the voice.

"Ugh, I can't tell yet. Say some more," Rudy asked.

"Well, you haven't heard my voice in a few weeks." This was the only hint Rudy needed.

"Neal. Right?" Rudy guessed. "Neal Ebler."

"Right. You're pretty good."

"Well, how're you doing?" Rudy asked.

"Great. How're you doing?" Neal asked.

"Great, too. I've met some friends here and we're having a pretty good time. Where you calling from? Boston?"

"No. I'm calling from Columbus, Ohio," Neal answered.

There was the slightest relief in Rudy's mind. He wasn't sure why but he didn't want to have to entertain Neal right now. He was sure that Neal would not like his friends, or what he and his friends did for entertainment.

"You know one of my friends is from Ohio," Rudy volunteered. "He's from Wooster. Ever hear of Wooster?"

"We've got a big church in Wooster," Neal admitted. "I get there about every other week."

This worried Rudy a little. This could be another complication. They talked for about ten minutes. Neal wanted to know if Rudy was going to church and how his spiritual life was going.

"Not well, I'm afraid," Rudy admitted.

"You know, Rudy, I pray for you by name every night," Neal said.

"Wow, thanks," Rudy said.

"Would you mind if I sent you some tapes of some of our sermons?" Neal asked. "There's a great minister in Wooster and he has some sermons that I think you'd really be interested in."

"Do I have to return them or anything like that?" Rudy wanted to know. He didn't want any hassles with shipping stuff around.

"No. Just listen to them and do what you want with them."

Under the circumstances Rudy didn't feel like he had any choice. "Sure. That'd be great," Rudy agreed.

"I wish I could get up there and see what Harvard's like." Neal volunteered. "Maybe I'll have a holiday when you don't and we can get together."

"That'd be great. I'd kinda like to see Ohio State. Maybe I can fly over there some time. Do they have an airport in Columbus?"

Neal was amused by Rudy's New York attitude. "Of course, Rudy. Columbus is the state capital, for Pete's sake."

Rudy sensed the gentle admonition in Neal's choice of words and apologized. "Well, maybe I'll surprise you some long weekend."

"If you do, call ahead. I go to Wooster a lot."

So Neal gave Rudy his address and phone number. Rudy wrote it in his Bible, guessing that if he ever went to Columbus to see Neal he'd probably take that along anyway.

This call would have left Rudy in a pensive mood had it not been for Craig ringing Rudy's bell and their going off to some school activity.

Neal, on the other hand, went into action. He had a set of twenty tapes from a minister in Wooster ready to send. He just wanted to have Rudy agree to it first. He planned on sending Rudy one almost weekly thinking that it would be like attending church regularly. Even as Neal packed the twenty tapes he feared that there were too many, but he couldn't stop himself.

CHAPTER 22

Over the next few months Rudy's attention shifted from school work to partying. His grades didn't suffer, but he was bringing no creativity or brilliance to his work, just going through the motions.

His parents came up for a Harvard/Yale football game and took Rudy out for dinner. He suggested Trecaso's and they actually drove past it before vetoing the idea. They suggested "Ye Olde Oyster House." To salvage the evening Rudy invited several of his friends: Craig, of course, and a girl named Pam.

Before inviting them, Rudy tried hard to get Renee up from New York. Her father had gone to Yale and he thought it would be fun to put the families together. Rudy made this the highest priority but in the end it failed.

Pam was the exact opposite of Renee. She bore a striking resemblance, cruel as this sounds, to the Muppet character Miss Piggy. She was stout, round faced, with straight, straw-colored hair. She had the same loud personality, quick to fly into a rage over some perceived insult she received, and usually from men. Everyone called her "Miss Piggy" behind her back.

Pam was rude about psychiatrists from the first course of Oysters. She admitted that she had been sent to one for years with no observable change, in the opinion of her parents.

She opined that: "The whole profession is founded on a bunch of myths that people have to pretty much close their eyes and believe. It's a case of everybody agreeing not to ask too many questions of a group of people that hate to answer any."

Rudy enjoyed the discomfort to his father. He thought she hit the nail on the head with that last remark.

"What does your father do?" Peterfield asked without the slightest indication of anger in his voice.

"Oh, he's an ophthalmologist in Atlanta, and he's gay."

It seemed to Rudy's parents that everything this unfortunate creature said was designed to upset people. So Peterfield, typically, offered that impression.

"You seem to calculate every comment you make to be shocking.

Do you ever say anything lovely, gentle, or kind?

"What're ya gettin at?" she wanted to know.

Peterfield lowered his stare right at Pam. He gave what he was about to say one last wash through that labyrinthine mind of his before he opened fire. Rudy and his mother recognized these expressions. Rudy's mother's anxieties rose as she wanted to sink deeper into the seat. She reached reflexively for the wine. Rudy started to smile. He knew his father was about to hit Pam right between the eyes with something even she wouldn't expect.

"I'll tell you what," Peterfield began. "I'll give you one thousand dollars right now if you suddenly remember something you have to do that requires you to excuse yourself from this luncheon, that you say nothing more than excuse me, and if you leave."

"You're on, pal," she said.

Peterfield pulled out his wallet and handed her ten hundred dollar bills. She said, "Excuse me, I just remembered something I have to do." And she left.

Rudy's mother immediately felt a great sense of relief. Even Rudy realized that she had been a poor choice. Craig was too shocked to feel relief. He knew Rudy's dad was rich but he would never have guessed that he was this unashamedly rich. Craig knew some other rich people through friends he had at school. Most of them behaved as if they were embarrassed about their money. They tended to deny that they had a lot of money. They certainly would not have bribed someone to leave a luncheon just because they were bored with the person or the person was making a bad time for them.

Rudy's dad seemed to not care in the least what people thought of him. In this respect he and Pam had something in common. But Rudy's dad was so much more polished. He spoke with charm and dignity while he was expressing hostility and loathing. He insulted people in such a smooth, cultured way that they didn't know they were being insulted. He showed that his time was too precious to be ruined by an unpleasant experience and that he was willing to pay to ensure that he only had pleasant experiences.

Craig considered acting rude so that he might get bought off. He could use the money, but he didn't.

"You didn't care for Pam?" Rudy asked his father.

"She's an unhappy child," Peterfield diagnosed. "I don't think it was wise to allow her to make the rest of us unhappy too, do you?"

"No," Rudy agreed. "You're right. She was a poor choice."

Then, as if suddenly aware that it was rude to critique Rudy's guest in front of another one, Peterfield turned to Craig and asked, "So, who's going to win this afternoon?"

"We're gonna get our butts kicked," Craig said without hesitation. "Yale's been having a good year."

"Each game's a separate contest," Peterfield reminded.

"That's true," Craig agreed.

They finished the huge meal and headed for the stadium in the limousine. Dr. and Mrs. Peterfield were dressed to kill. They were perfectly coordinated in tweeds and fall colors with layers of scarves, sweaters, lining, and gloves.

The game was a disappointment. Craig had been right. Peterfield looked angry as he and his wife said good-bye to Craig and Rudy and went off to one of the top-shelf after-game parties. Rudy and Craig went to one of their own. Craig noticed that Rudy looked relieved to be away from his parents.

"Wow!" Craig mentioned, "You're dad really looked pissed that we lost."

"Oh, don't think about it. He's just trying to get worked up so that he can act mad around some of his friends."

"I don't know. It looked pretty real to me."

"I don't think my dad's shown a genuine emotion in thirty years," Rudy complained.

Craig noticed that Rudy got more drunk and obnoxious than usual that night. He wanted to talk about parents. He had some pretty odd opinions about parenting.

"Who are you more mad at, your mom or your dad?" Craig asked.

"They work as a team," Rudy said.

"Why do you say that?"

"I don't know," Rudy answered. It seemed to Craig that Rudy wanted to drop the subject, but a few minutes later he brought it up again.

"My parents are like strangers," Rudy said. "I have absolutely no idea who they are. You know what I mean?"

"Yeah. My folks are pretty strange too," Craig agreed.

"No. I mean its like knowing your parents only as well as you know people you read about in a magazine. You get to know some personal things about them, but you don't know what they mean. I mean, other people get to be real close with their parents, right?" Rudy was speaking in a drawl and was more emotional that Craig had ever seen him.

"Some do and some don't," Craig explained and then struck on an idea to change the subject. "Your dad sure got rid of Pam in a hurry."

"Oh, great," Rudy said. "I almost forgot about that. That's gonna be all over the campus, now. How embarrassing."

"Why would Pam spread that all over the campus?" Craig asked.

"Because it makes my dad look like the jerk he is," Rudy explained. "I mean, who'd be that rude even if he wanted to be? Only my dad."

"I think you're reading it wrong, Rudy. I think your old man'll be a campus hero. Nobody likes Pam. Why'd you even invite her, anyway?"

"That's a good question. I don't know what I was thinking."

Their conversation was interrupted by a small fight between two girls. The group broke into cheers for the girls and they started wrestling and pulling each other's hair.

Rudy had been pouring the beer down until he suddenly felt sick. He tried to hold still till his stomach settled. When it became obvious that wouldn't work he started looking for a bathroom. They were at another student's apartment and the bathroom was being used. Rudy pounded on the door and told them it was an emergency. There was no answer. The sink was out of the question because it was in the middle of everywhere with bottles and ice trays all around. He found a waste paper basket and used that. He hated it because you couldn't be cool and throw up.

Surprisingly few people noticed him being sick. He was in a corner of a bedroom and there was lots of other commotion. He put the can back and dropped a pillow over it to keep the stink down and left. As he walked back to his apartment he got sick again along the way. He was feeling terrible when he arrived at his apartment. He had chills. He climbed into bed with his clothes on and fell asleep hoping that he wouldn't be sick again. He promised himself never to do that much drinking again.

He woke up the next morning earlier than usual and feeling terrible. He didn't want to move because every movement made him feel sicker. Fortunately it was Sunday. The phone viciously started ringing. After five rings the answering machine began. It was Neal from Ohio. He was in Wooster and was just talking to someone about Rudy so he decided to call. He hoped that Rudy was enjoying the tapes and that he was still praying for him. This gave Rudy a slight convulsion. He hadn't listened to any of the tapes yet even though more than twenty had arrived. He was glad he didn't have to explain that to Neal.

He decided that he was really messing up with all this drinking. He wasn't going to drink a thing for a while. The thought of a drink made him shudder.

That resolution, like so many resolutions about drinking was abandoned in only a few short days. Rudy was drinking so much and getting drunk so often that he was called the campus lush by his friends. He decided to turn his apartment into a private bar for his friends. He remodeled his apartment with leather furniture, thick carpeting, and high priced paintings for the walls. He bought a huge entertainment system that had every conceivable component. He had dozens of extra speakers installed around the apartment. The whole system was driven from one huge remote control panel that looked like three calculators glued together back to back.

Rudy went completely wild at a record store. He bought crates of CD's and cassettes of all kinds of music. His friends wondered what had gotten into him. His interest in turning his apartment into a first class lounge was driven by a compulsion no one had ever seen in him before.

He had a full bar installed complete with fountain service. This was all done even though he was still under the legal drinking age for Massachusetts.

Rudy's parties were legendary. His stereo equipment was able to break glass. His apartment was considered the hottest place to go on or around campus.

Early in Rudy's bar-running days he met a coed named Diane Hart. It was too bad that he was in such emotional turmoil because Diane was one of the two most remarkable girls he would ever meet. She was bright, witty, quick, and beautiful. She was studying foreign languages and pre-law. She wanted to go into international law.

Diane's father was a surgeon in New York City and her mother was an editor for Teacher's College Press. She had her father check out Rudy's father and learned quite a bit about him. She liked what she heard about Rudy more than what she saw. She was impressed with his intellectual accomplishments and the solid beginning he had made at Harvard. She decided to get to know him.

Rudy was impressed with Diane upon first meeting her. He asked his father to check out her family. She was poised, charming, but much alive and three-dimensional. She had a brilliant mind and it showed in an unpretentious way. When he talked to Diane she made him feel like he was the most important person in her life.

For a while it looked like Diane might rescue Rudy from his drinking. They spent lots of time together. He took her for weekends to Martha's Vineyard. Rudy could be quite affectionate. He wanted love and he gave love. He was tender, caring, and thoughtful. While they never had sex, they did spend weekends together even sometimes platonically sleeping in the same bed. They enjoyed many similar interests and Rudy spoke about her several times to his mother over the phone. They both felt comfortable with each other. They didn't need to compete to impress one another. But the timing of this friendship was tragically wrong.

Gradually Diane was having a helpful effect on Rudy. When they were together he was not home to run his bar. She was no temperance crusader, however, and was usually along when he had friends over for parties.

During this time Neal was sending Rudy regular sermons from Ohio. Sometimes Rudy would start to listen to one, but he would rarely finish it. Neal also sent Rudy long letters. These letters would contain long persuasive arguments for why Rudy should turn to Jesus Christ. Neal went to the trouble to print out the scripture verses he referred to believing, correctly, that Rudy would never look them up. Neal's effort was remarkable. Letters could easily be eight or ten pages long.

Rudy would occasionally write back and thank him. He could not seem to write more than a few lines. He was constantly sending excuses about why he couldn't write at the time. He promised to write a "proper" letter at a future time. This obvious inequity in their efforts made Rudy feel guilty, which he resented, because he didn't want to feel guilty.

In addition to letters and tapes, Neal made periodic phone calls. These weren't as frequent because they cost more and Rudy never answered them. Rudy didn't want to admit that he hadn't listened to the tapes so he never picked up the phone, even when he heard Neal leaving the message.

Neal wasn't naive about what was going on. He knew that Rudy wouldn't listen to too many tapes. He knew also that he wouldn't listen to any if he didn't send them. He was encouraging in his letters and tried to tell Rudy he understood that he might not be as ambitious about writing.

Rudy was being pulled from several directions. He knew that he would have to decide which direction he wanted to go, but he didn't know how. He felt like he was standing in the center of a square room. On each of the four walls was one door. Each door was a different choice in his life. One door was to get involved with Diane. One door was to party. Another door was to get involved in a career. The fourth door was to get involved in Neal's church. The problem was that choosing any one door seemed to lock the other doors. So it was hard to choose any single door, not for what was behind that door, but for what would be missed behind the other three doors. He was as trapped in the center of this hypothetical square room as if he were chained to a post, trapped by his reluctance to close any other option.

Being between these four choices was stressful. This was making him irritable, and causing him to drink much more. He wasn't the carefree Rudy that he used to be.

Diane never knew the carefree Rudy. She heard that he was a cool guy. He was lots of fun now, but he was more intense than he would have been normally. They both enjoyed some common interests, particularly career goals in law. Diane was relaxed. She could talk to anyone about almost anything. She did have a big blind spot about religion, however. She didn't reveal much about what she thought of it. She usually just cut the conversation off abruptly when the subject came up. She knew that Rudy had some interest in the subject. She decided that the safest thing to do around Rudy was to drop the subject, discouraging discussion. Around other people she could be aggressive and cruel on the subject. Those who knew them both knew this to be an area of ultimate incompatibility.

At one of Rudy's parties Diane dropped her guard. She had plenty to drink and found one of the tapes that Neal sent. She shoved it in the cassette recorder and played part of it for the crowd. She stood in front of the group and lip synced as if she were preaching. The crowd thought this was hysterical until Rudy came into the room. He completely freaked out, ran over to the system, and jerked the tape out of the machine.

He screamed at Diane, "What are you doing?"

She backed up a little, stunned by his overwhelming emotional reaction.

"You've got no right to do that," Rudy yelled still louder.

Diane didn't know what to say. She apologized sincerely, grabbed her coat and left. The whole party quickly broke up and Rudy was sitting in his living room alone. He thought of what Diane did, what he did, and couldn't understand either. It seemed like everyone thought what she did was funny. He wondered why he didn't think so. Was he losing his mind? Should he go back and see Keller? Would anyone come back after tonight?

CHAPTER 23

Rudy's blow up with Diane marked the last of his parties. While he and Diane were still cordial, something changed permanently. Rudy's social life chilled. He spent more time in his apartment alone. He wanted it that way. It gave him time to think. Things moved too fast recently. He wasn't sure he was doing what he wanted to do. He listened to some of the tapes Neal sent him. He was at home in one of these moods when Neal called again. Rudy, as usual, didn't answer the phone. When he heard Neal's voice he thought of answering the phone; but he was motionless in a numbed silence.

Then Rudy realized that he had been listening to the tapes. He didn't have to avoid Neal. So Rudy called him back. In fact, he was excited to hear Neal's reaction to this call.

When he called, Neal was out. He left a message, but Neal got back too late to call. Neal tried several times the next day; finally, after three tries he got through.

"Hello?"

"Hey, Rudy, how're ya doin?" Neal asked.

"Hey, listen, give me the number of the phone where you're at and I'll call you there right away."

"That's OK," Neal said. "I can afford the call."

"No, come on, give me the number, come on, come on," Rudy persisted. So Neal gave him the number and Rudy called him right back.

"You've made so many calls to me, it's time that I call you," Rudy argued. "How're things in Ohio?"

"Fine," Neal said. "They're really pouring the work on us, though. I can't believe how much work they dish out."

"Yeah, here too," Rudy agreed, although he really believed that he had been coasting the last month or so.

"They don't care what anybody else is assigning. They act like their course is the only one you're taking," Neal complained. "Some weeks they really pour it on heavy. Well, I guess I'm returning your call. What's up?"

"Oh, I just wanted to hear how you're doing," Rudy said. He

wasn't sure how much he wanted to tell Neal. "I've been listening to some of those tapes you sent me. Thanks."

"My pleasure," Neal said.

"Those preachers sure make it all sound so simple," Rudy said. "I wish life was really that simple."

"You mean you don't think it is?" Neal asked.

"Well, mine isn't."

"I wish you could come here," Neal said. "We could spend some time together and maybe I could help."

Neal said this without thinking there was a chance that is was possible.

To Rudy the idea suddenly had tremendous appeal. He thought it would be good to get out of Cambridge for a while. He wanted to think this over before committing himself but suddenly heard himself saying, "I guess that could be done. I could fly down there for a long weekend. Maybe this weekend."

Rudy was shocked to hear himself say this. He was going to think about it first. It was like coaching someone in a movie not to do something and sitting there powerless as he did it. The only difference was that he was watching himself and it was happening to him.

"Are you kidding?" Neal asked in bewilderment. "That's great. Just tell me when your plane arrives and I'll be there to pick you up. Man, we'll have a great time. I'll show you the campus. Maybe we can drive up to Wooster for church on Sunday."

"I'll get a flight and call you again, but I don't want to go to Wooster. It's too much sitting."

As the week wore on Rudy got several offers of things to do around Cambridge. Several times he considered canceling the trip but said nothing more to Neal.

A friend, Pam, dropped Rudy off at the airport a full hour before the plane took off. Since she came in to wait with him, Rudy related some of his uncle's experiences with flying.

"I have an uncle that flies a lot on business. He gets to the airport at the last possible minute. One time," Rudy went on, "he had a rental car and was stuck in traffic on the ramp to the airport. He waited until the last possible minute then pulled the car halfway onto the sidewalk, turned it off, left the keys in it, and ran to the gate and flew off."

"Your uncle just left the car there?" Pam asked.

"Yeah, and I don't think the rental company ever charged him extra for that. I guess the airport security notified the rental company pretty soon."

Conversations in airports are stressful. You sit in bench-like seats not facing each other. You resist talking about anything serious from a perception that there is little time, but you cannot think of enough short topics to talk about. You wrack your brain for something superficial to talk about, adding to the wear and tear of travel.

Anyone who has flown more than twice knows this and prefers to be dropped off at the curb. But Pam had plenty of time and thought it would be fun to spend it with Rudy before he left.

"So why're you going to Ohio, anyway?" Pam asked.

Rudy thought it would be playful to tell her the truth. "I'm going there to go to church."

"Oh, lots of people fly to Ohio for church," Pam joked. "See if they have a synagogue there? It's been a while since I've been to one."

"I'll check it out," Rudy joked back.

"No kidding, why are you going to Ohio, or is it none of my business?"

"Well, I can't see how it's any of your business but it's not a secret, either," Rudy admitted honestly. He was having fun with an honest interpretation of what people were saying. "I met this guy last summer in Connecticut and he's going to Ohio State University. He calls me occasionally and we decided to get together. He's going to show me around Ohio State and Columbus. I've never been there and I decided that this was a good time to go."

"What's that got to do with going to church?" Pam pursued.

"Well, he's really involved in his church. It isn't easy to explain. He goes to this real cool church where they really try to follow the Bible." Rudy felt the frustration of trying to explain this to Pam. For some reason it was important to him that Pam not lump Neal in with the mainstream Christian experience. He felt a pressure to defend Neal because an interest in religion was so uncool. Perhaps he was testing to see how acceptable his explanation could be.

Sensing Rudy's sincerity Pam decided not to make any derisive remarks about religion. Instead she turned the conversation to some subject that could be discussed in two minutes. So off they went on this verbal leap frog until mercifully it was announced that first-class passengers could board. Rudy leaped up from his seat, thanked Pam and boarded. He never boarded this early but he was so relieved to get away from Pam.

After waiting more than half the time of the total flight, the plane pushed away from the terminal. A wiry older man in a business suit sat next to Rudy. They were the only two in first-class. The man introduced himself as being a college professor from a small but highly respected community college. He was off to a larger campus to give a lecture on twisted American values and the evils of rock music. He pointed out that rock music promoted destruction and things that ruin people's lives like promiscuous sex, drug abuse, and rebellion against families.

"You know," he said, "Some rock stars will ruin more young people's lives in one concert tour than a college professor will help in a lifetime; and that same rock star will make more money in one tour than a college professor will make in a lifetime."

He obviously felt strongly about this. He was annoying. Rudy shifted in his seat and wondered how he could get away from this man. He considered going to the bathroom, or claiming that he wanted to sleep and moving to another row. Finally the man stopped.

Against all better judgment, Rudy said, "It sounds like you're a preacher."

"Oh, no!" the man exploded catching Rudy completely off guard. "Religion's the only thing I can think of that has ruined more people than rock music."

"Oh, surely you don't believe that," Rudy protested.

"Surely I do." insisted the professor. "The name of religion has been used to shed more blood, torture more people, and confuse more people than any other cause on earth."

This confused Rudy somewhat.

"I've seen people badly mistreated by religious groups," the man went on. "It's amazing how people turn their lives over to some pretty reprehensible people who tell them what to do and how to live their lives. It's just unbelievable that people can be that gullible on the subject of religion. Perfectly bright and talented people, capable of good thought in nearly every other area of life, just seem to suspend thought in the area of religion and buy the crap their told."

"Do you feel that way about all religions?" Rudy asked.

"I don't know about all religions. I suspect it's true of all religions."

"Do you think some groups are worse than others?" Rudy inquired.

"I don't want to mention denominations. I'm not an expert in comparative religions. I just don't like the way people hand over power to people who are too stupid and lazy to earn that power in any other field of work. It seems like people who can't make it any other way just become a preacher and talk people into handing over lots of money to them. It's really outrageous."

Rudy was amazed at how strident this man was on this subject. It reminded him of what his friends on Martha's Vineyard said about religious people. Rudy was amazed to see how strongly feelings ran against religion. He realized that religious people could easily be a new hated minority group and marveled at how universally they seemed to be hated. Who would stand up and defend them against such powerful feelings of contempt so universally held? Rudy made a mental note to send a contribution to the American Civil Liberties Union. He decided that they would probably be the ones left with that thankless job.

The plane stopped in Pittsburgh where Rudy had to change planes, which he did in merciful silence. He was the only one in first class on this flight where he caught the attention of an attractive stewardess. She seemed to like him and mentioned that she was based in Columbus. Rudy told her that he was meeting a friend and that his stay was tightly booked up. They had a nice talk.

Neal took Rudy to a place called Schmidt's in German Village, a section of Columbus that was restored to look like a 19th century community in Germany. It was now a tourist attraction and substantially improved the property value of a section of Columbus that had been heading for the wrecking ball just a few years before.

They went to Neal's dorm, where Rudy got a sample of dorm life. On Saturday Neal took Rudy around the campus. The word "compression" came most frequently to Rudy's mind. It seemed like the campus was not larger than Harvard's, yet they packed lots more students in the same space. The buildings were not as old or as ceremonial looking. There seemed to be a greater sense of rush here. No one stayed as long in the coffee shops, people walked faster, and it seemed like many people lived off campus.

Rudy decided that Neal had almost no social life in Columbus. He didn't go to movies, he didn't go to sports events, and he didn't get together with a bunch of friends and drink. Neal thought a social life was going to lectures, plays, and the youth group of their church in Columbus. On the weekends he usually went to Wooster.

That Sunday they went to the Columbus church. It was a small group of about thirty-five, as Neal had promised. A young minister preached an unremarkable sermon after which lunch was served. Rudy was introduced to the minister and his wife and sat with them for lunch. The conversation went well, so Rudy felt comfortable bringing up the conversation he had with the professor on the flight.

"It seems like a lot of people feel that way," Rudy added. "Do you ever feel like part of an unpopular minority group?"

"That's easy," said the minister. "The founder of Christianity, Christ, Himself, said that if the world hated Him, it will hate us. He also said that in the world we will have persecution but that we should be of good cheer because He has overcome the world."

"So you know about this feeling of other people towards Christianity?" Rudy asked.

"Oh yes. And I'd like to point out that you're running into those feelings in what's called a `Christian Nation.' Just think of what the persecution is like where there aren't so many Christians.

"But you know, Rudy, it's a little like the bullies at school. They only pick on you when they're in a group. When they're with you alone they like you and consider you a friend. Many people have Christian backgrounds and turn to Christianity in a pinch but in a group they mock and ridicule Christians."

"I think you're right about that," agreed Rudy. "I've seen that a little myself."

"That professor on the plane was partially right," the minister went on. "There are lots of abuses done in the name of Christianity. It seems like that's always been the case. There have always been scandals that give Christianity a black eye. But let me tell you what Christianity's all about."

Rudy liked this guy. He leaned forward, interested in learning what Christianity was all about.

"Christianity is about what you're afraid of when you're alone. It's about those thoughts that haunt you that you don't talk to others about. Maybe you can't even put those fears into words."

Rudy thought about this carefully.

"Did you ever wonder when you were a kid what would have happened if you never existed? Have you ever wondered if there would be anything if you had never been born?" the minister asked.

"Yeah. I did," agreed Rudy.

"Well, people can't stand those questions, so they stop asking them early in life. But people realize that those questions are sometimes close under the surface. Thinking about those questions can make a person depressed. Thoughts along those lines are triggered sometimes during a sad song."

"Yeah. I know that feeling," Rudy added.

"Well Christianity, true Christianity, takes a person face to face with those thoughts. Christianity comes to terms with those thoughts and gets them resolved once and for all in a person's mind. And once they're resolved, a Christian has a lot more peace about those matters. Fears and anxieties along those lines are completely removed. It makes them more powerful, less vulnerable to depressions, or those sad moods."

"You know, I've never heard it expressed that way," Rudy mentioned.

"Neither have I," added Neal. "That's good. You should write it down."

"It's just something I've been thinking about lately," the minister went on. "I think it's a key concept to understanding Christianity. A Christian goes boldly right into the face of those fears and thoughts of nothingness and gets past them. But I'm talking about true Christianity, now. Not some of the popular Christian movements of today. I think that many Christian movements of today have shrunk from this important function of religion and settled for something incomplete, inadequate, not powerful enough when the tough times come."

"So when the tough times come," added Neal, "or the temptations and tests, they fail, creating some of the scandals that are giving Christianity the bad name it has today."

"That's right. Let's go one step further," added the minister.

"A true Christian isn't fighting off the tough times by himself. It's the power of the Holy Spirit that lives within him. You see a Christian abandons any hope of self-control or self-determination just as surely as any heroin addict or any advanced alcoholic does. In the conversion experience, the self is destroyed by the power of the Holy Spirit, which assumes control of that person's life. The thing is that the self cannot be completely destroyed as long as the person is alive. It has a way of returning again and again. That's why the Apostle Paul said he had to die daily. We need to subjugate our self-control to the control of the Holy Spirit every day. Even moment by moment during a day.

"The Bible says that God is strong in us when we are weak, and His strength is made perfect in weakness. This is speaking, again, about this voluntary killing off of our own self-determination and abandoning ourselves to His leading and guidance.

"This notion is not emphasized in such a complete and radical way in most Christian teachings today. It's regarded as too mystical, too superstitious, too unmeasurable—and therefore too uncomfortable. But when churches move away from this principle, they move away from the essential power of Christianity and open themselves up to what the Bible calls `having a form of godliness but denying the power thereof.'"

"You know, I've read some of those verses you're referring to," Rudy said. "But I've never put them together in that way. That makes sense as I hear you say it."

The rush of the schedule interrupted his appreciation. They helped put the tables and chairs away, then returned to the sanctuary for a sermonette by another minister. Before he knew it, Rudy was back on the plane heading to Boston.

Rudy tried to remember some of the comments of that minister in Columbus. Again, however, he found he could not retrieve much of the information. He wondered if he was being hypnotized during these experiences. He wondered if religion was something like drugs dulling your criticism and making you in awe of the most ordinary things.

He knew this wasn't true but couldn't explain why he could not remember more of the impressions he had while there. This feeling happened so often when he visited one of Neal's churches that it was annoying him. He didn't like the fact that he didn't understand it. It was as if he was learning something in a different part of his brain and could not shift the learning to another part. It could not be stored up. It was an unfamiliar kind of mental activity to him, but challenging.

CHAPTER 24

When Rudy returned to Cambridge he felt like he had been in a foreign country. He had the uneasy feeling that he was walking into someone else's apartment. Suddenly the decorations, and the fact that everything revolved around his bar, was embarrassing to him. He felt he had let the pendulum swing too far, perhaps in reaction to Neal's friends. He felt his friends were too superficial, and Neal's too intense.

So for the rest of that academic year he returned to serious work. He abandoned most of his friends, worked hard, and spent much time in libraries. He was surprised to learn that none of his friends bothered him or wondered what happened to him. They went to other places to party. When he did see Diane she was friendly and they talked. She never asked why he seemed to drop out of the social scene. There was never any awkward questioning.

His friend Craig was the closest to him and lasted through both of his changes that year. He was able to talk freely to Craig about Neal's church and how attractive he found it to be. Craig thought he understood this because his parents had been "Jesus freaks" in the 60's and it seemed to stick. Craig didn't show much interest but he understood that some people respond to Christianity more than others. It didn't matter to him one way or the other.

Rudy removed the bar and redecorated. He was striving for a Colorado cabin look with lots of wood and earth tones. Overstuffed cloth furniture with lots of pillows. It was warmer looking and more relaxing. He kept the stereo equipment but the music changed. He liked a wide variety of music but stayed away, suddenly, from heavy metal.

In addition to studying, he was reading a good bit from the Bible. He listened to the tapes Neal sent him.

Rudy finished his first year of college as he had begun it. He came to the attention of the administration for outstanding work and intellectual contributions to the life of the college. This resulted in another letter being sent to his father commending him on his first year, which pleased his father who showed it to his wife. His father knew nothing of Rudy's continued interest in Neal's church. He believed that he had gone through some rough times with Rudy when he was younger but that things were looking encouraging now.

Rudy kept in closer touch with Neal. He sent him letters and cards. He liked sending interesting postcards. There were also occasional phone conversations. This was most convenient for Rudy. After a few frustrations getting through, the two established a regular schedule.

A year passed since they first met. Neal was back in Connecticut. Rudy was in New York. Rudy's friends seemed to be busy doing other things or away for the summer. Renee was in Europe for the summer. She wanted Rudy to follow her. He didn't want to but promised to look into flying over for a short stay. When she left, the plans were incomplete, suggesting to Rudy that she didn't care.

Rudy didn't care either. He had gotten a lot more serious about life and his friends had not. His only friends who seemed to have their heads screwed on right were Neal and his friends. So Rudy made frequent trips to Stamford to participate in all their activities, becoming a regular in their functions. He even thought about moving there because he was spending all his time there.

Rudy's parents spent little time in the city that summer. He had lots of time to think in solitude at home. He spent nearly every weekend of that summer in Connecticut.

He noticed a growing concern, or longing, to participate in Neal's church. He felt a subtle fear that he might not. He hadn't felt this for any of the other groups he attached himself to in the past.

He was concerned about the life-long commitment of these people. He had always been a dilettante about life, jumping from interest to interest rapidly but superficially.

This came up in a conversation at the cabin. One of the campfire speakers mentioned that he put off converting due to the fear that he would not be able to remain faithful all his life. He explained that this is common and it stalls a lot of people. He said that it didn't matter if you were never good at sticking with anything because no one can stick with Christianity without the power of the Holy Spirit. He also pointed out that, obversely, the weakest person can remain faithful with the power of the Holy Spirit. He informed them that the whole issue was whether you were utilizing the power of the Holy Spirit or not.

During the conversation after that meeting, Jim brought up the subject of Rudy's spiritual life.

"How're you coming spiritually, Rudy?" Jim asked.

"Well, I don't know what you mean, exactly," Rudy admitted.

"Well," Jim added, "It looks like you kinda like our church. You come to almost all the services. I was wondering if you were thinking about converting?"

"I guess I have been. But what that guy said tonight is kind of on my mind, too," Rudy admitted. "I've always jumped from one interest to another and I know you shouldn't mess around with religion. It's serious and in your church it's for life."

"All that's true," Neal added. "But you've got to realize that it isn't you doing it. You may have jumped from thing to thing in the past but the Lord doesn't. He's the One Who will come into your life and empower you to finish the job and keep the job done."

"I know. I've heard that, but it's hard to believe when you haven't experienced it yet," Rudy argued.

"Don't forget, there's a verse that says something like I am persuaded that He is able to keep that which I've committed until the end." Jack contributed. "That means He keeps what we've committed. He's so thrilled that you have chosen Him that he rushes in and gives you all you need to do the job."

"It's kinda like the way a college coach acts when a top-rated player decides to come to that college to play a sport. He's excited about what the team can do with that player. He's thrilled that that player has decided to come and join the team. He makes whatever provisions He can because that player has made that decision," Jim added.

The conversation went on for some time. Rudy admitted to being highly interested for the first time. And the other guys were excited for him and willing to give him all the help they could. So Rudy came to every service he could. He considered this church *his* church, quietly contributed money to help support it, and gradually became more involved. People were growing comfortable with him and he was fitting in nicely. He was grateful that he was being accepted so easily.

So that was his summer. He didn't get to Martha's Vineyard or to Europe to see Renee. Toward the end of summer they planned to go to a youth rally in Ohio. Rudy wanted to go along. He looked forward to going back to Ohio and seeing another of their churches. He had a memory of learning cool things on his last visit to Ohio. This youth rally was supposed to be in their biggest church, the one in Wooster, Ohio.

CHAPTER 25

The next three days passed quickly. Rudy did a lot of reading, got together with Jim and Jack in New York one afternoon, and went to Connecticut for a youth group meeting on Wednesday night where they finalized their plans for the big trip to Ohio. People signed up for rides. Neal had a full van. Neal was able to leave around noon on Friday so he took a lot of the younger kids and Rudy.

The Wednesday evening program didn't have a speaker. They broke up into groups and had "buzz sessions." The topic was "Knowing what God's will is for my life." Different members of the group were appointed to lead the discussion, with another member of the group recording minutes. After the discussion the group was to get back together and listen to the reporters' summaries.

To create the groups they counted off by fours. Since Rudy was sitting beside Neal, Jim, and Jack, he was put in a group with people he did not know as well. He decided to say little and see what these people were thinking.

The leader of his group started by reading a few verses from the Bible. He read Psalms 40.8: "I delight to do thy will, O my God: yea, thy law is within my heart." and Psalms 143.10: "Teach me to do thy will; for thou art my God: thy Spirit is good; lead me into the land of uprightness." He also read Matthew 12.50: "For whosoever shall do the will of my Father which is in heaven, the same is my brother, and sister, and mother."

Someone else in the group volunteered I Timothy 2.4: "Who will have all men to be saved, and to come unto the knowledge of the truth."

Another asked, "If it's God's will that all people are saved, then why aren't they?"

There was an awkward pause. Some looked surprised that the question was raised. Rudy thought it was an excellent question. It was on his mind as well.

"We know that the will of God would never violate the Holy Scriptures," said one participant. "So the Holy Spirit would never lead you to do something contrary to the Bible."

Another added, "We know that Christ, just before ascending to Heaven, told His disciples three times to feed His sheep."

"But what does it mean to feed his sheep?" asked another.

"I think it means to preach the Gospel to them," answered one.

"How about providing food for the starving across the world? Wouldn't that be feeding His sheep?"

"I heard it took the UN years of bitter negotiations to finally agree to spend about as much on feeding the starving of the world as the governments spend on weapons in one hour," said still another.

"Yes, but does anyone really need to be hungry anymore? Aren't our taxes going to that?"

The discussion went back and forth for a good twenty minutes. Nearly everyone in the group added to the discussion. Rudy kept his promise to himself and said nothing. He observed that, on the whole, the conversation was rather superficial. These were not deep thinkers. They were not all like Neal, Jim, and Jack. There were no opinions that were far off the group opinion. Everyone seemed to have a pretty canned opinion of the subject.

After most of the groups seemed to run down, Jack called the group together for summaries. As if to underscore Rudy's observation that the opinions were pretty much the same, that is what the subsequent reporters said after the first one gave his report.

The one question, however, concerning God's will that all are saved, did come up again. One of the girls came up with the most impressive answer, in Rudy's opinion.

"The problem is that God doesn't force people to convert. He calls gently and lovingly. He's given people the freedom to choose whether they want to follow or not. So there's more than one will involved here. Sure it is God's will that all are saved. He didn't give His only Son to be crucified without proving that. But it has to be our will to be saved also. Some people just don't want that," she said.

"That's right," said another. "I've often wondered why God would permit His Only Begotten Son to be put to death in such a humiliating and painful way. But it occurred to me that that is the loudest God can insist that we convert. He has imposed upon Himself the restriction that He will not force any one of us to convert; however, He wants that badly for us. So, He uses this form of death to dramatize how far He's willing to go for the love of us."

"That love should draw us, not compel us," added another.

This seemed convincing to Rudy. He believed that man had some freedom to choose in his life. It also seemed to him that giving man this freedom to choose has created all the major problems in the world. Mankind has created all his own problems. Sure, there are natural disasters like hurricanes, tornadoes, earthquakes, forest fires started by lightening, but these have only caused a fraction of the death and destruction that man-made events have caused.

The meeting closed with prayer and refreshments. That evening it was prearranged that Neal would take Rudy back to the city. Neal had to take a few others back to Brooklyn anyway. They made plans before leaving about where and when to meet on Friday to go to Ohio.

Rudy asked Neal to drop him off at the same place as before. Rudy got out and watched as Neal's van faded to a tiny speck as it traveled down the long row of green lights into the blur of the city. Rudy was in a pensive mood as he walked slowly toward his parents' apartment. He thought about free will, and what people choose to do with their lives.

He thought there were times when choices seemed easier to make than at other times. If most people are agreed on something, it's easier for an individual to decide that same way. At the same time, some people are oppositional by nature and are inclined to decide against the main flow of the culture. When the culture's position is clear, however, even this is not a free choice for that oppositional person.

He thought that people's choices are strongly dictated by their parents, or upbringing. He, of all people, knew that was not entirely true. He turned out differently than his parents would have wished for him. He wondered how he made the decisions he did make. Was Keller right, that his decisions were mainly reactions to his parents? Were his actions rebellions designed to anger or hurt his parents? Was he trying to get back at his parents? If yes, then where is his freedom to choose in all of this? Was his freedom to choose just now being introduced to him directly by God? Was his being picked up by Neal that one evening an act of God—like the blinding light to the Apostle Paul?

If this was his first opportunity to make up his own mind, how could he persuade his parents that this decision was his own and not still another way to get back at his parents? How could he persuade himself or Keller of that? What would his father's reaction to his new interest in religion be? On that last question, he felt fairly confident that he could predict. His father would be just as bored with this development as he had been with every other development in his life. This, he thought would be no problem whatsoever.

These were his thoughts as he walked around the park toward his parent's apartment. He walked slowly with his head leaning forward looking at the details of the sidewalk.

Rudy came home to an empty apartment. His parents had gone to Martha's Vineyard for a long weekend, and had given the staff the weekend off. Paulette left a note for Rudy telling him where food could be found and how to heat it up in the microwave. There was no note from his parents.

Rudy went through the apartment turning on all the lights. He was in a strange mood. He moved in a steady but slow pace. He was deep in thought as if he was in some kind of a hypnotic trance. He was struck by the stark contrast between this place and the home in Connecticut where he had just come from. He thought about the small rooms of that Connecticut house, the layers of wallpaper, the white paint covering the woodwork molding around the rooms. The plastic light switches, the ceiling lights covered with glass bowls. He was not too young to realize the relative difference in standard of living.

At the same time, he was touched by the love and generosity of the people in that house in Connecticut. How the mother glowed with warmth and love as she saw how much the young people enjoyed her baked goods and refreshments. There was an unmistakable atmosphere of acceptance, even gratitude, for the young guests. How tender, kindly, and generous they seemed to Rudy.

His parent's apartment, by contrast, seemed a stage upon which to flaunt their wealth. The purpose was theater; a kind of macabre theater designed to intimidate, bully, and impress the audience. You could put that entire Connecticut house in his parent's living room. His parents had entertained groups much larger than the group he was with that evening. Yet there was no impression of generosity, or charity. There was, instead, the cold, steellike purpose of putting on a better show than the rest. It was more than keeping up with the

Jones; it was making the Jones's wish that they were never born.

Every social interaction his parents seemed to have was of this competitive nature. Rudy tried but failed to think of one friend of his father's who could be described as a confidant with whom his father had stuck through thick and thin. Perhaps that was the greatest contrast, even greater than the difference in the living spaces. In the group he had just been with there was a strong feeling of love one for another, an appreciation for each other's friendship and companionship. Among his parents' associations there was backbiting, gossip, and jealousy.

Rudy walked through the apartment. His parents had separate bedrooms with spacious sitting rooms, dressing rooms, and baths. Everything was quite correct, much in place, and sterile. There were other rooms that were equally well appointed but totally lacking in any human softness, or lacking in any sign of normal human wear and use.

There were times before when his parents were away that Rudy jumped into action and threw wild parties. This place had everything for the greatest parties imaginable. But tonight, Rudy sat in the middle of it all deep in thought. "What is coming over me?" he asked himself. "I used to go wild when my parents were away. I would see how loud and long I could party before they came back."

He went up to his room and flopped down on his bed. Almost reflexively, he reached over and hit play on his answering machine. There were five or six hang ups, and two messages from Renee which he ignored. As he laid there drifting closer to sleep, he felt too lazy to even get up and take off his clothes. Then he remembered that he left all the lights on. He dragged himself down and turned them all off.

How different this was from the Rudy who left the sweeper running in place. But that he did to annoy people around him. As he thought about that he realized that that was theater too. How much of what we do is designed to cause someone else to think in a certain way, he thought. He began to wonder if there were any unselfish behaviors motivated entirely for oneself and not designed to impress, depress, or anger someone else.

CHAPTER 26

Friday rolled around and Rudy was ready to attend his first Youth Rally. He had flown to Ohio but never driven there. Neal told him it would take about eight hours to drive. Neal stopped for Rudy after making his circle through Brooklyn picking up some of the younger kids.

Rudy took a stack of fifty dollar bills, and a credit card, in case he needed to make other arrangements. He didn't expect an unpleasant time; however, he didn't like to be without options. He walked back to the drop-off site the same way he came the other evening but more quickly to get there before Neal.

The appointed time had come and gone and still no Neal. Rudy became uncomfortable standing in the entrance of a strange building. Residents walked past and stared at him suspiciously seeming to ask, "How can you be so stupid? Don't you know the unwritten rules about being in the wrong place with the wrong stuff, and not moving when you're stared at?" And, of course, Rudy did know these rules.

After a while, Rudy tired of standing there. He was afraid the building security would call the police so he crossed the street and sat on a park bench.

Forty-five minutes later, Neal showed up at the curb. Rudy had been sitting there so long, he had half fallen asleep. Rudy looked at the van without seeing it until Neal got out. He was on his way to the directory of the building when Rudy called out, and climbed into the van. Neal was apologetic but had good reasons.

The van swept efficiently up Broadway to 125th, under the bridge work, up the s-curved entry ramp, and moved easily onto the Henry Hudson Parkway.

They met a small caravan in New Jersey and headed West on Route 80 beginning the long, boring count of exit numbers through the wide state of Pennsylvania. After five hours of driving, they pulled off for something to eat.

Neal wanted to go to a truck stop because they had "class." They sat around a yellow Formica table on steel polled chairs with red vinyl cushions.

The food, served on thick porcelain plates, was incredible for its fat content. The restaurant's one effort at sanitation was to give each place setting a paper place mat with puzzles and jokes printed on it. This occupied the patron's attention for the interminable time it took the cook to produce the food. For those who didn't want to do the puzzles, there was a juke box playing such immortal hits as "Dead Skunk in the Middle of the Road."

Neal thought he had died and gone to Heaven by picking this place. He pronounced it a monument to middle America, and the trucking industry. Rudy, who never thought of himself as a snob, was gaining sympathy for those who gave Neal a hard time. The younger passengers of the van went along with anything Neal wanted.

Rudy ate without complaint. He reasoned that no one died on one of these trips. He decided that the only way to experience what they experienced was to do what they did. He suspended any censorship on his part, and did whatever they did. He hoped to fully experience what they experienced. He looked forward to each odd choice of activities with curiosity and interest. He took it in with sportsmanship, willingness, and participation.

He wondered what his friends would think if they could see what he was doing. He couldn't imagine Renee or Craig sitting in this truck stop eating this food. In fact that image made him chuckle audibly.

"What's so funny?" asked Neal

"Oh, I've got this friend named Craig who's fussy about his health. He's always complaining about the food we eat. He'll act horrified if we order a hamburger because it's red meat. I just pictured him sitting here and tried to imagine what he'd say," Rudy explained.

"Well, I'd like to meet him someday,"

"He's a real freak," Rudy volunteered. "I doubt if you'd like him. He likes to shock people if he thinks they can be shocked."

The waitress in this restaurant was short, solid, and competent. She knew when they would want more soda. She brought things out as quickly as they were ready, and she made sure that every time they wanted something she was near to be asked. She wrote all the orders on one check, however, and handed it to Rudy sensing that he was the authority figure in the group.

There was a small argument about the bill but Rudy insisted on paying it for two reasons: the younger ones didn't have that much money, and Neal wouldn't take any money for gas.

The second half of the trip was more boring. Most of the guys in the back took naps. Neal drove again because he was the only one with a driver's license. Rudy kicked his deck shoes off and put his feet on the dashboard. He slouched down so that his back was along the seat with his head propped up on the back. The scenery, so interesting at first, became so monotonous that he closed his eyes and fell asleep.

Neal drove silently along. He still couldn't believe his luck that Rudy would be willing to go on this trip. He wondered what the chances were that some sophisticated guy from the city would be willing to pile into a van and drive all the way to Ohio. He still hadn't figured Rudy out. He was just glad that he was interested.

After a while Rudy's neck got stiff and he straightened up. As they got closer to Wooster the guys in the van bounced back to life.

"Hey, Neal," one guy asked, "Where's Rudy going to stay?"

"I don't know," Neal answered. "I told them he should stay with me."

So the conversation revolved around the rally. Everyone was giving Rudy advice about youth rallies. They were having a little fun at his expense, being the new kid on the block.

The laughter and excitement was genuine, sincere. Whether Rudy thought it funny or not, these guys were doing what they liked to do. They were having a great time; and Rudy was getting caught up in the humor in spite of himself.

Neal drove the van skillfully on the narrower roads off the main highway. Rudy was surprised to see so much unsettled wilderness. Rudy was impressed with how Neal seemed to know the way so well. Neal, of course, had been there often the previous year.

Shortly they were driving through a residential section of Wooster, a small college town. Their church was a large building located on the outskirts. Neal pulled into the parking lot some distance from the building. The lot was already full of cars and people. There would eventually be around a thousand young people for this special weekend. Rudy was fascinated to see that they were all neatly dressed, and conservatively groomed. These were plain people who were full of energy and enthusiasm.

They left their things in the van and went to the registration table. Neal introduced Rudy to some people standing around. At the table a beautiful young woman handed him a name tag and asked him to put his name on it. Rudy was struck by her natural beauty. She had a sincere, innocent smile that Rudy thought radiant. She was shy, and quiet. Rudy wrote his first name and started to make a capital letter "P" then caught himself and wrote "Horace" as his last name.

Rudy felt a twinge of guilt at writing this false last name. He didn't like the name in the first place, and he knew if he ever got involved in this church he'd eventually have to tell them his real last name. So he tore up that name tag and noticed that this cute girl was watching him the whole time. She was already handing him another tag. On this one he just wrote his first name.

"Do you live here?" Rudy asked her.

"Yes. I'm on the registration committee," she said.

"You don't have a name tag. Here," Rudy offered, "let me make one out for you. What's your name?"

She said, "Gail Schmidt." Rudy wrote it down correctly without asking the spelling. He looked up and was surprised to see her blushing. He handed it to her delicate, slightly trembling hand. She was laughing self-consciously trying not to reveal that she was embarrassed by this gesture. Rudy was smiling also. He walked away from the table caught up in the natural flow across the registration line and looked back several times and saw her looking at him. He liked her. He wanted to see more of her.

Gail, too, was struck by the looks and style of Rudy. She found him smooth, polished, polite, a real gentleman. There was something about him that was powerful yet so perfectly in control. He appeared to have naturally good manners and a kindness or gentleness that was rare among the guys who normally came to youth group meetings. Most of the guys she had grown up with were always joking around, a little immature.

Gail found herself curious about who Rudy was. She followed his movements around the group with her eyes. She and some of the other girls at the reception table whispered about him and wondered who he was and where he had come from.

The registration went from early afternoon until late into the evening. People were arriving from all over the country at all hours. Arrangements had to be made for overnight guests. This could never be quite finalized because unanticipated guests would show up late in the evening. Gail had to stay at the reception table.

Neal introduced Rudy to hundreds of people. At first Rudy tried to remember the names but realized that it was impossible. He would shake hands—something this group did a lot of—smile politely, and say something vague about how nice it was to be there. They would smile and tell him how nice it was to have a guest.

Rudy was fascinated by these people. It was like no group he had ever seen before. He kept thinking of those primary reading books of the 50's about Dick, Jane, and their dog Spot. Those books were known for their sterile, middle class idealism, and it was commonly believed that that did not exist anywhere in the real world. Here, parading around in front of Rudy's unbelieving eyes, were people like that.

The impression on Rudy was strange and complex. It was like Neal's van was a time machine taking him into a land of the past. Rudy knew that these people came from all over the country. He recognized some from Connecticut. He learned that some had come from Virginia, Michigan, Indiana, Illinois, Pennsylvania, and even several provinces of Canada. He had seen a small group of them looking and acting like this in the Connecticut group, but here they were in huge numbers. Here, for this brief weekend, they could experience being the majority, the mainstream, the norm.

Rudy didn't stick out dramatically because he didn't wear any jewelry as a rule. His hair was longer and his clothes more stylish. Everyone seemed to know he was a guest.

Gail learned that Rudy was with the Connecticut group, so she asked one of the Connecticut girls about him. She didn't know much about him. She mentioned that he had been coming for a while and was a friend of Neal's. She thought he lived in New York City but that was about all she knew. They both agreed that he was handsome and had nice manners.

Gail knew Neal so she decided to ask him about Rudy when she got the chance, which came during the evening meal. Because of the crowd, they had to eat in three shifts. All the local kids were on duty either setting up new place settings, washing silverware, or hauling trash. The food was served cafeteria style.

Rudy was still eating the main course when Neal was going

through the dessert line. Gail was putting more things out on the dessert tables and she asked Neal to come over for a minute.

"Tell me about Rudy," she asked.

"Oh, he's someone I met in Connecticut. I've brought him to a few things. He seems to like our church."

"Where's he from?"

"He lives in New York City. I don't really know too much about him other than that. He's a nice guy. He seemed to like you," Neal teased.

"He does seem like a real nice guy," Gail agreed. "Don't tell him I asked about him."

Rudy observed that there were no structured activities scheduled for several hours, but no one seemed to need them. They seemed to be completely entertained standing around talking to one another. Rudy left Neal for a while to walk around the church. He listened to conversations for a few brief moments as he walked past clusters of people. They seemed to be talking about friends, what's going on back home, who is engaged, that sort of thing.

The church, a large brick structure in a colonial style, was located in the middle of a five acre lot in a residential section of Wooster. It had huge white pillars on the front porch, coined corners in the brick work and was impressive in its size and basic simplicity. Like the people who attended it, there were no ornaments attached to it on the inside or outside like crosses, or symbols. It was elegant in its simplicity.

As Rudy walked around the outside he noticed that it was well maintained. Everything that needed painting was freshly painted. The flower beds around the church were bordered by rubber trim keeping the thick, brown mulch in the bed, and the rich green grass outside. The shrubs were all the correct size for the proportion of the building. Everything was clean, neat, and tasteful. Again, Rudy could not help but think of what a church would look like in one of his elementary basal readers. This, with the exception of having no ornamentation, was it.

These observations were interrupted by Neal. "We're supposed to go in now, Rudy. They want us to sing for a while before the program begins. What do you think so far?"

"Great," Rudy answered. He was not sure what he thought,

but it was clear that these were nice people. They were different from any group he had ever met before. They were having a great time so far, and nothing, really, had happened yet.

CHAPTER 27

Neal and Rudy found seats about half way into the sanctuary, near the center aisle. Rudy noticed that members of the church tended to bow their heads in a short prayer after sitting down. The evening program was scheduled to begin at eight. Neal and Rudy sat down at seven-thirty and space was already rapidly vanishing. Before long people would be crowding in, sitting on folding chairs in isles, standing in the foyer, and spilling out the doors onto the yard.

The church had a piano on one side of the pulpit and an organ on the other. Young people were playing quiet music as people filed in. A director got up and asked for an opening song. Someone in the audience called out a number and, with a brief instrumental introduction, the director began what was the most amazing musical experience of Rudy's life.

Living in New York City, Rudy had been to many impressive musical performances. Every year at Christmas time there was a special production of the "Messiah" where the whole audience sings along. While that impressed Rudy much, this singing was even better. They sang four-part harmony with enthusiasm and skill. The singing was thunderous but beautiful. Rudy wondered how far down the streets of this neighborhood the music could be heard. He wondered what the neighbors thought of the music, and if they ever complained.

There was such an eagerness to sing that the last note of one song was not even finished when someone called out the next number. Often there were two or three numbers called at once.

Rudy noted that it was nearly eight and wondered what he would be doing if he had stayed home. He wondered what his friends were doing, or his parents.

Rudy thought he was in the last place they would predict. The thought amused him. As time passed the singing got bolder. They added variations to the way the music was written. Some basses sang an octave lower than the printed notes when they could. Some men sang in unison with the soprano music in falsetto. Some sopranos or tenors added obbligato parts to some songs, which gave a richness and texture to the otherwise common Christian hymns.

After a half hour of singing, a program leader suggested that they all rise and sing a greeting hymn in their church hymnal. Everyone put away the large hymnal and pulled out a black covered book. Rudy recognized it as the same book that Neal gave him on his first visit. They turned to the announced number, stood up, and Rudy thought the roof would blow off the building. His hair stood up on the back of his neck. Chills shuddered down his back. He never heard singing like this in his life.

When the song was over everyone sat down, and the program leader gave a standard welcoming speech and then asked for greetings from the other churches. People started standing in their places and giving greetings from the cities they were from. There were greetings from about forty churches.

The program began with several quartets and duets. Neal noticed that these songs seemed to touch Rudy as he wiped tears from his eyes several times. Then a young man about their age gave what was called his "Testimony." He told about how he had become involved in a world of sin, and how he had enjoyed the pleasures that the world had to offer. Then he told about how the Holy Spirit of God convicted him that it was sin, it was wrong, and that his life was an utter waste. He told about how he began his repentance, about the struggles he had, and about the victories he enjoyed.

Neal thought the story was long, but Rudy thought he was talking directly to him. He didn't move. He didn't even shift in his seat. Rudy thought that this person was speaking exactly about his own life. He could agree with everything he said about his former life. He, too, felt his life was wasted, worthless, and filthy. So when this young man described the steps of his conversion, Rudy listened carefully. He described how he talked with an elder of the church who guided him to important scriptures for the struggles he was having. He described how the elder listened to his complete confession and the relief that that had given him. He described how he had made restitutions and the feeling of victory and peace that each restitution had given him, and he described the final gift of peace which God had given him when he knew that he was truly forgiven by God.

Rudy noticed many similarities in this story to the experience Jack told him. The experience was similar to the biblical character of Zachaeus who wanted to see Jesus so he climbed up a sycamore tree. Jesus stopped at that tree and spoke to him. Jesus saw Zachaeus's faith and called him down and went to his house. Zachaeus was so inspired that he gave half his goods to the poor, and agreed to repay everyone four times if he had taken anything dishonestly. This notion of voluntarily repaying what was taken dishonestly was new to Rudy. He heard of giving to the poor, but restitution was something new.

Several other musical groups were scheduled next. During these songs Rudy felt a powerful conviction to begin this process of conversion himself. He could not shake it from his head. He could not concentrate on anything else. It was as if some voice was screaming at him to do it but no one else could hear it. It agitated him. He was uncomfortable sitting there. He squirmed in his seat. He wanted to jump over Neal, run down the center isle of the church, and go outside where he could breathe, where he could think.

The question kept coming back whether he should convert. Finally, he closed his eyes, lifted his head slightly upward and told himself, yes, of course he should convert: "This is what I should do. This is what I *will* do."

When he agreed to do this, it was like someone turned off a switch to all this noise in his head. He was at peace with the decision; and he had the clear belief that if he changed his mind the noise would come back.

The speaker that evening was a young elder from the Midwest. He was a powerful speaker. While he preached everyone in the audience seemed frozen in attention. This was something no one noticed while it was going on, but was immediately obvious when he stopped preaching and sat down. Suddenly, everyone shifted, coughed, and otherwise tried to correct the slight discomfort that resulted from sitting in the same position for twenty minutes.

After the preacher sat down a quartet got up and sang "Just As I Am." This song seemed to speak directly to Rudy as well. If he had any fears that he was too sinful to approach a minister this song removed them. He wanted to talk to the elder who spoke, if possible. He was anxious to get started. After the last song there was a prayer and then someone from the local placement committee got up and read the names of the guests and hosts. She asked them to stand to be identified.

Rudy leaned over to Neal and said, "I have to talk to that

preacher. When's the best time to do it?"

"Go to him right after this is over," Neal advised. "There's no hurry for anyone to leave. You'll have lots of time to talk to him." Neal could hardly hide the excitement in his voice. He closed his eyes and silently repeated, "Thank you." to God for working so powerfully in Rudy's heart. It was the natural flow of gratitude for a person he had come to care a great deal about.

It was a boost to his own faith watching someone turn to God in faith. It impressed Neal all over again of the power of the grace of God and the convicting power of the Holy Spirit.

After the service the crowd was incredible. There were more than twice as many people as the room could comfortably handle. Rudy moved with determination to find the elder who preached that night and introduce himself.

"Hello," Rudy began. "My name is Rudy. May I talk with you tonight?" They shook hands.

"Of course, Rudy. My name is George Bender. Let's go over to one of the Sunday school classrooms where we can have some privacy."

On the way, their progress was slowed by frequent contacts between Bender and others in the crowd. Some thanked him for the sermon. Some wanted to counsel with him also. Rudy was surprised that he had gotten to him first. Rudy was also surprised to observe how completely approachable Bender was. He gave every sincere impression that he was vitally interested in what they wanted to talk about, and showed no sign of fatigue or regret with all the help he was asked to give.

They found a Sunday school classroom toward the back of a long hall, well away from the main crowd. The further they got away from the crowd the more Rudy worried about the wisdom of his actions. He doubted that Bender would be interested in him. He wondered why he should trouble Bender when he was not brought up in his church. He began to doubt whether Bender would understand him. He started feeling silly about this as they turned two chairs to face each other. He was suddenly aware of powerful feelings of doubt. He then remembered some of the words of the last song that was sung: "just as I am." These words gave him a certain boldness to go forward no matter how absurd the situation may be. He was past caring about looking stupid. He was motivated by the Spirit to take this first important step.

"Just relax as much as you can in this situation, Rudy," Bender told him, "and tell me why you want to talk to me." His voice was soothing, relaxed, and patient. This tended to relax Rudy and slow his thinking somewhat. He felt less panic. He could think more clearly and deliberately.

"I want to convert," Rudy said. "I've been coming to your church in Connecticut for some time, and I realize that what you have is something I want for my life."

"That's wonderful," Bender affirmed. "Tell me how you came to find our church. Tell me more about yourself."

"Well, I had been in a bar in Connecticut and I got pretty wasted. I left the bar and passed out on the side of a highway just outside the bar's parking lot. One of the youth group kids in Connecticut happened to be driving by and pulled over and took me to his home. The next morning we struck up a friendship and he introduced me to some of his friends. We hit it off well and he asked me if I wanted to go to their youth group. I guess I was curious about this guy and the way he lived. It was so different from the way I lived. So I went to the youth group meeting. They had a speaker that night, Theo Venzel, I don't know if you know him or not."

"Oh yes, I know him well."

"Well, he spoke to us and I never heard a talk like that. I was amazed at the wisdom he had. So I decided to look into this group more closely. I came back for several of their services, and more of their youth group activities, then we came here."

"That's interesting." Bender encouraged. "It sounds like you are a serious young man."

Rudy snorted a laughing cough he could not prevent. "I've never been called that before.

"I've read quite a bit from the Bible, but I'd like some advice from you on what I should do next."

"You may want to make a complete confession to get started," Bender advised. "This will help you reach a certain milestone and make progress somewhat easier in the future."

This seemed wise to Rudy. It seemed more confidential to confess to Bender than someone in Connecticut. At the same time

Rudy was aware of a fantasy to just get up and run out. Some voice told him to flee, not to paint himself in a corner.

He became nervous. His hands became moist and sweaty. His mouth got dry. He felt like he was sinking into a deep tile pipe where he was unaware of anything around him. All he could see were the eyes of Bender. He began his confession as if under someone else's control. It was like he was listening to someone else talk although he knew it was his voice.

"Well, ugh, I've been sexually active for the last two years. I've been disrespectful to my parents. I've had big fights with them over the years. I've stolen small things out of stores just for fun, really. I've never had a lack of money to buy things I've wanted. I just did it for kicks, I guess." Rudy looked closely in Bender's eyes to see what his reaction was so far. Bender looked attentive, sympathetic, and understanding. He showed no surprise, shock, or curiosity. He seemed to admire Rudy's ability to make this confession and conveyed a hopefulness that this was the right thing to do, and that it would really help Rudy.

"I haven't really given Jesus Christ and God much thought most of my life," Rudy went on. He was running out of big things to confess. "I guess I've been selfish. I thought everything was just to enjoy and use up. I never thought much about sharing with others or helping out in Christian missions, or programs." There was a long delay while Rudy was trying to think of more things to confess. Instead of being awkward and putting extra pressure on Rudy, Bender's patient bearing made the silent moments productive, helpful, and comforting.

"I can't think of too much more," Rudy added. "I've been mean to people. I've mocked people, and I've gotten in a few fights. But I can't remember any specific ones. I guess that's about all I can remember."

"That's interesting, Rudy." Bender said in a soothing, reassuring tone. "Would it be helpful if I would ask you a few questions that might remind you of some other things that you might want to talk about?"

"Sure. Go ahead."

"Have you ever gone to pornographic movies, or viewed pornographic magazines or pictures?"

"Oh, yes. I'm not into them much. But I have in the past."

"Well, how do you feel about those now?"

"Ugh, the Bible advises us to flee youthful lusts," Rudy answered. "I'm sure that those things are harmful and should be avoided."

"That's right," Bender agreed. "You said you have stolen small things before. Have you ever cheated or lied about anything?"

"Sure. I've lied about things. I can't remember any lies right now. Most people say I'm pretty open and honest, but I'm sure I've lied about lots of things, probably my share. I've never cheated in school or anything like that." Rudy went on. "I can't think of ever cheating on anything."

"Have you ever done any vandalism?" Bender inquired.

"Well, I've broken some vending machines before, and I've thrown rocks at passing cars, which must have done some damage. That was a long time ago. I really can't remember who was hurt by it."

"I can see what you mean that people say you're pretty honest. You have been open and honest with me."

"Thanks," Rudy sighed, breathing a little easier, a little more relaxed. He was relieved to find that confessing these things did seem to take a load off his back. He was feeling more relaxed, more at peace with himself. He was unaware of the passing of time, and was thankful that this confession was out of the way.

"Why don't you take a few minutes and think more about the subject of lying. Are there some lies that you've made but can't remember without a little more time?" Bender asked.

Rudy was a little puzzled. He felt that there must be; but he could not remember them. He thought for a while. He realized that there must be more in this category, too. He was not irritated with Bender's asking more about this. He was just perplexed that he could not remember more. Then suddenly, like a bolt hitting him in the chest, he remembered his main problem of the moment. He was using a false identification. He was lying about his name, and who he was.

"Oh, yes, there is something kinda big. I don't know just how to explain it," Rudy said.

"Take your time. Remember a confession is confidential." Bender reassured. "We can discuss anything and clarify it if it doesn't come out the way you intended it." He wondered what could be kinda big to an eighteen-year-old who just confessed being sexually active for the last two years. He braced himself for whatever else Rudy might say trying, successfully, not to betray any anxiety.

"Well, I lied about my name." There was a brief silence in which Rudy realized that more explanation was needed. "You see, I wanted to get to know these people in Connecticut before they learned about who my father is. Nobody ever sees me anymore after they learn who my father is. They just see the son of this big shot in New York. I wanted to be taken as an individual, as myself."

"I'm sure that's a noble intention, Rudy. However, a lie is a lie."

"Yeah, I know. And I want to clear this up, but I don't know how to."

"Could you tell me more about what you told them?"

"Well, Neal—that's the guy who picked me up in Connecticut, Neal Ebler—asked me what my name was. I've been through so many experiences where people acted differently when they learned about my father. My real name is Rudyard Horace Peterfield, but I just said Rudy Horace. It was not quite a lie, but I permitted him to believe that Horace was my last name."

Bender tried to recall what famous person in New York might be called Peterfield. The name did sound familiar but he couldn't quite place it.

"Now everyone in Connecticut thinks my name is Rudy Horace and I'm going to look like a jerk when I tell them my real name."

"What does your father do?" Bender asked. He was wondering if Rudy was fantasizing an imaginary famous father.

"My father's a psychiatrist. It's just that he's got a lot of money and a lot of famous patients. He's like one of the mental health experts for the media, or something. He's always being quoted in the media."

"Oh, I recognize the name now." Bender added. "He's quite influential throughout the country, not just New York. If your father's who I've read about, he has more assets than Wooster's largest bank."

"That's the one," Rudy said with thinly disguised irritation. "I can't be taken seriously for myself because of what everyone thinks of him. That's why I lied about my identity. In your church I'm accepted for myself. I'm really scared to change that."

"Well, if the Spirit of God is working, you've nothing to be scared of," counseled Bender. "You must obey the scriptures. You must tell only the truth. Let your yea be yea and your nay be nay. God doesn't look on the outward things of man, but on the inward condition of the heart. God's people will do the same. You must trust that. Just go out in faith and make this lie right by telling the truth.

"You must also go back and apologize to those you've wronged in your past—that is, as many as you can remember. You may find that as you do this God will remind you of some other things. Make sure that you leave nothing undone. To be at peace with God you must be at peace with man as much as you can possibly be."

"What about past sexual partners? How do I make that right?" Rudy asked.

"That's an excellent question. What do you think you should do?"

"I should probably go and tell them that I now think it was wrong, and apologize to them."

"I think you're right, Rudy," Bender agreed. "You should also tell them why you now think it's wrong. Tell them what the Lord has done in your heart. Maybe your testimony will be a turning point in their lives too."

"Wow! That won't be easy," Rudy said. The image of going up to some of them and saying that came graphically to mind.

"None of this is easy," Bender said. "But with God all things are possible. Did you think talking to me would be easy?"

"No, I sure didn't."

"But now that it's almost over how do you feel?"

"I feel relieved to have it over."

"That's the way all these steps will be. You'll be given the strength to do them, and you'll be given a large measure of faith after having done them. These experiences are your first steps in faith. The first chapter of John, verse 12 tells us: `But as many as received him, to them gave he power to become the sons of God, even to them that believe on his name.' God will see you through to the blessed end, Rudy. Just go forward in that faith."

"Thank you, sir," Rudy said with sincerity. He was not accustomed to calling people "sir," but it seemed so appropriate at this time. Here was a man who had done a great deal for him. This man, who had never seen him before this night, had done this for no pay, no glory, and no requirements of Rudy in return. Rudy realized that this man had the Spirit of God, and the Christian charity or love that is so important.

"Oh, there's one more thing," Bender remembered. "How do you get along with your parents?"

"Not well. We're a distant family. We hardly see each other. My father's too busy to know where I am or what I'm doing, and my mother just doesn't have the interest."

"Well, you should ask them for their forgiveness if you have ever done anything to hurt them and explain to them what you're doing. After all, they are your parents."

"Is that important? That's going to be hard, I think," Rudy said.

"I think it's important. You need to make a public declaration of your intentions. When your parents know, they're around to keep an eye on you and keep you honest when your efforts start to flag."

"Well, I don't think my parents will care if I stay on the goal or not."

"Then why would it be hard to tell them?"

"I don't know." And Rudy did not know. He just had a feeling that this would not be something his parents would like to hear.

"Is that everything you can think of at this time?" inquired Bender.

"Yeah. That's it."

"Fine. I think we should have a prayer. I can pray alone, or we can both pray with you finishing the prayer."

"What do you recommend?" Rudy asked feeling a little self-conscious about even asking.

"I think we should both pray. I'll start and you can finish."

"OK"

"Let's pray. Dear Heavenly Father, we thank You for the miracle of faith in Jesus Christ. We thank You that turning to You in faith brings to us a rich outpouring of Your Good and Holy Spirit to continue the work that has been begun in faith. And we now pray for this precious soul, Rudy. Flood his life and being with Your Good and Holy Spirit that what he has begun might grow to fullness, bearing much fruit for Your Kingdom. Give Rudy the strength, the courage, and the determination to complete the miracle of conversion which he has begun. When the tempter comes and tries to discourage him, may he know certainly that that comes from Satan and should be ignored. Give Rudy the power to do whatever needs to be done. Give him the grace to find salvation in Your Son, Jesus Christ. This we pray in Jesus name—"

There was a long pause and Rudy got the message that he was to start praying at this point.

"God, help me to find You, to understand Your will for my life, and to obey You. Help me to make a complete conversion. And forgive me. Amen."

There was a moment of silence after the prayer while they both reflected on the things that were said. Then there was a slight awkwardness about leaving. Bender advised Rudy to talk to Theo Venzel as soon as he got the chance back in Connecticut. There would be many more steps that he would have to take and Venzel would be helpful in walking him through those.

Rudy was in no big hurry to rejoin the group. He wanted to think about things he said and promised. On the other hand, Bender had a few other people to see after Rudy left. So Rudy left and walked slowly down the hall toward the dining room. He wanted to rehearse the things he was told in his memory but he seemed unable to. He could not focus his thinking on those events, and the nearer he got to the crowd of people the more distracted he became.

CHAPTER 28

B ack in the dining hall Rudy wanted to find a table, a piece of paper, and write down the steps of what he must do. As he was doing this, his father, at the Edgartown Yacht Club, was sitting down at a table writing down the names of the two workers who pulled him out of the harbor near the dock where people were picked up and dropped off from their yachts.

After the race was over everyone in the Peterfields' circle went on what they called "a progressive party." They went from one yacht to another for drinks and hors d'oeuvres. Peterfield planned no sailing or driving, so he dove into the gin pretty heavily. He liked to drink. He was the kind of drinker who could pour it down and show little outward effects. He loved gin and tonics made with Bombay gin and lots of lime. Everyone knew this and made something of a show to produce this when he arrived.

His wife, Carol, was pouring down her usual: vodka martinis, dry, no garbage, with a shot of scotch on top. There was a polite fiction that Peterfield did not drink excessively. People were only too quick to make excuses for him. They reasoned that since he hears the problems of so many people every day he needs some escape from those tremendous burdens. This was a convenient fiction as well. Peterfield was perhaps more powerful in Edgartown than he was in New York City. So to believe a fiction that caused one to be kind to Dr. Peterfield was in one's best interest. His power here, as in New York City, came from his enormous wealth. He was needed for contributions and gave them freely when pleased or pampered. This gave him a tremendous power to veto plans and blackball people if he chose.

So the fact of the matter was that as people were coming to the dining room of the Edgartown Yacht Club for the main meal, Peterfield was drunk. Not drunk in a loud way, just subdued; he moved about more slowly, and he seemed warmer, friendlier, less dangerous. He took his seat in the elegant dining area and began working his way through the various courses, punctuated by various fine wines, enjoying the meal and especially the wines with abandon.

Also punctuating the meal were occasional impromptu speeches and performances. These were carefully planned by a committee. They were designed to give the impression of spontaneity, and of being casual, but were carefully engineered to be flattering to the right people. There were many deferential remarks made about Peterfield and his past sailing successes. He was given numerous opportunities to speak, or comment, all of which he wisely declined. He was not so out of control that he did not know his speech would be slightly affected, and he felt no obligation to speak.

He did get in a friendly argument with a woman sitting near him at his table. The argument seemed pointless, like most arguments seem upon reflection. She bragged that there was no navigational instrument that she could not run. Peterfield knew that he had just had installed some new, expensive instrument and believed that there was no way this woman would even know what it was, to say nothing of how to use it.

Peterfield loved gadgets. You could not put a quarter down on his yacht without hitting some high-tech electronic gadget. This woman was a gadgeteer also. She was married to a real estate broker in New York City, and she was in computer design for IBM. The probability that she was right was high. She was from a wealthy family herself and was not inclined to be patronizing to Peterfield. She held her ground until Peterfield had had enough. He challenged her on the spot to come out to his yacht and run this new instrument.

Peterfield's wife graciously declined to come out and be a witness. So Peterfield, this woman, and two other men marched purposefully to the dock where the launch would haul them out to his yacht. It was well after dark, and the lighting was not adequate. Peterfield was ahead of the group when he marched right off the side of the dock and into the water. It happened so quickly that no one could grab him. There was a stunned silence of disbelief. Then people rushed over to the edge looking for him. Two men came out from a small office beside the dock and pushed their way to the front.

"Where'd he go?" they asked.

"I don't know. He just walked off the edge and fell in," said one in the party.

"Who was it?"

"Dr. Peterfield," said the lady.

"Oh, no!" said one of the men. They dove in to search for him. This quick action proved to be brilliant, and necessary. One of the men caught him and brought him to the surface so that he was not under the water more than forty-five seconds. He did not breathe during that time so was unaffected by being under water. He was pulled out by four or five men and taken into the office to sit down. Someone handed him several towels to dry off and wrap around himself. He was quite a sight, dressed so fashionably but soaking wet.

"What happened?" he asked. "I was walking along the dock and the next thing I knew I was being pulled out of the water. I didn't see the end of the dock."

"Well, sir, it's not well lit tonight," one of the men working there told him. "They're working on the lights and we don't have the usual lighting up."

"Well, you men have saved my life," Peterfield said with conviction. Everyone seemed relieved that there was something else to blame besides his drinking.

"This is terrible," said the lady he had been arguing with. "Are you freezing?"

"No. The water's actually pretty nice," Peterfield chuckled. "Let me have your names." he said to the workers. "I certainly owe you a great debt of gratitude."

There was a sense of great relief in this little office by the dock. It was as if everyone knew what a huge disaster had been averted, and much trouble and pain had been saved. There was also no little relief that Peterfield was taking it all so well. There was the sense of sport in the air. There was also the sense of curiosity about what shape Peterfield's gratitude might take. Stories of his gratitude, like his anger, were legendary. He could be a creative giver.

Someone called up to the dining room and got Mrs. Peterfield out of the banquet. She looked shocked and concerned until she saw how well Peterfield was taking it.

"Really Horace," she teased, "haven't you had enough water sports for one day?"

"Yes, indeed I have," he answered. "Let's get the car and go home." One of the waiters found a blanket and wrapped Peterfield in that. He and his wife climbed into the back of the station wagon, and John drove them back to their cottage.

They were waved off by well-wishers. He never did find out if that woman could operate the equipment on his yacht. Most who heard the argument, however, were pretty sure that Peterfield was in for a disappointment. The woman could have probably run the equipment better than both Peterfield, and his pilot. In fact, she probably would have been able to teach them a few new features of the equipment.

The Peterfields left for New York City the following day. Peterfield did not forget the two men who fished him out of the harbor, though. He called the yacht club and talked to their supervisor. He learned that one was on a summer job after his first year at college, and the other was much into sailing. To the first one, he had his secretary check out what college tuition and books would cost for the remaining three years, and he sent him a check for that amount. He gave the equivalent dollar value to the second one in the form of a gift certificate for sailing equipment and boats.

Peterfield may be a powerful man, and he may be intimidating to people most of the time, but he knew when he had taxed people's sense of fair play. He was good at rewarding people for being kind to him. He did it in a personal way. His giving showed research, care, and a personalized touch which people appreciated.

In spite of it all, he had greatly enjoyed himself that night. He relaxed and really felt far removed from his hectic schedule and busy life. A few close friends teased him gently about his late night swim. But the whole matter was quickly forgotten. As everyone knows, every boater has a silly story about walking off a dock with the dumb look of shock and embarrassment on his face. No long-term boater is immune, drinker or non-drinker alike.

CHAPTER 29

Rudy finished the note to himself and moved around the groups of people standing around talking. There was a slowness in getting acclimated to the pace and activity. He slowly walked out to the parking lot and Neal's van making sure he was not holding up Neal or their hosts.

He stood on the far side of the van away from the church building. He wanted some quiet time to think and enjoy the spiritual experience that had just happened to him. He was leaning up against the van just letting his mind wander. The sounds from the church were faint, some talking, some laughing. In the distance there were twenty or thirty people standing around a piano in an inner room singing.

After enjoying this for about ten minutes he began to wonder if Neal might be inside waiting for him. So, as much as he enjoyed this quiet setting, he tore himself away from the van and walked back into the church.

"Have you seen Neal?" he asked someone walking out.

"No, not recently," the person said.

"Thanks," Rudy said absently. He walked into the main fellowship hall of the building. There was Neal sitting talking with a small group.

"Rudy," he called, "ready to go?"

"Yeah, I guess I am. Are you waiting on me?"

"Yeah, we're ready to go." So they folded their chairs and returned them to the neat rows that other people had put them in. They would be put back into use in nine short hours. "We're off to Ferrell's Ice Cream Shop," Neal declared. "You're not gonna believe this."

"What am I not gonna believe?" Rudy asked catching some of the enthusiasm in Neal's voice.

"This place is great. They have every kind of ice cream imaginable and huge servings. We always go there."

Just as Neal had promised, Ferrell's Ice Cream Shop was great. They had to wait even at ten in the evening for a table. There were lots of other people from the church there. They were sitting with a different group than before.

"Hi. My name's John Schmidt," volunteered someone to Rudy's right.

"Hi. My name's Rudy Peterfield. Where're you from?"

"Toronto. Ever been there?"

"Oh, sure. I've got an uncle who lives there."

"Really? What's his name? What's he do?" John made a point of asking people if they knew anyone in Toronto because he believed in coincidences. He knew that Toronto was a big city but if he did know someone it would be great fun. He never did.

"His name is Charles Kupferschmidt. He's a lawyer."

"Kupferschmidt, eh?" he asked. "Well, his name ends up on the right note anyhow."

"Who knows?" Rudy speculated, "We might be related. Your ancestors almost certainly shortened your last name to Schmidt. Maybe it was originally Kupferschmidt. You might be a long lost cousin?"

"Could be." Everyone around the table was enjoying the joke and glad that Rudy was joining in so easily.

Neal waited until the conversation came to a natural end and nudged Rudy on the arm. "What did you just say your name was?"

"Oh, yeah, I've got to tell you something kind of serious. Promise you won't be mad? Let's go out in the parking lot for a minute."

"OK" Neal told someone next to him what he wanted to order in case the waitress came while they were gone. He ordered a "Monster Pail." This was fifteen scoops of ice cream, covered with various toppings, nuts, whipped cream, and cherries. Rudy, distracted by the conversation of his uncle in Toronto, did not have time to look over the menu so he ordered the same thing.

They walked out to the parking lot where Rudy began the conversation.

"Listen, I hope you won't be offended. I lied somewhat about my name. It really is Rudy Horace but those are only my first and middle names. My last name is really Peterfield. This came up in my confession tonight and I want to straighten it out before it goes on any further."

"Why couldn't you tell me your last name?" Neal asked.

"Well, it's probably dumb, but my father's this big shot in New York and a lot of people don't pay any attention to me when they find out who my father is. It's like I don't have any identity of my own once people know I'm his son. I wanted to get to know the people in your church without any of those problems."

"You didn't have to worry about me. I don't recognize the name. You'll have to tell me more about your father," Neal said.

"I will, but not now. I'm sorry I lied to you about my name. I hope you don't think it's dumb. I thought I had to do it but I realize now how dumb it was."

"That's OK Rudy. I'm glad you told me the truth now."

"Let's go back in there and see if the ice cream has melted yet," Rudy suggested.

Rudy felt relief after telling Neal the truth. Neal was deep in thought as to who Peterfield might be. Was he a politician, an entertainer, a mobster? Neal was unable to put these speculations out of his mind, while Rudy found that he could join in the fun with no worries.

"What do you bet I could eat three of these Monster Pails?" asked one guy at the table.

"If you can eat three, I'll buy them," Rudy offered.

"You've got a deal," he agreed and ate them.

"Well," said one of the hosts, "we'd better get home or we'll be in big trouble with our parents."

"What time is it anyway?" asked one.

"It's after eleven o'clock."

"Oh, man, we've gotta get going. We've gotta get up early tomorrow morning to set up chairs and get things ready."

So the group broke up and headed to their hosts' homes for the night. They never stayed in hotels when they visited other towns. Visiting was strongly encouraged. All you had to do was show up at one of their churches and you would be invited by any number of people to stay overnight for as many nights as they could talk you into staying. This was true in Europe, South America, anywhere there were churches of this denomination.

So Rudy and Neal were put up in the bunk beds of the younger brothers of the youth group member they were staying with.

Shortly the house became quiet. After kneeling by the bed and praying, Neal climbed into the upper bunk. Rudy crawled into the lower.

"Do you want to talk or just get some sleep?" Rudy asked.

"Let's talk. I'm not tired yet."

"What do you want to talk about?" Rudy asked.

"What does your father do that's so powerful?" Neal asked.

"He's a psychiatrist with lots of famous, international patients. He gets interviewed a lot by the media when mental health issues hit the news."

"I guess I've heard of him." Neal admitted. "I would have never associated you with him, though. Is that what makes him so powerful?"

"That and his money," Rudy admitted.

"His money?"

"Well, he was an only son of an only son and the amounts of money involved are really big. He donates money to politicians and causes and calls in favors as he sees fit. He knows how to throw his weight around because of his money—and he frequently does."

"Wow. I've never known anybody from that kind of money. What's it like?"

"Well, it's hard to be taken seriously for who you are. As soon as everyone hears about it they say, `Wow. I've never known anybody from that kind of money.' And they usually never think of you and your personality again. All they think about from that time on is your father's money."

"Well, I don't know what to say. Sorry. I hope I won't be that way, but I am curious about that kind of life."

Rudy admired Neal's honesty. This openness was what he admired most about Neal and his church. Rudy believed that if any group could see him beyond his father's money it would be this group.

"I'll admit it's nice to not have any long-term money worries," Rudy said. "But you don't end up spending money carelessly. The problem is that you just don't have any friends that like you for who you are. Everyone seems to understand perfectly what your family's worth. They know vividly where you are on a sort of status yard stick. If you're above them they want to bump you off. If you're below them they're more worried about those above them than you. No one seems to have the kinds of friendships that you and Jim and Jack seem to have. Everything is a sort of theater rather than real feelings."

"How'd you get to know this? That seems so wise." Neal said.

"I'll tell you what my father said when he got the first test results ever run on me as a preschooler. He said, `He's a smart little guy.' My father may not think about me often, but at least he's pleased that I inherited his intelligence." There was real hurt in Rudy's voice as he told this to Neal.

"What makes you think your father doesn't think of you much?" Neal asked.

"He's always got so many other projects going that he never knows what I'm doing. I can leave the house for weeks and he won't even miss me. He believes in letting kids grow up in good schools and beyond that they're on their own. There's nothing you can do to shock him, or make him angry. He sees us as independently developing individuals who have nothing to do with him other than an accident of biology putting us in his family."

"You mean your father never spanked you or punished you?"

"No," Rudy said. "He may have told us to leave a room, but he never got angry about it, and wouldn't have gotten upset if we wouldn't have. Pretty strange stuff, huh? I tell you he's the human iceberg. He cares professionally for so many people that he's all out of care for his family or anyone else. I suppose you'd like to meet him?"

"Yes, I would," Neal admitted. "I've never known anyone like that. Oh, Jim's dad's pretty rich, being a surgeon and all, but they live a pretty normal life."

"No one in your church leads a normal life," Rudy corrected. "That's what you can't understand."

"Well, I mean that they live pretty much like the rest of us."

"I know what you mean, Neal, but if you're going to go into psychology you need to know how different your background is."

"Yeah. I think I understand that, but maybe I don't fully," Neal admitted. "You probably don't either, though, coming from your background. Maybe mine's more normal than yours."

"Maybe you're right. Well, you might get the chance to meet my father. We'll see," Rudy said.

"Hey, it's nearly two," Neal said. "We've got to get up early tomorrow. Good night."

"Good night."

Neal lay thinking about who Rudy was, about his famous father, and about the motivation Rudy seemed to have to get to know his church. He noticed that Rudy was right. He couldn't quite get the money out of his mind. He knew this would be a challenge but he was not going to disappoint Rudy.

Rudy couldn't fall asleep quickly either. He remembered his meeting with George Bender. He was suddenly aware of where he was. He was struck by how unlikely it would have seemed to him two months ago that he would be at a church meeting in Ohio. He remembered the first talk of Theo Venzel's when he said that no one exposes himself to the preaching of Jesus Christ and is not changed. Those words seemed to challenge him but he could not have predicted how quickly they were to be true in his life.

Rudy thought back to his friendship with Renee. It seemed like a lifetime ago. It seemed like someone else. He was excited about this change. He marveled at how powerful the change was in his life, how constructive it seemed to him, and how it was done without drugs. It was actually stronger than drugs and it was lasting longer than drugs. He hoped it would last all his life. He liked what was happening to him. And with those pleasant thoughts he drifted off into a peaceful sleep; a sleep cut short by the clock, but elongated by the sense of peace and unity with the Creator of his soul.

CHAPTER 30

Neal and Rudy were awakened by church music playing on the family stereo. They showered, shaved, dressed, packed, then walked to a kitchen radiating the smells of a Midwest breakfast. There were eggs, bacon, hash brown potatoes, toast, juice, and coffee. It was the kind of breakfast after which hard physical labor was intended.

Due to limited space, the young people rode in a separate car. Arriving early, they helped set up the chairs for the Bible study. The Bible study was a discussion format lasting forty-five minutes. There was a ten-minute break before the morning worship service.

Rudy noticed that here, too, people sprung into action and made the job look quick and easy. No one worked grudgingly. People were eager to pitch in and make the job easy for everyone.

Shortly, people were ushered into the main sanctuary. There was a reverent hush in the cavernous room.

Rudy looked around the big room. It was impressive for its simplicity. There were no ornaments on the walls, or the pulpit. The absence of these customary Christian symbols gave the room an even more formal appearance. The people, too, were dressed in suits and attractive dresses but with an absence of ornamentation.

Someone called out a song number and, after the introduction by the organist, the congregation burst into four-part harmony. He had the feeling of sitting in the middle of a choir.

After the song three ministers walked up to the pulpit. One, who happened to be the local elder, welcomed everyone. The elder then suggested that the congregation stand and sing their traditional greeting hymn. This hymn was obviously familiar to most of the people. Most sang the first three verses without a book.

The singing seemed almost heavenly. Rudy was almost overcome by this singing. His eyes teared up and he was struck with an unfamiliar thought. He thought that if he died now his life would have been fulfilled. He was filled with the conviction that this was the best that life had to offer.

The congregation was asked to remain standing after the singing for prayer. Another minister spoke: "We pray for the Holy Spirit to be our teacher, to fill our speaker with thoughts and words that are directly from the heart of God, and to cause all of us to cherish and treasure the words as the divine seed, the wisdom of God sewn abundantly for everyone to hear. Dear, Lord, if you would do these things, we will not fail to give you all the thanks and the praise."

Even this simple, utilitarian prayer struck Rudy as unique, and rich in faith in God. These were people who were used to talking with God. These were people who listened to God and tried to obey what God taught them. Every aspect of this service was different and more authentic than anything he had seen before.

Then, still another preacher walked up to the pulpit and delivered the morning sermon.

"I would like to remain, basically, with the theme we had this morning: 'The Bible Our Guide.' There is one thought, particularly, I would like to stress a bit that becomes important to me, especially when I read the Bible myself. It has to do with the attitude we take towards the Bible; and the approach toward reading. I don't like to think of the Bible just as a book. I think the Apostle John conveys so beautifully the point I would like to underline, namely, that when we talk about the Bible we should feel like we are dealing with a person. We heard this morning about Jesus Christ who was the Word and became flesh and dwelt amongst us.

"The apostle so beautifully describes here how they fellowship with Him. He talks about something that's not just past, but is still alive from the beginning. It is something they had seen, something they handled. Their hands have handled that Word of life. A life that was manifest and a life that is eternal. That we declared unto you that you may also have fellowship with us and truly our fellowship is with the Father, and with His Son, Jesus Christ.

"Maybe that's why the apostles were so successful. They were able to convey a knowledge of a Savior with Whom they had fellowship. They invited other people to have fellowship with them together with the Father Who is in Heaven. If we could portray to our fellow man an active vibrant fellowship with the Father, a living God, and that the Bible means something living and vibrant that transmits itself in our lives—down to how we behave, what we do, and how we plan—we might be able to attract yet more people to have fellowship with us, and together with the Father.

"There is a little saying that says something like this: `You can tell people, or know people, by the company they keep.' The disciples were known by the company they kept and by the fellowship they had. I'm reminded of a portion of scripture in John, where Christ also talks about that fellowship which He had with the Father. In chapter eight it says: `Then said Jesus unto them, When Ye have lifted up the son of man, then shall ye know that I am He and that I do nothing of myself, but as the Father hath taught me, I speak these things. And He that sent me is with me. The Father hath not left me alone for I do always those things that doth please Him.'

"I wonder, are we left alone sometimes, or do we feel alone because we are not doing the things that the Father wants us to do? Christ said here, I have fellowship with the Father and the Father does not leave me alone because I do the things He wants me to do. Is the Bible our guideline to the knowledge of the will of God, and also to lead us not only to an understanding of His will but also to the Source of strength—and that's the beauty of the Bible—of Christ our Savior? There is actually no excuse for not cultivating and having this beautiful fellowship with the Father through Christ Jesus.

"I think we all have that battle, both initially as we know we are to surrender our lives unto Christ, but also I think in many details and facets of everyday life. I'm speaking from experience, from defeats I've suffered, from lessons I have learned. It's difficult sometimes to cut our mooring lines and to surrender ourselves completely unto the Lord. We like to hold onto things or the limited degree of security we have in the use of our own judgment, reasoning, and personal resources. Sometimes I think the Lord has to bring a storm over our lives to rip those lines so that we might drift and be loosened from our self-reliance.

"Oh how beautiful it is when we can give ourselves over and cut loose the mooring lines to go out to sea on the beautiful swelling tide of Divine purpose. Beauty in the faith does not manifest itself until we are loose from self-reliance, and give ourselves over unto the Lord. How close is our fellowship, to what extent can we pass it along unto others is the recommendation. There is something beautiful when we see how close John was, and also the other disciples, but I think particularly John. His writings both in the Gospels and also in the Epistles show a great sensitivity unto his Master; and a deeper feeling and a greater affection than maybe some of the other disciples had.

"It shows especially that the relationship was a personal one. Did you read in the paper a few weeks ago about the complaints of some of the people we heard about down in Washington? They complained because they were worried that the boss would become inaccessible because they hired or appointed a chief of staff through whom all the information might flow. They felt that much of what they wanted to say or communicate was going to be lost by the barrier of that position. They were afraid he might surround himself like other presidents did and alienate his helpers or at least not have communication as it should be.

"The beauty of the Gospel is that you have direct access unto God. Christ is your intercessor. He doesn't hold you off. He helps to groom you, prepare you, and present you unto the Father. I'm often glad, just the other day I prayed and thanked the Lord, my Savior, that He is better able to convey unto the Father my needs and my wishes because He knows them first of all. He's not a barrier. He's a beautiful Helper. That is through Christ Jesus, our beautiful High Priest and Redeemer. If only we would use and believe in Him as the scripture says, we are able to come unto the Father.

"Think of the Bible as something personal. It is a personal communication and contact of fellowship with the Father through Christ Jesus. Then it becomes beautiful; and then it's meaningful.

"I had a conversation a few weeks ago with a business friend. We happened to have dinner together and somehow, I don't know how, unexpectedly the conversation drifted into spiritual things. He knows pretty much where I stand on things. He started telling me of some of the problems he had with some of his children. There were problems of communicating and problems of correcting them sometimes. He admits that he's rather emotional, and his temperament sometimes is hard to control. So I told him that faith properly practiced is something beautiful. Our relationship with our children is more successful if we can convey to them that we are not here to impose our own will or mere parental authority, but rather to convey to them and interpret to them the will of a Higher Authority to Whom we also bow, and to Whom we would like them to bow. It takes out the stigma, the personal enforcement, of parental will and makes it a joint venture to bow to Higher Authority.

"He said, `That's great. I'm going to try that.' But then we kept on talking about it and I said, `You know if you do that, you have to know first the Father's will.' I pointed out to him that he stands, in certain respects, on the wrong footing himself. He was quite receptive. He said, `You know I don't read the Bible too much.' I said that's the first thing to do. The Bible is our guidebook. How can the blind lead the blind? It's hard enough when we know the Bible. We have to wrestle to subordinate ourselves unselfishly to the Bible and what it says, so that we are free from the selfish imposition of our own will that we might practice what the Bible says.

"The guide is the Bible. We must know it. We must study it, and also be obedient to it. I remember reading years ago about all the victims on the Eiger Mountain in Switzerland. I can still see the pictures of dead bodies frozen stiff, dangling for days off the cliff on ropes. Victims of vanity and their personal ambition venturing forth into difficult and dangerous areas against the expressed advice of experienced guides . The guides even had to risk their lives to try to salvage some of them. They saved some, but many died. If we ignore the expert advice of the guide and venture forth ignorantly or self-determinedly into dangerous areas we're on difficult ground.

"The guide is here to council but also to be obeyed. Anytime we are outside of that fellowship, outside the orbit of the Spirit and Word and Influence of the Master, we are in danger. We alienate ourselves, or separate ourselves from that fellowship that's so precious and so beautiful.

"The Apostle James, someplace, talks so beautifully about the Word of God, the Bible, in a different aspect. He talks about the mirror. How we should not just stand in front of the mirror and walk away. I would like to have a show of hands, although I'm not going to ask for it. How many of you use a mirror? What do we use it for, and how well do we remember what we see? I used to travel with a cousin of mine years ago. I tell you it always used to impress me or make me almost laugh a little bit. He had a tiny little mirror in his pocket and every once in a while, or before he saw somebody, he pulled it out and looked at his face and that's all he could see in that little mirror. It's almost comical in a way. That's all he could see. Many of us operate in a small mirror sort of way. We see certain aspects or certain small portions of our being.

"Last night we talked about mirrors at home and one of my daughters complained she hasn't got a full-sized mirror. Ladies like a full-sized mirror. I do too, sometimes. I like to see the whole me. If, for instance, we look at ourselves the way the Apostle Paul talks about us as soldiers of Christ, we want to see all the way from the top to the bottom. Do we wear the helmet of Salvation, and our feet, are they prepared with the preparation of the Gospel. We can't just look at sections and think we are fully clothed to go to battle.

"When we are selective when we look at the Word that is supposed to be our guide, when we are picky and make our own selection of things we want to obey, and things we discard, that is not the proper mirror and we are foolish. We deny ourselves the fellowship with the Father. Christ unqualifiedly said, in a beautiful example, `I do all the things that I see my Father do and what He tells me. That's the basis, the key to my uninterrupted fellowship with the Father.'

"Where, if we did, have we lost the fellowship with the Father? The vibrant, indisputable, unmistakable awareness of being His and freely communicating with Him? In one place the Apostle said, `In all these things we tell you, that your joy might be full.'

"Being in the Poconos a few weeks ago we had a little map, a rather poor one, as a guide. You couldn't read the street names, and my son and I were looking for a certain place. It took us twenty or twenty-five minutes instead of two minutes. I was the navigator and, of course, I was a bit hasty. We went in the wrong direction. We got all tangled up. What did we do to find our way back? We looked at the map and asked a lot of questions. Finally we found our way.

"We cannot be too flighty. We cannot be careless studying the guide, the Word of God. The beautiful part is, too, if you are not sure, ask questions. That's how I found my way back. The Lord wants to answer questions. He might even point some brother or sister, a fellow-believer, to help you find the answers. Search the scriptures, it says, read it diligently. Communicate, have fellowship, fellowship with the scriptures with Christ, our Savior.

"In this way we have a life that is full of fellowship, divine meaning and personal interpretation by the guidance of the Spirit of the will of God as it was meant to be implemented in our own daily lives, which may vary for each one. That's why it is so important to have fellowship with the Father to know His purpose with us.

"Are we teachable? We had an experience not long ago. We tried to help somebody for weeks. Almost every week that person lost a friend because we couldn't tell her a thing. She always knew better. She brushed help aside. She kept asking for it all the time but not accepting it except on her own terms. It's hard to take. I wonder how often the Master finds us that way. In dire need of help but not accepting it on His terms the way He presents it, so things get worse all the time.

"John, who speaks about that vibrant relationship, was an apostle who stayed in the presence of Christ and learned as he went along. Sure the disciples made mistakes. We do too. But as long as they stayed in the orbit within the closeness of Christ they kept on learning. After Christ was gone, the Spirit taught them and they developed and maintained that fellowship and it was beautiful. Others, like the Apostle Paul, express the wisdom, depth, and the riches in the knowledge of Jesus Christ all because they were digging and looking for it in the Bible as something living. This was with the Bible not even fully developed yet like it is today. Paul even contributed to the Bible we have today while living in that fellowship with Jesus Christ the Master.

"'The Father hath not left me alone for I do always those things that please Him. As he spake these words, many believed on him.' Now listen to this, 'Then said Jesus unto those Jews that believed on Him, If Ye continue in my word,' He says if you continue to live within the guidelines or the guide of the Bible, 'Then Ye are my disciples indeed and ye shall know the truth, and the truth shall make you free.'

"The other day I watched a certain sorting machine for money. You put a whole bag of coins in a funnel, and it grinds away and in a couple minutes all the various denominations are carefully sorted out and counted. What has that got to do with the Gospel? Not much except, I thought to myself, I wish I could take the whole bag of last week's activities and throw it in a divine sorting machine and see what kind of value my activities actually had. I might be surprised. The low values, possibly, of certain thoughts, or certain deeds, the many actions outside the fellowship and close awareness of Divine will. Then the absence of the joy that gives strength and vitality.

"Somebody said once, a Christian will never get old. Judging by my bones and a few other things, I think I am getting older. But I firmly believe that the mind of a Christian and his being can stay young like Isaiah said, like on wings of eagles. Because what makes the person young or a child is the wonder and the anticipation of the new things he can see all the time. You can do that in spiritual life because in the fellowship with the Father in Christ Jesus there is something new everyday.

"I was driving back to the Poconos early the other day. I sometimes have a sermon that I play back on a tape player but I saw the beauty and the quietness of the hills and the valleys. I thought to myself, here in silent eloquence speaks that word by which all things are made by my Master. How in the world can He bother with individuals? With all His omnipotence, and greatness, He deals with me.

"Sitting out on the porch I said to my son, 'Hey.' (I tried to test him because he's studying landscape architecture.) I said, 'How about this tree? What do you call it?' So he told me a fancy Latin name. 'What else can you tell me about it?' He told me quite a few things, how many needles to a bunch, and all kinds of other things. It was great but the greater thing behind it is that it's the Lord's handiwork. There's no end to wondering how great our Father is. But the greatest thing is this, that He wants to bother with us. That all this means nothing, it's going to be destroyed. He's interested in your soul and mine. That's all. And in extending unto us a fellowship on the basis that we always want to do His will, the same basis that Jesus Christ had that precious, inseparable fellowship.

"Are we willing to pay the price? We come back again to that human attitude, or part of it, we'd rather hold onto that little security we have based on what we can do ourselves, rather than the promises that look intangible on the surface. We'd rather almost say one bird in the hand rather than two in the bush. Somebody once said, `Yes but the Lord wants to give you the whole bush and all the birds in it.' The more you trust, the greater, I think, the surprising wealth of divine generosity and divine wisdom, and divine depth at dealing in a personal way with your life.

"There are certain beauties to looking back sometimes and seeing how certain things that you could not understand ten years ago, fifteen years ago, or five years ago suddenly prove to have been the beautiful guidance of the Lord. Did you ever travel on a highway and come to an intersection with many different ways to go, a cloverleaf? Just the other day I stopped. I was so confused I didn't know which way to go. Do you know why? Sometimes the direction it shows you to go is not exactly the direction a certain city or place you want to go lies. Sometimes you think, if I want to go west I better get on a highway that shows west, rather than take the clover leaf that goes in the opposite direction. But yet if you take that cloverleaf you find out you wind up in the right direction and you find out that the other one goes wrong.

"Sometimes you have to listen to instructions and take your mind captive and it works out quite well. Sometimes it takes years to see how that cloverleaf led in the right direction. But you are glad if you are obedient. Sometimes it takes years to find out that we would have been better off following those directions because our own mind led us in the wrong way.

"'My Father never leaves me alone.' Why? 'Because I always do the things that please Him.' This is the basis of fellowship, the basis of constant wonder, the basis of growth, the basis of a deeper appreciation of the glorious plan of salvation, the basis of a growing anticipation of meeting Him someday. Life does not come to a halt or ebb into uselessness, but rather works into a climax or a culmination of a life's endeavor. Fellowship with the Father through Christ Jesus is available here, now, on the basis of obediently following the guide, His will, enjoying that fellowship through all eternity."

CHAPTER 31

The rest of that special weekend was filled with similar activities. There were songs, meals, special numbers, sermons, and campfires in the evenings. The last activity was a picnic on Monday morning before everyone left for home. Many fond farewells were said, as no one wanted the weekend to end.

The excitement of traveling with friends took some of the sting out of the long grind on Route 80 through Pennsylvania. Even with the lively conversation, however, a numbing sense of tedium set in by the time they reached the Delaware Water Gap.

On the ride into the city Rudy knew he would be dropped off first. He no longer had to pretend that he lived on the Upper West Side. He could be dropped off in front of his apartment building. He was glad that he could be himself now.

"Well, I've got a lot of restitutions to do," Rudy said as they were pulling up to his apartment building. "Pray for me. I'm going to try to get them over with quickly. I hate to have things like this hanging over my head."

"We will," Neal assured. "Keep in touch. Let me know if there's anything I can do for you. Oh, by the way, what's your phone number?"

Rudy wrote down his private number, making a mental note to change the recording before Neal called him—another reminder of how much he had changed. He found it amazing that such a dramatic change was possible.

As Rudy got out he said, "Thanks a lot, Neal, for everything you've done for me. You'll never know how much you've changed my life."

"Glad to do it," Neal said, his voice choked with emotion and gratitude also. Words seemed so inadequate.

Rudy walked into the building with the strange sensation that it was all new. He had the illusion that he was walking into the building for the first time, yet he knew all about the place. It was the same security people, the same elevator, the same decorations. The only thing different was Rudy.

When Rudy got to the floor of their front door he found it wide open. The apartment was filled with the guests of a party his parents were having. There was lively music and it looked like a young crowd. Some of the guests wondered who he was, not knowing much about the Peterfield family. His mother, with a nervous eye on the front door to be sure to welcome anyone who came in, was surprised to see him.

"Rudy, my love, where have you been?" she asked.

"I've been to Ohio," Rudy said in a proud voice like one would say they have been to the mountain. "I have to tell you what wonderful things have happened to me there."

"Yes, dear, but not now. You're welcome to change and join us if you like," she volunteered

"No thanks. I don't want to get out of this mood," Rudy said.

"Well, maybe I'll come up later, dear. I must see to my guests right now. You understand."

Rudy went to his room and unpacked. Finding his Bible he realized that he had some restitutions to do. He wondered if he should call Renee to get them started. This reminded him to change the message on his answering machine.

After changing the message he started to dial Renee's number, but hung up telling himself that this would not be a good time. Then he recognized that this was a trap to keep him from following through on these restitutions. He was told that this would happen. So he picked up the phone and dialed again. He hung up again wondering what he would do if Renee's parents answered the phone. He realized that this, too, was ridiculous and paused for a while.

He laid silently on his bed for a while, wondering what to do. He rehearsed what he would say in his mind before dialing the phone. He told himself that he should have it all worked out ahead of time. He couldn't think clearly, though, and this plan didn't seem to work either. He sensed that he was getting nervous about this and couldn't believe how difficult it was. He knew what he wanted to do but was finding it difficult to simply do it.

Finally, with hands that were literally shaking, he picked up the phone and dialed Renee's number. Even now he told himself to hang up again; but he held onto the phone while it rang three times. Then, a click, and Renee's answering machine told him she was not home. Rudy burst into laughter at the agony and the irony of worry-ing about what to say to Renee when, all that time, she was not even home. He hung up without leaving a message.

Then he realized that he should have left a message. He mar-veled at how stupid he could act when under this emotional turmoil. So he dialed Renee's number again and waited to leave a message. This time Renee answered, "Rudy, where've you been all my life?"

This development sent a new shock wave through Rudy as he tried to collect his thoughts and answer her question. "How'd you know it was me calling?" Rudy asked.

"Cause I heard you laughing when you called just a minute ago. When it rang again so quickly I guessed that you had forgotten to leave a message and were calling again. I was gonna pick it up the first time but you hung up too fast," Renee explained.

"Oh, I see," Rudy stammered. "How're you doing?" he asked. His tone of voice was tentative and shaky.

"You all right?" Renee asked. "You sound sort of strung out."

"Oh, I don't know. Listen, I've got to talk to you. Let's meet at F.A.O Schwartz and we'll take a walk." Rudy picked this place because it was about halfway between their apartments. It was a regu-lar meeting place for them.

"Sure. What's up?" Renee asked.

"Nothing serious," Rudy said. He didn't want to worry Renee. He believed it was serious, personally. It concerned the most impor-tant decision he ever made in his life, but he didn't want Renee think-ing about that ahead of time. "Don't worry about it. It's no major deal. I just want to talk to you about some things I've been thinking about lately."

"Sure. I'll see you there in thirty minutes, that OK?" Renee asked.

"No. I won't be ready that fast. Let's make it an hour."

"Fine. See you in an hour at F.A.O. Schwartz."

Rudy took a shower and put on fresh clothes. He was feeling better, but the anxiety of confessing his decision to follow Jesus Christ to Renee was causing him tremendous discomfort and nervousness. He was surprised at how difficult this was. It had seemed like he could share anything bad with Renee all his life. He and Renee were always getting into trouble and they felt comfortable through it all. Now, he couldn't help feeling concerned about the news he was planning on sharing with Renee. He imagined all kinds of terrible reactions in Renee. He wondered if she would become angry, or would she ridicule him. He wondered if Renee would try to talk him out of it.

Rudy found his hands shaking as he got dressed. He marveled at this experience. Was this the hold of Satan on him, he wondered? Were these Satan's ways of trying to get him not to tell Renee? This nervousness was real. He realized that this was the tangible battle between good and evil in his life. This shaking was the struggle between the fledgling little spiritual side of his life trying to gain control over his whole life, a life that had been given to pleasures and selfishness.

Rudy remembered what he was told about the Holy Spirit giving him the power to do things that seemed impossible. Speaking to Renee about this subject seemed impossible to him. He realized that he was only responsible for the choice itself, and not the power to follow up on the choice. He wanted to tell this news to Renee and make this his first restitution but he couldn't understand how he was going to get the job done. He had no idea how difficult the process would be. He was never this nervous about talking to anybody before.

Rudy went downstairs the back way and into the kitchen. Paulette greeted him with a curiosity about his weekend. She made him a plate to eat while he told her about going to Ohio. He left out all mention of the church. He wanted to talk to Renee first about that. This diversion with Paulette did nothing to take away his nervousness. She noticed that he picked at his food and was nervous but she didn't mention it.

There was a tense silence between them where there was usually bantering and playfulness. They both noticed it but didn't know what to do about it, so they ignored it. Paulette acted like she was busy. Rudy left his tray of food largely untouched and headed for the front door. He hoped that he wouldn't have to stop and talk with anybody and he didn't.

Rudy got to the toy store in a few minutes. Renee was standing in the courtyard in front watching the people walk by.

"Hey, Rudy, over here," Renee said. "Have you had anything to eat? Maybe we can get something."

"OK I grabbed a bite on the way out, but I could have a soda."

They walked to a chain restaurant that served burgers and brews and found a table. Rudy asked for one in a quiet corner. This was not hard to find. It was early for dinner.

"OK so where've you been?" Renee asked. "What's up?"

Renee noticed that Rudy was more nervous than she had ever seen him. He was rolling up and folding his napkin, drinking all the water, and playing nervously with the flatware. This caused Renee a little panic. She feared that Rudy was going to say something upsetting. She was beginning to have regrets that she agreed to meet at this hour. She was wishing it would not have happened. She was creating a storm in her own mind about what Rudy wanted to talk about.

"Well, Renee, I don't know just how to say this to you so I'm just going to blurt it out. I've been to Ohio this weekend. I went there with some people that I met recently from a church in Connecticut. I've been impressed with their lives. I've found out that the reason is because they believe in Jesus Christ, and I've decided to become a Christian myself."

Rudy took a big shaking breath and made a big sigh of relief after he got that out. Renee looked stunned. She hadn't seen Rudy for some time and had no warning that he was even thinking about this. She was a little confused.

"I thought you were a Christian," Renee reasoned. "Weren't you baptized? I thought your grandmother made sure of that."

"Yes, I was baptized, and yes, my grandmother did make sure of that. I just can't really tell you the last time I was in a church before meeting these people. Listen, you've got to meet these people. I've never meet people like this before. That's it. Why don't you come with me the next time I go over there, and you can meet these people I'm talking about. You've never seen anything like it. These people are so sincere, so open and truthful, and so loving."

"Well, I don't know. That might work out," Renee said, still not believing she was hearing right. She wondered what had happened to Rudy. "Did you get mixed up with some religious fanatics?" Renee pictured Rudy being brainwashed for an entire weekend.

"No, you didn't hear me. I said these are wonderful people. They really practice what they believe. There's no hypocrisy among these people. They're true believers in God's Word."

"Well, what does that mean?" Renee tried to understand. "Are you going to go join some monastery somewhere now?"

"No. I'm just going to have to start living by the Bible and the leading of the Holy Spirit. I'm going to have to make my life all over again. I have to apologize for all that I've done wrong, pay back all that I've taken, and live a good life."

"You've always been good," Renee said. "You're one of the nicest people I know. You've never taken anything. You've never lied. What have you done that's so wrong?" Renee was sincere. She always thought Rudy was a great guy. She always thought she was lucky to have him for a friend. She always felt unworthy, like she was undeserving. There was always a little fear in the back of her mind that her luck would run out and Rudy would stop being her friend. Now, she was feeling a little panic like this was what was happening; but she always thought it would be for another girl, not a church.

"Well, I've lied and stolen things. And, I now believe that having sex outside of marriage is wrong. I'd like to apologize to you for that, and ask your forgiveness. I value your friendship highly, and want to continue as friends. Please try to understand me. I'm not dumping you as a friend."

Renee was confused and shocked. She heard Rudy apologize to her for having sex with her, but she didn't feel hurt by the sex. She was being hurt now by this news; but this was not what Rudy was apologizing for. In fact, Rudy was inviting her to think the same way. Renee felt confused that Rudy was pulling away from her on an intimate personal level, yet assuring her that he wanted to be her friend. Renee felt that Rudy expected her to be friendlier, yet she felt she was being pushed away by him. In this confusion, Renee remained silent.

Rudy was relieved that Renee was not visibly angry or violent. The silence, however, was awkward for both of them.

"Look, Renee, I don't expect you to understand this all at once. I hope you'll give me some time. I hope you'll come with me and visit this church. I think you'll understand this better when you get a chance to meet these people."

"I hope so," Renee said.

"Thanks for being such a good listener," Rudy said with great sincerity. "You'll never know how much this means to me that you're as accepting of this news as you are."

Renee couldn't say a word. She was getting more and more upset as she sat there. Then when she heard Rudy compliment her on being so accepting of the news, the contrast between Rudy's compliment and what she was feeling in her heart almost caused her to break out in tears. She got up fairly quickly and did manage to say, "Hey, I've got to get back home, it's a family thing. Call me. I'd like to visit this church." She just got the last few words out and walked quickly out of the restaurant. When she was out of sight of the restaurant she broke down in tears. She pulled out a handkerchief and sobbed loudly into it as she walked back to her parent's apartment.

Rudy was oddly grateful to be left alone. He had a feeling of joy that he had accomplished this, his first restitution. He had a feeling of success, of victory over Satan and the temptation to put it off, or never do it. He enjoyed that feeling. He felt warmed by that feeling. He did not want it to end quickly. He ate what he ordered with pleasure, when it came. He took his time. He walked slowly back to his parents' apartment feeling like he heard the sounds, smelled the smells, and noticed the trees, birds, clouds, and flowers for the first time in his life.

CHAPTER 32

For the next few days Rudy made restitutions. He went to stores where he had stolen small items, offering to pay for them. He decided that he needed to tell his story briefly to each person he spoke to. He understood this to be part of the purpose, to witness to others of the wonderful work of Jesus Christ in his life. He heard many dramatic stories about this.

One story was about a young man who used to go to a restaurant with a friend and kill time. They would mix salt in the pepper shakers, give waitresses a hard time, and skip out on the check. During his conversion the Holy Spirit convicted him to go back and pay for what he had stolen.

When the manager heard the story he told the young man to wait there while he walked into an office. He wondered if the manager was going to call the police, or make him fill out a long report. Instead, the manager came back with a handwritten letter. In the letter, this guy's best friend, who had walked out on the meal with him and had since moved to the Washington, DC area, had written that same restaurant confessing the same crime. The manager was in tears. He told the young man that he had never heard of people making restitutions before that letter, and now he was seeing it twice within the same month.

There was another memorable case in Ohio where a young man actually broke into a home and robbed a house at night, using a gun. Years later he was convicted of the Holy Spirit to convert. He had never been caught for this crime; in fact, the local police closed the case, considering it unsolved. He realized, however, that he would never fulfill the scriptural requirement of having peace with man and God until he confessed this crime to the police.

He didn't know what to expect, but one day he went into the police station and told the clerk that he would like to confess to a crime. He explained that he was converting to a Christian life and the Spirit of God compelled him to confess this crime. Because of the seriousness of the crime, a criminal trial had to be held. During that trial he was able to give a testimony of how Christ had come into his life and required of him to make this confession. The trial didn't take long, of course, for a confession, and the only real decision was the sentencing.

This occurred in a small town and the judge knew many of the people from that church. Some prominent members of the community who went to that church contacted the judge urging him to be lenient due to the circumstances. The judge could plainly see that this was an unusual situation and indicated that he had some latitude about the sentencing. Some thought he might get only thirty days in jail. On the day of the sentencing the court room was jammed with concerned people from the local church.

They all listened carefully as the judge made the following explanation. "There are three major reasons for sentencing people for crimes. One is for rehabilitation, one for punishment, and one for a public example to warn others of the consequences of crime. It is clear that the first reason is not necessary in this case. This young man has gone through a personal rehabilitation that has even brought this case to conclusion through his own confession. However, the second two reasons require me to sentence this man to sixty days in jail."

There was some shock through the audience. There it was. Final. There was a hesitation as if people believed that if they waited longer something more could be done, things could be fixed even better. Gradually, however, the finality of the decision encroached upon their awareness like sunlight spreading at dawn. Nothing remained to be done. They rose, and filed out stunned. The sixty days came and went. The young man found them to be difficult; but his life went on, and he had done his duty as required of him by God and the law of the land. The story has proven helpful to others in the churches. There have been testimonies of young people who said that even before they converted they didn't get into the bigger sins because they always knew that some day they would have to confess them and make restitutions for them.

Rudy's restitutions were not that dramatic. They were occasionally embarrassing. Some store owners asked him to pay for things, most did not. His restitutions to friends and former lovers were more difficult. He couldn't explain his motives without appearing to say that he condemned them for continuing to do the things he was apologizing for. He did not, in fact, condemn them. He was only practicing what he believed and what had been recommended to him by people he trusted, admired, and wanted to follow. He tried to explain that, but many people misunderstood him and ended up feeling offended.

Rudy spoke about this to the local elder, Theo Venzel. He asked Venzel how this could be helping, since he seemed to be losing all his friends that he spoke to. Mr. Venzel showed him I Corinthians 1.18 - 25: "For the preaching of the cross is to them that perish foolishness; but unto us which are saved it is the power of God. For it is written, I will destroy the wisdom of the wise, and will bring to nothing the understanding of the prudent. Where is the wise? Where is the scribe? Where is the disputer of this world? Hath not God made foolish the wisdom of this world? For after that in the wisdom of God the world by wisdom knew not God, it pleased God by the foolishness of preaching to save them that believe. For the Jews require a sign, and the Greeks seek after wisdom: But we preach Christ crucified, unto the Jews a stumbling block, and unto the Greeks foolishness; But unto them which are called, both Jews and Greeks, Christ the power of God, and the wisdom of God. Because the foolishness of God is wiser than men; and the weakness of God is stronger than men."

Venzel informed Rudy that Christ did not come into this world to make peace but rather strife. He said, "This world is Satan's. He is the ruler of the air. Those that want to separate from this influence, this grip, must tear themselves from this world, and this tearing will sometimes be offensive to some."

He also quoted Romans 9.33: "As it is written, Behold, I lay in Sion a stumblingstone and rock of offence: and whosoever believeth on him shall not be ashamed." He also advised Rudy to read Matthew 10.34 - 39 where Jesus said, "Think not that I am come to send peace on earth: I came not to send peace, but a sword. For I am come to set a man at variance against his father, and the daughter against her mother, and the daughter-in-law against her mother-in-law. And a man's foes shall be they of his own household. He that loveth father or mother more than me is not worthy of me: and he that loveth son or daughter more than me is not worthy of me. And he that taketh not his cross, and followeth after me, is not worthy of me. He that findeth his life shall lose it: and he that loseth his life for my sake shall find it."

Venzel acknowledged, "These are hard words, but you may not permanently lose your friends. Your friends will remember your honesty, your reliability, and your integrity. When they really need a friend, you'll be one of the first they'll think of."

"I see that," Rudy admitted.

"Have you made restitutions to your parents?" Venzel inquired.

"Not yet. It's odd. I'm a little afraid of my mother's reaction. My father will probably forget whatever I tell him seconds after I mention it, if he hears it at all, but my mother might be somewhat hurt by these things. I have a feeling that this might be a problem."

"I usually advise people to speak to their parents very early," Venzel advised, "but your situation might be different."

"I have to tell you those words about setting a man at variance with his parents are not too reassuring," Rudy confessed.

"Well, I wouldn't wait too long," Venzel advised.

Venzel had seen this before. Sometimes major hurdles like this spring up and derail a new convert's plans and efforts. Venzel had seen some give up rather than overcome this fear. He saw this concern grow in Rudy and he put as much pressure as he felt he could on Rudy to take care of it soon.

Venzel had received a letter from George Bender, the elder in Ohio to whom Rudy made his confession. The letter merely confirmed that Rudy had taken this step and did not relate any of the content of the confession which, of course, is kept confidential.

Rudy noticed that with each restitution he experienced a greater sense of freedom or peace. Just like the feeling of relief and joy he had after first talking about this with Renee, he got the same boost after making each restitution. He recognized powerful feelings going on inside himself as he went through these actions. There was usually some hesitancy, some nervousness, sweaty palms, dry mouth, and making of excuses to put off doing it. He often was tense and spoke with a breathless, shaking nervousness. Afterwards he was joyful, thrilled, exuberant with a feeling of victory. Both of these feelings were powerful. They were more powerful than feelings or emotions he usually had in his life.

This, too, he discussed with Venzel. He described these feelings in one of their meetings, which did not follow any particular schedule. There was not, for example, a six-week catechism that was prescribed by the church. It was more on an as-needed basis.

He described these powerful feelings he was having as he

went about these restitutions. Venzel told him, "This is normal. Your life is the battle ground between the forces of good and evil."

He quoted Ephesians 6.12: "For we wrestle not against flesh and blood, but against principalities, against powers, against the rulers of the darkness of this world, against spiritual wickedness in high places."

Venzel went on to say, "You must fight for your conversion and the gift of peace as if your life depends upon it. You should consider it a warfare."

He quoted I Timothy 6.12: "Fight the good fight of faith, lay hold on eternal life, whereunto thou art called, and hast professed a good profession before many witnesses."

Rudy was amazed. He never believed in ghosts. He was not a superstitious person. He always relied on his intellect to understand things—to see the rational connectedness between things. Here he was getting his introduction to the spiritual world. Here were things that were not rational. Here he had to learn to suspend his rational judgment, much like the Apostle Paul had to learn to do, described so graphically in II Corinthians 12.5: "Casting down imaginations, and every high thing that exalteth itself against the knowledge of God, and bringing into captivity every thought to the obedience of Christ;"

As Rudy struggled to learn these things, he was quick to talk about his experiences with the people at church. He found that everyone had many similar experiences and had thought about them seriously as well. Most people had useful, favorite verses that they would share with him. He found it amazing how rich with depth of meaning the scriptures were. He had read them through first on Martha's Vineyard, and had read much again over the last few weeks. As he was shown various verses that were favorites of his friends, he discovered that verses he had read over rather quickly could, upon closer examination, be rich in meaning. They were like tiny green plant buds. They could be easily ignored initially but, given time, developed rapidly into ornate, intricate, creations of shimmering beauty.

Rudy was amazed at how these ordinary-looking people who went to this church, with ordinary jobs, cars, and houses, possessed such an incredible knowledge of deep spiritual matters. This was not a function of traditional intelligence like verbal memory, vocabulary, or overall fund of information. This was a discreet, thin, wedge-shaped section of the pie that made up overall intelligence. He mentioned this to Neal.

"I don't think these people realize how unique and special their knowledge is. They seem to have a much better grasp of what life is all about."

"I'm sure you're right," Neal agreed. "They have a valuable knowledge, and they don't appreciate it. It's like the restitutions you're now doing. They're good for so many people on so many different levels. They're a testimony of God's power to those you talk to; but, at the same time, they're taking you through valuable experiences. Experiences, not just lessons. You learn best by doing, and doing restitutions gets you started on the right foot in making important experiences about the power and help of God in your life. They tend to humble you as you discover that it's only the power of God that can do these miracles in your life. This gives you the early training in humility that you need, and sets you up with the right expectation of dependence upon God that you'll need all your life."

"It seems like everything is so well thought out. How'd your church learn how to do all this?"

"It's all in the Bible. We didn't think up anything. Oh, I could tell you that our founding father was an ordained minister in the state church of Switzerland. I could tell you that he was well educated in theology. But the fact of the matter is his training didn't emphasize these issues of the Bible. He started reading the Bible open-mindedly as a result of a promise he made on his death bed. He promised that if he'd be healed, he'd study God's Word, and try to obey it entirely. He didn't know then what he was promising. His studies caused him to believe things and preach things that quickly got him kicked out of the state church. He was forced to form a new church. This new church, and his preaching, were so exciting for the people to hear that it grew rapidly. It was like another reformation in his time and it's survived till today, even though the state church did all they could to stop it."

"But why don't all churches emphasize these things if they're in the Bible?" Rudy asked.

"The Bible is a highly subjective book, open to many inter-pretations. People decide they don't want to believe this anymore, or they want to emphasize something more than they have in the past. That's why there are so many denominations."

"I don't see why people don't want to obey these things, they seem so powerful."

"You will. Wait till some of these observations cause you some inconvenience. Wait till the tests come. Then you'll see why people decide to give up on some."

Rudy found that once he got started, his restitutions went fairly easily. He was poised and confident by nature. He was not easily embarrassed. If he believed in something he had little trouble living up to it. This helped him greatly in discussing his religious beliefs with his friends. He quickly went through the list of restitutions that he could think of. Soon the only ones remaining were his own family. In this respect his experience was just the opposite of young people brought up in the church. The usual practice was to talk to one's parents first.

With each restitution Rudy felt better. It was great clearing his conscience and living an honest, open life. When all his restitutions were done, he reached a plateau. Previous gains were fading somewhat. The fact that he had to talk to his parents loomed larger and larger in his mind. He noticed how easily he could ignore or put off talking to his parents while there were other restitutions to do. Now, however, this unfinished business seemed to scream in his head all the time. This had to be done, and had to be done soon.

CHAPTER 33

"Mom, Dad, I want to talk to you about something serious," Rudy said with a shaky voice. He was more nervous than usual because he had to wait more than a week to talk to them together. Finally, one night, they were all together at dinner.

"Of course, dear," Rudy's mom said. "What is it?" She, too was anxious. No son in history started a conversation this way without making his parents nervous.

"I, I, don't know if you've noticed anything different about me lately. . ."

"Notice anything?" Peterfield injected. "My dear boy, how could we? We seem to see little of you. But, then, I guess we're all busy."

"Yes. I've been busy, too. You know what I've been doing?"

"No, frankly, we don't," his father said.

"I've been going around to everyone I've ever known and apologizing to them for what I've done wrong to them."

Rudy thought this would impress them but they both nearly dropped their dessert spoons. They were in shocked horror at the thought of their handsome, bright, and socially confident son groveling in public. He could do few things to embarrass them more, they thought.

"And do you know why I'm doing this?" Rudy's tone of voice was optimistic because he thought he had taken a clever tack in breaking the news to them in this way.

"Oh, no, don't tell me you've joined a cult," Peterfield burst out. He no sooner said it then he searched his mind for places where he could send Rudy to deprogram him.

Stunned by his father's emotional reaction, Rudy said, "No, No! It isn't a cult. It's a Christian church. I'm doing restitutions as part of a true conversion."

Rudy's mom sank back into the cushion of her chair. If she had planned on saying anything she believed her chance gone now that her husband had reacted so emotionally. She sat there in the dull shock of one who has been engaged in the same, repetitive, pointless argument regularly for years. The possibility of hearing something exciting from Rudy cheered her for one brief moment; but reality came crushing down on her shoulders.

"What do you mean restitutions?" Peterfield asked. He asked it with the mean, metallic, clinical sound of a hammer hitting an anvil.

"Well, do you know the story of Zachaeus in the Bible?" Rudy asked, all hope of this being cheerful completely destroyed.

"No. I can't say I do."

"Well, there've been children's songs written about it . . ."

"I listen to surprisingly few children's songs," his father interrupted with growing contempt.

Rudy was shocked at the hostility his father was displaying. He was distracted by it. He would have expected his father to care the least; yet, he was almost coming out of his chair.

"Well," he started to explain but his father's behavior got to be too much to ignore. "Wow, I can't believe you're reacting like this."

"Stop right there," Peterfield ordered. "I'm not going to listen to this." He got up to walk out.

"I'd like a chance to explain myself . . . "

"Later."

"Please don't do this to me." Rudy pleaded. "At least let me say I'm sorry for all the hurt I've caused you in my life. I know I've been a monster at times. Sometimes I've tried to make you mad, and I'm sorry." There was real panic in Rudy's voice. He wanted to say these things, and had hoped that they would bring him the final peace he was looking for, but it seemed like it was all going wrong. This was not the way he had planned it. He never dreamed that his father would react this way.

"Don't do this to you?" Peterfield asked with the most arrogant emphasis on the last word. "What do you think you're doing?"

Rudy couldn't answer. His mouth hung open. His head was leaning forward, and he was speechless as he watched his father march out of the room. The only familiar signal that his father had given was slamming the door so hard that a painting bounced and tilted on the wall.

There was a moment of silence as Rudy and his mother sat in the big dining room alone. Then, suddenly, the silence was broken by his mother's laughter. First she laughed a little, then a little more, then for a short time she just shrieked with laughter. Then, quickly it reduced to giggling again. The irony of what was going on between her husband and son was too much for her. She was aware of how cold and unemotional her husband was toward any misbehavior Rudy had ever done. And now, when Rudy was trying to apologize for whatever reason, he couldn't handle it, and actually left the room. Her husband, Dr. Peterfield, master of decorum and the cool exterior, had to leave the dining room before Rudy was finished. He just got up and walked out.

"Mom." Rudy whispered. "I'm sorry." He hesitated for a long time listening to her giggle. "I'm sorry for all the hurt I've caused you."

She turned to him with tears running down her cheeks and Rudy was stunned by the double illusion of giggling and tears.

"Mom, don't," he begged. "Please don't be upset. I've never been so sure of what I'm doing with my life. I want you and dad to be happy for me."

"Rudy," his mother finally said. "You've never hurt me. You're the most beautiful child a mother could have. You've nothing to apologize to me for." Rudy went over to his mother's chair and she stood up and they hugged. She sobbed on his shoulder and they just stood there hugging.

Finally, she grabbed her napkin and wiped her eyes. "Well, I don't feel like eating any more of this either, do you?"

"No," Rudy agreed. "Thanks for saying that to me, Mom. I've never been a good enough son to you. I'm not sure I even know how."

Rudy's mother allowed Rudy to have the final word as she walked through the door he was holding open. She went to her office area, pulled out her journal, and added the evening's events to her book.

Rudy went to his room in a numbed confusion. How different the evening's events went from what he had planned. He was overjoyed with his mother's reaction. He was dumbfounded at his father's.

Why would his father react in such a strong way, he asked himself. It had the appearance of being almost satanic. Was his father possessed with an evil spirit? He knew that those who were not regenerated through conversion in Jesus Christ were enslaved to sin. Tonight he saw where his father, who was normally so self-disciplined, out of control. His father did not know how to handle the situation. Rudy could not get over how totally out of character his father had reacted.

Rudy received some peace of mind after talking with his parents. He went to his room and thanked God for the chance to talk to them, and for his mother's wonderful reaction. Rudy was glad that he was able to apologize to his father before he left the room. He was glad that he just burst out with it no matter what his father's reaction was. Now he could rest knowing that he had apologized to everyone who came to his mind that he might have ever wronged.

He had a sense of completion about his restitutions, and some sense of peace, but he could not say that he was overwhelmed with the kind of peace he had heard other people talk about. In other people's testimonies they would talk about a feeling of freedom, rest, total peace that was so overwhelming that there was no mistaking that it was a gift from God. So while Rudy had a wonderful sense of accomplishment for having finished his restitutions, he did not yet possess such a peace.

His father was on his mind. He didn't see his father for several days afterward and even then they didn't take the time to talk. His father acted like nothing happened. It was as if his father believed that Rudy would soon forget this interest like he had so many other interests in his young life. His father treated Rudy no differently for having made this experience with him. He didn't act embarrassed. He didn't feel the need to instruct him. He basically ignored him like he always did.

Rudy went on with his life, even though his interests and activities were different from what they used to be. He was aware that in New York City it was rare to get a feeling of being close to God. Little of what you viewed in everyday life could be directly attributed to God. Most of the view was man-made.

From the black pavement abutted by curbs, sidewalks, cold iron fire hydrants, parking meters, metal sign posts, street lighting posts, the walls, entrances, doors, railings, and glass of the various buildings—all were man-made. One could look up the sides of buildings to a great height and see only cement, marble, brick, stone, glass, and metal. All was gradually becoming gritty with the dirt of the city. All was surrendering its newness and shine to the relentless march of man and his inevitable decay.

Even the trees along the sidewalks, which are traditionally attributed to God, were not thriving. The stubby little trees struggled for life in that stunting atmosphere. They stood there in a silent crisis of ecology until they finally gave up their botanical spirit and died. Then someone came along and replaced them with other trees budding with new hope, innocent of the tragic prognosis ahead of them.

Rudy never had these thoughts before. He lived in the city all his life and had never been aware of the absence of thriving natural things to see which might draw one's mind to God. There was Central Park, of course, but even there was such a press of people during the day that it had a worn, unnaturalness to it—unlike that lake in Connecticut.

One had to look up, almost straight up, to see the sky to even be aware that man needed anything made by God. In fact man seemed to be annoyed by things made of God. Cockroaches, pigeons, rats, rain showers, these were the things not made by man and from which man was struggling to rid himself.

Rudy found himself searching out places where he could contemplate the creation of God. He went to the Museum of Natural History. He had been there many times before. He never looked at the displays like he did now. He was enthralled at the variety and intricacy of God's creation. He wondered why he had never appreciated this before and at how completely his opinion of these things had changed.

Rudy also liked to take the Staten Island Ferry just to be on the water, and to look out across the Harbor. He would take the ferry over to the Statue of Liberty. He didn't go in the statue, he sat on the patio outside the snack bar and fed the gulls and watched them as they searched for food.

The other thing that New York City had an abundance of that was made by God was mankind itself. Rudy found himself noticing people more. He was amazed at the variety here as well. Where he used to think of people as obstacles in his way he now saw them as part of God's creation. He used to be impatient with them, and now he found himself interested in them. He was curious about each of their life stories. This curiosity about God and His creation occupied Rudy's thoughts over the next few days.

CHAPTER 34

While Rudy was making these new experiences of getting to know God's creation he was attending the regular services of the church in Connecticut. Every time he thought he understood the whole of Christianity, someone would casually mention another aspect which would open up a whole new level of experience. He mentioned it to someone who agreed and described it as a precious diamond that has many facets which catch the light and shimmer as you turn it and look at it.

One example was when Rudy heard a minister preach on Mark 12.41-44: "And Jesus sat over against the treasury, and beheld how the people cast money into the treasury: and many that were rich cast in much. And there came a certain poor widow, and she threw in two mites, which make a farthing. And he called unto him his disciples, and saith unto them, Verily I say unto you, That this poor widow hath cast more in, than all they which have cast into the treasury: For all they did cast in of their abundance; but she of her want did cast in all that she had, even all her living."

The minister invited the audience, "Go to this synagogue in your imagination and watch, with Jesus, what is going on. She must have been ashamed of the little that she had to offer. She probably waited till the end of the line so that she would not be near a rich person to avoid comparison. She probably tossed her two mites into the treasury quickly so as to be as inconspicuous as possible; quite different from those who made a big show of their giving.

"Yet her giving caught the attention of the Master and this is still true today. This kind of giving continues to catch the Master's eye. This giving does not only apply to the giving of money. The last phrase of these verses mentioned that she gave all her living. Clearly the word `living' usually applies to the sum of money a person earns in a given period, but it is probably no accident that this particular word was used here. In the New Testament we are asked to give our living, our whole life, our motivations, goals, aspirations, our all is to be given unconditionally to Christ. Unless we surrender control of all of our life in this way we are not worthy of Him.

"This giving does not stop at conversion. We are saved by the grace of Christ Jesus to do that kind of giving all our lives. That giving should be as private as possible. There is a little known section of Christ's Sermon on the Mount that exhorts people to do their giving in private. Found in Matthew 6.2-4, it reads, 'Therefore when thou doest thine alms, do not sound a trumpet before thee, as the hypocrites do in the synagogues and in the streets, that they may have glory of men. Verily I say unto you, They have their reward. But when thou doest alms, let not thy left hand know what thy right hand doeth: That thine alms may be in secret: and thy Father which seeth in secret himself shall reward thee openly.'"

The minister asked, "Do we really believe this? If we did there wouldn't be a secret job to be found. People would be running around aggressively doing them because the Lord promised to reward them openly if they did. Since we don't see people scrambling around doing this, we can conclude that people lack the faith in this passage, and in The Father.

"In fact we have quite the opposite problem in the world. People are unwilling to do the grunt work. They want to be the leaders. They want to have the so-called 'glory jobs' or they won't be involved. Many churches find it necessary to put plaques on everything notifying people of who gave what. How shocked those people are going to be when they learn that they mortgaged their eternal rewards in Heaven for that cheap bronze plaque that tarnishes and falls off in time.

"What a suitably divine consequence that God made the conditions clear in a humble sermon, and people simply ignored it. God didn't force them to obey, neither did He keep His instructions hidden from them. No one getting to Heaven and receiving no rewards will be able to argue with the judgment of God. No one will be able to claim that that lesson was not clearly spoken in understandable language in the Sermon on the Mount by none other than the Son of God, Himself."

The minister went on to say, "The Sermon on the Mount was revolutionary because people had become selfish about their giving. If they were going to give at all, they wanted recognition for it. Sometimes they sounded trumpets before giving. Things are not all that changed today. There is little faith that giving in this secret way will be worthwhile."

Rudy thought about these things for the first time. His father never talked about giving. When his father did give it was for political influence. Rudy was not as political as his father and so was not interested in this kind of giving. He had never considered that there might be other reasons for giving. Even though he thought about these ideas, there was no immediate change in his behavior.

One day, quite unexpectedly, this changed. Rudy was sitting alone in a booth in a small grill on the lower east side. It was the kind of place that Neal liked to go to. Not much to look at, but good food.

Just when all the booths and tables were filled, an old, thin, wrinkled man in wrinkled clothes and a three-day beard walked in. Seeing no empty tables or booths, he walked over and sat down, without asking, across from Rudy.

"Kinda crowded today, ain't it?" the man asked Rudy as if they were long lost friends and this was the most natural thing in the world. Rudy's mind raced through all the options open to him. He thought of insulting the man and making him leave. He thought of leaving himself. He wondered if someone else would leave shortly and the man would move away. Rudy's initial reaction was disgust. He didn't like the looks of the man. He saw no hope of finding the man's conversation interesting. He was annoyed that the man would intrude on his privacy in this way without asking.

"Yes it is," Rudy answered in a sheepish, friendly tone of voice. In spite of all the aggressive plans he considered, he decided to simply wait and see what was going to happen. Rudy already ordered and was waiting for his lunch to come. The waitress took the old man's order which was a simple stew dish with water to drink. Rudy noticed that the choice was one of the cheapest options, and concluded that the man was poor.

"Whatcha do?" the man asked.

"I'm on summer vacation," Rudy answered. "I'm going to school."

"What school you going to?"

"Well, Harvard." Rudy was a little self-conscious about this answer. This did not seem like a place that would appreciate academic excellence.

"Oh, you're one of them brain types," he said.

"Yeah, I guess so," Rudy agreed. "What do you do?"

"I'm retired from the railroad," the man said. "Worked fifty years on the railroad." The waitress brought their meals. Rudy's fish sandwich, salad, and iced tea looked regal compared to the man's stew. He ate with poor table manners. He mopped his bread through the thick soup and chewed with his mouth open. He also talked with food in his mouth.

"Railroads ain't what they used to be. No siree," he volunteered. "They ain't taking care a the tracks. Don't surprise me there's so many crashes. They're just taking all the money out of it and lettin her go down hill."

"Ugh," Rudy grunted. He was willing to listen to this man but he had little to say and he was a little concerned that the man was going to spit in his food while he talked. Rudy found himself pulling his plate further and further toward himself. He moved his iced tea over to the wall.

He felt revulsion for this strange man. At the same time, he was mad at himself for making such hasty judgments from appearances alone. He felt like a snob. Rudy thought of some at church who would be friendly to this man. They would think of lots of interesting questions for him making him think he was valued by them. For Rudy it was doing well just to sit there and listen to him and not walk away. Rudy wasted no time finishing his lunch. He left a reasonable tip and got up and walked toward the cash register to find the waitress with his bill. He said a brief goodbye to the man.

On his way to the cash register a thought occurred to him. He decided to ask the waitress for the man's bill as well. He paid the man's check without telling him. As he carried this out it really thrilled him. He told the waitress to take him a piece of pie after he left as well. He became excited about this simple form of giving. The waitress was cooperative and shared in the excitement somewhat. Rudy left the diner without saying any more to the man in the booth. He never saw the man's reaction to the news. For all he knew the waitress gave the old man a bill anyway and kept the money; however, the idea was probably unusual enough that she told the old man. She would probably be curious about his reaction too.

This event took place several weeks after Rudy heard the sermon about secret giving. The idea of paying for this man's meal came from the Holy Spirit only after Rudy's heart was prepared for this lesson over the intervening weeks. The bill was less than ten dollars; but it represented a much bigger event in Rudy's life. He was genuinely surprised by the excitement and joy he received by this giving. This was unique. All his life other people were doing things for him. Mostly out of a grudging duty to his father, or because they had been hired to do it. This was Rudy's first experience of doing something for someone else. He liked it. He resolved to look for other opportunities.

In one of his counseling sessions with Venzel he talked about this experience. Rudy told him the whole story and particularly about how good he felt after giving even this small amount to this stranger.

Venzel showed him a verse in Hebrews 13.2: "Be not forgetful to entertain strangers, for thereby some have entertained angels unawares."

"Wow, that's amazing. I'm sure I've read that verse but I didn't see what it meant until now."

"That is why some people call the Bible a *living* book," he explained. "Certainly if you read any book more than once you notice things in it that you didn't notice reading before; but the Bible continues to do that no matter how often you read it. I have known people to spend a great deal of thought on only a few words in one verse. I have read passages and have actually wondered if the passage wasn't rewritten, somehow, because I saw things in the passage that I had never seen before."

"So you never really get to know the whole of it?" Rudy asked.

"It is a well that never runs dry." Venzel said. "All life is constantly confirming the truths of the Bible. No one can ever know the whole of it. It also seems like people need to learn some lessons over and over again."

"Well, I'll never forget this experience of buying that lunch for that old man. I'm eager to look for other opportunities to buy people things. That's one advantage I've got. I've got some money to do kind things with."

"Yes, Rudy, let's talk about that a little bit."

Rudy was surprised at this suggestion. He immediately wondered what he had done wrong.

"Giving to others requires a great deal of judgment. The way you gave to that man was fine. He had no idea who you were. You gave anonymously. Also, the amount was modest.

"You must be careful about money. It's something that is dear to the hearts of most people. Surely you know that not everyone has as much as your family. In some cases it's hard to come by. There are people who have real money struggles, yet, some of their struggles are necessary for them. It's part of God's training for them."

"I guess I never thought of it that way."

"Money is an artificial power, but a serious power all the same, and few people really know how to handle that power. It's also a great responsibility. Luke 12.48 records, ` . . . For unto whomsoever much is given, of him shall be much required: and to whom men have committed much, of him they will ask the more.' In fact several verses of this chapter of Luke talk about our stewardship of what we possess, or what God entrusts to us. It's a great responsibility. We must not waste it, or use it foolishly."

"I see what you mean," Rudy admitted. "I am interested in using it wisely. How can it be wrong to help people with your money?"

"Well, as a church we have helped several families who were in real financial jams. In some cases they were so embarrassed about even needing the help that they drifted away from the church. It was like coming back here kept reminding them of their dependence upon the church. Perhaps they lacked the humility to receive help without feeling guilty about it."

"I see what you mean."

"I know one person who goes to great lengths to send his financial help to people through the most elaborate channels," Venzel added. "He sends a check to people living hundreds of miles away and asks them to get a money order from there, and send it to the family he wants to help in his own area. In that way the local people have no clue who sent it to them.

"He has done other highly creative things. He has indirectly helped people find a job and has arranged that the new employer gives them a sizable fee for starting. In this way the people retain a sense of earning their own way. He has had stores call up people and tell them that they won a grand prize, that they were picked out of a telephone book, or something, and has given help to people in that way."

Rudy did not wonder how Venzel knew all this. Anyone going

to those extremes to avoid someone's finding out about their generosity would also not tell others about their methods. But this never occurred to Rudy. The fact of the matter was that Venzel was talking about himself in all these matters. He was not a wealthy man. He was of comfortable means with simple tastes. That combination left him with plenty of discretionary money with which to do charitable things.

Rudy frequently sought opportunities to counsel with Venzel. He seemed a wealth of wisdom, and every time he spoke Rudy found himself engrossed in what he had to say.

Rudy noticed that after a short while in conferences with Venzel he would become less and less aware of anything around the room except Venzel's eyes. It was a strange feeling for Rudy. It was like he zoomed in on his eyes and everything else disappeared. Rudy didn't know what that meant. It was just remarkable that it happened every time they were in counseling for any length of time.

"The Lord has blessed you with a rare opportunity, Rudy, and that is great wealth. You should think about these things because you can also cause great offense with the same wealth."

"I certainly will," Rudy agreed, "but I don't really have that much money myself. I certainly have enough to do some good things with, but the really big chunks are all tied up and I can't touch them. May I ask you another question?"

"Of course."

"How do you get this peace that everyone is talking about? I think I've done all my restitutions, and I've had a feeling of peace or accomplishment after each of them, but I can't say I have been overcome by a tremendous feeling of peace like most people describe."

"There is no one answer to that question. Everyone makes that experience in their own way. For some people it is a big dramatic experience, for others it is a quiet, private experience. You just have to pray about it and keep seeking it."

"I do," Rudy said. "I just don't know how long it will take."

"Of course you don't. God's time table is different from our time table. One thing, though, you have to seek God with all your heart. You can't hold anything back in reserve. You must abandon yourself to His will totally. Many people unknowingly hold onto one thing long after they have surrendered everything else. They don't permit themselves to think of this for a long time. Then, finally, after a long struggle in which they wear themselves down quite a bit, they suddenly realize that they have not surrendered all to Jesus. At this moment they have a decision to make. They usually decide to abandon even this last holdout and that is the exact moment when they receive this tremendous feeling of peace which is unmistakable."

"I see," Rudy whispered, deep in thought.

"Throughout the Bible there are references to seeking the Lord with all your heart. It has to do with the Lord's being a jealous God. He will not share your heart—His future temple, hopefully—with any other passion or interest on the same or higher level."

"I can't think of anything like that," Rudy said. "I guess I'll just have to keep praying about it."

"Do you remember reading King David's prayer in Psalms 139?"

"No, not off hand," Rudy admitted.

"In it King David asks, `Search me, O God, and know my heart; try me, and know my thoughts: And see if there be any wicked way in me, and lead me in the way everlasting.' You might read that psalm. It is all about how the Lord knows us better than we even know ourselves."

So that is how the next few weeks went with Rudy. He would read his Bible and pray and when he had the opportunity he would counsel with Venzel. He also talked with other members of the congregation. He found that they all had a good knowledge of the Bible. These were people who were encouraged to read and study the Bible for themselves.

CHAPTER 35

Rudy's life changed considerably. He was not seen at any of the clubs anymore. He didn't hang around with Renee or any of his other friends. He spent a lot of time at home reading the Bible, or around the city looking for natural places where he could feel a closeness to God and His creation.

His friends missed him. They talked about him at parties as if he had died. Those that knew him ran him down for the changes he was making in his life. Most of his friends abandoned him. This was oddly a relief to Rudy who didn't want to participate in the things they did anymore anyway. Renee, however, was different. Renee was hurt and confused for several weeks but gradually told herself that it was not true. She had convinced herself that Rudy was just the same and all she had to do was call him and they could get back on track.

Renee called and caught him at home.

"Hello?"

"Hi. Rudy, that you?" Renee asked.

"Yeah, Renee, great to hear from you. How're you doing?"

"Oh, not so good. I really miss you."

"Thanks. I miss you, too," Rudy admitted.

"What're you doing?"

"I'm just sitting here reading the Bible," Rudy said.

"Oh, are you still into that?" Renee asked. "I'd hoped that was old news by now."

"It is old news, Renee. It's one of the oldest stories on earth. But it's amazing. It's really true. You've gotta find this for yourself."

"Listen, ugh, can we get together or something?" Renee asked.

"Sure, sure. You name it. How about now? This can wait."

"OK Where do you want to meet?"

"How about Central Park, the restaurant near the old zoo?" Rudy suggested.

"Fine. I'm on my way."

Rudy noticed an excitement in his mood. It had been several weeks since he saw Renee and he was eager to tell her some of the things that have been happening in his life. He rushed to get ready, walked briskly out to the street and to the park.

Rudy got there before Renee so he sat down at an outside table, ordered mineral water, and waited. Fifteen minutes had passed. He was beginning to wonder if Renee was waiting somewhere else. Thirty minutes later Renee finally showed up.

"Hi. Been waiting long?" she asked.

"Yeah, but I got here early," Rudy said.

"Sorry. I just can't seem to get going. It's like slow motion. I sleep all the time. I hate to get up. I don't know what's the matter with me."

"Sounds like depression," Rudy diagnosed.

"It probably is. I'll tell ya, since you've turned religious, I've gone nuts."

"I'm sorry about that. Maybe you should look into religion too."

"Maybe I should. But to be honest, the only reason I would would be to get back together with you. I need you. It's like a drug thing."

"Well, why don't you come to church with me a few times and see if it will help?"

"I can't see myself sitting in some church listening to some preacher talking about world politics. If he knew anything he'd get into something that really made money."

"Listen, it's not like that in this church. This is the real thing. You've got to check it out."

"I don't know."

"Listen, if you really care about me at all you'll come and see this. I've never asked you for a favor before. Now I'm asking. Please."

"Well, maybe we can swap favors. Let's do the clubs tonight. Let's get back to our old routine."

"Not tonight. I don't trust you. You've got to come to church first."

"Listen, Rudy, how can you do this? Don't you have any feelings for me?"

"Of course I do. You're my closest friend."

"How can you change that much?" Renee asked. "Didn't we have fun? Didn't you enjoy that?"

"I don't know how I could change that much. There is a verse in the Bible that says something like old things shall pass away and all things will become new. Maybe that's what's happened to me."

"But didn't you have fun when we went out together?" Renee continued.

"Yeah, I think so. It all seems pretty mechanical to me now. It seems like a long time ago, another life."

"Another life?" Renee asked incredulously. "Boy you're cracking up. Listen, pal, you've only got one life to live and you're screwing yours up with this religion. Everybody thinks you're a freak now."

"Do you think I'm a freak, Renee?"

Renee thought for a moment and looked straight into Rudy's eyes.

"Rudy, nobody buys this religion stuff anymore. How can you get so sidetracked? No you're not a freak. You're a classy guy. You've got everything going for you. You're rich, you're smart, you're going to Harvard. You've got it all, don't blow it."

"It's funny. You see it as blowing it, and I see it as the best opportunity of my life. I see it as a miracle that I could be given the chance to see what life is all about. I know it sounds corny, but it's the meaning of life. I know I sound like an idiot even saying it that way."

"You do sound like an idiot," Renee agreed.

"You know, if I hadn't been there I would be saying the same things you're saying right now. I can just see it. I was never serious about life, was I?"

"No. You were always a little crazy. You were interested in everything a little but not too deeply. You never took anything seriously. That's one of the things I liked most about you."

"That's what I mean. Doesn't that prove anything to you? I'm really into this church. It isn't like getting hooked on heroin and I can't get away. I want to go back. I like what I'm learning about life in this church, and with these people. I've never seen or heard of anything like it."

"I guess it's just the idea that it's a church. It's like a cult or something. Why can't you just learn this stuff on your own? Why do you have to go to a church? And why do you have to get me to go?" Renee asked.

"Look, maybe this'll explain how I feel. Suppose you found a fountain in a jungle somewhere that gave off water that made you live forever. And suppose that this water ran continuously; there was no worry about running out of the supply. Wouldn't you want to tell your friends and have them come and drink out of this fountain too?"

"Well sure, why not?" Renee agreed.

"Now suppose that you went to your friends and told them about this fountain and they didn't want to even go and look at it. Just think of how frustrating that would be."

"Well, we're not talking about a fountain of youth, here. We're talking about going to church. Nobody wants to go to church anymore, Rudy. What can you learn in a church that you can't learn on your own?"

"I don't know. All these people seem to be so knowledgeable about the Bible, and what it means and how to interpret it. You just keep learning new things even during casual conversations with them. Just come, will you? Listen, how much will it take to get you to come once?"

"Hey, Rudy, I know my dad's not as rich as yours but I don't need your money."

"I'm sorry. I didn't mean to suggest that. It's just that I'm so desperate to get you to come and see. Why can't you see that?"

"I can see it," Renee agreed. "It's just causing me some confusion. My feelings are mixed between being flattered that you care enough about me to want me to come so badly, and amazement that you have fallen so hard for some religion. I don't know what to do."

"Well, are you afraid to come? Are you afraid that you'll be brainwashed if you only come once?"

"I don't know. Maybe I am. I mean you weren't like this just a month ago or so, were you?"

"OK, that's at least understandable," Rudy sighed. "I've got to admit that I wish you would become just as interested in this church as I am, but I'm not at all sure that that will happen. I mean, they don't do any brainwashing or mind games on you. They just read and practice the Bible as it is written. It's really just that simple."

"OK, Rudy. I'll go to your church; but for tonight, lets just hit the clubs again like we used to. What's it gonna hurt?"

"After you visit church. That's the deal."

"But I want to go tonight," Renee said in an aggravated tone of voice. "You're not gonna go, are you?"

"Not tonight," Rudy said. "I said I'd go if you visited this church."

"Just forget it," Renee said in obvious irritation. "Look I gotta go. This should cover my bill." She pulled out a five dollar bill and tossed it on the table.

"Hardly. The sandwich alone costs that, not to mention the drink and tip."

This really enraged Renee. She pulled out another five dollar bill and told him to leave the difference for a tip. She marched off purple with rage. Rudy sat there a little embarrassed. This looked like a lovers' quarrel and he wondered who would believe that the argument was about going to church.

Rudy enjoyed sitting there in the silence. There were birds around the perimeter of the tables eating crumbs from what was dropped or deliberately thrown to them. Rudy waited for the food and ate both the sandwiches. He threw little balls of bread out for the birds too.

Rudy decided to rent a bicycle and get some exercise. He pedaled around the park stopping by the pond to watch some men sail their radio-controlled sail boats. He enjoyed how quiet and pleasant the park was. You could easily forget that you were in the middle of New York City if you didn't look up at the skyscrapers around the border of the park.

He spotted the windows of his parent's apartment and marveled at how closely he had always lived to this place, and how little he had appreciated it in the past. He wondered, "Wouldn't this be a great time to have peace?" But he didn't believe that he had it even yet. "What's so hard about finishing this up?" he asked no one in particular.

CHAPTER 36

The next Sunday the morning sermon was powerful. It occurred to Rudy that this sermon would be a great way of introducing this church to his father. They recorded all sermons to send to shut-ins, or those living too far away, so Rudy decided to buy a tape.

Rudy walked back to the recording room and asked the technician to make a copy for him. The room had lots of high-tech equipment and a copy was made in minutes on a high-speed duplicator. The fee for this tape was four dollars. Rudy gave the man a ten and told him to keep the change.

The man seemed grateful for the donation, causing Rudy to wonder if he had done the right thing. He wondered if he should have waited for change and given the change secretly like he had learned from Venzel. He then told himself that six dollars was not really that much money in anybody's book, and no harm was done. This is how carefully Rudy was trying to put into application every lesson he learned from this church.

The rest of the day went rather routinely, but Rudy frequently tapped that cassette tape in his pocket, reassuring himself that it was there. He believed that this tape would capture the curiosity of even his father, so brilliant was the persuasion contained in that sermon in Rudy's view.

The next four days went slowly for Rudy. His parents were out of town. He rehearsed how he would present this tape recording to his father. It seemed like his parents would never get back. They did get back, however, and his father went on hospital rounds and came home for an eight-thirty dinner.

The conversation was stilted but pleasant. When asked how he liked Martha's Vineyard this time, Peterfield complained that there may not be enough excitement there. He suggested moving to Monte Carlo, but his wife told him he couldn't afford it.

Everyone was in good spirits. This encouraged Rudy. He believed that tonight would be perfect to talk to his father about this new church. Rudy couldn't believe how nervous he was feeling, though. This surprised him because he was capable of great boldness with his father in the past.

"Well, father, are we going to have some time to talk after dinner?" Rudy asked.

"Yes, son. Just let me digest this dinner a little more."

"Sure," Rudy agreed.

"Rudy," his mother asked, "Why don't you go ahead and your father will be along in a few minutes."

"OK mother," Rudy agreed. This seemed like an unusual request for his mother. Rudy assumed that she would be urging his father to be cooperative.

After Rudy left his mother began, "Horace, I do hope you'll try to be understanding with Rudy."

"You hope I'll be understanding?" he asked in a slightly testy tone of voice.

"I mean you were noticeably upset the last time we dined together. I hope you and Rudy can talk about difficult subjects without getting upset easily."

"I wasn't upset."

"Well you left the dining room before finishing your meal. That's quite unusual for you."

"I was just tired, dear. I just couldn't listen to any more conflict just then."

"I think Rudy is serious about this religion thing," she went on. "I think it could be a good influence on him."

"I don't know. Look at Julia." This was the first time he had mentioned her name for several years—a fact not lost on either of them. There was a pause in the conversation, burning this awareness into their minds. "Our children seem to jump to passionate extremes in things. It seems like the more extreme and the more different from our own lives the better they like it."

"I just hope you can find a way to end the conversation tonight on a positive note. I'd hate to see the happy mood of this evening ruined."

"I don't see why anything should be ruined," Peterfield said pompously. "I suppose I should go up there and get this over with," he said, rising from his chair and giving his wife a peck on the cheek. "Don't worry about a thing."

"Thank you, dear," she sighed; but drifted quickly to the bar for the comfort brandy would give.

Rudy got his cassette recorder ready to play the sermon. He wanted his father to see what he saw in these people, their honesty and sincerity. He didn't expect his father to want to join the group. He just wanted him to understand why he wanted to. He dared to allow himself to believe that this recording would do that.

His thinking was interrupted by his father's entrance.

"Well, Rudy, now what is it that's so important?" There was no anger in his voice. There was no enthusiasm either.

"Well, father, I want to explain why I am interested in this church. It's important to me that you understand what I see in it."

"Oh?" his father said. This was a common expression that meant "go on" as far as Rudy could determine.

"This church is not a bunch of fanatics. These are sensible people who are remarkable in their honesty, their love for mankind, and their obedience to the Word of God."

"I'm sure they are, Rudy," he agreed. "You've got enough sense not to get caught up in some cult, don't you?"

Rudy was caught by surprise that his father agreed with this point so early in the discussion. Rudy had rehearsed a list of arguments to fortify his point. He had dozens of first-hand accounts of these people and the things that they have done. None of these things were necessary now, it seemed; his father had simply accepted his word.

"Listen, father, I'd like to play a tape of one of their sermons. It'll show you how unique and rational they really are about their interpretation of the Scriptures."

"Oh, I don't think that'll be necessary, Rudy," his father argued, holding his hand up in a signal to stop.

"No, it won't take long. I've forwarded it through all the singing and stuff, although you should hear the singing someday."

"No. Rudy. Don't turn that on." his father protested in a somewhat strained voice. He was trying to keep calm, but he was obviously having difficulty doing so.

"It's really part of what I want to say to you, father. I hope you'll listen to just the sermon. It only takes about twenty minutes."

"I came up here to talk to you, Rudy, not listen to some tape of a preacher. I was under the impression that you wanted to talk to me."

"Father, I want you to listen to this preacher. I think you'll be impressed with the wisdom of this man."

"I don't want to," Peterfield said through clinched teeth.

"What are you afraid of, I think you should." With that Rudy punched the play button and the tape began. The preacher began by reading some scripture.

Upon hearing the first few words come out of the tape player, Peterfield, got extremely upset. He stood up and shouted that Rudy should turn it off. His face became red, his veins popped out. He pointed a finger at the player and shouted that Rudy should turn it off.

Rudy was so surprised by this anger that he turned it off. He had never seen his father that upset. He wondered what kind of spirit was involved here. He became fearful for his father. He knew that this preacher was inspired by the Holy Spirit of God. He was afraid that the only spirit that could get someone that upset just by listening was an evil spirit. It was the intensity of his father's reaction that alarmed Rudy. It raised the possibility in Rudy's mind that his father was possessed with an evil spirit.

"OK, father, I'll turn it off," he added quickly to try to salvage the talk with his father.

Peterfield was aware that he was overreacting, but was unable to stop it. The awareness of how badly this was going caused him more anger. He decided to get out of Rudy's rooms in a hurry. He seemed ashamed of his emotional outburst, but unwilling to think or talk about it.

He had just enough control to say, "We'll talk about this some other time, Rudy," and grabbed the doorknob.

"No, wait, father," Rudy pleaded. "Can't we talk some more right now. I'm afraid you'll still have the wrong impression about this church."

Peterfield said nothing more. He turned the knob, walked quickly through the door and closed it firmly without slamming it. Rudy sat there in silence for a few minutes. His mind racing with all kinds of thoughts about what had just happened.

Why would his father feel so strongly about not listening to this tape? He refused to permit himself to believe that his father was possessed by an evil spirit; but his reaction was so violent and out of character that he could not understand it.

Rudy turned off the stereo system. He sat in his room for some time listening to absolute silence. The house was unusually quiet. He was aware of a sad feeling developing for his father. This was unusual for him, or anybody for that matter. He began to think of his father with pity instead of irritation or anger. How unfortunate that he couldn't permit himself to be exposed to the truth of God's Word, Rudy thought, this Word that has done so much for me. He recalled all the wonderful feelings he had experienced as a result of obeying this Word of God.

He remembered the feeling of forgiveness he felt after each restitution. And now, with this experience, he was motivated to think of his father compassionately for the first time. Just as he became aware of this dramatic change in his thinking of his father, he suddenly felt overwhelmed with the most profound feeling of peace. It was as if his heart was beating twice as quickly with half the effort. It was as if there were no irritations, no pains, no discomforts. He was beginning to draw the awareness of what was happening to him and he was overjoyed. This was the answer to his many, many prayers for peace. He now experienced that elusive peace that he had looked for.

After only a few seconds of being aware of this peace, he felt some doubt creep in. Then, wonderfully, he recognized that doubt as coming from the Devil. Even in this priceless, precious moment, the Devil was making an effort to take it away, to cause doubt. This awareness, this attributing of that doubtful thought to the Devil, caused an even greater peace in his heart. Now he had found the sense of salvation that he had been waiting for. Now the work of conversion was done. Now his soul belonged to Jesus Christ Who had purchased it with His blood on Calvary's cross.

Rudy was overjoyed. He walked around his room feeling like he could jump twenty feet in the air if there wasn't a roof over his head to stop him. He quickly got dressed. He wanted to take a walk. He wanted to run, to get under the stars and just treasure this moment as long as he could.

He bounded down the stairs toward the front door. He looked overjoyed. He was singing, jumping, and in a great mood. His mother noticed this and asked him how the talk went.

"Oh, mother, I feel wonderful. I'm totally at peace. I'm the happiest person in the whole world."

"I'm so happy for you," she managed to say before he was out the door. She was deeply relieved to learn that the talk had gone so well.

Rudy left the building and walked into the park. It was starting to get dark but there was still some light. Rudy ran for a while and jumped as high as he could. Then he ran a little more. He became aware that it was going to be dark soon so he grabbed a cab. He wanted to go to West Battery and take the ferry back and forth to enjoy the water, and get away from the city. As he was sitting in the cab for the long ride to West Battery he thought over the experiences he had just had.

He realized that the last thing holding him up was his opinion of his father. He thought of how mysteriously the Lord works. This terrible reaction in his father was what Rudy needed to change his mind about his father. What he thought was bad news was really good news. He thought of Romans 8.28: "And we know that all things work together for good to them that love God, to them who are the called according to his purpose."

"How foolish," he thought, "to have had my own ideas of how this talk should have turned out. This could not have been better."

Rudy got out of the cab, boarded the next ferry, and stood outside on the top deck against the rail looking at the Statue of Liberty. "Liberty," he said to himself. "What a new meaning that word has for me now."

CHAPTER 37

Rudy got back from the Ferry shortly after eleven. He still had a warm, glowing feeling of well-being. No obstacle was an irritation to him. He gladly waited on others to go through doors first, he waited patiently for elevators. He was untroubled by the hundreds of little things that used to irritate him in the past. He slept the untroubled sleep of the saved in Jesus Christ.

The next day was Friday and Rudy and his friends had planned to go to the cabin for Friday night and Saturday. They would all go home on Saturday except for Rudy who planned on staying with Jim Stander for a change. Rudy was looking forward to sharing his good news with them. He knew they would be thrilled.

Rudy knew where Neal worked his summer job and took a bus to within a few blocks of the factory well before Neal's quitting time. He had time to walk around a little. There were sidewalks never walked on, grassy sections never used for football games, or strolling. The factory was located on a large lot bordered by a tall chain link fence. At the top of the fence were two rows of barbed wire mounted on holders that jutted outward. The fence was beginning to rust and some poles were bent from minor automobile accidents.

From the factory Rudy could hear heavy machinery grunting and groaning at regular intervals. There were dull thuds, high-pitched screeches of escaping air, and metallic clanking all at an unnaturally quick pace. As Rudy listened to the rhythms of this factory, he noticed a similarity between these sounds and the rhythms of rock music. He got a definite impression of power from these sounds. The power of expensive machinery. The power of corporate America. The power of money. These are the sounds one hears during the making of money.

Rudy walked toward the main gate of the factory. Signs were attached to the fence near the entrance gate advising the workers to be safety conscious and to eliminate errors. They were the kinds of signs that are all over America. They colorfully advised people on how to use things, how to avoid accidents. They suggest a caring concern to have people informed of dangers as much as possible. In spite of all the warnings, or maybe because of them, people take them for granted and don't read them. But when you come across one for the first time, as Rudy did, you are aware of all the trouble to design, manufacture, distribute, and hang the sign. It seemed to Rudy like a lot of effort.

The security guard at the gate wouldn't let Rudy past the gate even after hearing his story. So Rudy waited along the gritty, gravel-covered sidewalk at the side of the gate. Suddenly a bell went off like a school bell letting the children out for the day. And, just like children getting out of school, some men ran out of the doorway to their cars. There was a mad race to see who could get out of the parking lot first.

Neal was neither one of the first anxious ones to leave, nor was he slow. He was ready to get out and get on with the plans they had for the weekend. He looked around the parking lot and around his van but didn't see Rudy. An old fear came back. It was the fear he had the first full day they met when he wanted Rudy to be interested in the church but wasn't sure that he would.

He glanced up at the gate suspecting what might have happened and was relieved to see Rudy waiting on the sidewalk. Neal pulled his van into the line of cars waiting to get out. When he got past the gate Rudy ran over and climbed into the passenger side of the van.

"Well, we're off," Neal shouted with excitement. "Have you been waiting long?"

"No. The bus schedule was just right," Rudy answered. "How do you like working in a factory like that? What's it like?"

"It's OK for now. I think it's pretty interesting, but I wouldn't want to do it all my life. I'm glad I'm going to college to get out of a place like that."

"What's interesting about it?" Rudy asked.

"The people, I guess. There's an odd mixture of fun and sadness in them all the time. It's like they're somewhat sad because they ended up there, but fun because they do a lot of stuff to make it fun."

"What do you mean sad to have ended up there?"

"Well, it's like, everyone that goes to school hears the teachers say that they should get a good education so they don't end up in a factory job. It's like everyone was hoping that the teacher wasn't talking about them, like it was some sort of shame. Then one day they end up in a factory job and they're somewhat embarrassed. They stay embarrassed for a while until they realize that the whole factory is full of people who ended up with factory jobs. Then they sort of develop a sense of brotherhood about that fact and do things to make it more fun and special."

"What sorts of things do they do?"

"Well, they play practical jokes on people. For example, most of the guys bring lunch pails instead of buying their lunch in the vending machines. One day some guys took the food out of one guy's lunch pail, nailed the pail to the top of the work bench, and then put the food back in. When the guy came to pick up his pail he tore the handle off it before he realized that it was nailed down."

Rudy didn't look highly amused.

"I guess you have to be there to appreciate how funny this stuff is, Neal added. "Maybe it's the contrast between these silly jokes and the monotony of the work. I don't know, exactly, but it's funny when it happens."

Neal swung the van into Jim's driveway. Jack was to meet them there and they were all going to go to the cabin in Neal's van. Jim's mother wanted them to stay for dinner, but the guys wanted to get out on their own. (Rudy wanted to stay and eat Mrs. Stander's home-cooked meal but he got voted out by the other three.)

The guys piled into the van and headed for the cabin. There was a small bar-type restaurant near the cabin that they called "Harry's Bar,"that they stopped at for supper. It had old red vinyl booths with chrome coat racks sticking up like antlers on the ends of each seat. There were no table cloths on the Formica table tops. There was no carpet covering the shrinking, loose, dirty floor tiles. There was a bar along one wall of the building, but there was never anyone in there when these guys were there. Harry's had no menu. All they ever ordered were hamburgers. They were unceremoniously served on a thin bun with grease.

Harry had no personality, he was of nondescript age but well over sixty and had not taken care of his health. He was of amorphous shape, balding, with a face that is quickly lost in a crowd. He spoke in a bland voice barely above a whisper. He always had a cigarette butt hanging out of the corner of his mouth.

The guys enjoyed a fantasy that Harry liked them and was glad to see them come in. To the less biased observer, Harry's expression didn't change before, during, or after they were there. They talked to Harry as if he was an old member of the family. He did nothing to discourage this. Perhaps he did appreciate their patronage, although he gave no impression of it.

For the guy's part when they were there they believed that they were part of a well-worn tradition—something people their age seldom felt. They felt like oldtimers. After delivering their hamburgers and cokes, Harry disappeared, giving the guys plenty of time to talk.

"Well, guys, I've got some great news for you," Rudy began, not able to wait any longer with his good news.

"You've got peace," Jack guessed.

"Yeah. It's every bit the miracle everyone says it is. I can't describe it. It's just there."

"That's great!" piped in Neal and Jim. The joy on their faces was sincere and genuine. "Tell us how it happened."

Rudy told them of his experience with his dad. They all agreed that it was an unusual experience, a fact that made it all the more believable. The story had an originality to it, an important test for these guys.

"I just can't understand how it happened under those circumstances. I guess I expected it to occur when everything was resolved in my life. The fact that my father doesn't understand doesn't seem to be important. I'm glad. I just can't believe it in a way. It's the greatest thing that's ever happened to me."

All these comments were both unique to Rudy and familiar to the other guys. They had heard these comments many times before. Each time the comments were made in a different way, using slightly different words, but always containing the same basic meaning. The person making the comments believes he is discovering something for the first time; and in his life he is. People in this church, however, who have guided so many other people to a genuine conversion experience, have heard these ideas expressed many times.

After eating, they piled into the van and headed for the cabin. It was a warm evening so they headed down to the lake for a swim. They played some ball tag and clowned around a while until the air started getting cool. Rudy was the first to suggest that they head back to the cabin. They changed into warm clothes and Jack began the duty of building a fire.

They wanted to make some popcorn in an antique popcorn popper over the fire. It was a long-handled screen basket. The plan was to put the kernels in the basket, close the cover, and hold it over the fire. It turned out to be terrible. Most of the kernels burnt while they were waiting for the others to pop. It tasted dry, not being popped in oil. They decided that there was a good reason why they don't sell poppers like that anymore.

They decided to run out and get a pizza instead. This area had several big name chain pizza restaurants. The locals, however, preferred a small shop run by a colorful local character. It was called the Leaning Tower of Pizza and it was in the basement of a small, run-down, brick office building. You entered the shop from a side street entrance. Once there you were overwhelmed with the decorating. All possible surfaces including the ceiling were covered with pictures either taken or clipped out of magazines. It was a photo history of the 60's, a time when the owner was a part of the hippie movement and never seemed to leave.

During the early 70's the shop was chic, and people believed they were in the middle of "The Movement" when they went there. As time went on the shop became dated. Now it was like a museum, an opinion that would offend the owner.

After pizza the guys decided to play a game of Monopoly. This was a game that Jack took seriously. He usually won and, on the rare times that he did not, he usually got pretty upset. He took the game seriously, had all the rents memorized, and bragged that he never missed a rent. He usually tried hard to get the green monopoly and it turned out that Rudy had one of the properties of that color. He tried to make a trade with Rudy and found him difficult to trade with. Jack found this irritating and got somewhat annoyed about it. Eventually Rudy traded when he got several monopolies, and Rudy took most of Jack's development money. Rudy popped hotels on his monopolies and Jack promptly landed on one. Jack wanted to talk a deal but Rudy pointed out that the point of the game was to run the other players out. While this was not lost on Jack, he didn't believe that it applied to him. He was run out of the game to his annoyance, and to the satisfaction of his opponents.

Jack was not a poor sport about it, but he was annoyed. It seemed natural to Rudy that Jack should be annoyed, especially if he took the game seriously. Jack developed a bad conscience about it, however, and apologized to Rudy later for being such a bad sport.

Rudy told him that he had nothing to apologize for, but liked this attitude. These guys were concerned about one another's feelings. They apologized for things that they didn't always need to, which kept things positive between them.

During the rest of the evening they talked more about Rudy's experience. They urged him to tell Theo Venzel the next day, which he did. His conversion was faster than the average. But bright people often did get down to business quicker.

Rudy explained to Venzel what happened , who agreed that it was an unusual sequence of events, but that it had the unique signature of the Holy Spirit. The Holy Spirit has a way of creating each conversion in a unique way.

Rudy was invited to Venzel's house for one more conference regarding his experience during that following week. Then, on the following Sunday, his conversion was announced to the rest of the church. This was done in a brief announcement after the usual morning service. Venzel simply went up to the pulpit and said, "We are pleased to announce that Rudy Peterfield confesses he has found peace with God and is awaiting baptism. For those few of you who may not know Rudy, he has been fellowshipping with us for some time now. He has no family background in the church. If you have any questions to ask him, the next few weeks will afford you the chance. Since there are several others awaiting baptism, we will be setting a date fairly soon. The date has not yet been determined."

The whole church seemed to share his joy. On the way out many people encouraged him. He was not sure whether there would be a lot of questions since Venzel invited people to ask them, but he got none that day, and few over the next few weeks. He was amazed, however, at how pleased everyone was. It was as if his coming to this church and being so completely involved somehow renewed their faith in their own belief. It was a kind of reminder that their faith still worked, in a way. That this plan of conversion was still powerful and of interest to contemporary young people like Rudy. Everyone seemed to get a real boost out of it.

One of the things that Venzel wanted to know was whether Rudy was living in peace with his parents, and if they knew of his experiences with this church. Rudy assured him that he had told his parents; but that he was not at all sure that his father was pleased with the plan. He explained how strong his father's reaction was and how completely out of character it was. Venzel didn't like the sounds of that. It had no reflection on the genuineness of Rudy's experience, but the church was cautious about proceeding without communicating clearly with the parents, particularly if the family did not have a background in this church.

Within the next week a date for baptism was scheduled. The order of events was that the church would meet on a Saturday night and hear the testimonies of each convert one at a time. They then decided by unanimous vote whether they were led of the Holy Spirit to accept them into membership. Everyone was accepted in this way. The baptism, itself, was on Sunday. It was made up of three parts: a sermon, water baptism by complete immersion, and the Baptism of the Holy Spirit. This consisted of the elders of the church laying their hands on the converts' heads and praying over them.

The date for this baptism was one month away. Rudy was given the assignment of inviting his parents to come to the service, or at least getting their permission for this undertaking. So Rudy went home after that meeting with mixed emotions. He expected to have no difficulty with his mother, but he didn't know what to expect from his father. Nevertheless, he had never been too shy to confront his father about things he wanted in the past, so he was determined to head into this experience with boldness.

CHAPTER 38

When Rudy got home that Sunday night, he left word with Paulette that he wanted to talk to his father as soon as possible. They were dining alone that evening, making that a good time to talk to both his parents.

Knowing that his father liked formality, he dressed for dinner. He was surprised at how nervous he was. Before he was never afraid to say anything to his father. This time he wanted his father to be understanding, supportive, or at least permissive.

Venzel encouraged Rudy to try and get his parents permission for baptism, and to attend if possible. It would not prevent him from being baptized if his parents refused, it was just nicer if they agreed.

Rudy walked in the dining room feeling a little like an outsider. He could count on one hand the meals he ate in this room with his parents in the last six months.

His dad was in a good mood. Rudy took his place and bowed his head to say a short prayer.

"What are you doing?" his mother asked.

"I'm praying before eating," Rudy said. "Like grandpa Kupferschmidt used to do. I think, maybe we should do that."

"That's nice. You go ahead dear," his mother told him. His father remained silent, but Rudy thought he was being particularly observant, like a deer that keeps its eye on an intruder from far off to see if any of its movements look suspicious.

During soup, Rudy wondered how to introduce the subject, or if he should try lighter conversation at first. He wanted to take advantage of his father's good mood. Paulette sensed that Rudy had something difficult to talk about with his parents so she prepared some of his father's favorite dishes. It started with a rich, thick crab meat bisque.

"I think this is Paulette's best effort for this bisque, don't you dear?" he asked his wife.

"You like it better than I do, dear. It's nice," she said in a vapid, drained way. She sensed danger with both her husband and her son in the same room. She remembered another time they dined together. She sensed a rising anxiety level. She wondered if she could fake being sick and leave the room. She reproached herself for wanting to flee.

Finally the suspense was broken by the doctor's conversation. "You know where I went last week, Rudy?"

"I believe you were in Europe, weren't you?" Rudy asked.

"Yes," the doctor agreed somewhat surprised, "I didn't think that you paid any attention to my movements."

"Well, now, let's see," Rudy speculated, affecting an analytical expression. "You like to find some excuse to go to St. Moritz. You went hiking at St. Moritz."

"No. But a good guess. I'm impressed."

"Don't tell me," Rudy interrupted. The playfulness in his voice, and the little game that they had devised, impressed his mother. Rudy couldn't help but think that he was getting off to a good start. "You went to a boat show in Monte Carlo and bought a huge boat."

"Wrong again," the doctor said laughing a bit in spite of himself. "You were warmer with the first guess."

"OK, OK, I've got it. Don't tell me," Rudy continued the game. "You went mountain hiking at Zermatt."

"You knew all along. You were only faking," his father said.

"No, I didn't. Is that it?"

"Yes. How could you have guessed that?"

"Well, you've probably been thinking about Freud again. Whenever you get a little nostalgic about Freud you go off mountain hiking."

"I can't believe that you guessed that. How did you put that together?"

"I know more about you than you think," Rudy said, fearful that he went too far with that remark.

"Well I'm really impressed," Peterfield confessed. "I had a great time. We rode most of the way up on lifts. We packed a picnic lunch with cold meat, cheese, bread, pickles, and wine. We hiked for about an hour, thinking we would make more progress, and we finally stopped and had our picnic.

"The wild flowers were out. It was breathtaking. I've never seen a picture that could capture the enormity of the mountains, the peaks and valleys. They seem to go on forever. You really get a sense of the eternal there, of the timelessness of the mountains.

"That's great, father. That must have been a great feeling," Rudy said excitedly, thinking he had found an entrance to the topic he wanted to talk about.

"It was. I think that I've been the happiest in the mountains of Europe. I only wish your mother would go with me." This he said teasingly looking in her direction.

"Did you bring me a cuckoo clock?" Rudy was really pushing some sentimental buttons here. One of his favorite gifts his father had ever gotten him was a cuckoo clock from a trip to Europe. The clock was still hanging in Rudy's room, although it stopped working a long time ago.

"That's right. You always did like that clock I brought you, didn't you?" his father remembered. There was a smile of recognition on his face while all three enjoyed this unusual moment of family memories.

"As a matter of fact, I did find a cuckoo clock in Luzern. There's a small antique dealer just off the main square. We had a few minutes so I dropped in. They had a huge cuckoo clock about two feet square. It needs some work but I bought it and it's being shipped right now. I'm not sure whether I'll use it somewhere, or whether you can have it. Would you like it?"

"That's OK See what you want to do with it first," Rudy answered.

The meal was already more than half over and Rudy realized that time was slipping through his fingers. He couldn't decide when to bring it up. He was getting a little panicky but wasn't clear what to do. In his confusion, he suddenly heard himself talking.

"I do have something rather serious to talk about tonight, if you don't mind."

"Sure, Rudy, what is it?" his father said. He showed no signs of concern about what the subject might be. His mother, on the other hand, allowed her hand to flutter up and cover her mouth as her anxiety level rose.

"It's about this church I've been going to in Connecticut. I would like to join it."

"Fine. Join, join," said his father. "Why do you have to talk about this to us?"

"Well, you can't join this church unless you've had a true

conversion experience, which I think I've had, and after you've had a conversion they want to baptize you."

"I'm still not clear on why you are bringing this up with us? You've done lots of other things on your own. Why exactly are you talking about this now with us?"

"Well, this church recommends that our parents understand completely what we are doing, and why. In fact, they'd like your approval—or blessing they call it—if possible. You're invited to attend the baptismal service."

"Well, haven't you been baptized? Carol, didn't your parents have the children baptized?"

"That's right, Rudy. You have been baptized already," his mother quickly agreed hoping that that would end the subject.

"I know that," Rudy said. "But that baptism doesn't really represent anything to me. That was what my grandparents wanted, but it doesn't represent anything I chose to do. This baptism is my choice following a conversion experience."

"You keep saying a conversion. What do you mean by that?" his father asked.

"Well," Rudy began, "the Bible requires that people both repent and convert in order to become a child of God and to be able to inherit the Kingdom of Heaven. So a conversion involves both repentance and conversion."

"This sounds kind of cult-like to me," his father said.

This was the one remark Rudy had hoped would not be made.

"It's not cult-like. It's just a more faithful interpretation of the Holy Scriptures than most churches are observing these days. I happen to think that they are right, and that there's a great power and joy in interpreting the scriptures that way."

"You know, here we go again," his father reacted. "Didn't we just have this conversation a week ago? Nobody gets involved in churches these days. How can you be attracted to this church like this? I think you're ruining your mind with these beliefs."

"How does it ruin my mind just because I decide to believe the Bible? Lots of other people believe the Bible."

"Nobody does anymore. It's just too childish."

"I don't understand how you can form that opinion without looking into it a little more deeply," Rudy argued.

His father nearly rose out of his seat with that remark. "You don't think I have looked into this deeply?" he shrieked. He surprised himself and everyone else in the room with the emotion expressed with this question. "I work with people almost daily who are all screwed up because of religion. Practically everyone I see has been through some huge religious experience before finally breaking down and coming to me. And, as far as that goes, I've read the entire Bible from cover to cover. What do you think about that?" This last question was practically shouted.

Rudy's mother sighed and sunk down a few inches in her chair in total despair. Paulette was watching some of the conversation from the kitchen and realized that her efforts at cooking the doctor's favorite foods were not enough to avoid this conflict.

"I agree that a lot of people are screwed up because of their religion," said Rudy. "I think this church that I am going to would agree with that totally, too. The problem with those people is not the Bible, but the fact that they've had the wrong interpretation of it, or the church they went to didn't preach the whole Bible."

"Well, whether that's true or not, maybe the world would be better off if there were no Bible, and if there were no churches. And whether the world would be better off or not, I know you would be. For that reason, I'm going to do something I've never done before in your life. I'm going to forbid you to go through with this baptism. Your church wanted my approval. Well, I'm not giving it. They can just forget about getting a Peterfield in their congregation. I don't approve. I forbid it. Finally, I'm leaving this dining room again for the second time as a result of a conversation about your religious ideas. Please do me the courtesy of never bringing this subject up at dinner time again. I never want to disturb a meal with this subject again. Do you understand that request?"

"Yes I do," Rudy agreed. He was so upset and frustrated that he was afraid he was going to break down and cry. Peterfield left the room and Rudy was not far behind him. Rudy went up to his room, slammed the door, threw himself on his bed and wept. Peterfield went to his study, slammed the door, and seethed with anger. Rudy's mom went to the bar and poured a liberal amount of brandy and sat down in her reading chair.

While Rudy's father was sitting there, his anger was building. Within a half hour he was at the boiling point. He decided that he had not been firm enough. He called his wife and Rudy to the living room.

"Rudy, I fear that I have not made my position clear enough at the table," Peterfield began. "I mean that I clearly do not want you becoming involved with that church in Connecticut. And if you continue to become involved, I shall cut you off from your inheritance, disinherit you. You shall no longer be a member of this family."

"What!?" Rudy gasped. After some hesitation he continued, "Would you mind telling me just why you're taking such a strong position? Look at some of the other things I've been involved in that you said absolutely nothing about. Would you tell me what's so different all of a sudden? Why are you suddenly so concerned with my development and with what's good for me?"

"I have always been concerned with your development," his father screamed. "It's just that I believe that religion, and religion alone, is the worst thing you can do to yourself and I'll not stand around and let you do it."

"Oh, Horace," Rudy's mother added, to everyone's amazement, "you're making it forbidden fruit, can't you see that?"

"All I know is that I don't want my son going to any holy roller church in Connecticut or anywhere. It's the only thing I really care about as he just said. Now why can't he honor this one request? I'm giving you an ultimatum."

"So now you're pushing your last remaining child out of your life," Rudy screamed. "What's the matter with you? Are children too much bother for the great Dr. Peterfield? Is the great Dr. Peterfield too important with his world tours, his media appearances, his world famous clientele to be bothered with the different opinions and lives of his children? Are you driving us out so that you won't be bothered?" Every time Rudy said "the great Dr. Peterfield" the anger was so intense it was like dripping acid on the soul.

"That's enough!" Peterfield said. His voice was quiet again. Clinical, final. "I've said my final word on the matter." With that he left the room and went back to his study. Shortly he went to the gym to burn off some steam.

Rudy went back to his room reeling in a confusion of feelings, emotions, and fears. He wondered how this would interfere with his plans at the church. He wondered if Venzel would be willing to baptize him anyway. He was sure of one thing: he would not change his mind. He was resolved to follow through with this church no matter what his father threatened.

Rudy's mother just sat in her seat. She was stunned by her husband's performance. She was surprised to hear herself speak to him in the way she did. And she was wounded by what Rudy had said about their family. It was true. Her husband had in one way or another driven all their children out of the house. Her own mother had said so about the first two, and now Rudy was being treated the same way. She was furious about this and would have given a lot to prevent it, but she felt powerless.

Rudy's words kept going around in her mind. She realized that he was right. She, too, was angry because it seemed to her that her husband was making decisions about her family that affected her but over which she had no control. She did not like the way the family was turning out. She felt victimized by her own husband.

CHAPTER 39

The next day, after a wretched night's sleep, Rudy left. He moved into a hotel in Connecticut to think things through. He needed to talk to Venzel. In the harsh reality of the morning he realized that his situation was far more grim than he realized the night before. His father, who never cared about what he did before, actually forbade something, and made his membership in the family conditional upon that. This step stunned him. He had to think clearly.

Rudy checked into a discount highway motel in Stamford. He was placed on the top floor in a room with two double beds, a table, two chairs, a desk-like counter with two sets of drawers below, a color TV, and a full length picture window view of the parking lot, some old buildings, some determined sumac trees, and Route 95.

His friends were all working summer jobs, so Rudy called Venzel, who advised Rudy to read Matthew 10 while he was waiting for him to drive over.

Rudy read Matthew 10, learning that those who follow Jesus Christ can expect to have the most trouble with their own families. Rudy wondered why this was true. Wouldn't families have similar interests? Wouldn't they be inclined to participate in the same religious beliefs? His situation still had not quite sunk into his consciousness.

Venzel pulled into the parking lot in a late model Oldsmobile sedan that was cream colored, unremarkable looking. It had vinyl seats cluttered with reading material. Venzel was an irregular driver. He was short so his seat was pulled up close to the steering wheel. He gunned the accelerator and then coasted and then gunned it again. Rudy had to fight to keep from laughing.

Venzel picked a family-style restaurant that he liked because it was bland and easy to digest. After eating they settled back for a long conversation.

"This is so unlike him," Rudy said. "He has never tried to guide my decisions before in anything. He could passively sit by while I made some of the dumbest decisions. I'm not saying that this is a dumb decision...."

"I know what you mean," Venzel assured.

"It's the enormity of his reaction that baffles me," Rudy admitted. "Why does he suddenly care?"

"It's the first of many obstacles that will be put in your path over life," Venzel told him. "Life is full of these frustrations. Part of the human condition is continually struggling with them."

"I'm not sure I care to face any more of these kinds of situations. It seems so unnecessary. So dumb," Rudy sighed. "It just kind of knocks the wind out of you."

"You need to think of life as a process of these struggles, not as an end goal or a product. You never reach a place where everything's calm and there are no challenges or frustrations," Venzel explained. "Religion is not supposed to do that for you. True religion is supposed to give you confidence and peace along the way, as you're going through these challenges."

"Things seemed to be going so great. Things seemed so wonderful and now this has to happen," Rudy said.

"What is great or wonderful in your life doesn't depend upon other people's reactions to your life. Or shouldn't. You have to be sure of your beliefs and of your decisions so that they stand up in spite of other people's reactions. Otherwise you're always a hostage to other people's reactions or feelings. Your happiness can't be conditional or dependent upon others.

"It isn't that we aren't going to try to convince your father," Venzel added. "It's just that everything doesn't depend upon his approval. We'd like to have him approve but it's not absolutely necessary."

"How are we going to do any more work on that?" Rudy asked. "I don't ever want to talk to him about it again."

"No, right now I don't think you should either," Venzel agreed. "Perhaps I should make an appointment with him. Maybe I can explain things to him in a way he'll accept where you can't."

Rudy doubted that this was a good idea, but kept quiet. It was clear that Venzel didn't know who he was dealing with. Rudy recognized that this would have to be a great inconvenience for Venzel and was that much more impressed that he was willing to try it.

So, armed with that plan Venzel dropped Rudy off and went home to call Rudy's father. Rudy gave him an unlisted number to his father's desk. His father wasn't there on the first few tries but, eventually, he did get through.

Venzel was well experienced with making such calls. Even with this experience, however, there was the slightest hesitation. He had never talked to a psychiatrist before. He held some almost superstitious fears about these healers of the mind like many of his generation.

Finally the two got connected on the same phone call.

"Dr. Peterfield?"

"Speaking."

"I'm Theo Venzel. I'm the elder of the Stamford, Connecticut Church your son has been coming to for some time now. I would like to meet with you and explain some details about our church that you should know in the important decisions you are making about it."

Peterfield's first impulse was to get jealous about his time. Feelings of resentment flashed through his mind at how this man got through to him at all. He thought of handing him back to his receptionist, giving him an appointment and then losing him through a series of "emergency" cancellations. He thought of just simply telling him off and hanging up. He sorted through a series of options, none of which included meeting with this man.

"I've talked with Rudy about this," Venzel added. "He wants me to try to explain this to you, although he doesn't hold out much hope that it will be effective."

"What does effective mean?" Peterfield asked in a confident, direct manner.

"Well, Rudy indicated that you were strongly opposed to his becoming involved in our church. We both feel that that is because you don't appreciate some of the nuances of our faith that may separate it from some cult. I would like to have the chance of explaining this to you clearly, so that you could make an informed decision."

This last phrase struck a responsive chord in the doctor's mind. So he made an appointment for lunch with him in two days. He asked Venzel to come to his office and they would go from there. This gave the doctor all the flexibility in time. Venzel agreed.

As the day approached, Venzel grew more apprehensive. What he thought was going to be a routine visit with an unsympathetic relative grew more intimidating in his mind as it approached. He knew

Rudy's father was a prominent psychiatrist in New York City, and wealthy. Both of these, alone, would tend to intimidate anyone. So he wore his best suit and polished his shoes.

He drove into the city since he was going in after rush hour. He found a parking garage near Peterfield's office and followed Rudy's directions to the office.

He was reminded of how Moses must have felt going to Pharaoh's court negotiating for the release of the Israelites.

He told the receptionist his name and purpose and was invited to take a seat. He noticed how comfortable all the furniture was. Knowing something of Peterfield's reputation, he wondered who might have sat where he was sitting. Along one wall was a sizable mirror. He wondered if it was a one-way mirror and if Peterfield was watching him through it. He decided to look directly into the mirror at about the height where Peterfield's eyes might be. He looked into the mirror with confidence and serenity because he knew he had nothing to lose. He would try his best to communicate with this man but if he couldn't he realized that that wouldn't be entirely his fault.

Peterfield was inside a small room behind the one-way mirror when Venzel was looking at him. Venzel would have been amused to learn that Peterfield found it a little disconcerting to have Venzel look right at him in the mirror. But Peterfield wanted to look over Venzel before meeting him. He wanted to be prepared. He felt he had something to lose if he didn't handle it well. He felt he had to be in control because inside he was raging at the need for this meeting in the first place. While Venzel was taking some strength from the knowledge that he had nothing to lose, Peterfield was losing strength from believing that he had something to lose.

When Peterfield thought he had the man sized up, he worked his way through the labyrinth of inner doors to get to the waiting room. Venzel heard some doors and had the feeling that Peterfield was coming. Venzel fought the urge to stand up even before he came into the room.

"Mr. Venzel, I'm Horace Peterfield," Rudy's father said as he assertively strode up to Venzel's chair. Venzel rose to his feet and shook his hand with a firm, sincere handshake.

"I'm Theo Venzel. It's a pleasure to meet you, Dr. Peterfield."

"Please call me Horace," Peterfield urged. "and the pleasure is mine."

"And you must call me Theo," Venzel returned.

"Fine. I hope you don't mind, Theo, but I've taken the liberty of making reservations at my favorite restaurant for lunch. Will that be all right?"

"Well, since I asked you to lunch I'd like to pay, but we'll have to go to a place within my budget."

"That's nice of you, but entirely unnecessary. I understand you've been nice to my son. The least I can do is buy your lunch for coming down all this way to meet with me."

They agreed with that plan partly because Peterfield offered a gracious excuse for doing it; but mainly because they both knew that Peterfield could well afford it.

They rode an elevator to the street level in an awkward silence broken only occasionally by efforts at conversation on topics of mutual interest. On the street they climbed into Peterfield's waiting limousine.

"This is the first time I've ever ridden in a limousine, let alone a Rolls Royce," Venzel said.

"It's the best way to get around New York if you can afford it," Peterfield assured. "I've got it set up as a sort-of portable office. I can actually get a lot of work done here if I get stuck in traffic. I answer nearly all my correspondence here."

"What would a car like this cost?" Venzel asked.

"I really haven't the slightest idea. I don't think I own it. I think we lease it."

"It must be expensive," Venzel ventured. "It sure is beautiful inside. You feel so comfortable."

Peterfield was listening to the man's remarks with his clinical ear. He wondered if Venzel was clever and making suggestions of comfort to raise his tension level, or if he was some kind of boob who didn't know anything about cars. To test it he decided to put a question to him.

"What kind of a car do you drive?"

"I drive an Oldsmobile," Venzel said. "It's a basic four-door family car."

"Yes, I know what an Oldsmobile is," said Peterfield showing slight tension.

"I didn't mean to suggest that you didn't know what an Oldsmobile was," Venzel apologized. "I was just filling in some details for conversation."

The conversation got off to a bumpy start. But it was off. They pulled up to an awning on a side street and went into a door that looked rather ordinary. Venzel would not have known it was a restaurant had he walked along the street and seen it alone. Inside they were greeted enthusiastically by a French maitre d' who ushered them quickly to Peterfield's usual table.

"Do you speak French," Peterfield asked, "or can I help you with the menu?"

"I don't speak French. Please, you do the ordering."

"Fine, just tell me what kind of meat you want."

Peterfield fired off a flurry of colloquial French and ordered in a familiar way. He and the waiter carried on a brief, knowing conversation which gave them both something to chuckle about. Then, with all the formalities finished, the attention was finally turned to their business.

"Perhaps I should start, Theo, by saying that you should make yourself as comfortable as possible. You can say anything to me. I am here with an entirely open mind."

"Thank you, Horace," Venzel said with a smile. "I am here to explain our church to you so that you can understand what it is that Rudy wants to join. Rudy tells me that you've strongly forbidden his participation in this church, and we can only conclude that you probably don't know what we're all about."

"Fine," Peterfield agreed. "That agrees with my understanding of what we're here for. Please continue."

"I realize that there are many different kinds of Christian churches today. I realize that they vary so dramatically that the descriptor "Christian" does not really explain anything anymore. Our church basically broke off of the state church in Europe because our founding father believed that the state church had gotten too far away from a basic literal interpretation of God's Word, the Bible. So our church tends to follow the Bible literally. We are not an overly emotional church. Your son did not respond to an altar call. We don't do that. He was not steamrolled into a conversion experience. We simply preach the whole Bible and encourage people to read it for themselves and make their own decisions about what it says."

The conversation went on at an intense level for nearly forty-five minutes with Venzel essentially covering all the distinctions of this church in a brief, concise, but honest way. Peterfield interrupted him only twice to ask for a simple clarification. Otherwise he listened intently.

Venzel had two overpowering impressions as the conversation went on. He was surprised at himself for being able to explain the church so clearly in such a short time. He knew he did not have the ability to do that of himself. He believed that the Holy Spirit was speaking in his behalf. He also believed that Peterfield was impressed and was able to appreciate how Venzel's church is different, and perhaps worth Rudy's interest.

Venzel's explanation came to an end over dessert and coffee. At that point he got a reaction that he had not planned on. Peterfield abruptly changed the subject as they prepared to return to his office. Venzel was shocked that Peterfield could listen to him talk for nearly an hour and not feel the need to add anything, challenge anything, or ask any additional questions.

They were riding back in the limousine when Venzel asked him, "Did I make everything clear? I realize I monopolized the conversation. Do you have anything to say to me?"

"You made yourself perfectly clear, Theo," Peterfield said in a sterile clinical tone of voice. "Oh, by the way can I drop you off anywhere more convenient for you than my office?"

Venzel was confused by Peterfield's total lack of interest in any further conversation. He told Peterfield where the parking garage he parked his car at was. He was dropped off there.

As he was getting out of the car he thanked his host for buying lunch. He pronounced it to be the best lunch he had ever eaten, which it was. Peterfield assured him that he was more than welcome to it. The door was shut and the car drove off. Venzel realized that Peterfield did not thank him for coming down, or for explaining his church to him. In fact, he had no idea what Peterfield's real reaction was. He marveled at how cold and neutral Peterfield could be. He wondered if this was the way psychiatrists talked to their patients. He began to get a glimpse of what Rudy was talking about when he mentioned that his father was as cold as an iceberg.

Venzel drove back to Connecticut in some confusion. He could not say whether he was successful or not. He did have some vivid impressions of Rudy's father, however. He couldn't help but be impressed with the wealth that Rudy came from. He was amazed at how nice Rudy had turned out, considering his father. He concluded that Rudy's mother must be a warm, loving, devoted mother to make up for this cold paternal influence.

CHAPTER 40

As Venzel drove home in the light early afternoon traffic, he reviewed his conversation with Peterfield. He thought it went well. He believed he described the church in as clear a way as he ever had. He believed the conversation was a success, even though Peterfield had been unnervingly neutral in response to him.

That evening he shared the experience with his wife. "Peterfield was friendly. We went to some kind of private luncheon club. It was French, and I can tell you it was the fanciest lunch I ever had. We rode there in a Rolls Royce limousine. I'm sure he was the richest person I've ever meet. You can't believe the kind of wealth Rudy comes from.

"Sounds like you had a nice time," Mrs. Venzel offered.

"Yes. What puzzles me is that I'm not sure how he took it." I tried to look carefully at him to see if he was pleased with what he heard. He was impossible to read. I have no idea what his true reaction was. It was kind of spooky."

"You make him sound pretty cold."

"That's the funny part. He was warm and charming, but I never really felt like I got past a polished exterior. It was like he had a lot of cassette tapes of pleasant conversational bits and he would play an assortment of them to fit any conversation. Each tape was designed to be kind, courteous, and warm, but each was prerecorded and may or may not have expressed his sincere feelings. I guess I would have to admit that I still don't know his true feelings."

"Oh, I'm sure you made a good impression on him," Mrs. Venzel assured. "You always work so well with people."

"Well, I hope you're right. I pray you're right. I should go get Rudy. Want to come along?"

"No, I've got some last minute cooking to do."

They arranged to have Rudy over for dinner that night so that Venzel could share his impressions of his meeting with Rudy's father. On the way back they talked about other things. Rudy was in no hurry to hear how the talk went because he feared the worst. Venzel was in no hurry because he didn't have anything certain to report.

Toward the end of dinner, however, they did get into the subject.

"I'm not really that hungry. I'm still full from lunch. Your father took me to a fabulous French place for lunch," Venzel began. "I've never eaten anything like that in my life. It was quite fancy."

"That sounds like my father," Rudy agreed. "He likes a big fuss at meals."

"We had a pleasant visit. He was extremely warm and friendly," Venzel added. "I'm just not sure I really talked to him. I mean I'm not sure he really heard what I said. He listened attentively but gave no outward sign of his feelings or reaction."

"That sounds like my father," Rudy repeated.

"It wasn't that he was quiet, or sulky," Venzel thought out loud. "He just treated what I had to say with no reaction at all. I imagine that must be what it's like being in therapy with a psychiatrist. I guess they listen without reacting much of the time."

Rudy listened as Venzel told him what so many others told him before. He listened carefully for some evidence of his father's behavior that he would understand. There was nothing. Venzel tried hard to put a positive spin on the meeting but Rudy was not convinced and neither, really, was Venzel.

"So where do we go from here?" Rudy asked.

"Well, perhaps you need to give your father a little time to think about what I said and then talk to him and ask for his support," Venzel offered.

This was not pleasant news to Rudy. He would have liked to be done with it.

"Can't we just send him an invitation?" Rudy asked. "Whether he supports it or not really doesn't change my mind or my intentions."

"I'm glad to hear that, but we can take a little time. We're talking about a life-long commitment here. We don't have to make any hasty decisions that we might regret later."

After dinner Venzel drove him back to his motel. "I don't know why you don't move back home," Venzel said, "Your father didn't kick you out of the house, did he?"

"Not yet."

"It doesn't seem natural your living at a motel. I think it would be better if you lived at home."

Rudy was silent for a while. Venzel had pulled up to the motel and they were sitting there for a few long seconds in silence.

"Well, you think about it Rudy," Venzel urged. With this, as in all his suggestions, he was gentle. Rudy didn't sleep well that night. He was disturbed by the prospect of needing to talk to his father again. He felt an overpowering wish that the whole thing would be over. He wondered why he had to be put through such aggravation. He wondered why it couldn't be simpler. Then he realized, somewhat to his embarrassment, that he had relatively few problems in his life. He realized that some people live with conflicts daily. He decided that this was just part of life. He realized that this was just his next challenge or battle. After this one, he realized, there would be another and another.

So the next day he took a train back to New York. He took a cab to his apartment building. The apartment was quiet. He poked his head in the kitchen to see if Paulette was there. She was shopping. He called for his mother and a maid said she was in her sitting room. He threw his pack in the direction of his rooms and went to his mother's sitting room.

"Can I come in?" Rudy asked knocking lightly on the wide open door.

"Of course, Rudy. Come in," his mother beamed. "What have you been up to?"

"I've been up in Connecticut for a while," he said.

"Still going to that church up there?" she asked.

"Yeah. Has dad said anything about that recently?"

"No. Not that I recall."

"Well, Mr. Venzel came down yesterday and had a talk with him about the church. I was just wondering if dad mentioned anything about it."

"He may have mentioned that he met Bensel…"

"Venzel."

"Oh, sorry. Venzel. I don't remember him saying any more about it. I'm sorry that your dad has taken such an unusually strong position on this. How are you taking it?"

"I can't believe it," Rudy said. "He's never supported or opposed anything else I've ever done. How'd he decide on this?"

"That's a good question. I was shocked by his reaction too. I think he'll change his mind. Or maybe you could put this on the back burner for a while, couldn't you?" his mother asked.

"No, Mom. That's something I could never do. This is the most important decision I've ever made in my life. I've never felt this right about anything. I've looked into this deeply. This is the most important thing I could do."

"All that sounds so dramatic, Rudy," his mother reflected.

"Mom, don't you think I've got any brains?" Rudy asked.

"Yes, of course…"

"I've thought this thing through. This isn't something I decided in one weekend of indoctrination in someone's basement under hot lights. I've read the Bible carefully. I've talked about this decision with lots of friends at college and around. I haven't made this decision because everyone thinks it's a good idea, either, I can tell you that. Most people think it's wrong.

"Well, what does that mean?" his mom asked.

"It means that Christianity has somehow turned into the most hated minority group in America. Unlike other minority groups, though, everyone accepts the idea of ridiculing them. It's even fashionable to hate them."

"Oh, I don't think that," his mother protested. "Some of my best friends are Christians. I'm sure of it."

"OK, ask them when they last attended a church service to worship Jesus Christ. Ask them when they last mentioned the name of Jesus Christ in public. For that matter, ask yourself if you don't feel uncomfortable that I am even mentioning Jesus Christ right now in this conversation."

"Well, yes, I would have to admit that I do."

"That's just it, mom. It's become fashionable to talk openly about every taboo in the book. You can walk on any talk show in America and talk about murder, homosexuality, bestiality, crime, incest, but you mention Jesus Christ and you're suddenly rude, impolite, you're creating an awkward scene, you're embarrassing people. What kind of a Christian nation is that? Christianity is the new taboo. Face it."

"What has that got to do with you? Is that why you like it?"

"No. It's just that I can't talk with my friends at school about this because they don't listen long enough to give it an honest chance. And they don't listen long enough because of its being a taboo. So I'm saying that my interest in becoming a Christian for the last year or so has been in the face of this social pressure against it. I'm saying that it is not a light decision. Can you appreciate that?"

"I can when you put it that way. I'm sure that I have no opposition to it. And I don't know why your father should care either."

"If I do go ahead with my baptism will you come even if dad doesn't?" Rudy asked.

"Am I supposed to come? I guess I would, it depends upon what goes on there. I'm not interested in snake handlers, or altar calls, or things like that."

"No, mom, nothing like that goes on in this church. It's really a calm, unemotional church. It's just a bunch of nice people trying to respond to their God along lines prescribed in the Bible."

"Well, don't we all?"

"Not really. Why don't you read some of the Bible and decide for yourself? I don't want to get into all the details now. You should read the book of Matthew or Luke for starters and see if the friends you thought were Christians are following the advice in those books."

"Well maybe I will," his mother agreed.

"Well, I need to talk to dad sometime. When's he getting home again."

"He's off to Switzerland for a few days. He'll be home late Sunday night."

So Rudy had to wait a few days before he could find out directly from his father what he had decided about Venzel's visit. The longer he waited the more sure he was that the visit was not a success. Rudy went back to Connecticut for the weekend but the weekend was clouded by the prospect of talking to his father on Monday night.

CHAPTER 41

Rudy returned home late Sunday night. His father was home but Rudy sensed that it was the wrong time to talk to him.

"Your father will be home tomorrow night. Why don't you talk then?" his mother asked. "But please don't talk about it at dinner. By the way, Rudy, I read the book of Matthew like you suggested."

"Yeah? what did you think?"

"Well, I was really surprised by some of the things that were in there. There's some really scary things in there."

"Yeah, like what?" Rudy asked.

"Well, Christ said, that He didn't come to give the world peace, but a sword. And that He would set a man against his father and a daughter against her mother. He taught against divorce, and a lot of other things. I really don't ever remember hearing any of those things taught about Christ."

"Of course you didn't," Rudy assured her. "That's because nobody reads the Bible seriously anymore, and those who preach explain everything away by either saying it's not to be taken literally or that it was for a different time and culture."

"Well, I have to say you're absolutely right about that. I've found what you said to be true," his mother said. She had a certain finality to her voice like she didn't really want to continue the subject. Rudy caught the hint and went off to his room.

The following evening Rudy avoided dinner altogether. He ate out with some friends and returned home to meet his father at a prearranged hour.

Rudy walked into his father's study and sat down in a dark green leather chair which sat facing a matching chair near a fireplace. His father was comfortably settled in the opposite chair reading some of Kipling's "Barrack Room Ballads" while drinking some cognac.

"Well, dad, I understand that you got to meet Mr. Venzel," Rudy offered to get the conversation off to a good start.

"Yes, mediocre fellow," his father answered. He returned to his book as if this was just casual, unplanned, conversation. This irritated Rudy because he understood they were to talk. It looked like his father was suggesting that he drop it. Perhaps that was what he wanted.

"Didn't I make it clear, father, that I wanted to talk to you tonight?" Rudy asked with some irritation in his tone of voice.

"Yes, of course you did. Just let me finish this one stanza," Peterfield paused after reading it, chuckled slightly, slowly closed the volume and laid it on a small table beside his chair. "Now then, Rudy, what's on your mind?"

Rudy sensed that his father had decided to play hardball with this conversation so he decided to go straight for the question he wanted.

"Did Venzel's visit with you change your mind about my becoming involved in his church?"

"Would you answer one question of mine before I tell you my answer to your question, Rudy?" his father asked.

"Sure," Rudy agreed.

"Would you give me the line of argument that they used on you that caused you to believe what they are saying." There was some delay while Rudy was trying to figure out what his father was asking. He was unable to grasp his intention.

"I'm not sure what you mean, father. Could you rephrase the question?"

"Certainly. What specific argument did they give you that convinced you to make this step? What specific things did they say that persuaded you that this was the right thing to do?"

"Oh, I see," Rudy said. "Well, that's hard to say. There's no single argument or a single line of reasoning that can be put into one statement that can convince someone of something as important as this."

Peterfield displayed himself to be somewhat annoyed with that remark.

"I didn't make this decision in a hurry," Rudy said. I didn't decide this over one weekend, or even one month. This decision came as a result of more than a year of studying the Bible, talking things over with friends and other people, and lots of thought.

"In fact," Rudy added, "My answer to your question is similar to a famous gospel song. It goes something like, `I know not how this wondrous love to me He hath made know. But I know Whom I have believed, and am persuaded that He is able to keep that which I've committed unto Him against that day.' Those words sort of sum up my feelings."

Peterfield shuddered. He was repulsed by the image of his only surviving son being into Gospel singing like some kind of television evangelist. Rudy grew more confident, missing his father's signals of disgust. Then came the detonation. Rudy decided to ask for the sale.

"Well, I hope that satisfies you, and that you won't object to my becoming involved in this church."

Peterfield blew up. "Satisfies me? I should say not. I've brought you up in a colorful world of ideas. And what do you do? You go straight to the worst choice in the whole menu. Nobody with at least a room temperature IQ goes to church these days. And you send down this Venzel person thinking that that's going to help me like this church? Take a good look at this Venzel. Is that what you want to end up like? How can you be impressed with his life?"

"How do you know anything about his life?" Rudy answered back. "And why now, all of a sudden, do you care what I do, where I go, or what I believe? You never even knew where I was half the time. You probably don't know what I'm studying at Harvard. . ."

"Stop right there," Peterfield ordered. "You're studying law. Your department chairman has written me two letters commending your first year efforts. I never interfered with your choices in the past because I had respect for your ability to make the right choices. This choice, in my opinion, is not only wrong, it's dangerously wrong. It may be wrong for an entire misguided lifetime. I know more than you think about religion. I've seen too many people who are suffering from the effects of religion. In fact, the whole world has seen too many people who have suffered from the effects of religion. It was in the name of religion that some of the worst crimes the world has ever seen were performed."

"Don't you think I know that, too? Do you think that's some kind of new discovery?" Rudy shouted. "Give me more credit for thinking than that. What I'm trying to tell you is that this particular religious group is different. I'm telling you they are unique. I'm sorry that you didn't get a chance to see it in Venzel. It's there but you probably didn't give him a chance to show you. I wish you would give them a fair chance. And, yes, I would like to grow up like Venzel. I don't want to do what he did to earn a living; but I would like to do what he does for his life. It boils down to whether you respect me for being able to see the difference between a bunch of fanatical Bible thumpers and this group. I think that you need to visit this church, get to know these people before you form any opinions about this particular religious group."

"I don't need to visit this group. I met Venzel. I'm not impressed. I don't need any more normative data. The answer's still no. I haven't changed my mind. Give this up. You'll get over it."

At this point Rudy was very upset. "You don't know what you're asking me to do. You don't know what you're talking about. That's it. That's what's so unusual about this conversation. For once the great Dr. Peterfield doesn't know anything about what he's talking about. I'm not going to give this up. There's nothing in life more important than this and I'm not going to miss this."

"I'm sorry to hear that," Peterfield said in a nearly inaudible voice. He reached for his book again. As far as he was concerned the conversation was over.

"Well, I'm not sorry to say it," Rudy said and stomped out of the room. At the door he turned around and looked at his father sitting in the green leather chair. He had the jolting realization that he didn't really know who the man sitting there was. He realized that he was his biological father, that he shared many genes in common with him, and that he received his physical life because of him, but he felt no spiritual connection to him. This awareness gave him a spasm of revulsion. He was going to slam the door as hard as he could swing it before he looked back and saw his father sitting there. This view of his father took all the hatred out of him. All he felt, again, was pity.

His father sensed that he had not left the room. He braced himself for another attack or the slamming of the door. When there was a delay he had the slightest sense of fear. He wondered what Rudy was going to do, but he didn't want to look over and encourage any more conversation. So he sat there much attending to whatever he could sense or hear coming from Rudy. And Rudy stood there for a few seconds feeling pity for his father. Then he quietly closed the great door without a sound and walked pensively down the hall toward his rooms.

CHAPTER 42

Events passed by quickly after that. Rudy shared the bad news with Venzel and his friends. They decided that they had done all that they could do and went forward with the scheduled baptism in three weeks. Rudy sent an invitation to his parents, and spoke with his mother several other times. His mother was making something of a change herself. She had always enjoyed Rudy. She liked his energy, and she took a vicarious pleasure in his exploits.

She deeply resented her husband's decision to disinherit Rudy if he went through with this. She resented the fact that he never discussed this with her, and she resented the fact that he appeared to be pushing Rudy out of the house like she believed he did their other two children. She shared her mother's opinion that Peterfield was not a good parent. This crisis polarized Peterfield and his wife.

Discussing this with her mother, Rudy's mother grew bolder at exercising her options. In discussions with Rudy she believed that he was better off with this new religious interest. She thought Rudy was happier and more directed in his life. She supported Rudy in their frequent conversations.

In one unprecedented move she decided to talk to her husband about it.

"Well, I think that Rudy seems happier than I've ever seen him before in my life. And I think that counts for something."

"It's a fool's hope," Peterfield said. "The Bible has long ago been found to be historically inaccurate, and no one takes the social recommendations seriously anymore. The idea of anyone taking Christianity seriously is intellectually embarrassing, let alone it being my own son."

"Our son, Horace," Mrs. Peterfield corrected. "And can't you imagine that there may be another way of experiencing this instead of intellectually? Let's face it, in intellectual matters you're the best. Your thinking is clear, incisive, accurate, the best. But this may be more of a spiritual matter. Maybe you just can't operate on that level."

"Well, maybe I'm a one-trick pony," Peterfield quipped, not taking his wife's remark too seriously. But that evening when he was opening his personal mail he received a letter from Venzel saying the same thing. Ordinarily he would not have given the letter any time at all, but because it came on the heels of his wife's remarks he became distracted by the contents of the letter. Venzel had spent much thought and research on this letter, writing it with great concern and love. He wanted to see this matter end happily for this great family.

"Dear Dr. Peterfield," the letter began, "I have learned that I was not successful in making myself clear about the great change that has taken place in your son. I realize that this failure is not due to my lack of effort or caring, nor to your inability to understand. The failure may be due to something else entirely. These ideas are spiritually discerned, not intellectually discerned. This is made clear in I Corinthians 2.13–14, 'Which things also we speak, not in the words which man's wisdom teacheth, but which the Holy Ghost teacheth; comparing spiritual things with spiritual. But the natural man receiveth not the things of the Spirit of God: for they are foolishness unto him: neither can he know them, because they are spiritually discerned.'

"I wish you could understand what a priceless gift your son has found. But there is almost an enemy relationship between these spiritual matters and the wisdom of this world. And those who trust in earthly wisdom are unable to see the abundant riches in Christ Jesus. But that doesn't mean that those riches aren't there.

"Possibly the greatest intellectual of Christ's day, Saul, was converted to Christianity in the midst of his persecution of the church. He wrote the words I quoted above and also wrote II Corinthians 10.5, 'Casting down imaginations, and every high thing that exalteth itself against the knowledge of God, and bringing into captivity every thought to the obedience of Christ;' This is what this great intellectual did. He brought his own thoughts into captivity to the obedience of Christ. He surrendered his own reasoning to follow the glorious path that Jesus Christ would lay out for him.

"There is another principle of spiritual matters that I feel compelled to share with you. These matters tend to offend the intellectuals of our world. The prince of this world, Satan, wants it that way. He does not want people believing that the way of Jesus Christ is the right way. So he promotes intellectuals who are hostile to Jesus Christ and gives them great reputations on this earth to insure that the way of Jesus Christ will always be in disrespect among the intellectual community. The Bible also speaks of this in several ways, such as Matthew 11.25: `At that time Jesus answered and said, I thank thee, O Father, Lord of heaven and earth, because thou hast hid these things from the wise and prudent, and hast revealed them unto babes.' And I Corinthians 1.27 - 31: `But God hath chosen the foolish things of the world to confound the wise; and God hath chosen the weak things of the world to confound the things which are mighty; And base things of the world, and things which are despised, hath God chosen, yea, and things which are not, to bring to nought things that are: That no flesh should glory in his presence. But of him are ye in Christ Jesus, who of God is made unto us wisdom and righteousness, and sanctification, and redemption: That, according as it is written, He that glorieth, let him glory in the Lord.'

"There, in the black and white printing of the Bible, Dr. Peterfield, is the reason you have the problem of understanding and approving of what your son is doing. I cannot add any more to what I have quoted in this letter, except that you can be sure that I am praying for you and your family. I am praying that you, like that intellectual of Christ's day, might see these spiritual matters clearly and transform yourself into one of God's most powerful servants for modern times. Your least servant of Christ, Theo Venzel."

Venzel believed privately that he could not possibly have put the argument any better. He had searched his soul and written what he felt were the most persuasive words possible. Yet, privately, he believed that unless the Holy Spirit of God would convict Peterfield of the truth of these words, that they would not be understood any more than Peterfield understood any other words spent on him to explain his son's experience.

As for Peterfield, he was annoyed. This letter sounded to him like the rattlings of an insane man. He thought them to be delusions of grandeur, or one who walks and talks with God when, in reality, he is really a disappointing little person who has not worked hard enough in life to achieve any grand goals on his own merits. Then Peterfield made a big mistake. He walked out to his wife's sitting room and tossed the letter in her direction.

"Here, read this if you think Rudy is in such good hands with this old maniac."

With that he turned around and went back to his study to

address some of his other correspondence. He was not troubled in the least with lingering thoughts about the letter. He had dismissed it without any affect on him whatsoever. This would not be the case with his wife.

Mrs. Peterfield read the letter carefully and was struck with the parallel with what Venzel was writing her husband and what she had just told him. Venzel demonstrated with appropriate scriptures exactly what she felt was interfering with her husband's ability to understand their son. She was confused, however, by her husband's attitude. He didn't seem to be impressed with the letter. His expression, in fact, was one of derision. She wondered why he had given it to her. The letter seemed to support so well what she was saying. Why would he put this letter in her hands?

She thought about these matters for another day before talking about it again. She was surprised to notice that she was growing more angry every time she thought of it. She finally confronted her husband one last time.

"Horace, I've got to talk to you again about Rudy and this church he wants to go to."

"Oh, no," Peterfield began to whine. He contorted his face to look extremely put upon.

"Stop that, Horace," she scolded. She was surprised by her emotional urgency. He felt slapped in the face.

"I want to ask you a question."

"Fine," he agreed.

"Why did you give me that letter Mr. Venzel sent you yesterday?"

"I don't know. I thought it was funny."

"You thought it was funny?"

"Well, not funny, really, kind of pathetic. This Venzel is a dangerous man, don't you agree?"

"No I don't agree," she said. She let a short silence sink this reaction in a little deeper before she went on. "Do you realize that Mr. Venzel's point in that letter was exactly my point to you just before you opened it and read it?"

Peterfield thought for a minute but could not honestly remember what either of their points were. "No, I don't realize that," he admitted.

"You probably don't even remember what the point was," she said even louder. "Well, I'm going to tell you another point that maybe you will remember."

"Now, wait just a minute, Carol," Peterfield started. He was concerned that she would fly off the handle and say things that would create problems for them both.

"I'm not waiting any more minutes, Horace," she said in a voice that was paradoxically both shaky and resolute, a voice Peterfield had rarely heard, but when he did it was serious. "I've waited a minute while you basically ran the upbringing of our children and, frankly, I don't like the way you've handled things there. You may be a great psychiatrist but that hasn't been any help to your own children. Our first son killed himself with alcohol. Our only daughter rebelled and ran off to Africa doing who knows what because of you and your stainless steel, hands-off approach to parenting. And now there's Rudy. It looks to me like he's found something pretty solid. He looks happy to me. And I'm not going to sit by and let you drive him away. I'm going to support him in this. I'm going to his baptism.

"I think Rudy's onto something that's good for him and I see nothing wrong with it. So I'm going to his baptism and so are you. You're going to change your mind about disinheriting him, and you're going with me to that church for his baptism. If you won't, if I have to go there without you, then I'm ready to live the rest of my life without you. That's how strongly I feel about this."

At this point Mrs. Peterfield was shaking with rage. She dropped into a chair near where she was standing and closed her eyes. She did not know what her husband's reaction to these words would be and she was not eager to learn. She wished she could float there for an eternity in that beautiful place between the pride she had for making a bold stand and before experiencing the consequences of it.

Peterfield was stunned by the cruelty of her words. He was hurt that she felt their children's' behaviors were entirely his fault. But, instead of retaliating, he decided that this was not a time for reason. He spoke quietly.

"I see," he said. "I'll have to give your words some careful thought, Carol." He turned to leave the room.

"Horace," Carol said in, herself, a much quieter tone. "I realize that I was selfish in blaming you for our children's not turning out like I would have liked. I want to take that back. I don't want that to confuse the real issue here. The real issue here is to let Rudy do what he thinks is right, to support him, and to let him know we're proud of him. Let's do things differently with Rudy."

With those words Peterfield left the room. As he walked back to his study he experienced a feeling rare for him. He experienced the feeling of a student who didn't know the answer to a question on an exam and made up some answer and then had to verbally defend it before his classmates when he and everyone else knew that it was wrong. He felt the embarrassment of having done something wrong. Of being flawed, in error. He who had spent so much time being the expert, the network consultant, the healer. He was now briefly feeling that he was being judged for how his children turned out and that he was guilty of errors and omissions, some of them pretty glaring.

He sat in his study and gave his wife's words some serious consideration. He had been too angry to listen to her words before, and he couldn't remember what Venzel had written. He wondered if this, too, was an omission. He was no longer sure that this course was wrong for Rudy. He was not sure what his reasons were for ever thinking that. At the same time he was not sure that this course was good for Rudy. He was becoming increasingly aware that he had been making some pretty serious decisions about Rudy without much information. This, more than any other error, was intellectually indefensible.

In the midst of all this self-examination, he got a flash of inspiration. He didn't have to decide. He realized that he was grabbing up ownership of a decision that was Rudy's, not his. Suddenly the fact that had surprised and amazed Rudy and his mother came into focus to him. Why should he, who had given Rudy so much free rein in the past, suddenly care what his choices were?

His wife was still sitting in the same chair quietly crying. She was feeling sorry for herself because she didn't like the way two of her children turned out, and she felt more blame than she let her husband believe. She remembered her own college days, her dreams of marrying and raising the perfect family. She was not comfortable with how her own life had turned out.

She was definitely not feeling sorry for the ultimatum she had given her husband.

In the quiet of that pensive moment Peterfield spoke up.

"Carol, you're right. I've been wrong to be opposed to Rudy in this. I'm not saying that I support it, but it really is Rudy's decision. If he's happy with it, why should I block it?"

His wife rose from her chair and he walked over and they embraced. She was crying but said through her tears, "Horace, you're a big man." She was bursting with pride and appreciation. Pride that the right decision was made, and appreciation that her husband was so sensitive of her feelings that he did not make her wait long for his answer. "I love you, and I always will."

"We'll both go to that church for Rudy's baptism," Horace agreed.

CHAPTER 43

The next day Rudy called his mother.

"I've got some good news for you, Rudy," she said.

"Oh, what could that be?"

"Your father has agreed to let you make up your own mind about religion, and he has agreed to come to your baptism with me."

"Don't joke about that, Mom."

"I'm not joking. He really said that."

"How'd you do that?" Rudy wanted to know.

"A mother has her ways."

Rudy found the news almost impossible to believe. This news was like the point at the top of a roller coaster where the last hindrance is passed and nothing can stop the rushing advance of experiences ahead. Rudy informed his friends and Venzel. It seemed like only a matter of hours before the big weekend in Rudy's life was upon them.

It was the custom of this church to hold a meeting on the Saturday night before the planned baptismal service on Sunday to hear of the convert's experience. During this meeting the convert is required to tell what his conversion experience was like. Then the convert is asked a number of questions about his or her specific doctrine. This step requires that the convert make a public promise to uphold the doctrine and practices of the church.

Most converts found the experience far easier than it sounded. They believed that they were given the strength for this by the Holy Spirit. They found that the prospect of sitting in front of the congregation was not as terrifying as they at first feared.

The elder, Mr. Venzel, asked Rudy to relate his story. Rudy sat in the folding chair with the microphone pinned to his lapel and looked over the group. He felt a genuine love for each one of the people he was looking at. They really did feel like older brothers and sisters to him. It helped to know that they had all been required to sit in front of a congregation and tell their story just like he was doing. He knew that they felt nothing but love for him and were eager to hear the exciting story of his conversion.

So Rudy told his story in about twenty minutes. He was then

asked to express his support for a number of specific doctrinal questions. After that he was asked one more question by Venzel.

"Now, Rudy, who are these people sitting in the audience listening to your testimony in relation to God?"

"They are the children of God," Rudy answered.

"Do you believe that they possess the Holy Spirit?"

"Yes."

"Do you believe that the Holy Spirit has been witnessing to their hearts about whether this is the right time to baptize Rudy Peterfield?"

"Yes."

"And," Venzel pressed on, "What if the Holy Spirit instructs us that this is a little too early? Maybe Rudy should take it a little slower, dig a little deeper into God's Word. Would you be able to accept that as from the Lord?"

"Yes."

"You wouldn't get angry and say, `They don't want me'?"

"No."

"OK, We'll take you at your word and excuse you into the Bible Class Room for a little, while we counsel together and then we'll call you back."

So Rudy took off the microphone and walked out of the sanctuary and into the Bible class room. He sat there alone for what seemed to him like an eternity. He prayed. He prayed that the Lord's will would be done, but that he also really wanted to be baptized at this time so badly. He wondered how he would explain this to his parents if the church did ask him to wait. He was not sure how often this happened. He decided not to worry about that, either. At this point he decided to leave everything in the Lord's hands. This decision, itself, gave him a renewed feeling of peace. He realized that it really did not matter what was decided. He was at peace.

In the sanctuary Venzel arose, turned around and began to speak.

"This young man has no family in the church. It has been a real inspiration to see how he has grown in his spiritual understanding to this point. It has been a boost to my faith to see how the Lord can work so effectively in the heart of one who has had no background in our church.

"Even though he has no family in the church, he has some friends. Perhaps we should start with Brother Neal. Neal, how do you feel about Rudy?"

"I have to agree that it has been like watching a miracle to see what the Lord has done in Rudy's heart. I'm convinced that he's truly converted and ready for baptism."

"You've seen a big change, then, in Rudy?"

"Oh, yes. I've seen a big change," Neal agreed.

"He has some other friends. I'm not sure how many. I don't want to leave any out. Would anyone who would want to say something on Rudy's behalf feel free to speak up?" Venzel pursued.

There was a long hesitation and then Jack got up.

"Well, I've been one of Rudy's friends in the youth group. I can agree that he's made a big change and is ready for baptism."

"Thanks, Jack," Venzel acknowledged

"I've spent quite a bit of time with Rudy, too," Jim added. "I can certainly say that he's been truly converted."

Again, there was a long silence. So Venzel decided to ask for the vote.

"Will all those that believe that Rudy is truly converted, and have that testimony from the Holy Spirit in their heart, testify by rising."

Everyone in the sanctuary stood up.

"Thank you," Venzel signaled and everyone sat down again. "Did anyone remain seated?"

There was a pause while he waited for any objection. It was the practice of the church to only accept people into membership if the vote was unanimous. If anyone remained seated, or expressed a doubt, the convert was asked to wait and become a little more grounded in his faith. This was not common, but there were enough occurrences of it over time that it caused a little anxiety while Venzel was waiting to find out.

When Venzel was satisfied that no one remained seated, he decided to give a little more information about Rudy.

"You know, brothers and sisters, I didn't want to say this before your vote so as not to influence you in any way but I really think this young soul represents a remarkable miracle. His family is not at all religious and he has had no formal religious training. In fact, his father was strongly opposed to this for some time. He was so opposed, in fact, that he threatened to disinherit him and kick him out of the family if he went through with this.

"I can tell you that Rudy was absolutely resolved to go through with this no matter what. I am reasonably sure that few of us have ever been asked to make such a hard decision. But Rudy was determined to go forward with his faith even though he was certain that his father would never change his mind. It has only been in the last week that his father did change his mind. Fortunately, his father no longer stands in his way. In fact, If I am not mistaken, I think his father and mother will be here tomorrow for the baptismal service.

"You know, I have to tell you that watching this precious young soul find his way through conversion has been a tremendous uplift to my own faith. I'm sure that Neal, Jim, and some of the other young men in our youth group could say the same thing. I believe we have all witnessed a great miracle here tonight."

With that he called someone to go and ask Rudy to return to the sanctuary. Rudy came back in and was directed to sit down. Rudy did not dare think about what anything might mean. He just obediently sat down and waited on the news.

Venzel was smiling and was eager to relieve Rudy's fears.

"Rudy, we all like to give good news. And I'm happy to tell you that when I asked the congregation whether it was time for Rudy to be baptized, every brother and every sister stood up in testimony that it was."

Rudy felt a tremendous rush of acceptance. He closed his eyes and gave a brief prayer of thanks.

"Now Rudy, you will remember that my last question to you was whether you would accept the testimony of the congregation as to whether this was the time for you to be baptized, and whether they felt you were truly born again."

Rudy nodded yes.

"In the future, Satan will come to you and tempt you into doubting that this experience was real. He may try to say that this was just an emotional experience, or a figment of your imagination. You just tell him to get behind you because not only you, but every brother and every sister, through the inspiration of the Holy Spirit, believed that you were truly born again."

Rudy felt a powerful feeling of gratitude. It was a tremendous joy to know that you were accepted by everyone. He felt indebted to each of them, and a deep sense of love for each of them.

"Do you have any word of expression for the congregation?" Venzel asked Rudy.

"I'd like to thank everyone for your encouragement, your support, and your prayers," Rudy said.

"The Lord be thanked, Rudy," Venzel added. "Now you can take a seat with the brothers while we take care of a few more housekeeping matters."

Venzel announced the order of events for the next day. He welcomed their visitors who came from as far away as Ohio to be a part of this service. The congregation sang a song and Venzel asked one of the visiting brothers to lead the congregation in prayer.

Rudy and Venzel decided that it would be wise for Rudy to go home that night and come up with his parents the following morning.

Neal insisted on driving Rudy home. On the way there was a reverent silence for much of the way. Then Neal interrupted the silence.

"This is just how it all began, isn't it, Rudy?"

"What do you mean? You mean in your van?" Rudy inquired.

"Yeah. I must tell you that I'm completely blown away at what a big miracle this is," Neal said. "I get all choked up when I think about it. Who would've ever dreamed that it would've turned out this way a year and a half ago?"

"Yeah. It's really something, isn't it?" Rudy agreed.

Neal pulled his van up in front of Rudy's apartment building. Even this sparked memories in Neal's mind. He remembered how Rudy had him drop him off on the other side of the park to keep his identity secret. Neal was so full of these thoughts that he was hardly able to carry on a conversation. So, too, was Rudy.

"You can come up, if you want to," Rudy offered. But there was something in his voice that said he would prefer to be alone with his thoughts.

"Thanks. I think I'll get home," Neal answered. "I'm not in a talkative mood. I guess we've both got a lot to think about, don't we?"

"Sure do. Thanks for dropping me off. And, I don't know if I've ever said it before, but thanks for everything, I mean, you know.

Thanks, man. You've been the best friend I've ever had in my life." With that he offered his hand for a firm handshake. Neal shook his hand and Rudy was off.

Neal was deeply touched by Rudy's words. He knew that he was a good friend to Rudy, but it meant so much to hear it from Rudy in this way. He drove home quietly and slowly. He was in no hurry to get there. He wanted to savor that moment, and the entire evening. This was one of the best evenings of his life, too.

CHAPTER 44

On Sunday morning Paulette was working on one of her finest achievements. She was making an extraordinary egg-and-cheese breakfast casserole in honor of the occasion. She calculated it to be pleasing to Peterfield because she, naturally, was aware of all the developments in this drama. It seemed to have a positive effect on his mood because he, his wife, and Rudy climbed into the Rolls in a good humor for the ride to Stamford.

Peterfield expected to go to a great hall with a lot of ceremony. He got a jolt when the car pulled up to a modest-sized, attractive colonial church tastefully decorated in a conservative, subdued way. He climbed out of the car and led his family confidently into the church through the main entrance. While this was open and there were people standing around in the vestibule, most people went in through a side door off the parking lot. So entering through the front doors was, itself, a way of announcing that here were some first-time guests. Peterfield entered the room and inspired a hush of respect. A few people were bold enough to go over and meet him.

Rudy timed their arrival to miss the informal Bible Study and be on time for the formal worship service. This, he calculated, would make a better impression on his father.

The schedule of services for the day was a regular morning service, lunch in the church, and a baptismal service in the afternoon. Peterfield was a little put out with the length of this stay, but went through the process without complaint.

George Bender came from Ohio because he had a part in Rudy's conversion. Everyone was relieved that he was there because he was the most dynamic of their ministers. They wanted to make a good impression on Rudy's father.

Bender did give a moving sermon on the story of Zachaeus. During the meditation that followed the reading, he illustrated the conversion process with personal stories.

On the way to the dining room after the service, Peterfield spoke to Bender and complimented him on an outstanding sermon: "I've rarely heard the scriptures illuminated in such a comprehensible way."

Peterfield was equally impressed with the food at this cov-
ered-dish luncheon. Everyone went to some extra bother, especially
for the desserts. Peterfield took a generous sampling of those.

After the meal everyone stood around and talked for a while
before the afternoon service began. Rudy was nervous because of the
importance of this event in his life, and the wish that his parents would
form a favorable opinion of this church.

The afternoon service was conducted by Venzel at Bender's
insistence. At first, some were disappointed, but later everyone agreed
that it was Venzel's finest sermon. He read from the book of Romans,
chapter 8 verses 1 - 17:

> There is therefore now no condemnation to them
> which are in Christ Jesus, who walk not after the
> flesh, but after the Spirit. For the law of the Spirit
> of life in Christ Jesus hath made me free from the
> law of sin and death. For what the law could not do,
> in that it was weak through the flesh, God sending
> his own Son in the likeness of sinful flesh, and for
> sin, condemned sin in the flesh: That the righteous-
> ness of the law might be fulfilled in us, who walk
> not after the flesh, but after the Spirit. For they that
> are after the flesh do mind the things of the flesh; but
> they that are after the Spirit the things of the Spirit.
> For to be carnally minded is death; but to be spiri-
> tually minded is life and peace. Because the carnal
> mind is enmity against God: for it is not subject to
> the law of God, neither indeed can be. So then they
> that are in the flesh cannot please God. But ye are
> not in the flesh, but in the Spirit, if so be that the
> Spirit of God dwell in you. Now if any man have not
> the Spirit of Christ he is none of his. And if Christ be
> in you, the body is dead because of sin; but the Spirit
> is life because of righteousness. But if the Spirit of
> him that raised up Jesus from the dead dwell in you,
> he that raised up Christ from the dead shall also
> quicken your mortal bodies by his Spirit that dwell-
> eth in you. Therefore, brethren, we are debtors, not
> to the flesh, to live after the flesh. For if ye live after

the flesh, ye shall die: but if ye through the Spirit
do mortify the deeds of the body, ye shall live. For
as many as are led by the Spirit of God, they are
the sons of God. For ye have not received the spirit
of bondage again to fear; but ye have received the
Spirit of adoption, whereby we cry, Abba, Father.
The Spirit itself beareth witness with our spirit, that
we are the children of God: and if children, then
heirs; heirs of God, and joint-heirs with Christ; if
so be that we suffer with him, that we may be also
glorified together.

Venzel elaborated on this passage in a way that was quite
unfamiliar to Peterfield. He indicated that in this passage was both the
power and the accountability of Christianity. "The essential business
of Christianity," he said, "was to introduce people to this Divine Spiritual Power that enables otherwise normal people to join the Heavenly Family. This passage indicates that we actually take on joint-heir
status with Christ through the spirit of adoption. And the power to do
this comes from Christ's sacrifice of shedding His blood at Calvary,
and His sending His Holy Spirit to empower us after He ascended to
Heaven to return to be with His Father.

"We, as mortals, simply decide to allow this work to be done
with and through us. We choose to be partakers of this work, rather
than be bound to earthly matters, and partakers of earthly works. Once
we make that choice, spiritual powers take over. We witness the work-
ings of the Holy Spirit in our lives and make the same observations
that the Apostle Paul did in Romans 7.5, 'For when we were in the
flesh, the motions of sins, which were by the law, did work in our
members to bring forth fruit unto death. But now we are delivered
from the law, that being dead wherein we were held; that we should
serve in newness of spirit, and not in the oldness of the letter.'

"We see that the Spirit works powerful changes in our lives.
In the past, we enjoyed sin and evil works. We had pleasure in these
things. Now, through the moving of the Holy Spirit, we abhor these
things. We mortify these works in our bodies. The Spirit gives us the
power to turn from them not so that we can look good to others around
us, or not to put on a good show, but to please the Heavenly Father
Who dwells within us and motivates us. This transition is not intel-

lectual, it is not done through some powerful exertion of the will. It is done through the transformation of the spirit that leads us. It is transformed from our own spirit which is inherently evil, selfish, and sinful, to the Holy Spirit which is inherently unselfish, good, and giving.

"When this transformation takes place through conversion, the fruits, or the outward signs, are obvious to those around. The person has become a new creature. And this is what Christianity should be all about. It should guide people to where this kind of power resides, and help people utilize this kind of power for their lives."

These words about how no exertion of will could make this complete of a change were particularly effective with Peterfield. He was thinking those same thoughts as he was listening to Venzel preach. He knew of no therapy or self-hypnosis that could work such a change. And for one brief moment in the sermon, at least, he found himself in agreement with the preacher.

Venzel went on to elaborate, "Now the other part of this passage speaks to the accountability of the Christian. These fruits of the Spirit should be seen and evident in a Christian's life. Much of modern Christianity has abandoned this notion of the gradual, perfecting power of the Spirit. Out of a misguided sense of humility, they have insisted, too quickly, that they are imperfect. This essentially accurate admission quickly gave way to an admission that they were basically still sinners, which gave way to the verse in II Timothy 3.5, which says, `Having a form of godliness, but denying the power thereof: from such turn away.' We, today, are speaking about recognizing the power of this godliness. The power which is able to transform lives even today, as we have witnessed in the life of these converts."

Venzel continued talking about this transforming power for a while and then the sermon came to a close. Peterfield had to admit that this was unlike any sermon he heard in any other church. He was unmoved, however, when it came to believing that he needed anything like this for his life. He simply did not feel any need.

At the close of the sermon Venzel asked Rudy and the other converts to come forward and sit on a bench in the front of the congregation. Venzel read from Matthew 28.19-20: "Go ye therefore, and teach all nations, baptizing them in the name of the Father, and of the Son, and of the Holy Ghost: Teaching them to observe all things whatsoever I have commanded you: and, lo, I am with you alway, even unto the end of the world." "Rudy," Venzel asked, "Is this your faith to be baptized into the death of Jesus Christ, to arise a new creature in Him?"

"Yes."

"May it be according to your faith. You may go to the room on the side and get ready for baptism. The congregation will sing hymn 41."

Rudy went to the dressing room and got into some white painter's coveralls and a white T-shirt. It was customary to take someone with you to help hold out a towel when walking back to the dressing room, so Rudy asked Neal. They went through the process silently. Both knew what the other was thinking. Their thoughts raced forward but were keeping pace with each other. They knew what a miracle this was. They had both been part of an amazing act of God. It was too big for either of them. They could not hold the entirety of it in their minds at once.

They then walked behind the pulpit where there was a baptistery. When the converts arrived, the congregation stopped singing and Venzel asked Rudy to step down into the water. The church had a large bathtub behind the pulpit for this purpose. It was twice a long as a normal tub and twice as wide. The water was pleasantly warm, not shocking. Venzel grabbed his two hands with one of his hands, and the shirt at the base of his neck with the other.

Rudy glanced out over the congregation. The whole experience had an other-world feeling. It was hard to comprehend entirely what was going on. The process was moving fast, he thought. He would have liked to go slow and cherish every aspect of it. He felt unable to attend to all the rushing feelings and experiences he was making.

"Rudy, is this your own free will to be baptized, no one has forced you to do this?"

"Yes," Rudy answered. He wanted to make firm, loud answers. He wanted his parents to know that he was confident of this course for his life.

"And from henceforth, do you promise to renounce sin and Satan and serve him no more?"

"Yes."

"Because of these promises, and on the basis of your testimony before the congregation last night, I now baptize you in the name of The Father, The Son, and The Holy Ghost." On these last words Rudy bent his knees and leaned back to be immersed completely under water in the baptistery. He then straightened up, stood up, and walked back to the changing room. Neal handed him a towel but water ran off him all over the steps and the linoleum hallway. The entire congregation could hear the wet splats of his footsteps going back to the changing room.

After he was finished baptizing the converts Venzel directed the congregation to sing another song. Peterfield could not help but cringe at how primitive this ceremony seemed. He was uncomfortable with the proceedings but recognized his powerlessness about it. He sat there in some discomfort waiting for it to be over. He realized what Rudy was doing, but did not really enjoy being a part of it, or being there watching it. Ironically, everyone in the congregation was hoping that Peterfield and his wife would be impressed and would be interested in attending their church also.

After two rather long songs Rudy returned to the sanctuary dressed in his suit with wet matted down hair. He took a seat on the front bench again, and Neal joined his friends further back in the congregation. At this point Venzel got up again and read from Acts 8.14-17, "Now when the apostles which were at Jerusalem heard that Samaria had received the word of God, they sent unto them Peter and John: Who, when they were come down, prayed for them, that they might receive the Holy Ghost: (For as yet he was fallen upon none of them: only they were baptized in the name of the Lord Jesus.) Then laid they their hands on them, and they received the Holy Ghost."

"Rudy, last night you testified that you believed in the second part of baptism which is the baptism of the Holy Spirit. You said that if the elders laid their hands on you and the congregation prayed, that you would receive, or be sealed with, the Holy Spirit. Is this still your faith?"

"Yes," Rudy answered. The other converts were asked the same question.

"May it be according to your faith. If you will get up and walk behind the bench and kneel, resting your elbows on the bench." In a louder voice Venzel addressed the congregation, "And may the congregation please arise."

The entire congregation arose while Venzel, and later Bender, joined in a chain prayer. There were many personal references to Rudy, his family, and requests for the Holy Spirit to be his constant Companion and Guide. The prayer was unusually long and emotional. Many in the audience were crying, sniffling, and wiping their eyes with handkerchiefs. The whole experience was moving. Rudy's mother was deeply moved. His father was not. He thought it was pandering to people's emotions. In truth, however, he had expected it to be even more emotional. He was disappointed that he could not complain that the church's practices were highly emotional, bordering on fanatical. It really was as Rudy had described, a relatively unemotional church, depending much more on a rational commitment to the Bible.

After the prayer the converts were asked to stand in the front of the church while both elders greeted them with a holy kiss, and words of encouragement. This kiss amounts to one brief peck on the cheek. The ministers of the congregation were then invited to come forward and greet them. One by one they walked up and gave them this kiss and said some well-chosen words of welcome and appreciation. Mrs. Peterfield watched this part of the service with some surprise. Rudy had not prepared them for this. Everyone seemed to be overjoyed.

Then Venzel invited the family and close friends to come forward to greet the convert. This put Peterfield in something of a quandary. He could not remember the last time he kissed Rudy. It seemed so contrived to him to do it here. It seemed so out of place; yet he did not want to have all these other people kissing him and not his father. So when he got up to Rudy, he kissed him in the same manner that everyone else did. There was an obvious emotional reaction in the audience remaining. Everyone held out such powerful hopes for Rudy's parents.

"If you're happy, I'm happy," his father choked out. He was not happy to be there and be forced to go through this protocol.

"Oh, Rudy," his mother said, "I see what's so great about this church. You're really lucky to have found something like this."

Rudy's friends also followed closely after his parents. They had nervously said encouraging things to his father and mother while waiting in line. They felt stupid, intimidated, small. Still, they tried. If Rudy's parents were not so busy trying to comprehend the matter and act appropriately, they would have been able to see the sincere love and good intentions of his friends. The good intentions were focused on Rudy—and would soon be focused on someone else in an ongoing ministry of personal friendship and kindness.

Rudy's friends greeted him, after the holy kiss, in a sporty manner of slapping each other's shoulders and small punches. There were no actions big enough to cap this magnificent experience in all of their lives. They all shared the feeling of wonder that such an improbable miracle could occur. They shared a feeling of gratitude that it did. Deep in the recesses of their minds there was the anxiety of not knowing what the future would hold. What would they do now? Where would they go? They kept those questions suppressed today and enjoyed the glory of this gift from God.

To Neal, Rudy said, "I can't imagine where I'd be today if you hadn't picked me up and helped me out. Thanks."

Neal was deeply moved by the comment. He hadn't thought about that much. He was grateful that Rudy remembered it, but the experience was too much of a miracle for Neal to feel a sense of personal accomplishment. He was just overwhelmed with gratitude.

Rudy and the other converts were then asked to walk back to the vestibule of the church. Then the entire congregation was dismissed and filed past them. All the members of the congregation greeted them. There were lots of words of advice which were all blending into one general expression of love and best wishes. Rudy knew most of them. Seeing their faces brought back many memories he had of each of them. Rudy would be unable to remember much of the advice but one, which came after all the others had passed, he would never forget. Venzel waited with Rudy until all the others passed and then put his arm around Rudy one more time.

"Well, Rudy," Venzel said, "You have now just gotten your feet on the eternal running track. This is not the victory tape. It's the starting block."

About the author

Paul L. Weingartner is married with three college-aged sons. By the grace of God He and his wife have made conversion experiences and have been members of a Christian denomination much like the one described in this book for thirty-two years. All three of their sons also embrace this faith. He edited an international monthly publication for this denomination for twenty years.

Paul lives in Ohio where he works as a school psychologist in both a public and private setting. He has published books and numerous articles in the fields of Psychology and Religion. He has conducted workshops in: parenting, attention-deficit hyperactivity disorder, and pastoral counseling.

His vision for this book is that it will help others in their search for God's will in their lives. His philosophy about writing is that all writing should direct people to the knowledge of that greatest of all writers, THE WORD, Jesus Christ.

Paul@Just-One.net
www.Just-One.net